THE DREAMING BUTTERFLY

Philip Miers

The Dreaming Butterfly
by Philip Miers

Published in 2015 by Shaldon Press

A catalogue card for this book is available from
the British Library

ISBN: 9780993481802

Publication managed by TJ INK
tjink.co.uk

Printed and bound by TJ International, Cornwall, UK

THE DREAMING BUTTERFLY

or

LA VIDA ES SUEÑO

En esta vida todo es verdad y
todo mentira

PEDRO CALDERÓN DE LA BARCA

'Once upon a time, Chuang Tzu dreamt that he was a butterfly, a butterfly fluttering about, enjoying itself. It did not know that it was Chuang Tzu. Suddenly he awoke with a start and he was Chuang Tzu. But he did not know whether he was Chuang Tzu who had dreamt that he was a butterfly, or whether he was a butterfly dreaming that he was Chuang Tzu.'

Chuang Tzu, Daoist Sage: *The Dream of Life*

Row, row, row your boat,
Gently down the stream.
Merrily, merrily, merrily, merrily,
Life is but a dream.

Traditional

CONTENTS

PART ONE: ORIGINS AND MEMORIES

I

Was he really dead? That now seemed the only possible question.

For the last few days – or was it much longer? – he had certainly been dying, lying almost motionless, detached and confused with whatever drugs they had been pumping into him.

Propped up on three pillows in his enormous curtained bed in the Imperial Apartments in the core of that centuries old complex of palaces in the centre of Vienna called the Hofburg, he was conscious of subdued but restless activity around him in that high-ceilinged cream and gilt chamber and beyond – a humming, a murmuring, which rose and fell, advanced and receded. Besides the medical staff, the adjoining rooms, he knew, were full of his family, household officials, ministers, representatives of all his governments, clergy, senior military commanders and even a few approved court journalists, all coming and going and buzzing away indistinctly, just so many bees round a hive. Now and again sorrowful deferential faces swam out of the haze and gazed down on him. Nearby, discreetly parked in a courtyard were dozens of television vans bristling with antennae and satellite dishes, and tens of thousands of people packing the Heldenplatz to overflowing, keeping vigil in the September night.

The city, the Empire, the world, he knew, were watching and waiting.

Nevertheless all that he could think of was how pitifully little his life amounted to. His overwhelming all-consuming feeling was one of waste, the waste of a life. In fact he had hardly had a life at all. Not that he had not been kept fully occupied: his time had been filled with business – councils, banquets, investitures, state visits, tours of inspection, diplomatic receptions, speeches, reviews, endless minutely choreographed ceremonies, intriguing courtiers, oversensitive and harassed politicians. He had a dutiful consort with whom he had eventually managed to produce three well-conducted children, none of whom seemed to have any particular liking for him. But who was he at the centre of it all? His profile was on every stamp and coin, his portrait in every public building, behind every office desk, but his lengthy assortment of names: Theodore Anton Franz Joseph Otto Maria Nepomuk Karl Felix Gaetan Ludwig Heinrich Pius Ignatius Maximilian, and grandly sonorous titles that took fully twenty minutes to proclaim in full seemed to bear no relation to him at all. He signed 'Theodore Imp.' (for Imperator) but in the family his name had always been Anton, Antony in English, and once upon a time long ago he had even been called Tony. Essentially he was a hollow man, a public function rather than a human being. They had told him that he had successfully restored the Empire thus inaugurating, or at least presiding over, the birth of a new era in human civilization. He knew of course that that wasn't true, but even so would it have all been worth it?

He had been deprived, or had allowed himself to be deprived, of the only real life he might have had by being plucked from blessed obscurity just when he was in the process of becoming the person he wanted to be, in those far off days when he was engaged to Rosemary, an English girl whom he had met while studying agriculture in Scotland. After their final exams they spent six weeks together in the Highlands, which reminded him of Austria – hope-filled days that had been, looking back, the happiest of his life; now nothing but a barely remembered distant dream. They planned to marry and buy a farm, perhaps in France where there were generous grants. They saw themselves surrounded by a growing family, cultivating olives, making their own wine and – they were both musical – playing together in the evening, he on the piano, she on the cello. Chopin and Vivaldi were their favourites.

It was only in the autumn after they had qualified and Rosemary joined him in Austria that their troubles began. His mother vehemently objected to her only son, the heir of the House of Hapsburg, marrying a 'commoner', something, she said, that had never happened before in the centuries old history of the family. Not expecting this attitude from her – hitherto she had appeared to be quite unstuffy and enlightened on most issues – he was shaken. Rosemary was shaken too, and to his surprise and disappointment started talking about not belonging to his world and not being able to do that to his mother, when he was ready to defy her. However he was, he thought, well on the way to winning Rosemary round when suddenly the whole world seemed to turn against them. As they did not follow the news closely, Anton and Rosemary had no conception that a great historical process was in train that as one of its multifarious consequences would part them irrevocably and forever.

To pinpoint the origins of that great convulsion would be as difficult as to detect the first shifting pebble of a landslide, the first grumblings of an earthquake. Suffice it to say that in an unfamiliar and hazardous post-communist world beset by alienating American popular culture, an increasingly assertive and militant Islam, a resurgent Russia and the economic might of Asia dominated by China, India and Japan, it was understandable that the peoples of east and central Europe should be led to forsake the uninspiring economic bureaucracy that was trying to unify a continent still riven with national rivalries, and take refuge in something much richer and more deeply embedded in their historical consciousness. There were conferences in Paris, London, Rome, Madrid, Berlin, Vienna and, of course, Brussels; tortuous negotiations, declarations and deadlines until finally, after prolonged debate and soul-searching, Germany, Italy, Poland, the Baltic States, Austria, Hungary, the Czech Republic, Slovakia, Croatia, Slovenia and even that old Hapsburg nemesis, Bosnia, announced that they were binding themselves together in a federal union under the aegis of a sovereign prince, convinced perhaps that the best, indeed the only, adequate response to those whose ultimate aim was the reestablishment of a Universal Caliphate was the restoration of the Holy Roman Empire! (Significantly however no one seemed interested in reviving 'local' monarchies in Italy, the German states or Poland, and especially not the Hohenzollerns.) This great idea, which when first mooted seemed so outlandish that it was scarcely understood, soon began to stir up long-buried yearnings in the old Hapsburg heartland and within a few months swept whole nations.

The other countries of Europe that already had monarchies or that for various historical and cultural reasons, like France or the predominantly Orthodox Balkan nations including Greece, could not associate their future with the double-headed eagle of the Latin West (as opposed to the Byzantine East), went their separate ways, though not without a considerable amount of acrimony, regret and misgiving, agreeing only to maintain a free trade area with the Restored Empire – though there were those who harboured hopes that before long, the two halves of what had once been the Roman Empire might in these amazing times again acknowledge their common heritage under a single crown and a single eagle. Policy makers in the United States however, quite at a loss to understand this powerful atavistic resurgence shaping events in the heart of Europe, echoed certain French intellectuals in speaking of the revival of the concept of Mitteleuropa and even of the rise of something ominously like a Fourth Reich.

It was only when it emerged that the nations were turning ineluctably to the House of Hapsburg – where else? – to fill the new imperial throne, that this great turn in European history, as unpredicted and even more profound than the collapse of Communism that preceded it, erupted into the lives of the young couple who, naturally enough, had not been giving any thought current political events.

Anton was of course well aware that, following the tragic death of his sportier cousin Franz in a riding accident about five years ago, followed by that of his father a few months before he went off to study in Scotland, he was now the senior male member of Hapsburg family, but he never imagined that this distinction, apart from possibly making his mother more reluctant to accept Rosemary as a daughter-in-law than she might otherwise have been, would have any serious implications for his way of life. He and Rosemary were, as it happened, on a long planned skiing holiday in the Val d'Isère when they saw his face on the front page of a German newspaper. It was a moment he would never forget.

In the ensuing classic conflict between love and duty, love neither could nor would conquer all for this particular student prince. He remembered his Vergil, inculcated into him at his Jesuit boarding school – Aeneas forsaking Dido to fulfil his higher destiny, the founding of Rome itself:

At pius Aeneas, quamquam lenire dolentem
Solando cupit et dictis avertere curas,
Multa gemens, magnoque animum labefactus amore,
Iussa tamen divom exsequitur, classemque revisit.

He was never really sure whether he had been weak or strong to give her up. He only knew he had no real choice. He felt a mere twig borne along on the surging flood of world historical forces sweeping all before them. Nevertheless, unlike Dido, his English rose showed no inclination to tear her hair, rage or fling herself onto a funeral pyre; rather she was totally calm and withdrew from his life with scarcely a murmur. In fact, once it was apparent that they had no future together she packed her bags and left without even saying goodbye. At first he thought this was cruel but on reflection he considered that she had probably been right to avoid a painful farewell scene in which they could have said nothing positive to each other. At any rate after that holiday there was no further communication between them.

On the very eve of his coronation in Rome on Whit Sunday fourteen months later, he learnt from a notice in the London Times that Rosemary was to be married to some Englishman in a place called Great Missenden the next day. Could it possibly have been a coincidence or was she trying to send him some sort of message? In any case he had been sufficiently affected by the news to slip away alone from the Quirinal Palace where he had been staying and spend the day alone driving in the Alban Hills while frantic officials tried to locate him, only returning to their immense relief in the small hours of the morning.

In all his long reign it was his only serious lapse from duty. But when the splendid ceremony went ahead on the morrow in St Peter's, and the Crown of Charlemagne was placed on his head as he knelt before the Pope in front of a potential television audience of three billion – the first such occasion since Clement VII had crowned Charles V Emperor in Bologna in 1530 – Anton felt numb and at the same time strangely insubstantial as he moved trance-like through the august and well-rehearsed rites to thunderous applause and rejoicing – the closest he could come to describing it was that it was like being a character in someone else's dream, the projection of a massive collective fantasy. The only real thought in his head, the only real emotion that touched him, was for a much less august ceremony that was in all likelihood taking place simultaneously in some rural corner of south east England. Commentators spoke of his intense concentration, even of his devotion, throughout. In fact he was drawn and tired after a sleepless night, and it was all he could do to stop himself from yawning. But at least he had made his mother happy by fulfilling what she saw as his family's destiny.

As a constitutional sovereign he had proved, outwardly at least, a great success carrying out his duties with dignity and charm, and his historic visits to Paris, London, Madrid, Moscow and the Chinese border were seen as making a crucial contribution to mending the Restored Empire's fences with its neighbours and generally calming their apprehensions about this new great reality in world politics. True, the fact that his name was never linked with that of any attractive woman either before or after what was clearly an arranged marriage to a Portuguese princess, gave rise to rumours that he was homosexual, but these faded with the belated arrival of children.

His success might seem surprising at first sight since when he was growing up and before there was any thought of the imperial destiny descending upon him, he had been a rather withdrawn and solitary character who did not attach himself readily to other people, nor they to him. It was as if he exuded a certain subtle coolness that mildly repelled. In his own mind he was decisive, bursting with extraordinary ideas and possibilities, but with others he never seemed able to take the initiative; always on the brink but never quite prepared to plunge into a situation he might not be able to control. Too complex and self-questioning perhaps or just too diffident or too fastidious to simply get on and do things, he had tended to let life pass him by, drifting, procrastinating, avoiding the challenge of external realities. There seemed always to be an invisible barrier between him and the rest of the world.

He had thought of his future as inevitably a lonely one and his father's unexpected early death only served to reinforce this feeling. He might even have seriously considered entering a monastery had he not lacked religious faith; but Rosemary's advent changed everything. For a brief period he began to be warmed with a glow of self-confidence and became almost sociable, though it must be admitted that even in their relationship, initially at least, it was she who largely took the initiative.

However this awkward passivity of temperament which would otherwise have been a great handicap, proved something of an asset in an Emperor whose whole life was minutely planned and protected, and who always acted on advice. Moreover secure in the imperial persona, which made him not only socially invulnerable but mysteriously seemed to endow him with the capacity to bring confusion, joy and intense excitement to those who had even the briefest encounter with him, he could deal with other people invariably on his own terms. He even developed a certain dry ironical sense of humour which in a private person would have been quite unremarkable, but in one whose every utterance was received with rapt attention, was much admired and echoed. He derived a certain satisfaction from performing his duties effectively, never or only very rarely putting so much as a foot wrong and he was sustained year in and year out by the perfectly regulated rhythm and routine of a court life centred on himself that he found not uncongenial. But it was not living. The only time he had begun to feel truly alive, a full participant rather than an isolated spectator, was during his months – it was scarcely more than a year – with Rosemary.

Though the grand routine had kept him going, he had not

positively enjoyed his years on the imperial throne; indeed enjoyment was something quite foreign to his existence. To be the living symbol, the unifying icon of a great multinational empire and heir to over two thousand years of tradition, living always within the impenetrable shell of his great office, was a strange kind of existence. For all the overwhelming interest in 'The Emperor' or 'His Imperial and Royal Majesty' what difference had he as an individual really made? What difference could he make? What was he as an individual anyway? Could not a flag, a monument, a shrine or even perhaps a ceremonial cupboard have done just as well? Why not simply the proud initials – true once more – A.E.I.O.U: Austria Est Imperare Orbi Universo, emblazoned on a tablet of stone? But then could one have an Empire without an Emperor?

Though everything was done in his name and the constitution was judiciously and respectfully vague as to the limits of his own position, it was clear to him that, in practice, he functioned as a kind of ornamental screen to conceal the realities of power, the mystique of imperial authority dignifying, sanctioning or disguising what would otherwise be seen as naked and cynical politicking. If really dwelt on, the full consequences of all the decisions taken in his name, decisions some of which at least he might conceivably have obstructed if he had really exploited his huge influence and apparent popular support, he would have been unable to enjoy one night's peaceful sleep.

But at least he had managed to remain untarnished by the various political crises and scandals of his reign, forewarned by the sage advice of his great uncle Archduke Ludwig Salvator soon after he came to the throne: "Keep all the politicians at arm's length. Sooner or later, however popular they seem, they fall from grace. Never let their fall touch you!" Consolidating the position of the monarchy was what mattered above all and that was in the supreme interest of all his peoples, and he must never compromise that position by meddling in controversial matters however good the cause. That was what all his advisers told him. He accepted it and reigned largely untroubled by his conscience. He had not after all given up his whole life to duty. Who could ask more than that?

He had wanted to be a farmer and ended up ruler of the world. Somewhere out there he sometimes thought there must be a farmer who yearned to be an Emperor. Why couldn't they simply change places? The most impressive of his student contemporaries, the only person he had ever met – there is always one! – who unquestionably deserved to be called a genius, certainly had grand ambitions and his friends certainly took it for granted that he had the world at his feet. But for reasons never explained he took his own life at the beginning of his final year – a circumstance, Anton could not help feeling, that had cleared the way for his relationship with Rosemary, for it was inconceivable to him that she or any other woman could possibly have preferred him to that compelling and tragic young man that they had both so admired.

How infinitely long ago and unattainable it all seemed now. Another world. Another existence. And all the time his reign, the so-called life he had subsequently been called upon to live, had been eaten away with regret and nostalgia, more and more so in fact as the years passed, for a happiness he had barely begun to experience before it had been snatched away. Whenever he listened to music alone, especially Chopin (he no longer played the piano), he was plunged into a hopeless, fathomless longing for an irrecoverable past. At first he had imagined their paths might somehow cross, that he might somehow contrive to meet Rosemary again. He never stopped unconsciously searching for her face in every crowd, at every reception. Vivid imaginings of their reunion secretly brightened many daytime hours, to say nothing of his dreams and, however hopeless in practical terms, he never ceased harbouring them entirely. How could he? They were the only stirrings of real life within him, and though he had stuck to his duty to the end, to the consternation of the court he had ended up a virtual recluse.

II

Then the moment comes. Looking down from somewhere high up behind the glittering chandelier of Venetian glass he sees a flurry among the group below, and two nurses followed by half a dozen doctors approach the bed, then the tearful Empress and her three sons, pale and solemn. The Chief Court Physician feels the Emperor's pulse, nods gravely and closes his eyes. Then the Empress and the three Archdukes kiss his hand and kneel beside the bed. The news spreads to the adjoining apartments and those not obliged to scurry off also fall to their knees while the Cardinal Archbishop of Vienna recites the De Profundis. Outside a groan spreads among the vast crowd holding candles in the Heldenplatz and almost immediately the bells of the city followed by those of the whole Empire begin to toll. Somewhere in the depths of the Chancellery the Great Seal of the Emperor Theodore the Great, first sovereign of the Restored Holy Roman Empire, is shattered with a silver hammer. The forty year reign is over!

So he was dead, and witnessing his own death. How interesting! Latterly, as he tried to suppress grave worries about his health, he had become obsessed by the whole business of dying, reading extensively on the subject. Thus he was very intrigued by the nature and explanation of the frequently reported phenomenon of near-death out-of-body experiences, and in particular whether they offered any grounds for believing in the possibility of mental survival beyond physical death. Here was incontrovertible proof that they did, though frustratingly, he would not be able to share it with any one still alive! He *must* be witnessing his own death. What other explanation could there be? Someone was definitely looking down on the scene surrounding his own now lifeless body and who could that be but himself? Video ergo sum. He might be disembodied, hovering somewhere near the ceiling, but he undoubtedly existed!

Then he became so caught up in the scenes that followed as to forget his own predicament. He saw the 'in der Burg' courtyard below his windows packed with journalists and camera crews from almost every nation to hear a court spokesman behind a forest of microphones on an arc-lit platform in front of the Schweizertor – the gilded and painted Renaissance gateway of the Emperor Ferdinand I leading to the original fortress from which the palace grew – announcing his death to the world and outlining the solemn sequence of events that it would set in train.

No longer the Emperor Theodore but Anton, or simply Tony, or even perhaps just a nameless conscious disembodied point of view, he saw it all: the lying-in-state in the Burgkapelle of the Hofburg and then in the Schönbrunn Palace where mourners forming a queue that stretched back into the centre of Vienna filed past the open coffin, high on a bank of flowers and watched over by an ever-changing guard of soldiers from different regiments with arms reversed, in a continuous shuffling procession that lasted for an entire week. He witnessed the seven Great Electors of the Empire – the Archbishops of Mainz, Cologne and Trier, the Arch-steward or Seneschal and Elector of Bavaria, the Arch-marshal and Elector of Saxony, the Arch-chamberlain and Elector of Prussia and the Arch-treasurer and Elector of Hanover – foregather, in accordance with arrangements going back to the Golden Bull of the

Czech Emperor Charles IV in 1356, in the Wahlkapelle of Frankfurt cathedral formally to elect his son, the thirty year old Archduke Maximilian as his successor, and that election proclaimed by the Arch-marshal of the Empire and his heralds to vast crowds from the central balcony of the Neue Burg, the great curving nineteenth century addition to the Hofburg – the very spot where, in another age, Adolf Hitler had proclaimed the Anschluss. The ceremony was echoed in all the capitals of the Empire.

Then there followed the military pomp of the funeral procession to St Stephen's Cathedral; the muffled drums, the endless slow marching regiments, the troops lining the streets, the coffin on a gun carriage flanked by the most imposing plumed and bearskinned guardsman , draped with the Emperor's standard and bearing the Crown of Charlemagne, together with the orb, sword and sceptre, immediately preceded by the Great Electors and the highest dignitaries of the Court bearing the other principal regalia: the Austrian Imperial Crown of Rudolph II, the Iron Crown of Lombardy, the Crown of St Wenceslas of Bohemia, the Crown of St Stephen of Hungary, the Crown of Augustus III of Poland and the ceremonial grand collars of the Sovereign of the Order of the Golden Fleece and of the Teutonic Order, and followed by a riderless horse and then by most of the world's royalty, presidents and prime ministers led by the male members of the House of Hapsburg – the ladies, according to centuries old tradition, following in carriages.

At the requiem mass attended by over fifty cardinals, his son and heir – officially still only King of the Romans and Emperor Elect until his eventual coronation by the Pope – occupied a solitary throne on an elevated dais of the head of the great nave and just in front of the catafalque and its six tallow candles in massive candlesticks of beaten gold, with the heads of state and government of over a hundred nations behind him. He had always been distant from his sons, regarding them as an extension of their mother – if he had had a daughter he might perhaps have felt differently – and had little to do with them, but now looking down at that young man, so solitary amid all the sombre splendour in essentially the same situation as he himself had been forty years ago, he felt closer to him than he had ever done while he was alive. Though Max was eight years older than he had been at his election he had always thought him immature for his age, so it came to the same thing. Nor was the boy married, which was a cause for concern. But now the mantle had descended upon him – it was his son's turn to bear what could sometimes feel like the overwhelming burden of 'the hopes and fears of all the years', yet in a very different world.

He remembered, when the decision was finally taken to restore the Empire how, hesitantly at first, hardened politicians of all parties had come forward and kissed his hand, many with tears in their eyes, and the enormous crowds that greeted him everywhere in their almost frantic enthusiasm for a shy young man who, without in any way seeking it, had become the symbol of the renewal of the Old World. Wherever he had gone, not just in Austria but Hungary, Germany, Italy and even Poland, the police had been overwhelmed by the thousands who just wanted to touch him. That was the best part of half a century ago, but in spite of his somewhat secluded later years, or perhaps because of them, the reaction to his final illness and death and the hopes almost universally invested in his son, showed that the appeal of the restored dynasty and all that it implied, was stronger than ever and thus not the mere passing fashion of a generation. Rather than being the product of the age he had defined it, providing a dignified, stable and never-failing framework against which all the kaleidoscopic shifts and reversals of the passing scene had played themselves out, and many millions lived their lives in security and peace, the envy of other nations.

There was a panegyric by the papal legate and a secular valedictory address from the Grand Chancellor of the Empire, the wily veteran Polish statesman Count Lichynski who was obviously milking the great occasion for the all political kudos he could extract from it. He spoke of "our departed sovereign whom all mankind concur in calling 'the Great'" as not only the heir of Augustus and Constantine but a latter day Justinian, a true Restitutor Orbis whose reign of forty years "had brought unprecedented peace and prosperity to the heart of Europe from Sicily to the Baltic and from the Rhine to the Black Sea, and profoundly changed the order of the world. Well does he deserve," the Chancellor sonorously concluded, "the farewell tribute of all his governments and peoples." (Not perhaps the happiest of tributes Anton reflected, for Justinian's restoration of the Empire of the West, however glorious, proved to be only the last gleam in the long sunset of imperial Rome).

As he followed the ceremony in his disembodied state he seemed somehow to be aware, indeed to know with certainty, what his son was thinking as he was being subjected to all this fulsome oratory, namely that whatever his father's shortcomings as a parent might have been, it would be impossible to imagine anyone more perfectly suited to the role of Emperor than his late father and that he could not hope to equal his achievements. If only the boy knew. If only he could tell him, share the experience of a lifetime with him. Yet what had he got to say that his son might profit from? It would be just as hopeless to try to communicate with him now as when they had both been flesh and blood!

After the requiem in the packed cathedral, the end came with the final laying to rest of the Emperor's body among the generations of his illustrious ancestors in the Imperial Vault of the Capuchin Church. Following the ancient custom of the 'Anklopfzeremonie' the Arch-chamberlain struck the doors of the church with his staff of office, and in the traditional Latin formula demanded admittance for his Imperial, Royal and Apostolic Majesty, reading out the full list of his titles. The hooded prior answered from within that he knew of no such person. A second request referring to him simply as 'prince of the House of Hapsburg' brought the same denial. Finally the Arch-chamberlain knocked a third time and humbly asked the Capuchin friars to admit 'the body of your brother Theodore, a miserable sinner'. With that the coffin was at last allowed to enter, but when the doors heavily shrouded in black velvet closed behind the pallbearers, he knew he would not be able to join the privileged few inside.

Then it occurred to him that he had been watching events starting with his own death that had stretched over a period of more than a week. Could near-death experiences persist for so long in terms of 'earthly' time? Why had his whole life not passed before him? Why had he not been propelled down a tunnel to the Source of Light? What now? He had often felt no more substantial than a dream beholding the great imperial charade in which he was ostensibly playing the leading part. Now the dream was over, or perhaps changing into another dream altogether....

III

A hazy figure detached itself from the crowd in the high-ceilinged chamber, approached his bed and looked down at him. Close up he could see that she was a nurse. She smiled.

"You had a visitor a little while ago but I didn't like disturb you as you seemed so comfortable."

"A visitor? A man or a woman?"

"A man. He said he was an old friend."

"Has he gone?"

"Yes. I told him to come back another time."

"Good!"

So he was not dead after all. He was being nursed. He had not succumbed. He was resisting, if not recovering. This rally, he could well imagine, would generate immense hope throughout the Empire and around the world. Indeed he fancied that he could hear even now an excited murmur rising from the crowds keeping vigil in the Heldenplatz. But however much it might be good news for the world, the realization that he was still alive dawned on him with a heavy heart and a sense of profound, almost devastating, disappointment. So far from soaring far beyond his moribund body he was imprisoned inside it still, with the whole grisly business of dying yet to be undergone, to be followed in all likelihood not by continuing consciousness but by extinction. But terrible as this might be, his weakness, mental and physical, tempered any emotional reaction.

How very strange to reflect that he might well have slipped through life almost unnoticed, unmarried, with few if any friends and yet by a quirk of fate he had become one of the most notable figures in world history, at least never to be forgotten as long as civilization persisted. But somehow now regardless of what he had still to face, dying or not dying, alive or dead, it really didn't seem to matter. Maybe this was what dying meant: nothing mattering, not even having been Holy Roman Emperor for forty years!

At any rate his unfortunate son and heir Maximilian, together with the rest of the world, was still waiting.

IV

Now he could hear a tune, an English romantic song – songs somehow always seemed more romantic in a foreign language:

That certain night, the night we met,
There was magic abroad in the air
There were angels dining at the Ritz
And a nightingale sang in Berkeley Square!
I may be right, I may be wrong,
But I'm perfectly willing to swear
That when you turned and smiled at me
A nightingale sang in Berkeley Square!
The streets of town were paved with stars
It was such a romantic affair!
And as we kissed and said goodnight
A nightingale sang in Berkeley Square!

That certain night... that unforgettable night! Then as if by a miracle they were together again; if he had been dreaming, now he was waking to reality, his senses never more acute. He had followed Rosemary out of the stuffy marquee and into the voluptuous, velvety, starry night, a close night so unusual for Edinburgh in late June, heavy with the scent of syringa and honeysuckle and to his delight had found her alone for the moment in a secluded corner of the college grounds which were bathed in bright moonlight. 'In such a night as this, when the sweet wind did gently kiss the trees, and they did make no noise....' The pulsating music of the post-finals ball receded and faded away.

"Found you!" (He could tell immediately that she wanted to be found and that he wasn't interrupting).

"It was hot in there. I thought I'd come out for some fresh air."

"Me too."

"You know you're a very good dancer."

"Oh, it's just the way I was brought up."

That evening she had surprised him by wearing what was, in his eyes a stunningly daring dress which showed off her figure to perfection and he had spent most of the time trying not to look too obviously at her cleavage. Now, acutely self-conscious, he was determined not to appear overtly romantic in such an obvious situation.

"Almost like daylight isn't it," he observed with a fair impression of casualness. "Look at our shadows on the lawn – so clearly defined! Why do poets, I wonder, always compare the moon to a galleon?"

"The slow and stately way it sails through the clouds, I suppose. It looks much bigger tonight somehow."

"That's because it's the solstice moon."

"The solstice moon?"

"Yes, and after that it's the hunter's moon and then the harvest moon."

"Hunter's moon, harvest moon; sounds so beautiful – peaceful somehow. Do you ever think that there are some moments so perfect that nothing could improve them?"

"Can they last though?"

"I don't know, but it doesn't matter because in a way they're outside time, so whatever happens in the future they'll always be there. I don't know, it's something you can't really put into words. Do you know what I mean though?"

He nodded. Her impressive chest was gently heaving and he was aware of a low rhythmic thumping.

"What's that sound?"

"My heart I expect."

"Could this be one of those moments?"

She nodded.

Without thinking what he was doing he seized her hand overpowered by the sense that this was the now or never opportunity of his life.

"Will you marry me?"

For a few moments she continued gazing into the night sky as if nothing had happened. Then she said: "Look, shooting star!"

"I'm so sorry; I don't know what came over me...."

"Of course."

"You mean, yes?"

"I mean of course I'll marry you."

"But that's, that's wonderful! It's just that you seemed so calm. Not all surprised."

"I'd have been very surprised if you hadn't asked me – and disappointed. Don't look so confused." She kissed him on the forehead. "You haven't had a lot to do with girls have you, before me?"

"Not really. It's the way...."

"....you were brought up!"

Their laughter was followed by a long tranquil silence broken eventually by Rosemary.

"You know who I'm thinking about?"

"Rollo."

"Yes, I was wondering shall we, would you like to visit his grave? It would be like...you know..."

Anton nodded. This was exactly what he had been thinking of but didn't like to suggest. They seemed to understand each other perfectly!

V

Unlike his son who had been raised in palaces, he mused, there had been nothing special about his own upbringing which was in a world where the very name of Hapsburg was hardly known. His parents simply called him Antony – even from his earliest years he secretly resented the abbreviation 'Tony' as offensively familiar and an affront to his dignity. One might even say his origins were humble, for he first saw the light of day in suburban south London, not in the Victorian/Edwardian inner suburbs of Tooting or Battersea but in the vast inter-war sprawl of road upon road of indistinguishable semi-detached homes beyond. His part of the sprawl happened, quite arbitrarily it seemed, to bear the name of Raynes Park, but it might equally have been Morden, Surbiton, Tolworth or Carshalton.

When he was allowed to ride around the area on the second hand bike that he was given as a reward for winning a scholarship to the local grammar school (his mother had ruled out a new one as quite unmerited as well as a disgraceful waste of money), it only served to reinforce his dismal sense of not living anywhere in particular. Other people, he was only too well aware, lived in real places: castles on forested slopes perched above precipitous cliffs, thatched cottages far down country lanes, palaces in the heart of great capital cities, or at least in a trim old market town snug in a landscape of neat fields and rolling hills. Even the deserts of Arabia had the occasional oasis with pools and palm trees, but he lived nowhere, amid endless rows of divided houses and narrow gardens interspersed with the occasional parade of mean little shops.

Antony's father was only a clerk in an insurance office in the City, but he went up to town every morning in a bowler hat and carrying a tightly rolled umbrella, and his mother certainly considered herself a cut above her neighbours in the road (it was in fact called Fullwell Avenue, though bereft of any trees), especially the family three doors down where the breadwinner actually worked in a factory! Thus she derived a certain satisfaction from the fact that her house, separated by both a fence and a high impenetrable hedge from 'next door', was not only on a corner, but for technical reasons arising from the builder's division of the plots, had an extra patch of garden at the bottom making an 'L' shape rather than the standard straight strip. If truth be told his mother considered herself a cut above her mild-mannered husband as well; his father had only been an office worker like himself, whereas her father had been a schoolmaster and her mother a piano teacher. There was in fact a piano in the house but it seemed to Antony that it must be purely for decoration, just one more piece of furniture for his mother to clean, since it was never played and as far back as he could remember he had been strictly forbidden even to touch it.

Although it never occurred to him when he was little, Antony's parents were actually quite old, and sometimes indeed, to his father's acute embarrassment and his mother's indignation, mistaken for his grandparents. He was born in 1939 when his mother was forty and his father forty-five. They never expected or wanted to have any children, let alone at that stage of their lives, and though relieved that he proved not to be physically or mentally handicapped as they had feared, the child was a constant worry and a burden to them to be watched over with anxious care, rather than in any sense a source of happiness or a blessing. This would have been true at the best of times but the War made everything worse.

When Antony first got word of 'the facts of life' through sniggering playground rumour he confidently dismissed them as crude fantasy, since so far from practising the obscene intimacies he heard whispers of, his parents never touched nor seemed to display any particular interest in each other, let alone affection or any stronger attachment. They hardly ever even called each other by their Christian names and in his experience, which he naturally regarded as the norm, always slept in separate rooms. The very idea of either of them less than fully clad or behaving in any way indecorously was so incongruous as to be simply unimaginable.

His mother in particular was a woman of the most rigid propriety even by the standards of the day, but it was a propriety which seemed to be quite unsupported by religious convictions or larger moral views. Religion was in fact one of the very many things that were never mentioned at home. As soon as he could walk unaided his mother discouraged any displays of physical affection on his part such as kissing or hugging, dismissing them with "don't be so silly" so that he was made to feel that there was something rather unhealthy or unnatural about them. It certainly seemed that his mother, whose mouth was habitually set in a hard single line of disapproval without any sign of lips, would have been constitutionally incapable of kissing anyone. Their only physical contact was when she gripped his hand tightly as they crossed the road together. Tears were regarded by his mother as, if anything, less acceptable than displays of affection. Whatever their cause he was told that he ought to be ashamed of himself and to stop being a stupid little cry-baby.

His mother's disapproval, often expressed with a characteristic sniff, extended to almost everything and everyone in her world. Thus Antony would not have dreamt of bringing a friend home from school, and was never allowed to play with other children in the road, go to the cinema or even listen to the radio (in those days called the wireless), except for the news. His mother, as he recalled her, was never without her apron in the house and always joylessly busy day in and day out cooking, cleaning, scrubbing, sewing and darning. She seemed almost to take a perverse pleasure in the most tedious of chores, even spending most of Sunday afternoon scouring the oven clean. His father, on the other hand, when not at work spent as much time as possible gardening, sitting in his shed or in the attic where over the years he had assembled the ever more complex electric train network which gave him much quiet enjoyment. It was also the only place indoors where he was allowed to smoke his pipe.

Though pleased not to have him "under my feet" as she put it, his wife was contemptuous of his absorption with "toy trains" and professed herself unable to imagine why a grown man should want to waste his time playing with such things. On the grounds that the pipe smoke and the dust in the attic might affect her son's lungs (she made the most of the fact that Antony was mildly asthmatic) his mother forbade him ever to go up there, however briefly. Occasionally however, for a great treat when she was out, his father allowed him to come and look at the trains and even work them under his supervision. He also enjoyed helping his father in the garden until interrupted by a summons from his mother.

In her frequent bursts of what she considered well-justified exasperation with her mild husband, his mother was prone to refer to him as "your father" as if his defects were somehow Antony's fault: "Your father is much too easy going for his own good... He'd let people walk all over him if I let him... If only he'd stand up for himself more." (Needless to say she didn't mean that he should stand up to her.) Any flights of fancy, unusual exuberance or high spirits on Antony's part – and he was quite a high-spirited little boy – were regarded balefully by his mother as signs of what she called "bad blood", coming from her husband's side of the family, naturally. These dark hints, possibly of some unmentionable wickedness, seemed to Antony the only remotely interesting thing about his dismal home circumstances. Was this the reason, he wondered, why he heard nothing of his father's relatives? As his mother's mother was said to be 'in a home' until she finally faded from the scene when he was nine, Antony, unlike the children in the stories he read who all seemed to have grandparents, uncles, aunts, brothers and sisters to say nothing of numerous cousins as well as friends to play with, grew up in total isolation. His parents had no friends and never invited anyone round. The cards they received at Christmas were scarcely enough to fill one mantelpiece.

One way or another his father got blamed for most things at home but though he never stood up to his wife, he remained generally cheerful and never scolded Antony or tried to check his behaviour in any way. Indeed there seemed to be a tacit acknowledgement between them that they were both on the same side, both fellow sufferers, though because he never stood up for himself or his son, Antony could not respect him.

His mother had taken to the austerities and privations of wartime with relish and the subsequent gradual relaxation of rationing hardly affected the household. He never remembered his mother buying anything for herself or even for the house unless it was broken beyond repair and, though the content of the meals increased slightly, there was never any suggestion that food could be a life-enhancing pleasure. In fact she would have regarded any overt enjoyment of food as bordering on the indecent and, what amounted to the same thing, somehow un-English. As far as his mother was concerned, eating like everything else in life was just one more inescapable necessity to be endured as well as the occasion for a lot of hard work in the kitchen. Thus all through his childhood Antony suffered the same rigid repertoire of unappetising dishes prepared without any imagination or enthusiasm: a roast leg of lamb with mint sauce, hard potatoes and lumpy gravy on Sunday, the same meat cold on Monday and served as mince in a cottage pie on Tuesday, ham and salad on Wednesday, sausages on Thursday, steamed fish on Friday and corned beef and mashed potatoes on Saturday. But though Antony and his father ate all they were given, his mother, a scrawny, sharp-featured little woman, never seemed to need food at all.

Rationing or no rationing Antony was never allowed sweets and when he was deemed old enough to go to school by himself received such dire warnings about what they could do to his teeth and his 'insides', that he learnt to look on the gobstoppers, sherbet fountains, sugar cigarettes and wine gums which his contemporaries were allowed to indulge in, as a generation later he might have looked on cannabis and cocaine. As for chewing gum, in his mother's eyes it was a sign of irredeemable degradation.

He did have an annual seaside holiday, always sharing a room with his parents in the same boarding house (his mother called it a "private hotel") in Bognor Regis; but it was a gruesome business hedged about with even more restrictions, embarrassment, and discomfort than the ordinary routine of home. He was naturally forbidden to play with other children on the beach and as 'guests' were not allowed into their rooms during the day, many an hour was spent on rainy afternoons huddled in shelters on the promenade waiting for half past six. His father, Antony observed, appeared to enjoy his week by the seaside even less than he did.

Were it not for reading he might have regarded his bleak home life as typical of the human condition, but from even before he went to school at five and three quarters he had developed a passion for books. Though his mother disapproved of 'made-up' stories that would "only fill his head with nonsense" and would not have public library books in the house – not only were they 'common', a favourite term of disapproval, but a possible source of infection – she felt she could hardly stop him reading altogether. Through it he was transported from

Raynes Park to a vivid, vibrant and splendid world of enchanted forests, mystic quests, pirates of the Spanish Main, the Knights of the Round Table, King Solomon's Mines, the siege of Troy, the wanderings of Jason and Ulysses, the conquests of Alexander and Napoleon, the labours of Hercules; explorers, heroes, magicians, gods, legend, fairy tales, myth, romance and adventure against which the drabness of post-war suburban England faded into the unreality of utter insignificance.

The only part of his environment that he found tolerable was the secluded bottom corner of the garden from which, when the leaves were out, neither his own nor any other house was visible. Here there was an old stone bench on which he could sit and read out of the confines of the house in fine weather and enjoy a certain privacy, at least until the harsh intrusion of his mother's voice. He liked to imagine that the bench and the tall elm that stood nearby were the surviving remnants of some great estate that had formerly occupied the neighbourhood long before all the little houses were built.

When he got to grammar school, the rich but rather undifferentiated imaginative life that his reading created and sustained gradually crystallised out into an absorption with the great movements of history, glorious and soul-stirring but at the same time factual – he could no longer lose himself in something that wasn't true – in particular how it was that a family of obscure Swabian Counts, tenants of nothing but the fortress of Habichtsburg deep in the Alps on the Swiss/German border could gradually expand their land by conquest, but above all by judicious marriages, so that in the course of six centuries they had become not only the heirs of Caesar and Charlemagne but masters of the world beyond the Pillars of Hercules which those worthies had never even heard of – 'bella gerant alii, tu felix Austria nube!'as the old adage had it. His favourite book was Bryce's *Holy Roman Empire* which he permanently purloined from the school library. Fortunately because no one except him ever wanted to withdraw the book, his little crime passed undetected. It should be noted that the history of Britain, ancient or modern, including the great conflict that had overshadowed the first six years of his life, held absolutely no interest for him. In his mind it hardly counted as history at all.

Judging by his mother's horrified reaction when, as she was twiddling the knob to tune the wireless set in the sitting room, the odd phrase in a foreign language came over the airwaves, she would not, to put it mildly, have been sympathetic to his interests. But from his early years at grammar school he had learnt to avoid blank incomprehension or even outright hostility by letting his parents know as little as possible of what he was up to, his hopes and plans, and, while observing the usual courtesies, excluding them from his life altogether insofar as he could.

There was nothing really new in this. They had always been shadowy figures for him, never really impinging on his inner existence. Indeed he could never quite bring himself to accept that the ineffectual little man and the joyless narrow-minded woman with whom he lived could truly be his parents. They and he belonged, it seemed, to completely different worlds. As a child he had convinced himself that he had been farmed out to these obscure people either to keep him out of danger or to avoid some sort of scandal and that sooner or later the inevitable happy ending, the rescue that awaited all changelings in novels and fairy tales would be his fate too. One fine day a large black Mercedes car would draw up outside the house and central European gentlemen in black overcoats with astrakhan collars would get out. There would be lengthy confidential conversations in the sitting room, documents would be produced, money would change hands and he would be swept away to be reunited with his true parents – wealthy, attractive, sophisticated, sociable – in the chateau, schloss or palatial villa where he rightfully belonged, his dim life in the mean outer suburbs of London henceforth no more than a sad half-remembered dream. But though he looked out for it almost every day, that large black Mercedes never came.

However once he was established at secondary school he resolved, as soon as he was old enough, to get as far away from his parents, Raynes Park and indeed England, as possible. The first place he intended to make for was Vienna, followed by the cities of Italy and then Paris. Indeed from the time when he had first become conscious of his surroundings he had always yearned to escape, and up until he was about ten he derived some consolation from writing in every book he acquired:

If found please return to –
Antony T. Kilroy (his second name was Trevor and he hated it),
25 Fullwell Avenue,
Raynes Park,
Merton,
London,
England,
United Kingdom,
Europe,
Northern Hemisphere,
Earth,
Solar System,
Milky Way Galaxy,
The Universe.

Being so solitary Antony was not aware how widespread a practice this was among his contemporaries. But in his case it held a special significance, confirming just what an insignificant speck Fullwell Road constituted in the great scheme of things and what vast regions lay open for him to explore! In fact in his own mind he was already well on the way to doing so. From old guide books and street plans picked up in second hand bookshops he had arrived at a taxi driver's knowledge of the layouts of Vienna, Rome and Paris as well as their histories, palaces, museums, parks and grand thoroughfares. He knew every detail of the views from the Janiculum and the Spanish Steps, could have conducted guided tours of St Peter's and the Forum, and was intimately familiar with all the great public buildings round the Ringstrasse, as well as every detail of the cathedral at Aachen where Charlemagne was buried and the Kings of the Germans were crowned throughout the Middle Ages before going to Rome to receive the Imperial Crown. But though he would have been able to find his way all over Paris by Metro, he knew nothing of the Underground. London, where his father spent his days and which he had visited on various school trips (his parents never took him anywhere), was of no interest to him in itself. Entirely lacking the grandeur and exotic aura of the great cities of the continent, it seemed to have little to distinguish it from the ugly jumble of any commercial town except that it was larger, noisier, dirtier and more crowded.

Antony excelled academically at grammar school especially in English, History and Languages. His mother was both bemused and disgusted that a supposedly respectable school should waste time teaching boys French and German, especially after the War, to say nothing of Latin, which was, in her eyes, utterly useless. But in those far off days when parents were not consulted about their children's education there was nothing she could do about it. (Her reaction when he won a History prize in the fifth form and chose a book on the Emperor Franz Joseph may well be imagined.) Nor, in the early fifties, had the nascent teenage culture of teddy boys and pop music yet permeated the blazered and short-haired ranks of his fairly traditional grammar school. As for sex, among the decent upstanding boys it was never mentioned, and while a small coterie of the indecent might tell each other dirty jokes and comb their hair with Brylcreem, the notion of any of the pupils being 'sexually active', let alone taking drugs, would have been unthinkable. Depravity went no further than the odd furtive cigarette behind the bike shed.

But frail, bookish and apparently self-sufficient Antony had no real friends even among his most studious and upright contemporaries, and outside the classroom, where he shone, he was always on the margin of school life. Nevertheless he was respected as far as it went, and never bullied, chiefly because of his ability to make people laugh. He also revealed a surprising dramatic talent in school plays, finding that through acting a part, he could access and display personal resources that could find no expression in his socially and emotionally impoverished 'real' life. But though he was in many respects a model pupil he was convinced that for all the commendations he received, the masters didn't really like him as much as the sportsmen and rogues, however careless their prep might be.

Though he continued to have as little to do with his parents as possible, by the time he had reached his mid-teens he could not help becoming aware that his father seemed to be fading further and further into insignificance, becoming an even more shadowy and elusive figure. He said little, spending more and more time in his shed; even his quiet cheerfulness failed and he was given to bouts of abstraction when he seemed to be on the brink of tears. Antony could only assume that his mother was being more than usually unpleasant to him. But his parents' lives were so far beyond his ken that while he felt a certain pity for his rather pathetic father he could not really sympathize with him. As they seemed such incomprehensibly different beings, it never occurred to him to speculate as to what made them tick or even to regard then as people in their own right.

Antony's unusually wide early reading helped him to thrive when he reached the sixth form where for the first time in his life he had, to some extent at least, a feeling of coming into his own and, though not in the ordinary sense an extrovert, he excelled in the cut and thrust of public speaking in the formal circumstances of the debating society.

He received particular encouragement from the head of English who also produced the Senior School Play, the flamboyant and subversive figure of Mr Marjoribanks – pronounced 'Marchbanks', as he never failed to tell each new overawed form he taught. By far the most entertaining member of the staff, he habitually wore a bow tie, suede shoes, a silk waistcoat and a monocle, addressed his pupils as 'dear boy', told risqué stories in class and was even known to kick of his buckled shoes, put his yellow socked feet on the master's desk and wiggle his toes while eating what looked like caviar from a jar – such at least was the legend, and there were many legends about Mr Marjoribanks. His older and longer established colleagues might have found his crowd-pleasing eccentricities studied and tedious, particularly as they suspected, rightly, that he was quite capable of undermining them to the boys, but he certainly kept his classes on the edge of their seats and in spite of his eccentricities, his commanding presence and his penetrating personal sarcasm put any attempt to 'play him up' out of the question. He could silence the most high-spirited class in a moment simply by letting the monocle fall from his eye. Though he made no effort to organise his lessons or even mark books he nevertheless achieved excellent results chiefly because the boys hung on his every word.

Everyone knew that he had published poetry and detective stories under the name of Llewellyn Rhys, and he let it be understood that for him schoolmastering was only a small part of his rich and varied life – it was difficult to imagine the rest of the staff having any kind of life at all beyond the school gates. In contrast to the other masters – dowdy, unpolished, unsophisticated, in their brogues, crumpled grey flannels and leather patched sports jackets with pens in the top pocket – 'Marchers', as he was universally known, scintillated, fascinated and entertained. He was sui generis. The clear impression was given that outside the classroom he moved in very different circles, rubbing shoulders with the rich and famous on equal terms. He certainly had a way of talking about some celebrities and distinguished writers as if they were known to him personally. The rumour ran, and it seemed perfectly plausible to his sixth form admirers, that he was a déclassé aristocrat – Antony imagined an idyllic Edwardian country house childhood – who had broken with his family for a more bohemian life, or even to go on the stage. There was talk of his having made a young actress pregnant (subsequently famous naturally), thus precipitating a brief and unsuccessful marriage, or that he had some sort of connection with the secret service – a sort of Bulldog Drummond or Richard Hannay figure perhaps! No one of course would have dared to ask him any direct personal questions and he retained his aura of mystery.

Mr Marjoribanks took Antony under his wing, directed his reading, introducing him to Byron, Nietzsche, Hardy and Conan Doyle, and first planted in his mind the goal of an Oxford scholarship, as well as warning him against women or rather the snares of domesticity, citing Cyril Connolly's "pram in the hall" as the enemy of all promising young men. He also freed Antony from the temptation to take seriously the evangelical Christianity he had imbibed in Divinity lessons together with the restrictive moral code which it implied. From the perspective of his grim home circumstances the world beyond it was perhaps bound to seem more intensely attractive than to even his most imaginative contemporaries, but now without moral restraints, the possibility of Babylonian orgies beckoned as well; though he was still at the stage of blushing with embarrassment if he was ever required to speak to a girl.

However though the future now seemed limitless in its possibilities, dizzying, exalting, beyond all imagination, it was increasingly borne in upon him that the great condition of it all, the portal through which he had to pass in to enter in and enjoy it, was Oxford. But his mother, dismissive of any suggestion of his going to university, insisted that it was high time that he started earning a living and making some contribution to the expenses of the household. Marjoribanks advised Antony to secure his place but take it up after he had done his National Service. However in the event his asthma, which had been worsening with the approach of his all-important A levels and the inevitably looming conflict with his mother over his future, caused him to fail the medical. There then seemed nothing she could do to prevent the school from entering him for the entrance scholarship as a candidate for Mitre College as recommended by Mr Marjoribanks.

No one, not even the young Jude the Obscure viewing the distant prospect of his New Jerusalem from a ladder propped up against a barn on the Berkshire downs, could have felt a stronger yearning for Oxford. He devoured all the accounts he could find of Oxford and Cambridge life including novels from *Jude* and *Zuleika Dobson* to *The Longest Journey* and *Brideshead Revisited*. Indeed his reading and imaginings so coloured his anticipation, experience and even his memories of university life that ever after it was almost impossible for him to distinguish 'his' Oxford from everyone else's in fact or fiction ranging from Shelley's, Matthew Arnold's and Oscar Wilde's to those of Harold Acton and W. H. Auden. He first learnt the geography of the environs of the city not from a modern gazetteer but from *The Scholar Gypsy*.

One thing however that all the early chapters of biographies of distinguished Englishmen, be they writers, statesmen or scholars, seemed to agree on was that the subject spent his days at Oxford or Cambridge almost exclusively among a set of friends all of whom subsequently became eminent in one way or another. To get into any university in the late fifties was a signal achievement but for Antony it had to be Oxbridge or nothing, for that alone, on all the available evidence, meant a chance to associate with the soon-to-be great and famous of the coming generation and in all likelihood, given his talents and vivid if diffuse ambitions, win a prominent place among them.

The world was evidently divided into the Oxbridge elite and the rest. The sovereign importance of gaining admission to that charmed enclosure became his overriding obsession and he could see only too well how failure to do so might be the life-ruining tragedy that it had been for Jude Fawley. Fortunately his A level results were so good as to make it virtually impossible for his mother not to agree to his going back to school for a final term to prepare for and sit the Oxford scholarship. She had expected this absurd university business to have blown over long before now and had done her best to discourage him. All his life she had been telling him (as well as his father) that he wouldn't like this or didn't really want to do that, about any proposed novelty or change in their rigid and blinkered domestic routine, but on this she could see that her son was determined as never before.

Ever since he had been going to the grammar school she sensed that she had been gradually losing the influence and control over him that she had hitherto taken for granted. Now it had come to this. She blamed the school bitterly for having, in her words, "put ideas into his head." It was a rather alarming development which she had been quite unprepared for and did not know how to handle. However she continued to hope with some confidence that he would not pass the entrance exam;

after all, she reckoned, there must be thousands and thousands from all over the country competing for very few places.

VI

The week that he saw Oxford for the first time when he went up in December 1957 to sit the second and decisive part of the exam – it was also the first time he had ever been away from home on his own – was one of painfully mixed emotions. Though the old stones were not immediately as impressive as he had expected they worked their spell on him as he began to get the measure of the place. (Mr Marjoribanks had advised him that last minute revision was useless so he had some leisure time when not actually caught up in the toils of exams). But how could he surrender to its enchantment when wandering round the deer park of Magdalen – he knew it was pronounced Maudlin and spelt differently from the Cambridge college – or the cathedral of Christ Church, known to its members after its Latin name as 'The House' or the sumptuous library of Queen's, so spelt because unlike its Cambridge sister it was founded by only one queen, not to mention dining by candlelight in the medieval hall of Mitre College – not as grand as Magdalen or Christchurch perhaps, but a perfectly respectable centuries old Oxford college, with a sprinkling of real live dons above him on high table – *it was not his to enjoy!* Only by passing the exams he was daily sweating blood over with sixty others in the college law library could he possibly earn the right to make all that his own. Failure to do so would exclude him from it for ever and banish him to the outer darkness.

Few undergraduates were still up but how he envied those he saw during that fateful week slumped in hall wrapped in their gowns, mooching round the college and about the city, solitary or in groups, gossiping, complaining, emerging from libraries and diving into pubs. How could they appear so nonchalant, so unimpressed, so apparently oblivious of their immense and secure good fortune? It was as if they were flaunting their uniquely privileged existence in his face. He felt as never before the immense gulf that separated them, the élite that had 'got in', from himself, the humble aspirant.

Once he himself was 'in,' though with a place rather than a scholarship – that would have been too much to imagine – and installed in his attic room overlooking the Chapel Quad of Mitre College in Turl Street in the heart of the city, he found university life nothing like as exciting as he had imagined it to be from the outside. For one thing, knowing no one at all when he came up – he was the only boy in his school going to Oxford that October – and lacking anyone to show him the ropes, he felt very much alone. This was compounded by the fact that apart from a few tutorials a week he appeared to be left completely to his own devices. At school, whether he liked it or not, he had been part of a community where he was known and to some extent appreciated and in which every hour of his day had been timetabled and supervised. Here, had he wanted to, he could have stayed in bed on most days without anyone enquiring where he was. No one seemed to know or care whether he was in his room, the college library, the English faculty library, the Bodleian or the schools, or just wandering about the city, and neither lectures nor meals were compulsory.

The only people that he came into contact with regularly were the small group of freshmen reading English like himself and the people on his own staircase, none of whom seemed to be at all interesting. It was impossible to imagine any of them, even decades hence, being eminent in any field. The man he saw most of was a prodigiously boring scientist from Solihull with a droning voice and disfiguring acne. He lived in the room immediately below and kept coming in for coffee, probably because no one else would talk to him. While the more amusing freshmen proved elusive the man from Solihull clung to him like a limpet.

Antony knew that if he wanted to take full advantage of his time at Oxford he would have to push himself and make an active effort to meet people, but this was not his style. His diffidence was all the greater initially in that, though as a freshman he had the novel experience of being addressed as a 'gentleman' in official communications, apart from drinking beer and smoking pipefuls of aromatic tobacco, he felt very much as he had done as a senior schoolboy and was all too aware that he was totally inexperienced in the ways of the world especially where the opposite sex was concerned: though as far as he could see girls played no part in the day to day social life of the college. There appeared to be very little contact with the women's colleges which were all on the fringes of the city anyway and the young women he saw at English lectures seemed much more mature and self-assured than he was and kept very much to themselves. For the moment at least there seemed no danger of his being ensnared by domestic bliss to the detriment of his creative potential as Mr Marjoribanks had cautioned.

Though the notion of student life might have had alarming bohemian connotations for respectable folk such as Antony's mother, Oxford undergraduates, who were never then referred to as mere 'students' in any case, were at least a decade away from the permissive 'sex, drugs and rock 'n roll' lifestyle which began to emerge in the sixties. (Indeed the very concept of 'lifestyle' would have been totally alien.) It was still the age of short hair, grey flannels (if not plus fours!), college ties and scarves, rather than jeans, T-shirts and trainers, with not a guitar or a beard in sight. Subversive satire was still confined to few bright young men in the Cambridge Footlights and the 'Ban the Bomb' movement had barely begun.

Oxford life also seemed to Antony extraordinarily fragmented. Not merely were there the divisions into quite separate colleges but within the college as well. There were the ex-National Servicemen who really did stand out as men among boys, the easy mannered and socially confident public schoolboys, the hearty sporting fraternity of rowers and rugger players, the crowd who spent most of their time in the Mitre Arms and a few smaller groups like the actors and politicos, the religious and the handful of genuinely scholarly types (as distinct from the fairly numerous scholars) as well as a few who liked to think of themselves as aesthetes. Then there were the inevitable divisions by subject which also tended to create social divisions as well: lawyers, scientists, medics, classicists, historians, geographers, the English lot and so on. Naturally these college groups overlapped – most of the medics were drinkers and rugger players for example – but none of them held any attraction for Antony.

There were of course any number of university clubs and societies ranging from country dancing and bee keeping to the Communist Party which he could join if he wished, but only three conferred any real prestige: the OUDS, *The ISIS* and the Union. Being regarded as a potential entrée into the worlds of theatre, journalism and literature and politics respectively, they were said to be cliquey and difficult to make one's mark in. One was advised to establish a reputation in the college first before attempting to scale those dizzy heights. ('Getting in', it seemed, was still a problem.) But his immediate priority was passing the English prelims at the end of his second term. Though failures were rare he saw it as the final hurdle before his place at Oxford was really secure, so he bent all his energies to studying the rudiments of Anglo-Saxon and the two books of the *Aeneid* and of *Paradise Lost* that the exam required. But apart from the Anglo-Saxon which he rather enjoyed, it was all very familiar ground and he felt he was marking time. It was just like his first year at grammar school which, apart from French and Latin, was largely spent covering work he had already done. Freshmen had no contact with the senior English don. The junior don and a lecturer put them through their prelim paces and neither was anything like as stimulating as Mr Marjoribanks. He passed of course like everyone else and was able to enjoy his first summer term with a delicious sense of being irrevocably secure within the bosom of the university and finals a full two years away.

Rather than advance his Oxford career he preferred to spend that Trinity Term floating gently downstream in a punt beneath the overarching bows, metaphorically at any rate. He had, in fact, already dismissed the Union – one visit was enough – as a self-regarding little coterie of 'characters' strutting about, telling in-jokes and playing to the gallery while aping the procedure of the House of Commons and appearing inordinately pleased with themselves in the process; whether or not the Union was a nursery for future statesmen it certainly resembled a nursery. The level of argument in his school debating society had been of a much higher quality. Nor was he impressed by the quality of the college undergraduate magazine or for that matter of *The ISIS*, or the various other more ephemeral publications that appeared on an irregular basis. He could not believe that failure to be involved with such parochial, studentish publications might conceivably stand in the way of a future literary career. He did, it is true, have a dream of playing Hamlet before a rapt audience in the Playhouse Theatre but he found the theatrical types in his own college very off-putting. Did he really want to spend his brief undergraduate years mixing with all those self-obsessed, jostling, posturing and preening egos with very little likelihood that he would in the end get a part in an OUDS production, let alone successfully audition for a leading role? Those who made it there, as everywhere else if the truth be told, seemed either to have connections or be brazen and persistent self-promoters, and he fell into neither category. In any case trying to get into an OUDS show or on to the Union committee was evidently more or less a full-time occupation and his priorities were academic; not so much to get a first, but the very best degree he was capable of. Only then could he say he had not wasted his time at Oxford. And he only had six brief terms in which to do it. He simply did not feel sure enough that he possessed the rare brilliance that would allow him to squander his time on non-academic activities and still 'scrape a first'. It was not a risk he felt justified in taking.

Antony now went to tutorials with Mitre's senior English don Dr Aubrey Rameses who listened politely as he read his essays and afterwards delivered a few insightful aperçus on the week's author while at the same time subtly conveying the impression that he would rather be doing almost anything else than listen to the same naïve and derivative undergraduate ramblings year after year. Antony noted that whenever he tried to liven up an essay by introducing an element of humour his tutor would laugh heartily if he were quoting from an established author, however familiar the reference, but without exception studiously ignore his own original witticisms. And however hard he had worked on his essay he was always left with the feeling that he had somehow just failed in some mysterious way that was never quite made explicit, to get to the essence of the subject. The impression was reinforced by the way in which his tutor never failed to enquire politely, after Antony had finished reading him his effort, whether or not he was familiar with a whole series of apparently crucial works that Dr Rameses had previously omitted to mention.

As an academic subject he found English Literature unexpectedly frustrating and unsatisfactory, at least as taught at Oxford. He seemed to be spending much more time navigating his way through shoals of highly opinionated critics, all with their various axes to grind, than on the poems, plays and novels they were writing about, and quickly grew tired of the all too familiar categories of literary evaluation: character and plot, intention and achievement, style and content, and so on. Eng Lit seemed to inhabit its own rarefied and virtually self-sufficient world. Apart from the occasional disparaging reference to Freudian or Marxist interpretations, there was scarcely an acknowledgement of any social, intellectual, let alone international, context. An alpha essay consisted of a string of well-conceived critical insights or 'good points' on a given subject. The ability consistently to produce such essays denoted a 'first class brain' and the prospect of a first. Antony never quite achieved this trick. At least until the end of his second year, his laboriously worked over essays were 'beta plus plus' with just a dash of alpha; his was apparently a 'good second class brain'. Nevertheless he clung to the conviction that he was somehow better than this. He knew he had the makings of a don and scholar in him. If only he could acquire the knack of writing the right sort of essays!

At the beginning of his second year he had begun to wonder whether he ought not to have heeded Mr Marjoribanks advice and read History. (At that point he could still have switched schools.) But he had been deterred by acquaintances who suggested that the subject had nothing to do with the capacity to understand and empathize with the great figures of the past and be deeply stirred by great events (in both of which Antony felt himself exceptionally if not uniquely qualified), but was rather a matter of poring over Stubbs' Charters and other dry-as-dust source material and assessing the value of various documents and set texts as evidence, together with a lot of talk about fashionable and unfashionable views of a particular event or period. Oxford seemed to have a way of chopping even the most promising subject into narrow specialisms and petty arguments which made it almost impossible to see any wood, however magnificent, for the trees.

Thus Antony found precious little cultural or intellectual nourishment of any kind as an Oxford undergraduate. In those far off days before pop culture had carried all before it, the arts, as they were then called, were quite a demanding and high-minded business (even the avant-garde was respectable). They meant opera, ballet, the legitimate theatre, subtitled films, certain serious novelists, slim volumes of poetry, Picasso and Henry Moore, and precious little of any of this was available in those days in what was, when all was said and done, an English provincial town. When Antony ventured out to an outlying cinema on a chilly February evening to see Cocteau's *Orphée* he found the auditorium almost empty.

Apart from a few conspicuous poseurs, most of his contemporaries were unsurprisingly far more interested in beer drinking and the football results than culture. As for any discussion in the area of what might be called the 'Meaning of Life', he soon learnt that philosophy as currently practised at Oxford had nothing to say about morality or politics and was simply contemptuous of so-called ultimate questions. All metaphysics was simply the result of muddles with words, technically called 'category mistakes.' In fact if the terms were properly analysed it would be seen that there were really no philosophical problems at all! Fortunately for philosophy dons however, this analysis was expected to take some considerable time. As for existentialism, Jean-Paul Sartre, and the whole intellectual ferment of Saint-Germain-des-Prés, it did not even begin to warrant serious examination and had nothing to do with philosophy properly so-called!

Most of this he gleaned from Loader, a clumsy and dishevelled PPE man (reputedly brilliant and a regarded as a certain first) whom he occasionally met for coffee in the Cadena café – a hazardous business as Loader was liable to fling his arms round while expostulating, sending hot liquid flying in all directions. But though a robust, not to say scornful, Humean sceptic in philosophy, one morning to Antony's great surprise he produced with uncharacteristic diffidence a sheaf of dog-eared papers from his inside pocket which proved to be a collection of his own very sentimental lyric verse.

"Don't read them now," he added hastily, "but I would be grateful if you could go through them when you've got time and let me know what you think. There's no hurry."

Antony was flattered and more than a little embarrassed that Loader, who clearly did not have much of an opinion of his understanding of philosophy, evidently valued his literary judgement sufficiently to entrust him with these very personal poems. Their prevailing theme was loneliness and the inability to achieve any kind of intimacy with others; but the most remarkable feature was that they were punctuated with sploshes which had caused the ink to run making the writing quite illegible in many places. When Antony examined the stains in question later he discovered that they were not made by tears, as might have been appropriate, but by traces of whatever beverage he had been consuming at the time in the solitude of his room.

Thus by his second year Antony was considerably disillusioned with Oxford. For him it was dowdy, parochial, self-absorbed and lacking in any kind of intellectual excitement: difficult to believe that tucked away in panelled chambers in various crumbling sandstone eyries round the city were to be found some at least of the world's foremost authorities on their subjects! Oxford's prestigious history, he knew, was also something of a fraud. Founded in the first place only because English students were temporarily banned from Paris, it had been a notoriously sleepy clerical backwater for most of the post-Reformation period. Even in the nineteenth century when great centres of learning were flourishing in Germany it was still little more than a glorified training college for Church of England clergy.

Nevertheless gently and ineluctably the place had entered its soul. Its history might be less than glorious but in a very English way it had kept its fabric and its traditions intact through the upheavals of recent centuries in a way that few other major seats of learning had managed to do. In any case he liked being part of a community where, generally speaking, intellectual criteria prevailed. He might not have read anything like as much as the smug dons but at least he knew what knowledge and scholarship really were and could thus see through the crude simplifications, half-truths, imposture and propaganda of politicians and journalists. With all its shortcomings Oxford was infinitely preferable to the crass and unlettered outside world of getting and spending, and as the terms began, all too quickly to slip by, he yearned to be a permanent, rather than a temporary, part of it all; ultimately to be a don, absolutely secure and irremovable in his ancient and book-lined suite of rooms, ensconced in his favourite chair in a deep-carpeted senior common room and sipping vintage port on high table. 'Staying on' now became as great an obsession as 'getting in' and 'going up' had once been. As far as he could see, the thousands that left every year after their first degree did so for two reasons: either they had failed to make the grade or they were prepared to sell out in one way or another, compromising intellectual rigour and disinterestedness in the scramble for power, reward or notoriety. But of course 'staying on' meant getting a good enough degree – a first or at least a top second – to be accepted for a B.Litt. which might lead to a D.Phil., a lectureship, a junior fellowship... Such was his dream.

There was only one character at Oxford who really inspired him – in fact he was the only person he ever encountered in his whole life who seemed capable of genuinely penetrating and original insights into the basic problems of existence: a chubby fresh-faced unfailingly cheerful and incorrigibly disorganised young man with red hair and freckles studying Oriental Languages, called Rollo Mandeville. There was nothing pompous or didactic about him – his favourite recreation was playing jazz on the beaten up honky-tonk piano in the corner of his room – and he appeared much happier getting others to talk than holding the floor himself, but his luminous intelligence and absolute sincerity made him a genuinely charismatic figure. He had a gift for bringing out the best in the most unlikely people; stimulating them and making them feel they were able to make a valuable contribution to a discussion. No one could have made less of an effort to be impressive or impose himself – indeed he radiated a sort of childlike simplicity – yet everybody who was anybody in the undergraduate world seemed to find their way to his ground floor rooms, and though only in his second year he was, at least in Antony's limited experience, by far the most popular undergraduate in the university. Antony, who would not normally have intruded into such company, found himself a frequent visitor simply because, till Rollo was taken ill during the summer term, they happened that year to have rooms directly opposite each other on the same staircase, and everybody from the shyest freshman to aspiring presidents of the Union was made equally welcome.

Proximity made him and Antony friends where nothing else would have done. For all he knew Rollo might have had any number of intimates – they never met outside the college as far as he could remember – but nevertheless it was undeniably true that in coffee fuelled tête-à-têtes far into the night, Antony, who was little given to confidences, confided in him more than in anyone else before or since. It was not just that he found Rollo congenial and sympathetic; just listening to him, being in his presence, gave one the feeling that life was beyond question worth living.

The episode that most stood out in Antony's Oxford life however was when he was part of a crowd of about a dozen in Rollo's room – including Loader whom Antony had brought with him – late afternoon or early evening, comfortable even drowsy warmth, fug of tobacco smoke and one of those lively wide-ranging discussions that seemed to spring up spontaneously under his influence. Someone was going on about the various ways in which survival after death had been imagined down the ages: the immortality of the soul, bodily resurrection, reincarnation, eternal recurrence, apotheosis and so on, concluding that, of course, even when subjected to most cursory analysis, the concept of post-mortem existence could have no meaning.

Almost diffidently Rollo intervened, as if he were thinking aloud rather than joining in: "... life and death... past and present... perhaps it all arises from a confusion about time..."

"How do you mean?" asked the pipe-smoking Loader uneasily.

"Well, everything that happens, everything that we can possibly experience is in the present; even memories, thoughts about the future, they can only be present, they can only happen now..."

"Are you saying that the past doesn't exist any more than the future?"

"What I'm saying, I suppose, is that time isn't a series of events a lot of which have happened already with a lot more lined up waiting to happen... Think of a work of art. Madame Bovary exists now at every stage of her life in the novel – we describe all her actions in the present don't we? – even though we can only read about her one sentence at a time. It's the same with a symphony. Wouldn't it be absurd to suggest that the only part of it that exists is the note currently being played? Well, life is infinitely more complex and more inscrutable than even the greatest work of art... Material things decay but the essence of experience is timeless."

"Timeless?"

"Yes. It has to be. If experience were really nothing but a series of moments in time flashing without intermission from future to past, how could we possibly perceive anything? What would there be to perceive and who would be doing the perceiving? This linear sequence of time is just a way we have of arranging things, a pattern we impose – a quirk of our brains, I suppose. But who knows what other realities, alternative lives, other modes of existence, might be available to us if only we were open to them. Why shouldn't everything exist that can possibly exist...?

"So what about life after death?"

"It's simply the wrong question. Everything that exists, exists now, outside what we think of as time. Nothing is lost. How could it be? Don't be tricked by grammar into believing in the future conditional or the past historic, or the present indicative for that matter. It's all now."

Now, now, now, mused Antony dreamily as others intervened and the conversation droned on unheeded while he was absorbed in watching a plume of smoke rise in a speck-filled beam of light slanting down across the room, wreathe round itself, expand and flatten like a little galaxy and then slowly thin and disperse. That moment and every moment. Now and forever. Timeless. There was no point in any further discussion. He knew it was true; it must be true, all of it. Nothing lost, parallel existences – it corresponded to what he had somehow always known but had never been able to express coherently. What a universe away from the dry fare of current Oxford philosophy, or rather anti-philosophy!

Looking back, Antony could never quite decide whether it had been late November round a glowing electric fire with gathering dusk outside or May, with the last of the late spring sunshine filtering through the high sash windows. Whichever it was, in the middle of the summer term of that second year Rollo's room suddenly became empty. He had succumbed, it was learnt, to a rare form of leukaemia and he died in the subsequent summer vacation.

In retrospect the months of Rollo's influence had been the high point of Antony's Oxford career and his tragic disappearance, though he did not realise it at the time, marked the end of his Oxford dream. He often wondered whether his wonderful friend, who always seemed a picture of health, had known that he had only a short time to live. Had facing that knowledge led him to develop the distinctive philosophy which enabled him to live his life with that unique mixture of intensity, light-heartedness and serenity that made him such a compelling and attractive personality? Strangely, though on any reckoning he had been recognised as one of the most notable undergraduates in the university, in later years Antony was never able to find a single reference to him in biographical accounts and memoirs of student days covering that period.

Although by now he was well aware that such accounts inevitably tended to highlight only those contemporaries who subsequently became well known, he was more than a little surprised that Rollo Mandeville was passed over without any mention at all. It almost began to seem as if he had imagined him. In any case after Rollo's death Antony's driving ambition to get a good degree and 'stay on' faded, and by the time it revived, early in his final term, he felt he was so behind with his planned reading and revision that, after a day of heart searching, he persuaded his tutors, against their better judgement since they had him down for a first, to let him postpone his finals for a year. It was a momentous decision but Antony was convinced it was the only way that he would stand any chance of doing himself justice. But he never quite knew afterwards if he had done the right thing or impulsively thrown away his chances of becoming a don, and for years afterwards he had vivid waking dreams in which the decision was still before him with all still to play for.

However Oxford and the friends he met through Rollo remained with him, though he never had any more contact with them, as a permanent dimension to his life. He could almost always stop what he was doing and find himself back in that group in Rollo's room among all those as yet undaunted young minds putting the universe to rights – trading ideas, hammering out arguments and outdoing each other in the most audacious speculations which they naturally assumed were entirely unprecedented. The dons had only baffled and frustrated him. He had been made all too aware of his deficiencies and the academic game had been conducted on their terms so that he could only win such limited approval as he did by playing it their way. Only in the uniquely stimulating atmosphere generated by Rollo had he felt that his original qualities and insights might be truly understood and valued at their true worth. Only there, in that company, had he ever felt intellectually, or for want of a better word spiritually, at home.

VII

But Oxford was for the future. For now the great boon was that he would not be going up ('going up', what a resonance that phrase had!) until the following October – a full nine months away. Now at last was his chance to travel; to begin to explore that real world beyond the narrow confines of savourless, colourless, hidebound, philistine, suburban Britain, where in his imagination he had always lived and moved and had his being. He had never felt the ties of home, family or country. At heart he knew he was a gypsy, a nomad, a wanderer, a rootless adventurer! So as soon as the fateful envelope plopped onto the mat offering him his place, he made arrangements to leave the country.

With his father's connivance and without his mother knowing anything about it, he had procured himself a passport, taken his life savings out of the Post Office and bought tickets at Thomas Cook's. Thus he was able to confront his mother – who would doubtless have tried to get him to work in a local shop for nine months – with a fait accompli on the very morning of his departure, leaving his unfortunate father to cope with the fallout. In vain did he suggest to her mildly that it was natural for young people to want to travel and see the world, though he couldn't see the need for it himself. His wife was, predictably, implacable. For her 'the continent' was corrupt, unsanitary, dangerous, hostile and backward. In all likelihood they would never see their son again. Abandoning his home like that was a monstrously perverse act of ingratitude in return for the endless sacrifices she had made for him!

So it was that just after his nineteenth birthday Antony found himself on the deck of a channel ferry gazing back at the ever receding cliffs of Dover, feeling the pernicious imposed restraints and inhibitions of eighteen dim years in a semi-detached in Fullwell Avenue dropping away from him with every succeeding yard of the ship's wake. He was free at last, free to be himself, and the world was waiting for him! Then turning away from the sight of the English coast and not caring whether he ever saw it again, he made his way up to the other end of the vessel and strained for the first faint glimpse of the coast of France.

"...les voyageurs pour Paris restent dans leurs voitures!"

Antony caught the end of the announcement sitting in a corner seat of a crowded train, his knapsack in the rack above him, looking out on Calais-Maritime station. It was late afternoon in early February and all the lights were already on. Everything around him seemed interesting, vivid, appealing: the low platform, the police in their kepis and cloaks, the nonchalant railwayman walking along the track tapping train wheels with a metal bar, the smell of Gauloises cigarettes, the handshakes and shouted greetings, the signs and advertisements in French. The whole scene was so much more animated, more charged with energy than on the other side of the channel; even the station architecture was lean and functional, entirely lacking the ugly and rather pretentious solidity of Britain – and Paris lay just a few hours down the line. Paris! How much was summed up in that one word – glamour, sophistication, history, culture, political, intellectual and artistic ferment; the crossroads of the world and the capital of European civilization, the goal of every traveller and tourist who ever left his native land, and before the day was over he would be part of it all. Vienna might be his ultimate objective but where else but Paris could be his first destination. He was indeed a 'voyageur pour Paris'. Now he was truly abroad and it felt like coming home. This really was waking up from a sad and already forgotten dream to the reality of a bright morning. He was conscious of being full of life and its possibilities as never before!

After Amiens there was a call for dinner and Antony spent the rest of the journey in the shiny dark panelled restaurant car. He marvelled at the skill of the waiters who managed to serve him soup and then freshly cooked côte de veau and a selection of vegetables from piping hot metal trays with spoon and fork, while all the time adjusting so skilfully to the swaying and jolting of the train as not to spill a single drop on the white tablecloth. The meal, accompanied by half a bottle of red wine and completed by cheese, tarte aux pommes, coffee and brandy, served as he rattled through the dark fields of Picardy, was for Antony, brought up on his mother's cooking and school food, the most delicious as well as the most sophisticated culinary experience of his life. He lingered at the table after he had paid the bill savouring the whole situation and trying to make his cognac last as long as possible.

When he had finished cashing up, the restaurant manager, seeing that Antony was alone and no doubt feeling benevolent after having finished for the day, came over with a bottle and offered him another brandy. He sat down opposite and they fell into conversation, chatting away amiably (Antony hardly even aware that he was using his A level French in earnest for the first time), smoking and drinking together until the first lights of the northern suburbs of Paris started flashing by the windows. Back in England he would have kept himself to himself and avoided conversation with a stranger but in this new free life it seemed natural to be open, confident and spontaneous with other people, even to take the initiative. Now that he was able to begin again as it were, jettisoning all the baggage he had somehow collected in his past, there was nothing to stop him being the person he always knew he had it in him to be!

Though he did feel momentarily overwhelmed when plunged into the heaving anonymity of the Gare du Nord, the feeling soon passed as he reflected on how fortunate he was to be thus invisible to the world. He should make the most of this opportunity of being able to travel incognito and unobserved. How many more would there be before imperial duties and responsibilities engulfed him and the doors of the palace began to close behind him?

Antony installed himself on the very top floor of a cheap one star hotel, rather grandiloquently called Le Grand Hôtel du Globe, in the Marais which in those days was still a rather shabby and run-down area, its hôtels particuliers yet to be restored to their ancien régime glory, but quite conveniently central nevertheless. In the late fifties there were no credit cards, no hole in the wall cash dispensers on every corner and severe restrictions on the amount of sterling that could be taken overseas. He was only too well aware that in order to stay abroad for an extended period as he planned, he would have to earn some money. Accordingly, with his new found confidence, he asked in the local brasserie where he was to become a regular, striking up a cordial relationship with the 'patron', if he knew of anyone in the quartier who wanted English lessons from an Oxford student – he also advertised his services at the boulangerie on the corner – and before long he had enough clients to keep him busy for a few hours each day and longer on Saturdays, with the great advantage that all he had to do to earn his money was talk! This talking generally took place at a table in the brasserie (the patron was quite happy with this arrangement as it often brought in customers at quiet times of the day) and sometimes, if the weather was mild, in the Place des Vosges or the Tuileries or the Jardin du Luxembourg, but never in his cramped hotel room.

Antony spent his spare time reading and exploring the city he knew so well in theory, making Sunday expeditions to such places as Versailles, Fontainebleau, Barbizon, Saint-Germain-en-Laye, Chantilly and Chartres. He also kept a very detailed diary of impressions – which inevitably he hoped would one day provide the material for a novel – often writing it up during his solitary evening meal in the brasserie. (His proudest moment was when he overheard the patron describing him to a customer at the bar as a "jeune écrivain"!) Though he was on friendly terms with those he saw daily in the quartier and there was no shortage of people to talk to, he was essentially alone and, in fact, rather relished his solitariness which, for the first time in his life, allowed him essentially to do as he pleased without external demands or intrusions and free of the stifling constraints of his so-called home.

Before leaving England he had naturally imagined that once in Paris he would be swiftly initiated into a series of intense sexual adventures. But though he felt he was in many respects living a new and liberated life he had, as yet, experienced no sexual initiation. Fantasies of being taken up by some Trilby-like grisette encountered by chance in an artist's studio proved to be several generations out of date. The bosomy middle-aged woman with dyed hair who occupied the other attic room in the hotel across the landing from his was, as it happened, a whore – or so he assumed from the succession of men who went in and out of her room – but though she knocked on his door from time to time to borrow sugar or coffee and they sometimes sat and chatted together, she obviously regarded him as a neighbour and even a sort of confidant, rather than a potential client. In any case Antony, for all his increasingly elaborate fantasies of Babylonian orgies, would have been too fastidious and fearful of catching something to go with a prostitute, even had she been much younger and more attractive.

The weeks passed. Spring came to Paris, the city began to fill up with Americans and he was still a virgin and restless. He had begun to tire of the little world of the quartier and a routine so regular that if he missed his evening meal in the brasserie he felt constrained to explain to the patron where he had been and what he had been doing. So by the third week of April he felt it was time to move south and without telling anyone – he paid for his hotel room a week in advance – simply packed up his knapsack and moved on.

Hitch-hiking that morning at the Porte d'Italie, perhaps because he looked young, clean cut and presentable, he had the good luck to be picked up after a mere five minutes by an English family, the Dunmores – an attractive couple in their thirties, with two very bright little girls aged eight and six. They proved to be the sort of relaxed, happy, high-spirited family that Antony had thought only existed in fiction and before long he was on Christian name terms with them all. During the course of a stop for a late lunch at Auxerre, Alex Dunmore said he was on his way to Toulouse to take up a job with Shell Oil, but before he started work and they all got settled into their new home with the girls adjusting to life in a French school, they had decided to treat themselves to a month on the Côte d'Azur, making their way there at a leisurely pace with overnight stops at Vienne, just south of Lyon, and Avignon. When Alex added that Antony was very welcome to join them en route if it suited him, he naturally leapt at the offer. Though he had promised himself that as soon as he crossed the Channel he would eschew all contact with the British he unhesitatingly made an exception for the Dunmores and, it should be said, more than earned his ride by keeping the children amused in the back of the car, playing 'I Spy' with them and teaching them a little French.

By the time they got to the Riviera he had become so much part of the family that it was virtually assumed as a matter of course that he would be staying with them in the villa they were renting just outside Antibes. Antony was torn. He had grown very fond of them all, but being incorporated into family life, however congenial, was quite incompatible with being a free-wheeling and rootless adventurer. Explanations and goodbyes would have been painful and embarrassing. There was nothing for it but to be ruthless, so under cover of all the coming and going involved in the move into the villa he simply slipped away never to be seen again and half an hour later was looking for somewhere to stay in Cannes. Although he regretted what he had had to do and tried not to think of the Dunmores' reaction, his overwhelming emotion was exhilaration at having recovered his freedom, and very quickly the whole episode was forgotten except as elaborated in the pages of his diary.

It was the beginning of the tourist season with the town gearing up for the Film Festival in a few weeks' time, and places of entertainment all along the coast were taking on temporary staff. Antony with his English and increasingly competent French had no difficulty in finding work, first as a waiter then, when he tired of that, as a beach attendant and ice cream seller, supplementing his earnings with some judicious gambling on the roulette wheel in Monte Carlo which finally left him nearly two thousand francs to the good.

By the beginning of August he had saved enough to stop work and pursue his dream of visiting the cities of Italy and then, if there was enough time before the Oxford term began, the main archaeological sites of Greece. (When nowadays young people think nothing of backpacking round the world during their gap year this may seem a modest enough goal but fifty years ago Antony thought it quite intrepid.) Thus, hitch-hiking and spending the night in youth hostels, he made his way via Genoa, La Spezia, Parma and Bologna to Ravenna accomplishing the journey in a mere two and a half days. Hitching proved unexpectedly easy in Italy for not only did Italian drivers seem very willing to stop especially if they were on their own, but the number plates carrying city initials often indicated where the car was bound for and the roads were excellent. After spending three days absorbing the Byzantine splendours of Ravenna, last outpost of imperial rule in the West, Antony decided with regret under pressure of time, to postpone the exploring of Venice and the Veneto, its Palladian hinterland, till his next visit, and push on to Florence and the other major attractions of Tuscany and Umbria before getting to Rome where he intended to stay for at least a week.

Every detail of this journey, every impression, was meticulously and evocatively chronicled in his diary and he was as enchanted as countless travellers had been before him; but it was a lonely business conscientiously making his way round galleries, churches, palaces and villas with his Hachette Blue Guide only able communicate his responses to the pages of a notebook. If only he had more time, more money and someone to share his thoughts, then he felt he would really be able to experience it all to the full, to let it sink into his soul. At any rate he swore to himself he would return again and again. England had by now all but completely faded from his consciousness. He avoided English people as far as he could, never looked at an English newspaper and whenever possible, especially with Italians, spoke only in French which, as it happened, generally resulted in him being treated with considerably more consideration and respect. Moreover it seemed to be automatically assumed that anyone who spoke English was an American which in Antony's eyes was even worse than being British!

He lingered for ten unforgettable days in Rome until the end of August, in shimmering heat pervaded by resin scented pines, changing youth hostels three times before preparing to take the cheapest ferry to Greece which he discovered ran from Otranto, right down in the heel of Italy, to Igoumenitsa. By now an experienced hitch-hiker he managed the journey via Pescara, Foggia, Bari and Brindisi in just forty-eight hours and very much enjoyed the process. Not only was there a rather exhilarating element of chance involved but he found it the best way on his travels so far of meeting people. It was surprising what interesting and sometimes quite intimate conversations one could have when both parties were assured that they would in all probability never meet again.

The morning crossing to Igoumenitsa was rough. The small steamer which was nothing like a modern car ferry rolled and shuddered, reared and plunged down into troughs between waves. Cutlery cascaded onto the floor of the deserted restaurant. Glasses and bottles were thrown about and smashed. The few passengers staggering about on deck or clinging to the rails were liable to throw up suddenly and without warning. But Antony was exhilarated and proud to be one of the very few on board to be entirely immune to fear or sea sickness. Perhaps it was his evident enjoyment that attracted the attention of two members of the crew who invited him to come below and share some food with them. Once down in the hold however he found himself being crudely propositioned with increasing insistence by half a dozen Greek deckhands and it was only with some difficulty that he managed to extricate himself. Fortunately by that time the boat was rounding Corfu and approaching the Greek mainland.

Greece in those days was not a major tourist destination and quite untouched by the mass package holiday market. Young independent travellers like him (Antony would have indignantly rejected the label 'tourist') were a comparative rarity and he often encountered the same people among the small group visiting each archaeological site. As he made his way across the country to Larissa and down to Athens by narrow roads that in places were not even asphalted, in the backs of lorries and buses crowded with peasants and in some cases livestock, he had a sense that he was experiencing the real adventure of travel for the first time. The contrast even with the south of Italy was stark. Brindisi for instance was a substantial and imposing city while Greece was very evidently still a poor, down at heel and largely rural Balkan country dotted with classical, Mycenaean and a few Byzantine remains (though nothing as impressive as Ravenna) which apart from its language and Orthodox faith had little real connection with its brilliant past. This of course was what one might have expected after centuries of Turkish occupation. And unlike the Italians, the Greeks seemed rather sensitive and over insistent about 'their' great heritage, aware perhaps that modern Greece had not much to offer by comparison and that its connection with ancient Hellas was tenuous to say the least.

This is not to say he was not enjoying his Greek adventure. Youth hostels being thin on the ground he got used to unrolling his sleeping bag in any reasonably well protected spot he could find, and how could he resist sleeping on the lower slopes of Mount Parnassus! Delphi on its hillside overlooking olive groves stretching all the way to the Gulf of Itea was magical, even though it was difficult to imagine the Mysteries and Persephone being carried off to the Underworld in an Eleusis that had now become an industrial suburb of Athens where everything seemed to be covered in a fine dust of cement.

In spite of superficial similarities Antony was struck by the immense difference between Athens and Rome. Rome in its fabric and history epitomised almost every age of western civilization from antiquity to the present day. By one title or another it had never ceased down the centuries to be the City. Athens-Piraeus on the other hand was an undistinguished modern Mediterranean urban sprawl which had grown in little over a hundred years from a Turkish village of a few thousand people at the foot of the Acropolis – even in Byzantine times the capital of the Greek world was Constantinople, the Second Rome, not Athens. Of course when it came to antiquity Athens had the edge. Roman remains counted for nothing in Greece and when the Parthenon was built Rome was an unimpressive town struggling for supremacy in central Italy...

Antony was interrupted in the midst of these rather disorientating reflections as he stood on the Areopagus by a voice from somewhere behind him saying: "the young Englishman abroad, how charming!"

He whirled round irritated that anyone should be able to tell his nationality so easily. "How can you tell where I come from?"

The voice belonged to a youngish man in glasses with greasy black hair who was smiling rather disarmingly. "Oh, I'm a lover of all things English," he replied.

They got talking. He seemed interesting, well-educated and extremely knowledgeable about the ancient world. As far as Antony could gather he had some sort of civil service job. They went to a café together but when he started enthusing about the Emperor Hadrian's love for Greece and in particular his male favourite Antinous, then laid his hand on Antony's knee, suggesting that they take a 'siesta' at the apartment between Plaka and Syntagma Square that he shared with his mother, Antony, in the time honoured phrase, made an excuse and left. In fact he went to the toilet and out of a side door leaving his anglophile admirer to pay the bill.

But that evening his life changed. He was at Cape Sounion watching the sun set into the Aegean through the columns of the Temple of Poseidon, while trying to entertain a humourless Norwegian with a fixed smile and a curly beard who had attached himself to him, with a spirited discourse on Salamis, Themistocles and the Persian Wars, when he was accosted by an olive skinned and very brown young woman with swept back black hair wearing leather shorts, a check shirt and hiking boots.

"Do I know you?"

"I don't think so."

"I'm sure I've seen you some place before. Are you an actor?"

"What makes you think that?" (Antony was not displeased. It

was certainly more flattering to be taken for an actor than just another Englishman!)

"Oh, it's just the way you talk, your sense of humour I guess... You certainly know a lot of history. I'm very impressed. You make it sound so real. I'd love you to show me Greece!"

"Why not?

"Jesus!"

What's wrong?" He could see she was angry and frustrated.

"I was going to some place in southern Crete called Matala where you can sleep in caves by the beach but some fucking bastard's stolen all my money!"

"When was this?"

"It must have been this afternoon sometime. I've only just realised."

"You're very welcome to come with me; I've got plenty, that's if you don't mind doing the Peloponnese first!"

"Sure. When?"

"Now?"

Leaving the slightly bemused Norwegian, they hurried off to catch the bus back to Athens and were just in time for the last train to Corinth that evening.

"Do you feel safe as a girl going round Greece on your own?" asked Antony as soon as they were settled in the carriage.

"I'm not on my own, am I?"

"No, but when you were."

"Not in Greece. The men are all jerk-offs here or else they fancy each other. You know – Greek love. They've been at it for thousands of years. Boys, that's what they like!"

Antony told her about his own recent experiences in this area and made her laugh. Back in his old life in England he would have been too embarrassed to look a shop assistant in the eye let alone engage her in conversation, but now everything was different. Even so nothing had prepared him for his new companion. She so was totally unlike any girl he could have imagined. He had never even heard a woman swear before. The middle-aged prostitute he had come across in Paris was almost genteel by comparison!

In the course of the journey she told him a bit about herself. Her name was Laura. She had been born in New York – "half Jewish, half Italian" as she put it. Her parents had split up and she hated America anyway for its "conformism", so having dropped out of college she moved to Israel and went to live on a kibbutz. But the collective regimentation of kibbutz life didn't suit her either so now she was on her way to Italy to "check out" her other homeland. She was only two or three years older than Antony but with what seemed to him a lifetime's more experience. Nevertheless she apparently found him as fascinating as he found her, and they talked incessantly until they passed over the narrow strip of the Corinth Canal, seeing to their great surprise the funnel of a sizeable ship passing directly beneath them.

"Corinth," Antony informed Laura as they were pulling into the station, "used to be the 'Gay Paree' of the ancient world. The girls used to have 'follow me' stamped on the bottom of their sandals..."

Laura was intrigued. "Yeah? That was probably the Romans not the Greeks."

"It was, actually."

As modern Corinth proved to be what she called a "shithole" they walked off into the warm night in the direction of the site of Old Corinth, until they found a secluded spot by a stream where they could sleep. Then as Antony did his best to appear entirely nonchalant, Laura stripped without the least suggestion of self-consciousness, got naked into her sleeping bag and began to roll a cigarette.

"Would you like one?"

"I normally smoke Gauloises."

"You'll like this. It'll relax you."

"What is it?"

"Cannabis."

It did relax him. So it was under a glittering southern night sky punctuated by shooting stars, in a grove of cypresses overlooking fields of vines, that Antony finally and very comprehensively, thanks to Laura's accomplished efforts, lost his virginity. This was the night, as he saw it, when he ceased to be a spectator at the game of life and became a player. Now he really could call himself a free spirit. They finally got to sleep about three, and woke late discovering when they finally stirred, that in the clear morning light the spot they had chosen proved to be not nearly as secluded as they had thought!

Thus began a two week Peloponnesian idyll in which they went from village to village in a haze of pot, retsina and ouzo, eating in local kafenions where they were invariably invited into the kitchen to see if there was any moussaka on the stove; washing in rivers, relaxing in the shade of ancient gnarled olive trees, sleeping and making love every night under the stars, while they visited Mycenae and Tiryns, the theatre at Epidaurus, Argos, Sparta, the ruins of Byzantium's last redoubt at Mistra, Nestor's palace at Pylos and Olympia. What did it matter if Laura didn't really understand him or quite get his quirky 'English' sense of humour?

Though their arrival in a remote village invariably caused considerable excitement and they were met children running out to greet them with cries of "Inglis? Inglis? American? German?" the inhabitants were largely elderly with, as Laura pointed out, the men sitting outside the kafenion with the local priest talking politics while the women in headscarves toiled in the fields. More than once they were told that almost all the young people in a village had gone to Australia.

In mid-September they returned to Athens and caught the ferry from Piraeus to Heraklion in Crete. After an overnight stop in the youth hostel and a visit to 'the Palace of Minos' at Knossos they set out for the southern coast in a series of buses, the last of which bounced along a dirt road from Mires, where they had an evening meal, to Pitsidia stopping en route to take on a man with a goat. Though they had to do the last four kilometres on foot the journey was worth it. They arrived at the Bay of Matala as a blood red sun was setting into the turquoise sea of the Gulf of Messara. To their right, catching the last of the light, was a headland of sandstone honeycombed with caves, some of which were clearly occupied just as Laura had suggested, while rising from the curve of the beach was a small cluster of whitewashed buildings. A creature of impulse, she immediately stripped off and waded into the sea for a swim breasting the waves like some Minoan fertility goddess, while Antony had a paddle and guarded their knapsacks. It was a far cry from Fullwell Avenue!

On their first evening they did little more than take possession of a habitable cave, have a smoke, make love and fall asleep to the sound of a distant guitar. It was only the next day that they began to get to know the place they had come to. Matala, nowadays a fashionable commercial resort, though not yet then the haven for hippies and flower children that it was to become in the sixties and seventies, had already begun to attract a few people who for one reason or another wanted a freer way of life. This at last, he felt, was the bohemian world that he had sought in vain in Paris.

There was one small hotel and two tavernas, one of which was little more than a reed-thatched shelter on the edge of the beach. Perhaps because it was the end of the season there were only a handful of people in the caves: an intense young refugee from East Germany who as a socialist disliked the West almost as much as the GDR and was on his way to Egypt; an Austrian dodging National Service, which made him liable to a ten year jail sentence; his Swedish girlfriend and a rather straight-laced American college student with a very plain travelling companion, also a college student, that he insisted was not his girlfriend. The authorities, they were told by the East German, disapproved of the caves being occupied and periodically a couple of policemen arrived from Mires to inspect them. However as they came at the same time every week they invariably found the caves empty.

The main gathering place apart from the hotel and the tavernas was the house of one Nicos, whose wife and children it appeared, conveniently lived in Athens. Here they met the visitors who lived in the village as opposed to the transient population of the caves: a couple of chubby English-speaking girls of indeterminate nationality, both rather confusingly called Sylvia, who had been there all summer, appeared to be on fairly intimate terms with everybody and spent most of the time sunbathing naked on the beach; a Frenchman with receding blond hair in his early thirties called Serge, with two friends or acquaintances who had hitch-hiked from Paris to Matala with him; a Greek poet called Anastas; and Campbell, a black American living in Europe because of racial discrimination in his native Alabama, who played the guitar and supported himself by writing books about the Greek islands. There was also according to Serge "a very important writer" who lived in a secluded villa overlooking the bay, but he never appeared.

As for the real locals, apart from the proprietors of the tavernas, the one they encountered most was Costas, a wizened little man with a nut brown complexion and the face of a satyr. Reputed to be an ex-goatherd or fisherman, he now spent his days lurching about half drunk and leering at the sunbathing girls until told in most uncompromising language to be on his way. On one notable occasion during a boozy party at Nicos's, he fired a revolver three times into the ceiling after having been rebuffed by one of the Sylvias – "you fuck with everyone, why you no fuck with me!" This was also the occasion when their host introduced them to a murderer – "he has killed a man in the north of Crete and been to prison but the dead man's family still want to revenge so he stay here!" Altogether quite an eventful evening!

After a week Antony grew weary of the lotus eating little world of Matala, its petty quarrels and its cliquishness, not least because, after Laura had successfully taught him to swim, he felt he had constantly to compete with other people for her attention. He was also finding Serge a constant irritant. Not only was he given to extremely pretentious remarks but he insisted on patronizing Antony, treating him as a typically conventional bourgeois young Englishman, and though he felt that in his new life this charge no longer applied, it was nevertheless very galling that he could still be perceived in this way.

Laura however was clearly in her element at Matala, joining the sunbathing girls and showing no signs of wanting to move on. By this time the prospect of returning to England to take up his place at Oxford seemed so unreal and outlandish as not to warrant serious consideration. As far as the future was concerned he took it for granted that he would be staying with Laura and in due course accompanying her to Italy. At the beginning of the second week however, Antony suggested a visit to the nearby Minoan site of Phaistos and as she declined, went on his own. On his return, somewhat earlier than he had planned, he discovered Laura noisily making love with Campbell in their cave. Telling them to carry on, he immediately collected his things and made his way back to Heraklion, catching the ferry to Piraeus the next day.

Tired of Greece as well as shocked and humiliated, he was now intent on getting back to Italy as quickly as possible. By the beginning of October when he reached Genoa, though still hurt, he felt he had got 'The Laura Episode' as he called it in his diary, into some sort of perspective. He had always realised they were incompatible and therefore, he was now convinced, they could have had no long term future together. Evidently he had scarcely known her and she could have had no very serious feelings for him, so it was probably for the best that their relationship ended when it did. But he could not possibly regret having met her, and he now saw losing her as well as loving her, as an inevitable part of his initiation into the heart of life.

At Genoa, where he stayed for a week, he was confronted with a choice: a fork in the road, one of many such alternatives of which his life seemed to be constituted. There was an Italian liner in the harbour bound for Rio, which had an unexpected vacancy in the purser's office for someone who could speak English and very little time to fill it. Should he apply and continue to travel the world and forget about England for good? He knew now that he could support himself and was confident that with his enterprise and talents, and perhaps some help from the gaming tables, he could make his fortune as well as gaining the material for a whole series of novels. He yearned for a dangerous and adventurous life. Twenty years ago he would probably have gone to fight in Spain, but failing a good war he might still find some lost city deep in the Amazon jungle. Or should he return for three years to take his degree before launching himself into the world? Eventually he chose the latter course, catching the night train from Rome that ran via Chiasso and eastern France to Ostend, and for the rest of his life was haunted by regret for the road not taken, convinced that he had made the wrong decision.

There were of course other forays abroad, more exotic, more far flung, more comfortable, more eventful; moreover after Laura's initiation he enjoyed considerable success with women.

Though never a macho girl chaser he discovered that a great many responded to his discreet charm, humour and sensitivity. He became adept at detecting whenever someone was particularly attracted to him and encouraging her to make the running. But no subsequent trip came anywhere near that first life-changing escape and the possibilities it offered.

VIII

It was in the middle of his last autumn term at school, just as he was preparing to take the first part of the Oxford entrance exam which he was due to sit with a handful of others in the school library, that the shadowy and long disregarded world of his parents which he thought he was irretrievably leaving behind, burst into his life with the brutality and suddenness of a train crash, derailing all his hopes and plans and reducing his longingly imagined future to a heap of mangled wreckage.

He returned home from school one Friday afternoon to find his mother (whom he usually tried to avoid) actually waiting for him more than usually grim-faced and, for the first time ever in his experience, red-eyed. He had hardly closed the front door when she was telling him that his father had collapsed and been rushed to hospital.

"To hospital? Is it serious?"

"Of course it's serious. He's got prostate cancer. It's very far advanced. There's nothing they can do." She covered her mouth with a small crumpled handkerchief in a kind of strangled sob.

"But that's terrible. I'm so sorry."

"Sorry. What good is that?"

"But I had no idea he was even ill!" Antony, who had been brought up in a climate of euphemism and extreme reticence, was almost as shaken by his mother's frankness as by the import of what she was saying. As far as he knew, the word cancer had never previously passed her lips. "Very poorly" was as far as she had ever gone in the description of illness.

"That's you all over. So selfish you never think of anyone but yourself! I knew there was something wrong." Then she carried on as if talking to herself rather than to Antony. "Scared, that's what it was, scared of going to the doctor. Oh why didn't he do something about it before it was too late?" She accompanied this outburst by beating her fist on the hall table nearly toppling the rather dreary brownish green vase which had stood in precisely that place next to the telephone for as long as he could remember. He had never seen his mother express such emotion before.

Two days later he was told that his father had died. The funeral was a strangely muted and unreal affair at the local crematorium, with the duty clergyman going through the minimal ten minute service attended by a scattering of about half a dozen people. One or two of them he recognised as neighbours, the others he speculated might possibly be relatives or colleagues from his father's work; but as no one was invited back to the house and he didn't like to ask his mother about them, he never knew.

Once the initial shock had worn off, her overriding mood throughout the days that followed appeared to be one of bitter resentment. She did not conceal from Antony what she felt about her weak husband who had so tamely and irresponsibly succumbed to mortal illness, leaving her at the age of fifty-eight ineligible even for a share of the pathetically inadequate pension she would have been entitled to had he managed to survive the few years to retirement age. Even now Antony was not aware, or rather simply could not believe, that his father's death might also be fatal to all his Oxford hopes, vaguely assuming in his youthful unworldliness that his mother might be able to support herself somehow and life could go on as before.

The very day of the funeral these illusions were dispelled. As soon as they got home his mother began to look even more grey and ill and started gasping for breath. When she found she could not climb the stairs without sharp pain in her chest she telephoned the doctor fearing a heart attack. The doctor's opinion was that though her heart seemed sound she was suffering from acute angina brought on, or made worse, by the stress of recent events. He prescribed some tablets and urged on her the importance of taking life as easily and quietly as she could for the foreseeable future.

"He told me I mustn't do anything, not even go to the shops; any excitement could be very dangerous," was how she interpreted the doctor's advice to Antony. (Clearly there could be no question of her working or even having a lodger.)

"Couldn't you get some money by selling the house and moving to somewhere smaller? Antony volunteered rather desperately feeling the ground crumbling beneath his feet.

"Do you want to kill me? No, we must stay here. You'll have to leave school and support me. It's high time you had a job anyway. If you were only half a man you would have suggested it already!"

This was the coup de grâce he had been dreading. But how could he, as it were, consider abandoning his mother now? So she wrote to the headmaster withdrawing him from the school and Antony, unknown to her, sent a letter to Mr Marjoribanks to explain why it was impossible for his teacher's hopes for him to be fulfilled, receiving in return a cheerful and encouraging postcard spiced with literary quotations.

So at the age of only eighteen Antony, as he saw it, had had his life stolen from him before he had even begun to live it. The enemy of promise in his case had not been "the pram in the hall" but human mortality, frailty and sheer mischance. Once again he was conscious of having been confronted by a decisive parting of the ways and a road not taken. Yet had he really had a choice? In a sense of course he had. If only he had any love or affection for his mother or even believed in filial duty or self-sacrifice he might have derived peace of mind, even self-esteem, from the knowledge that he was doing the 'right thing' by giving up his chance of Oxford and travelling the world to look after his ailing mother, but he didn't. His heroes, Charlemagne, Napoleon, Nietzsche et al. would not have given in so tamely. In all honesty he had to admit that he had simply lacked the ruthlessness, the strength of will to break away and follow his destiny and instead had done what the world and moral convention, which in theory he repudiated, expected of him. He had failed to have the courage of his own convictions. But the dreadful question remained: how could he simply walk out on her?

If his mother had not planned her angina attack, she might just as well have done; at all events she had got her way. As the weeks passed during that bitter autumn in which his boats had been definitively burnt, his mother began to perk up somewhat and felt able to do some shopping and light housework. But though this change made his daily life considerably less arduous it increased his suspicion of her. Nor was his predicament made any more palatable by his mother's complete lack of gratitude or even acknowledgement of what he was giving up for her. The impression she gave was that it was the least he could do. Indeed he was often taken to task for his thoughtlessness and "lack of consideration". Now more than ever he identified with Jude the Obscure, Hardy's novel seeming uncannily prophetic of his own disastrous misfortune.

Determined to salvage what he could from the wreck of his life and not to allow himself to be entirely crushed by fate, he set about making the necessary business of earning a living as congenial as possible in the circumstances. In this at least he had some luck. The local bookshop where he used to spend most of his Saturday mornings in happier days browsing and dreaming of his brilliant future, offered him a job – a temporary one in the first instance as they needed someone extra to help with the Christmas rush. Furthermore with the courage born of despair, to fulfil something at least of his potential and to keep in contact with Mr Marjoribanks, Antony at last took up his invitation, first made over a year ago, to join the adult drama group he directed which enjoyed a considerable local reputation. (He knew where to apply from a poster in the bookshop.)

The Arden Players, who as the name implied specialised in Shakespeare, were by no means just a club for Marjoribanks' ex-pupils from the grammar school and in fact only included one or two of them. Most of the company had some sort of connection with the professional stage, a sprinkling were professionally trained and some had actually earned their living in the theatre for a period however briefly: in cricketing terms a good club side strengthened by a few ex-county second eleven and minor counties players. Though nobody got paid, "semi-professional" was how they liked to describe themselves. Hence Antony's severely damaged amour propre was more than a little comforted by his successfully auditioning for the part of Sebastian in the Players' Christmas production – their "panto" as Mr Marjoribanks called it – which was, appropriately enough, *Twelfth Night*. (Though his mother very obviously disapproved she was not quite as obstructive as he had expected; indeed she seemed almost resigned. Did she perhaps tacitly accept that it would not be wise to deny him any outlet at all in his new situation?)

The first thing that struck Antony was the difference between Marjoribanks the schoolmaster, the rather languid, grand, gowned and monocled figure, the school institution who awed and entertained succeeding generations of boys, and the impression he made as stage director working under pressure with adults to put a show on. At school he had been the dilettante amateur and man of letters, now in his pink shirt, yellow pullover and red corduroy trousers with his clipboard and glasses pushed up onto the crown of his head, he seemed sharp, practical, incisive and altogether very much more theatrical in manner and idiom, as well as considerably younger – he was in fact only forty-five – in short more Noël Coward rather than Lord Peter Wimsey.

Antony had been greatly impressed by Mr Marjoribanks – indeed he had been a crucial influence on his life – but now encountering him again with fresh eyes in a very different context and after his recent bitter experience, he was disillusioned. At school he had been treated as one of Mr Marjoribanks' star pupils and most promising actors – at times it had seemed as if his life's ambition was to get Antony into Oxford – but now he paid him little attention or at least much less than he had anticipated. In fact it soon became clear that he had only got the part of Sebastian because of an unusual resemblance to the young woman who was playing Viola, and because she was called Daisy, Marjoribanks called him "Daisy Two" which he resented. At first Antony even wondered whether his apparent coolness was because he felt let down by a potential scholar on whom he had placed high hopes, but from the few rather perfunctory remarks of commiseration at the end of the first week, it was evident that Marjoribanks had accepted the ruin of his ex-pupil's Oxford dreams with complete equanimity.

But there was more to Antony's disillusionment with his old mentor than the noticeable lack of regard he showed to him personally, though if he were honest, he would have to concede that this might have precipitated it in the first place. A schoolmaster is allowed to be a 'character' (or at least he was in those far off days), to dominate and enthral his captive audience if he can, to give his charges nicknames, to tease, cajole, ironize, make jokes and caustic comments at their expense and always have the last word, but towards a grown-up cast of volunteers such behaviour was, or so it struck Antony, quite inappropriate. In these circumstances his blatant striving to be invariably the focus of attention, to have the last word in every exchange, to cap every story, to say nothing of his remorseless angling for praise and complements revealed itself as crude and inexcusable egoism. Particularly intolerable in this context were his waspish personal comments which seemed designed to highlight the quirks and deficiencies of others and hold them up to ridicule especially when, as had almost never been the case at school, Antony was the butt of them. For instance Marjoribanks, sensing his diffidence with the opposite sex, was always urging him to be more physical with the girls he was acting with: "You are allowed to touch her you know... throw your arms round her; she's the girl you love, not an unexploded bomb!" and so on.

As far as Antony was concerned jokes at the expense of individuals did nothing to create the necessary sense of common purpose and camaraderie among the cast. But it was apparent that Marjoribanks was quite indifferent to people's feelings so long as he raised a laugh from an admiring audience. In fact in Antony's opinion Marjoribanks was a very poor director. For one thing he was far too egocentric really to engage with his actors and help them improve their performances – he only took any pains at all with the male and female cronies to whom he had given the principal parts, encouraging selfish prima donna-ish attitudes among them. (Only they were allowed to call him Leo; to the rest he was very firmly Mr Marjoribanks.)

Not one to underestimate his own talent he followed what he said was Shakespeare's example and took the part of the Duke himself, playing it, in Antony's judgement, in an almost ludicrously affected manner. To make matters worse the whole cast clearly thought he was wonderful, didn't seem to mind his giving them nicknames or his barbed personal comments and competed in flattering him and laughing at his jokes. Though it was difficult to believe that the company could be content with being patronized in this way, perhaps there was some excuse for those to whom he was a relative novelty. Antony however was by now all too familiar with the mechanics and repertoire of Mr Marjoribanks' wit. He knew what he was up to and it was all too stylized and predictable. Like watching a conjuror on stage from the wings – when one could see how the effects were achieved, the magic no longer worked.

He sometimes wondered whether if he had joined in the laughter and flattery instead of remaining aloof, Marjoribanks might have paid him more attention, but he was determined not to play his game. In any case it was highly unlikely that someone so self-absorbed and self-satisfied could possibly have conceived that a junior member of his cast might not be impressed with him. (In this however Antony was wrong. The cold appraising stare of his former schoolboy protégé had not gone unnoticed. No one was more aware than Mr Marjoribanks of who did and who did not admire him, or more sensitive to the least dissent from the general chorus of praise.)

During the first week of rehearsals Antony actually considered giving up and leaving the company; but then he asked himself why should he be put off by Marjoribanks and his cronies who seemed to be tarred with his brush. He had encountered these actorish types before and they had deterred him from taking part in drama at university, something he now regretted for who could say where it might have led. This was his last chance and he wasn't going to let it happen again. Most of the cast and stage staff were pleasant enough and he enjoyed acting, even under Marjoribanks direction. He found it liberating and though it was true he would have been confounded if required to 'chat up' a girl on his own account – when securely in character and speaking the verse he was quite capable – pace the director, of looking a young woman in the eye and giving an adequate impression of the emotions appropriate to recovering a drowned sister or being finally united with a lover, even though whatever rapport he might succeed in establishing as Sebastian with his twin, Viola ("Daisy One") and with Olivia, vanished as soon as the acting stopped.

Daisy was a dark, slim, pretty, lively, but as far as he was concerned, rather snooty girl who took little notice of him, and Olivia – who was married and nearly ten years older than him, almost a middle-aged lady in Antony's eyes – was civil but distant. Her husband was also in the cast playing the minor part of Fabian. Antony was convinced that apart from his natural diffidence the reason he failed to make an impression, especially with Daisy, was that he looked young and immature for his age, something that he had been self-conscious about even in the sixth form at school.

He had however another reason for wanting to stay in the Arden Players which he would not have acknowledged even to himself – Rosemary (he didn't at this stage know her surname); Marjoribanks called her Rose Marie. Friendly and outgoing (she was well cast as Maria) and aware that Antony was new and isolated, she alone quite early in the rehearsals had made a deliberate effort to draw him into the group.

"Hello I'm Rosemary. You're Antony aren't you?"

"Er yes, that's right. How did you know?" (It was the first time anybody in the Players had addressed him by his Christian name and he was quite taken aback.)

"Oh I keep my ears open. I think we must be the two youngest members of the cast."

"We probably are, yes."

"Do you know any of the others?"

"No, not yet. You seem to know your way around."

"Ah well I helped behind the scenes before but this is my first part. I'm quite enjoying it."

"I think you're very good, very... very natural."

"Oh I don't know about that – that's my cue. See you!"

After that they exchanged a few friendly words at every opportunity and on the first Saturday night about eight o'clock when the cast was dispersing – they rehearsed in a church hall in Mitcham – Antony felt a tap on the shoulder. It was Rosemary.

"Coming for a coffee?"

"Yes. Where?"

"The Cabana? That's on your way isn't it?"

Antony could hardly believe what was happening to him. He had noticed her from the first read through and though dismissing her as not his type – too bubbly and sociable, too superficial, too unreliable – he instantly experienced a powerful if deeply buried urge to place his head on her lap and be cuddled to her ample bosom with all the physical nurturing affection that his mother had been totally incapable of. But actually being asked out by her was completely beyond his expectations; her not being his type, whatever that was, only added an element of the dangerous unknown that made the whole situation even more exciting. He had never in his life been out with a girl nor for that matter had he ever been to a coffee bar. Yet here he was with his frothy coffee facing Rosemary across a flimsy looking glass-topped table and trying his best to look suave and relaxed.

"You don't mind if I call you Tony, do you? Antony sounds well, you know, a bit toffee-nosed."

He would have firmly rebuffed such a proposal coming from anyone else, but now from her he accepted it almost as an initiation into a new and exciting sociable life.

"Well it's certainly better than Daisy Two!"

Soon the unprecedented strangeness of his situation dissolved in lively conversation as Antony, rapidly gaining confidence, discovered that he could make her laugh; in fact she was the only person he had ever met in his admittedly very limited experience who seemed really to share his idiosyncratic brand of fantasy humour.

"I thought you were very quiet and reserved, but you're not at all really,"' she said.

Rosemary for her part, to Antony's delight and surprise, started treating him like a confidential friend offering her candid opinion of each of her colleagues in the cast and inviting his in turn, as well as initiating him into all the gossip, rivalries, flirtations and jealousies endemic to any amateur theatrical company. It was all a complete revelation to him.

"How on earth do you know all this?"

"I told you, I keep my eyes and ears open, and people tell me things!"

"I don't think Olivia's husband is much of an actor." (In spite of Rosemary's revelations Antony still found it easier to identify the actors by their roles rather than their names.)

"He's dreadful isn't he?" (She impersonated his wooden delivery.)

"And he doesn't even seem to be enjoying himself very much."

"There's only one reason why he's there."

"What's that?"

"To keep an eye on his wife of course! You know she was a real actress once, West End and everything. She's even had small parts in films. She gave up when she had children, but rumour has it that she's very flighty, always having affairs. They've split up at least once. He obviously doesn't trust her out of his sight."

"What about Daisy? Has she been a professional actress?"

"No, not her, though she thinks she is – stuck up cow! Sorry, I shouldn't be bitchy. Her uncle was Gary Goldsmith, big matinee idol before the war, wavy black hair, little thin moustache. England's answer to Errol Flynn."

"I didn't think we had an answer to Errol Flynn."

"No, but you know what I mean. Anyway I think that's why she fancies herself as a star."

Almost the only member of the company that Rosemary did not mention was Mr Marjoribanks and Antony could not refrain from bringing him up.

"Mr Marjoribanks? You mean Leo. Oh he's wonderful isn't he?"

Antony's high spirits were somewhat deflated by this declaration and he did not quite know how to react. "You don't mind him calling you Rose Marie?"

"Oh that's just his way. Mind you he makes me nervous sometimes. Don't you like him?"

"Well he was my English master in the sixth form at school."

"Was he a good teacher?"

"He was quite a character. He tried to get me into Oxford as a matter of fact."

"What happened?"

"Oh it didn't work out – for all sorts of reasons." Antony could see that she was curious, but though reluctant to go into the business of his father's death and mother's illness he surprised himself by adding instead: "I'm going to be a writer anyway."

"Well good for you!"

Antony had never expressed this ambition in so many words before, but once stated he immediately recognised it as both true and inevitable.

"I'll tell you who does give me the willies – Guy Halliwell, you know, Malvolio. He's a groper. All the girls say so!"

"You mean he actually interferes with people?" (Antony, who had thought of Halliwell as just a rather unpleasantly smooth middle-aged man, was obviously appalled, which Rosemary thought was rather sweet.)

"Well it's more like brushing up close in the dark."

"I can't understand how he gets away with it."

"Well he's very well off. Have you seen the car he drives?"

"What's that got to do with it? Is he married?"

"Divorced."

Divorce in Antony's experience was something that only film stars and decadent aristocrats went in for. It came as a considerable shock to encounter it within the very restricted circle of people he actually knew.

"The thing is he keeps asking me out. What should I do?"

"Asking you out! But he's years older than you. Just don't go."

"I might have to one day. I'm running out of excuses. He's what you call a lounge lizard. Ugh!"

They laughed but she could see that Antony was still uneasy.

"Don't worry about me. I can look after myself."

The fact that she had asked his advice and assumed that he might be worried about her was so deeply pleasing that, temporarily at least, it quite took the sting out of her admiration for Marjoribanks.

Suddenly Rosemary looked at her watch. "Good heavens! Look at the time. We've been here two hours. I'm sorry I've kept you so long – rambling on about myself as usual. Come on, I'll walk you to your bus stop."

(Fortunately he had not told his Mother what time to expect him home.)

During the following week's rehearsals he occasionally managed to catch Rosemary's eye when someone behaved in the way she had indicated on the Saturday evening, but though invitations to the coffee bar now became routine, Antony always found himself sharing her company with a varying group of younger members of the cast and stage staff, so that he began to wonder whether the purpose of her original invitation and confidences had simply been to integrate him into the company and make him feel part of things, as she had effectively done. In addition to this he was now much more aware how evidently charmed she was by Mr Marjoribanks and, worse, made every effort to impress him.

The more Antony became aware of Marjoribanks as an egregious phoney the more he could only wonder how he got away with it; the cast after all were not impressionable schoolboys but grown up and in some cases mature people. Antony kept hoping that he would so overreach himself as to seem ridiculous to these undiscriminating and imperceptive admirers. But it was futile to hope for the mask to slip, for him to be suddenly and dramatically exposed for what he really was. Such things, he was forced to recognise, simply did not happen in real life. In any case as he saw it Marjoribanks was inseparable from his public persona. He was, as it were, a phoney all the way through. In the end he had to conclude that most people were sufficiently unsure of themselves to be intimidated by the appearance of assured wit and sophistication from someone like Marjoribanks, who had the unquestioning self-conceit to assume as a matter of course that whatever he had to say was amusing and worth listening to.

Antony flattered himself that in his best moments he could be infinitely more amusing and original than him, but had to concede that he was not so sharp, polished and unrelenting. If they were ever to cross swords, by the time had come up with his telling riposte, his unanswerable put-down, Marjoribanks would have won by some cheap thrust and moved on. It was only in imagined exchanges in the bath that Antony got the better of him.

But why had he allowed himself to become so obsessed by a poor man's Noël Coward like Marjoribanks? If he were honest, the reason why he really got under Antony's skin was that Rosemary seemed so captivated by his tired old nonsense and to put it bluntly gave every appearance of finding Marjoribanks considerably more entertaining than him.

Antony was well aware that his humour was too subtle, too personal, too allusive for instant general appeal, but he liked to think that would have recoiled from displaying a crude travesty of himself even if he had the gall to do so, which he hadn't. It was an old story – the way of the world; whether in the OUDS or the Union at Oxford, or in the government of the Empire, those who naturally imposed themselves, who successfully thrust their way to prominence or power, tended to be single-minded, shallow, unself-critical, uncomplicated and insensitive to the feelings of others. How often had he thought as he received the sleek politicians who succeeded each other in his study at the Hofburg, that among his hundreds of millions of subjects there must be people with vision, insight, judgement and a sense of history, more capable of providing for the present and future well-being of the Empire than those hyper-ambitious mediocrities, demagogues and placemen whom a combination of luck, a certain plausibility and a remorseless dedication to their own self-advancement had brought to the top of the heap. If only he had been an absolute monarch like his predecessor Joseph II or a reforming Chinese Emperor, he could have dispensed with politicians who thought only of their own popularity and the next set of elections, and chosen disinterested and high-minded advisers to govern with; but that was another story...

At the end of a week in which Antony had striven to come to terms with the fact that there was nothing exceptional in his friendship with Rosemary, he found that he was not even included in the invitation to the coffee bar after the next Saturday rehearsal. What a difference one short week had made! He tried to work off his disappointment by walking slowly all the way home by a circuitous route only to be greeted by his mother who announced, not without a certain satisfaction, that because he was so late, the hot meal she had taken the trouble to prepare for him was now, in all probability, burnt to a crisp in the oven.

That evening with Antony in his lowest spirits since he had been forced to abandon his Oxford ambitions, the phone rang on its little table by the front door, an unusual enough event in itself. His mother answered and he was starting to make his way back upstairs when she called out: "It's someone who wants speak to you" and reluctantly handed over the receiver. Who could it possibly be? Apart from the odd school acquaintance asking about homework no one had ever rung him up before.

"Tony, it's me. Rosemary."

"Rosemary!"

"Why didn't you come for coffee this evening? You were missed."

"Was I? I didn't think I was invited."

"You are a chump. Of course you're invited. I just didn't see you to ask that's all. Listen, I hope you don't mind but I'd like to ask your advice. I'm not interrupting anything am I? Are you busy?"

The astonished Antony just managed to signify that he was indeed not busy.

"Well I want to know what to do about Derek."

"Who's Derek?"

"He's someone I've known for years. We practically grew up together. Our families are friends and all that and we used to say when we were kids that when we were old enough we'd get married; you know like you do. The trouble is I think he still believes it! When we're out together he keeps trying to hold my hand as if we were on a date and recently he's even taken to stopping in front of jewellers and estate agents and staring at the windows. It almost as if in his mind we're going steady."

Antony was a total stranger to this world of 'dating' and 'going steady'. It was the sort of thing he was only aware of from the problem pages of the magazines he glanced at in his dentist's waiting room or at the hairdresser's if he had not brought a book to read, and would normally have dismissed with scorn. Coming from Rosemary however he took it very seriously.

"Has he said anything?"

"Well no, not exactly, but he doesn't need to. It's his whole attitude, and his mother too. She keeps giving me these meaningful looks and little cuddles. The thing is I'm fond of him but he's just not my type. He's so correct and careful and... well, boring, I suppose. The trouble is the longer it goes it goes on the more he's going to get the wrong impression. Oh Tony, what am I going to do?"

"What you want is to find some way of discouraging him without hurting his feelings."

"You're so understanding. That's exactly what I want to do!"

"Well you're going to have to say something, aren't you."

"Yes, but the trouble is if I put it into words it might sound very presumptuous. I mean I'll be assuming that he wants to marry me when he hasn't even asked. Once these things are said they can't be unsaid can they? And I know he'll be terribly upset."

Rosemary, he was beginning to discover, was a difficult person to advise because she always tended to put the opposing case to whatever one suggested. Thus the conversation meandered on for over half an hour, prolonged to some extent, it must be admitted, by Antony who was keen to keep it going for as long as possible.

When she eventually rang off he was walking on air and completely impervious to the hostile reaction of his mother who had been hovering with growing disapproval throughout the unprecedentedly long call. As far as she was concerned the telephone was intended only for brief and necessary business transactions; to use it for personal chit-chat was an abuse of the official GPO apparatus, which was not only indecent but practically a violation of the law. The inevitable outburst, long brewing, was not slow in coming.

"And what was all that about I'd like to know? Have you any idea how long you've been talking?"

"It was Rosemary, mother. She's in the play. She just wanted some advice, that's all."

His mother gave one of her derisive sniffs.

"What you want to waste your time with that play acting for I can't imagine. Well she's not coming here, that's all I can say! Ringing up in the middle of the evening and asking to talk to you. The very idea! Advice! What advice can you possibly give her anyway? What do you know about anything?"

But Antony could not be provoked. "I can promise I won't ring her but I can't say the same for her. Don't worry, it won't affect our phone bill."

So with a serene smile which she was finding more provoking than anything else, he bade his mother goodnight and went up to his room while she called after him: "I would have thought at least you might have more consideration for me! You know how much I need to rest!"

At the beginning of the next rehearsal the following Monday Rosemary touched his arm and whispered: "I took your advice!"

He didn't like to ask for further details, but it was enough. However Antony's quietly triumphant mood was soon deflated for following this first furtive exchange she largely ignored him for the rest of the evening, spending most of her spare moments in gossipy huddles with female friends from which he was excluded. Then as they were all leaving she announced in his hearing that she would not be coming for a coffee afterwards because she had "a date". When Antony impulsively assuming what he thought was a confidant's privilege hurried after her to ask "who with?" she told him in effect to mind his own business.

After a miserable twenty-four hours during which, after the initial shock, he strove to convince himself that in reality whatever she might or might not say to him could be of no possible importance, at the next rehearsal Rosemary, whom he had been avoiding, sought him out, drew him aside and asked: "Tony, I was wondering if you would do me a great favour..."

Instantly he expressed his willingness to do anything he could.

"Will you be my dialogue coach; you know, go through all my lines with me and take the part of the other characters? You're so good with the voices, besides you're the only one I feel I can ask..."

In spite of having resolved in effect to keep his distance from her in future, this request, naturally, changed everything. Only afterwards did it occur to him to wonder whether she was conscious of having hurt his feelings and was deliberately trying to make up for it. He could not decide, but in a sense it was irrelevant. The fact was that from now on he would be closely and regularly associated with her in a role that excluded every other member of the cast. She might ignore him on occasions or get involved in confidential conversations with other friends – no doubt he wasn't the only person she rang up or asked for advice – but being chosen as her "dialogue coach" was a unique distinction!

Rosemary now rarely came along to the post-rehearsal visits to the coffee bar of which she had previously been the moving spirit. This suited Antony as he now had his exclusive time with her anyway and was thus spared the stress of trying to compete for her attention in a social situation while appearing not to do so. She did however ring quite often later in the evening just for a chat. These calls never lasted more than twenty minutes or so and ended abruptly with Rosemary saying she had to go. Nevertheless they were enough to provoke in his mother an intense restless agitation. Was it possible, Antony wondered, that she imagined that this young woman might actually attempt to steal him away from her? Though she never went so far as explicitly to forbid Antony to use the phone, she kept insisting that he might be preventing an important call from getting through. But with new found assurance that came with being a breadwinner and no longer a schoolboy or student, and perhaps also with being Rosemary's friend and confidant, he shook her by asking coolly: "And when was the last time you had a phone call, mother?"

"Don't you speak to me like that! Who do you think you are?" was the reply.

These gossipy calls in which she was just as frank and outspoken as on their first visit à deux to the Cabana, were a joy, a reaffirmation for him of their special friendship especially as at rehearsals she now seemed a little distant and preoccupied, even when they were going through lines together.

Then in the middle of a Sunday afternoon a few days before the dress rehearsal the phone rang. Although he was upstairs he managed to get to it before his mother. It was Rosemary! But her voice sounded different, as if she had been crying.

"Are you alright?"

"Yes, I'm OK. Have you got time to talk?"

"Of course."

She proceeded to give him a very open account, full of circumstantial detail, of what sounded like a highly unsatisfactory relationship that she had just ended when her suspicions that "he was seeing someone else" were confirmed. The man himself was not named and Antony felt he could not ask her – given that she had told him so much it could scarcely be an accident that she had withheld this crucial piece of information. The last thing he wanted to do now was to invite a rebuff from her. He had convinced himself that he would have noticed if the mysterious man were a member of the cast, that was all that he really cared to know; but at the same time he could not help wondering who was privy to the secret of his identity.

"How long has this been going on? I mean did it start the day you said you had a date?"

"Oh no, quite a bit longer than that, off and on. It seems I made Derek miserable for nothing."

"Well not really."

"How do you mean?"

"You don't really want to go back to Derek do you?"

"No, no, of course not. I've just hurt him so much that's all. Oh Tony, what am I going to do?"

"About Derek?"

"Derek? No about... my problem."

"You don't have to do anything do you. You've just ended it. Sounds like good riddance."

"Yes, but was I right? Oh why do I always fall for creeps!"

"So you did fall for him then."

"I suppose I must have done."

Antony was more than ever flattered that she had turned to him in this crisis and was determined to do his best for her as well as impressing her with knowledge of life, such as it was. But he was conscious of having to feel his way with great care, taking his cue from her responses rather like a clairvoyant and drawing on all his resources of intelligence and imaginative sympathy, supplemented by what he had gleaned from poetry and novels. His task was not made any easier by the fact that although her account of the affair was very graphic, she was vague about the chronology and very hard to pin down as to her precise feelings. In particular he found it difficult to determine whether any of her ex-boyfriend's defects, which she was so trenchantly analysing and so vehemently expounding, had been apparent to her before, or separately from, the suspicions that he had been "two-timing" her (as she put it) being aroused and then confirmed. And if, as she now knew, he was such a bad lot why, he wondered, had breaking up with him upset her so much. It will be apparent that he had a lot to learn about matters of the heart. He was however beginning to realise that it was no good trying to make her consistent by quoting back at her things she had previously said or try to confine her to either/or logic.

"Perhaps in future", he suggested tentatively after a long, exhaustive but frustratingly circular discussion in which he obtained no clear answers, "it would be better to choose someone you definitely like, respect and trust; someone you've got things in common with." (He nearly added 'someone who makes you laugh,' but this might have seemed too obviously like special pleading as well as being incompatible with his role as her 'disinterested' adviser).

"You mean like a friend? I might as well go out with Derek!"

"But you don't like Derek."

"Well he's alright. He's very sweet really I suppose."

"But he bores you!" For the first time Antony's voice betrayed a certain exasperation which he was doing his best to suppress. "I mean someone whose company you actually enjoy, someone more on your wavelength."

"You mean you think that love can grow out of friendship. But love and friendship, well they're just not the same thing are they?"

"They must go together surely, in any successful relationship, otherwise what is it based on? Better than always falling for creeps I should have thought. You may think that friendship can grow out of love but it's quite a risk to take."

"But you can't choose who you're going to fall for."

They were essentially at cross purposes. He sensed that for

the time being he was not going to convince her that love, as all the great happy endings of literature testified, could only be 'a marriage of true minds'.

"I don't know", she sighed. "Perhaps it's me. I must just attract the wrong kind of people... never anyone really nice like you!" There was a pause. Antony dared not say anything. Then she resumed: "Sorry to bore on and on about myself. I promise not to do it again – not for a bit anyway!"

Thus this important if unproductive conversation ended unexpectedly on a distinct note of hope for him to fix on, with his position as her confidant, if anything, reinforced. They had been speaking, he afterwards realised, for nearly an hour and a half! To conciliate his mother, who seemed disturbed almost to the point of collapse, he made her a strong cup of tea.

The protracted call had given him plenty to digest and reflect on. Rosemary, usually quite discreet and circumspect at rehearsals, always seemed a different person on the phone. Was it because there was no one else about or was there something about the quasi-anonymity of the disembodied voice down the line, the complete security and privacy of it, that promoted intimacy? He could not help regretting however that she had only let him into her confidence post facto as it were, so that any advice and guidance he might have to offer came too late to be of any real help; in this particular case at least. Perhaps he was expecting too much. But the more she admitted him into her life, the more he wanted to know and be involved – he just couldn't help himself.

The following week taken up as it was with the dress rehearsal and the three performances left little time or opportunity for them to speak to each other. Rosemary was more high-spirited than she had been for weeks and he was left to observe and reflect on what a complicated and perplexing creature she was. What a strange mixture for instance of frankness and evasion;

bold, impulsive, even reckless yet always asking for advice as if chronically unsure of herself and in need of moral support; at times outrageous and yet also discreet and self-possessed; sharp-witted and critical yet able to tolerate and apparently enjoy the company of the very members of the cast she had mimicked so tellingly when they had their first coffee together; shrewd and objective about herself and others yet on her own admission taken in by creeps and though completely open, down to earth and unsnobbish, impressed nevertheless by wealth, to say nothing of their pretentious fraud of a producer.

Everyone else he had ever dealt with, Marjoribanks excepted, was boringly straightforward by comparison. In the past he had habitually taken other people for granted at face value as unproblematic and of no particular interest in themselves. Characters in novels, he knew, could be complex and interesting, but at least they had a certain consistency and in the last resort one knew what to think about them. Rosemary on the other hand was too contradictory, too inchoate, too unpredictable, to be a convincing character in fiction, indeed she evaded all descriptive formulas, yet no one made a stronger impression as a distinct personality. Though it has to be said that Antony had never before scrutinized or sought to understand another human being with anything like this degree of intensity before, so that he found himself trying to construe her every gesture, looking for the least change in her mood or direction of interest.

Even had she not regarded his involvement with the Arden Players with contemptuous disapproval there would have been no question of his mother attending any of the performances, for increasingly nowadays she felt short breath in crowded spaces and feared that she was going to have what she called a "funny turn". Thus he was practically the only member of the company who did not require any tickets for friends and family.

In spite of pre-first night nerves and misgivings the theatre did not fail to work its magic and apart from a few hair-raising moments and the odd mistakes that the audience did not appear to notice, it all went off better than anyone except the producer expected. On the last night, in response to (deliberately orchestrated) calls from the audience, Mr Marjoribanks emerged from the curtains to make a long and witty speech about the trials and tribulations of putting on the show – in effect all about himself, and although he thanked everyone who should have been thanked, he somehow contrived to give the impression that the success of the production, such as it was, was ultimately entirely due to him and in spite of all he had had to contend with. But the cast and audience loved it. (Antony wanted to call 'author' afterwards but nobody except Rosemary thought that was a good idea!)

The last night was followed by a party on the stage for everyone involved. Antony had never been to a party before, not even as a child – being naturally reserved and not knowing what to say to girls, he had hitherto always avoided uncontrolled and unpredictable social situations, turning down the few invitations he had received from contemporaries in the sixth form at school with some lame excuse. But with the new found confidence that came from Rosemary's friendship he had nerved himself to attend. In any case, he told himself, he would know everybody there so the whole thing would simply be a continuation of the camaraderie of the rehearsals and performance. Anyway Rosemary would doubtless expect him to be there and think it very strange if he didn't stay for it.

By the time he had taken off his makeup and changed he found that the party was already under way. Everyone had brought a bottle so there was wine, beer and spirits as well as little savouries on sticks and sandwiches made by the female members of the cast and laid out on the tables used in the production. Proceedings began with the presentation to Leo Marjoribanks of a green and pink woollen sweater laboriously and lovingly hand-knitted by one of the ladies of the company who had skilfully incorporated into the pattern a line from the play, 'he hath been most notoriously abus'd', which had become a catchphrase of the production. Marjoribanks said that he would be delighted to do almost anything with it – except wear it! (No one else could have got away with a remark like that.) Then after toasting the cast in champagne, with a "toodle-pip kiddiwinkies, don't do anything I wouldn't do" , he was off.

Gradually as the alcohol had its effect the party grew louder and noticeably more relaxed. But Antony was not comfortable. Rosemary, who had kept on her Maria costume which revealed quite a troubling amount of cleavage, was at the centre of a group which included the older actors who had played opposite her as Sir Toby Belch, Sir Andrew Aguecheek and Malvolio, with whom she appeared to be flirting rather obviously (to Antony's surprise as he had understood that she didn't like any of them very much). Not only did she not speak to him but she never even glanced in his direction. She was also drinking rather a lot of red wine and as the evening wore on her behaviour became more raucous and her laughter more uncontrolled.

Antony felt he could no longer remain. His aversion to parties was totally confirmed – if only he had made his goodbyes and left early like Marjoribanks! Detaching himself from the group of stagehands in one corner by the wings, with whom he had been having a desultory conversation, he slunk away unnoticed taking with him the Victorian pocket edition of *Twelfth Night* that he had been so delighted to find in a second-hand bookshop and planned to give Rosemary on that occasion as a present. He never expected to see or hear from her again.

Antony's mother did not believe in Christmas or Christmas presents – the only decorations he saw were at the bookshop –

so as an additional consolation to reading during what would otherwise have been a very bleak season, he used his savings to give himself one of the new record players. Inevitably his mother told him that he didn't want to waste his money on such trashy novelties, adding darkly that it might dangerously overload the electricity supply. In fact she strongly suspected that he would never have dreamt of buying such a thing were it not for the influence of "that young woman" in the play.

Antony also brought two records to play on it; not current hits like *All Shook Up*, *Diana*, *That'll Be The Day* or that Christmas's number one, *Mary's Boy Child* (Rosemary he knew liked 'pop' music but that of course was no longer a consideration), but a couple of LPs which attracted him irresistibly by their titles: *Tales from the Vienna Woods and Other Waltzes* and *Vienna City of Dreams*. For the present that was all he could afford. But from the moment he heard the first bars of that lilting, free-flowing, effortlessly elegant music he had an overwhelming experience of recognition. His dreary, constricting, alien surroundings were exposed as nothing more real than a crudely painted stage flat, and then dissolved altogether as he was carried deeper and deeper into the world of imperial Vienna which he knew to be his home and where he was grounded in roots centuries deep.

He was filled with a heart-aching, yearning nostalgia for the city between the 1860s and 1890s when that music was new – still a golden age though politically and militarily after the heavy blows of Solferino and Sadowa, it might then have seemed an age of decline; but though generally seen as decadent, Vienna remained one of the cultural and intellectual capitals of the world right up to the catastrophe of 1914, and even afterwards until the rise of the Nazis. However the break-up of that great multi-ethnic Empire with no less than thirteen different languages on its currency into little nation states after the First

World War had proved to be an irreparable loss for Europe – irreparable that is until the Great Restoration – for it not only left the Austrian remnant of the Empire and its capital a prey to Hitler but destroyed the centuries old balance of power in the heart of the old continent. At first he listened intently to the music over and over again totally absorbed in the world that it evoked, and subsequently always put it on to accompany his reading or whatever else he happened to be doing in his room so that it still pervaded all his solitary hours.

IX

It often seemed as if his entire reign had been dominated by the melodies of the Strausses, that it had been in effect one long Kaiserwalzer, one ever restless sea of swirling couples filling hall after gilded hall, gliding over vast expanses of gleaming parquet under blazing chandeliers. There was the Opera Ball, the balls for the Emperor's birthday and his name day, the Corpus Christi Ball, balls for visiting sovereigns and balls to mark the anniversary of great events in the history of the dynasty and the Empire. But he had never really enjoyed them. Though he was no dancer, protocol dictated that he had to begin the evening with a few shuffling steps round the empty floor with a specially chosen and usually completely overawed partner, and even when that minor ordeal was over he was granted no peace. After all how could he relax and enjoy the splendid spectacle; the ladies' shimmering décolleté gowns, the white and crimson uniforms, the glittering orders and decorations, the gold encrusted court dress of his chamberlains and councillors, when he knew that every eye was on him, and his imperial and royal ear was constantly being bent by the unending stream of people who were being presented to him; politicians, marshals, admirals, diplomats, celebrities from the fashionable world, to say nothing of assorted members of the aristocracy and his own relations, however remote, who seemed to include half the royal and princely houses of Europe. To each he had to have something fresh and intelligent to say while ensuring, as hovering courtiers were constantly there to remind him, that not a single observation or opinion that he uttered could possibly commit him or his government to any specific course of action, or be in any way misconstrued. In this respect he preferred the Debutantes' Ball; debutantes curtsied but did not speak!

In the winter balls when his guests filled the marble columned Festsaal and the Grösser Redoutensaal of the Hofburg, it was stiflingly hot and such was the crush that there was scarcely any room for real dancing until the early hours, long after the imperial party had departed. It was much more pleasant in summer when the court was in residence at the Schönbrunn and balls were given in the rococo Great Gallery. Then on sultry Viennese nights the crowds could disperse down the ceremonial stone staircase and out onto the parterre lit with lanterns and torches, wander as far as the floodlit fountains and even climb to the neoclassical arcade of the Gloriette to survey the enchanted scene. But all in all he had to confess that he preferred to enjoy his waltz music sitting down hence, apart from the odd night of Mozart in the Imperial Box at the Opera where again he could never fully relax; his favourite musical event in the calendar was the Vienna Philharmonic's New Year's Day Strauss Concert in the Musikverein Hall, which he had never failed to attend.

X

One evening in the second week of the New Year, the melody of *The Blue Danube* was penetrated by the strident tone of the phone ringing. His mother was resting and he made his way slowly downstairs hoping that the noise would stop before he reached it. When he lifted the receiver the voice seemed at first like something from the remote past.

"Hi, it's me, Rosemary. Did you get my card?"

"Er yes, I think so." (Antony was determined to be cool and distant. He did of course remember her card – a vulgar comic one which he had thrown away as soon as he received it.)

"You didn't send me one...."

"Well we,... I don't normally..."

"I didn't see you at the party after the show. Did I behave very badly?"

"I don't know. I went home early."

"Oh did you?"

"Why, do you think you did?" In spite of himself Antony was slipping into the role of her counsellor again.

"I don't know. I can't remember. That's a bad sign isn't it? I know somebody had to take me home and I threw up. I must have been legless." She laughed. "The thing is I'm not used to drinking so much – pathetic isn't it!"

If he were honest, the notion of a girl like Rosemary getting drunk and then making light of it was quite shocking to Antony – as for his mother's reaction it hardly bore thinking about! – but it did not make her any the less attractive. On the contrary he had the feeling once again of being drawn into another world vastly more exciting and more promising than the one he knew.

"So I'm not in disgrace then?"

"No, of course not. Did you feel bad the next day?"

"Ghastly! Anyway what I really wanted to ask is whether you're going to audition for the new spring production."

Instead of a flat negative expressing his settled intention of having nothing more to do with the Players he heard himself saying: "Well, it rather depends on what it is."

"It's a musical – *Seven Brides for Seven Brothers*."

"A musical, that doesn't sound like the Arden Players. What does Marjoribanks think about it?"

"Oh he's mad keen. It was his idea. He said he wanted to do an all-singing, all-dancing show for a change – some of the older ones are against it though."

"Well it doesn't really sound like my sort of thing."

"Oh go on, don't be so toffee-nosed! I want people that I like to be in it. You can help with my lines again. It'll be fun, better than boring old Shakespeare..."

(Antony had the impression from the way that she entered into the role of Maria that she loved and appreciated Shakespeare, albeit in an unscholarly way. It was one of the things he felt they had in common. But now this hardly seemed to matter at all.)

"OK then. I'll give it a try."

Thus in one short conversation she had succeeded in completely disarming him, whether intentionally or not he did not even consider. To his mother who thought that Antony had definitely given up what she called his "play-acting nonsense" as well as severed his connection with the young woman who had kept ringing him up, his renewed involvement with both was a cruel blow, confirming her worst fears as to her insidious and dangerous influence over her son. Her chest pains intensified and her breathing became shorter and more laboured to the point where for a couple of weeks she could not go out of the house; but Antony did not allow this to deter him from going for the audition. In the event he did not get a part but was given the job of assistant stage manager.

"Bad luck," said Rosemary, who had been chosen as one of the brides.

"Marjoribanks doesn't like me."

"It's not that. You're a great actor but you're not really a dancer are you?"

"I suppose not. Do you really think I can act?"

"Of course I do. That's obvious. Everyone says so, not just me. You know Leo thinks very highly of you."

"You could've fooled me."

"No, he really does. He said you were one of the most talented schoolboys he'd ever directed, because you really understood what you were doing."

Antony couldn't quite bring himself to believe this but at the same time could not help being both intrigued and gratified. For all Marjoribanks' intensely irritating qualities and his disillusionment with the man he had once so looked up to, some part of Antony still wanted to be his star pupil and earn his praise.

When the production got into its swing, Antony, although without a part, found himself enjoying the experience considerably more than *Twelfth Night*. None of the theatrical old guard were taking part in the musical and Rosemary, as she implied, had no really established friends among the new cast and was clearly closer to him than any of them. He felt liberated from the constant sense that he was competing with others for attention. She might complain that there was not so much socializing in a group after rehearsals but naturally it didn't trouble him. In any case they seemed a much nicer and less pretentiously actorish bunch than the Shakespeare cast. It was all beautifully relaxed; almost, he mused, like getting her on a slow boat to China, all to himself alone. Looking back years later he often thought of it as their happiest time together.

The one fly in the ointment was Leo Marjoribanks, now more

flamboyant and outrageous than ever in his new role as producer of a Broadway musical and amazingly, going down well with the young singers and dancers. He showed precious little sign of his high opinion of Antony, and Rosemary appeared as intrigued with him as ever. But Marjoribanks, apart from being a grating distraction, could not seriously impinge on his relationship with her or the much greater opportunities they now had to be together uninterrupted. The man's one saving grace, in Antony's eyes at least, was that he kept his distance socially from his cast – his disappearing from the party was typical – and his private life or lives remained as mysterious as ever.

During the weeks of that production a relaxed and close friendship effortlessly established itself between them, and Rosemary, who continued to confide in him, was now almost as open with Antony during rehearsals as in their frequent evening phone conversations. She asked his advice on whatever happened to be on her mind: whether or not to go on a diet, buy herself a new pair of expensive shoes or even give up her office job and try to get into drama school. Though he began to think that he was more of a sounding board than an adviser, since for all his sage words and after the most minute dissection of all the pros and cons, she invariably came to the decision which he suspected she really had in mind all along. Nevertheless to be so earnestly consulted on all her personal concerns great and small did wonders for his self-esteem and even made him feel quite like a man of the world!

Indeed they were so often in each other's company and engrossed in conversation that other members of the cast, most of whom were about their own age, to Antony's deep inner satisfaction, treated them quite naturally and unselfconsciously as a couple, referring to them habitually as "you two", as in "are you two coming for a coffee this evening?" And more wonderful still it was a perception that Rosemary seemed happy to accept; at least she did nothing at all to correct it. Only when Marjoribanks made the odd barbed comment about them did she appear at all uncomfortable.

Antony never tired of her company or of dispensing sage advice, encouragement and support. Even if he had found her disconcerting in the past, Rosemary was now firmly established as his feminine ideal. In his bookish way he came to see her as representing the best qualities in the two girls in Jude the Obscure's life: the lively intelligence and sensitivity of Sue and the cheerful, earthy, well-endowed physicality of Arabella, in living breathing reality, sufficient to drive all thoughts of Babylonian orgies from his mind. Her friendship had healed in him the bitterness, disappointment and resentment of recent months and though like Jude he had been excluded from Oxford, which once seemed the only gateway to a life worth living, now at least he felt he had an enticing future again. He would have maintained however that this undeniable attraction to Rosemary had nothing to do with trite and conventional notions of romance, still less domesticity and the dreaded "pram in the hall". The last thing he wanted was to be tied down by marriage and family life, in any case unless and until his mother died or recovered that was out of the question anyway. He simply saw them coming closer and closer together, slowly but inexorably, until there was nothing for it but for them to become permanent companions and lovers. The details were vague and shifting, how could it be otherwise, but the precedent he had in mind was that of Irene and Young Jolyon, her befriender and adviser, in *The Forsyte Saga* – though he hoped the process would be somewhat quicker!

At times this outcome seemed inevitable, at times utterly absurd. Inevitable, because there appeared nothing to stop it and hardly a day passed without some flattering attention or sign of friendship on her part which he duly noted, analysed and recorded in his diary; absurd, because in his more sober moments it seemed simply too good to be true that such a lovely and desirable young woman would simply give herself to him. Moreover he had to admit when he was being ruthlessly honest that, however much he strained his analyses, there had been so far nothing in her attitude to him that could be unambiguously construed as going beyond friendship, however close and confidential, and it was difficult to believe that she was as aware of and as preoccupied by him as he was by her. Nor could he forget that in her experience friendship didn't grow into love, that the two were indeed virtually incompatible. But then experience might prove her wrong. After all there were any number of literary precedents for it – literature being Antony's only real source of experience in these matters. And they seemed so right for each other, so in tune with each other, so natural together and they laughed so spontaneously at the same things. Why otherwise would new acquaintances with no preconceptions assume quite straightforwardly that they were a couple?

Even the current constraints imposed on his life by his mother turned to his advantage with Rosemary. When a careless remark about his home life led to him admitting, in response to her insistent questions, that he had allowed his father's death and his mother's frailty to destroy his prospects of going to Oxford her response was shattering:

"Good for you! You know there are very few men of your age (she actually called him a man!) who would be prepared to do what you're doing. It's generally the girls who get landed with that sort of thing. But then I always knew you were different."

He thought his admission would have destroyed him in her eyes provoking at best incomprehension, at worst a sort of patronizing contempt. But it appeared that what to him had been a weak capitulation of which he was ashamed, was to her a mark of distinction, even moral courage.

So their friendly companionship continued though they never met outside the context of rehearsals and Antony could not quite convince himself that they were actually growing any closer – rather they seemed to have settled into a comfortable routine. But then, it hardly seemed to matter. There was no urgency, he told himself: they had all the time in the world.

Then the day before the dress rehearsal Rosemary, unusually flustered, took him on one side. Antony had been wondering if something might be up as she had, unusually, not rung him for several days.

"I've come to a decision and I want you to be the first to know..."

His heart leapt involuntarily in hope and expectation as, in spite of what sober reflection might have suggested, he could not but believe that the decision must somehow concern himself!

"I've decided to get engaged." (Paradoxically, with the word 'engaged' hope intensified even though he sensed that the way she was expressing herself was ominously strange.) "You won't be cross will you?"

(Now at last his surging hope died and he began to feel a little sick.)

"It's not Leo Marjoribanks is it?"

"Leo! Whatever made you think that – he's queer! Isn't it obvious? I thought you knew him."

"I suppose I just thought he was theatrical...."

"It's Guy Halliwell."

Just when he was beginning to regain a sort of wretched equilibrium with the relief that it was not Marjoribanks, the name stunned him almost to the point of incomprehension.

"Guy Halliwell! But I thought you..."

"I was going out with him before Christmas. I know you advised me against him... but I've been seeing him again."

"That was Guy – your mystery man!" (He restrained himself from saying 'your creep'.)

"Don't look so shocked. He's not so bad really. You'll like him when you get to know him. I want you two to be really good friends. Anyway the engagement party's next Sunday – we're getting married in June – do please come; a lot of the old *Twelfth Night* crowd will be there!"

"I'm sorry I don't think I can leave my mother."

Here, concerned only to preserve some semblance of dignity, he ended the conversation with a bleak smile and walked away. Rosemary however, relieved at having got the difficult bit over, went off merrily to tell some the girls in the cast whom by now she was quite friendly with.

Antony, who needless to say did not this time attend the post-show party, spent the next few weeks in a state of dispirited numbness while his mother made no attempt to conceal her satisfaction at Rosemary's engagement. He could not help reflecting, however little he tried to dwell on it, that she had spoken of her engagement in a rather curious way – "I've come to a decision", "I've decided to get engaged" – curious and defensive. But perhaps that was simply because he had been so vehemently critical of her fiancé-to-be to him only a few weeks ago. If he had known then she was talking about Guy Halliwell he would have been even more insistent that she should have nothing more to do with him! He could quite see now why she had withheld his name. What could have possessed her to do it? Surely it could not simply be his money. And getting married in June! She was only eighteen and he was more than ten years older. It was almost indecent.

How pathetically unworldly his cherished little dream of their coming together over an indefinite period of years was made to seem by contrast. He would never understand women. Now he could see why some men paid for sex. It cut out all nonsense.

Anyway that was that, and Marjoribanks would have been worse – scarcely tolerable in fact. With the appalling Halliwell at least there was just one seed, one grain of hope, albeit so small as to be practically invisible, and it was generated by his conviction that they could never be happy together and also that, at some level, she already knew it. However hoping for her unhappiness so that she might one day just conceivably turn to him was pale consolation indeed. He had perhaps however acquired some material for a novel and great suffering might well be a prerequisite of becoming a great writer.

There was one minor piece of good news to set against 'The Engagement': Antony, having impressed the manager by his efficiency and evident knowledge of what he was selling, had been given a permanent job at the bookshop, replacing a woman who had to move because of her husband's job.

PART TWO: DUTY AND FREEDOM

I

In the spring of 1958 two things were clear to him as a result of the Rosemary episode. The first was an irrevocable decision that, in spite of his talent and gift for entertaining, acting was not for him. Rather pompously he told himself that he lacked the shallow versatility, the mobilitas animae required to lose himself completely in a series of roles devised by other people. When it came down to it he was much too serious a person with too substantial and complex an inner life to make a real actor; though if Marjoribanks had offered him the lead role opposite Rosemary in some spectacular new production he might have felt differently!

The second was that he could no longer stay in England, not even for a permanent job in a suburban bookshop. In fact he bitterly regretted ever having come back. Now was the time to repair that mistake. But where to go? He decided against Europe. There would be plenty of time to explore the old continent later; Europe was home, where he intended to live one day, not real travelling. He longed to take the Trans-Siberian railway from Moscow to Vladivostok or travel the Silk Road all the way from Damascus to Xi'an (inspired by the books of Robert Byron that he had borrowed from the local library) but in those days free movement for westerners in Russia to say nothing of what was then Soviet Central Asia was out of the question. Similarly he thought it best to defer his dream of going up the Nile to Thebes as the British were, to say the least, likely to be unpopular in Egypt so soon after Suez. So he would resume the only life that he could live, that of a rootless adventurer with the world at his feet, where he had left off – in Genoa, and this time board a ship for Rio.

Rio, rebuilt and transformed in the early twentieth century from an insalubrious port into a great modern city, still enjoyed in those days the allure of its Twenties and Thirties heyday. Unscathed by the War and its aftermath, the city of samba and carnival with its beaches, casinos, nightclubs and vibrant, relaxed and racially mixed society seemed, in the late Fifties, to offer a freer way of life than almost anywhere else in the world. (This was before the crime, violence, drug trafficking and gang warfare nurtured in the favelas had begun seriously to impinge on the life of the city at large.)

Antony, now confident from his first trip abroad that living by his wits he could not only survive but prosper, had a vision of himself as having made it, standing in a white tuxedo on the terrace of a luxurious villa on the wooded heights overlooking Guanabara Bay at sunset after dinner, brandy and cigar in hand, looking out at the passing cruise ships, which through binoculars seemed so near that he had the illusion of almost being able to reach out and touch the passengers on deck, while all the time being totally secluded and secure on his property. Yet all this was really only a means to an end. However his adventure might eventually work out, he would have amassed invaluable material for novels and travel writing.

Such was Antony's confidence in his ability to cut a swathe through the great world like the hero of a picaresque novel that this time he was setting off with nothing more than his passport, a suitcase and the price of a single ticket to London and a few meals in his pocket – not much to get him to South America; but currently he had nothing saved and he was desperate to get away. If he succeeded it would make a better story, but at the time that was only a secondary consideration. So, leaving a note for his mother to spare himself futile argument and recrimination, he caught the Victoria train.

Getting on the Ostend boat train proved to be much easier than he had anticipated – he simply asked at the barrier a few minutes before the train was due to leave if he could go on to the platform to give the suitcase he was carrying to his brother: "He left it behind and he can't do without it. It's urgent! Please, I'll only be a moment." The busy inspector, aware that he could hardly expect the brother to get off the train at this late stage, with the air of making a great and generous concession, waved Antony through and thought no more about the matter. After all travellers were always panicking about something or other just before the train pulled out.

There was nothing particularly gullible about the inspector's behaviour. This was a generally more law-abiding age, concerns about terrorism were decades away and people in such situations were generally taken at their word except by the most officious and pig-headed. Nevertheless Antony settled into his compartment relishing his modest triumph. This was how an outsider and adventurer like himself ought to make his way in the world, by 'living off the land', exploiting the weaknesses and stupidities of conventional settled society!

After about half an hour he heard a man coming down the train clipping tickets. Antony avoided him by going into the toilet but not locking it – so that it showed 'vacant' – until the danger had passed. Another clever ruse, another success. He was beginning to feel invincible. But he was well aware that a more severe challenge awaited him before he could get on the ferry at Dover. Boat train tickets as well as passports would certainly be checked and he would not be able to rely on being waved through again. To avoid giving rise to any possible suspicion he returned to another compartment thinking furiously but all the time confident that somehow his luck would hold – and of course it did!

He found himself sharing the new compartment with an offensively large and loud-mouthed American student who persistently tried to engage Antony in conversation. On the basis of a few days stay in London he was full of complaints about Europe, even though he appeared to lack even the most rudimentary knowledge of its history, geography or culture. Eventually he announced that he was hungry.

"You might be able to get a sandwich at the other end of the train," said Antony encouragingly. By this time he had had more than enough of him.

"You think so, huh. In the States all the trains have dining cars."

The young American went off in search of food asking Antony to keep an eye on his rucksack. What an opportunity! As soon as he had gone he extracted the student's folder of tickets which were conveniently located in a side pocket and refastened its strap. In this instance he felt no qualms whatever about solving his problem in this way. On the contrary, it seemed the most satisfyingly appropriate punishment for an arrogant boor.

Antony was about twenty yards behind him in the walkway that led to the boat and though he passed swiftly on was able to hear the altercation that developed after the student discovered for the first time that he was unable to produce his ticket:... don't be ridiculous, of course I had one... how do you think I got this far?... call American Express... call the American Embassy... call the police... don't you understand English in this country?... you're damn right I'm not gonna pay... don't you want tourists in your goddam country?... I paid in dollars... can't you see it's been stolen... are you all thieves in Europe?..."

Antony was quite disappointed to find him on the deck of the ferry an hour or so later. "Hello, you made it then. I couldn't help hearing you had a problem with your ticket."

"Problem! It was stolen. I had to pay out all of that Mickey Mouse British money I had left to get another one. I'm gonna claim it back on insurance as soon as I get to the American Express office in Rome."

"Couldn't you just have lost it? I mean anybody on the train would've had a ticket already. Why would they take yours?"

He could see that the student was unconvinced by this very cogent argument and decided to waste no more words on him. Though they did not meet again, he did afterwards hear his voice in the restaurant car on the train about an hour out of Ostend, demanding to know why he couldn't pay for his meal in dollar traveller's cheques, to the embarrassment, it should be said, of several of his compatriots.

Antony explained to the couchette attendant that although his ticket was for Rome, his plans had changed because he was meeting a friend in Genoa so he would need to be called before six o'clock, and he was accordingly deposited in that great port city just as it was stirring into life. Following the encouraging smell of coffee he made for the first café he found open and, to revive himself after a largely sleepless night, spent his last remaining money on a caffè nero before making for the harbour.

Here he found, or rather saw from a distance long before he got to the quayside, the familiar high and graceful profile of the liner Giulio Cesare with its characteristic backward sloping red-topped funnel – and she was sailing for Rio, Santos, Montevideo and Buenos Aires in five days' time! This time there was no chance of a white collar job, but at least he knew enough about how things worked to get himself taken on as a deckhand with immediate effect to help get the ship ready for the voyage. If this attempt had failed he would have been prepared to try his luck as a stowaway; but how could he ever have imagined he would fail!

The Giulio Cesare called at Naples, Cannes and Barcelona to take on passengers before passing through the Strait of Gibraltar and out into the Atlantic; not that Antony as a mere deckhand saw much of these desirable places. But though the hours were long and the accommodation basic, his duties, which consisted largely of swabbing, polishing, scrubbing and sweeping, were not particularly arduous or dangerous – there was no shinning up ropes, climbing masts or being suspended over the side for example. The greatest hazard was being showered with water from another man's bucket.

After a few days Antony, because he stood out as presentable, hard-working, evidently intelligent and well educated and above all able to speak English – over half the first class passengers were Americans – was sent for by the purser and offered a job as a steward. Naturally he jumped at it; but the job, though better paid as well as offering the opportunity for tips, was also more demanding. It involved waiting in the first class dining rooms, running errands for the passengers as well as taking meals to their cabins if required, including morning coffee and breakfast which meant getting up very early in the morning.

A steward, he very soon discovered, had a more intimate relationship with the passengers than any other members of the crew. A number of wealthy middle-aged ladies travelling on their own appeared to take a special interest in him, most notably an Italian countess who was particularly lavish with her tips. The contessa started having breakfast in bed, and when he brought in her tray he found her sitting up in a negligée so diaphanous and revealing that he scarcely knew where to look.

One morning in mid-Atlantic – there was a heavy swell which made some of the passengers seasick so he had very few breakfasts to take round – he knocked as usual and entered to find that her bed was empty. He was wondering what to do with the tray when he heard a voice saying: "put it on the table." As he did so the door slammed behind him and he saw the contessa standing against it barring his exit, her pink silk dressing gown hanging open to reveal her naked body. At first he could scarcely believe the evidence of his own eyes. Deeply shocked and indeed physically shaking he approached her, ostensibly to leave the cabin, asking at the same time if there was anything more he could do for her. By way of reply she began to undo his trousers...

Thus, however shocked and surprised he might be, Antony found himself in a situation that scarcely offered him a choice. To reject her now, even if he had been able or inclined to – and though nearer to fifty than forty, she was still a remarkably attractive woman – would have been not only ungallant but grossly insulting. In the event she proved to be completely unrestrained and initiated him into pleasures that even Laura had not attempted. At last when even the contessa's erotic arts were incapable of coaxing any more activity out of him, Antony was dismissed with a wad of banknotes in various currencies from her handbag and told to come back at ten o'clock.

When he staggered into the stewards' mess still trying to come to terms with what had happened to him and feeling more than ever like the hero of a picaresque novel, he inevitably attracted the notice of his colleagues and before long found himself obliged to try to explain the extraordinary episode. To his surprise, little explanation was necessary. In fact he had hardly got beyond 'la contessa' than they seemed to understand and urged him to tell them all the salacious details, which he did in a mixture of English, Italian and graphic sign language.

"We were wondering", said Franco, the steward who spoke the best English, "how long it would be – we were taking bets!" He explained that the lady, a regular traveller with the line, was notorious – indeed she was generally known to the crew as 'la piranha' – for reasons which were now quite obvious to Antony! She lived in Rome, he was told, but her husband, an Italian count spent most of his time in Argentina: "He is an old man, very rich. She was an actress, a dancer, before she married him. She likes very much young boys, so we knew...."

Though 'la piranha' was especially notorious, being propositioned by ladies of a certain age or, in the case of some of the stewards, by gentlemen, was, he learnt, all part of the job. Those passed over because they were older or otherwise unappealing did not resent it provided that any extra money thus earned was shared out equally with all the other gratuities. This, it was made clear to him, was the absolute rule, whereupon Antony produced the contessa's money from his trouser pockets to general approval and congratulation.

Antony continued to visit her twice a day. What impressed him most about this remarkable woman, apart from her voracious sexual appetite, was that socially she appeared a perfect lady with exquisite manners who, when he served her in public, gave not the slightest indication of what was going on between them. But then of course, he reflected, she had been an actress! In private however, the contessa became if anything more demanding and insisted, begged would not be the right word, that he should come and work for her at her husband's villa outside Buenos Aires and then accompany her back to Europe as her personal servant. When, two days before they were due to arrive in Rio, Antony at last broke the news to her that he planned to leave the ship there, she made a terrible scene, calling him every name under the sun, scratching his face with her nails and throwing him out without the jewelled cufflinks engraved with her initials she had intended to give him that morning.

Passing her cabin in the evening Antony heard shrieks and groans and, without thinking, burst in to rescue her, only to find Franco naked from the waist down most energetically employed astride the lady who, as soon as she had recovered herself sufficiently to be aware of the intrusion, quite undaunted by the situation, shouted: "How dare you come in here without permission. I'll have you dismissed. Get out! Get out this instant!"

Within the hour he was sent for by the purser who said he had received a complaint from the contessa alleging that he had attempted a sexual assault on her from which she had been saved only by the prompt intervention of another steward who had fortunately been passing her cabin and heard her shouts for help. The other steward was Franco who, wearing a new pair of cufflinks which he had not put into the common fund, confirmed her account. Needless to say the lady herself did not appear in the purser's office to confront her assailant.

The purser, who knew all too well that the whole thing was extremely dubious, was sympathetic to Antony but made it clear that, in spite of his vehement denials, he had no choice in the circumstances but to sack him immediately. He would have to leave the ship at Rio but – and this was a clear indication that the purser did not really believe the accusation – with the pay he would have been entitled to had he completed the voyage. As for Franco, it appeared that in the past he had been the contessa's favourite, and that though he hadn't shown it, he resented Antony as an interloper and so naturally lost no time in exploiting his fall from favour. It had all been a very salutary lesson in the ways of the world. But he would be much better off than if he had simply jumped ship at Rio as he had been planning to do! Fortune was still favouring his adventure or rather, like a true adventurer, it seemed he was making his own luck.

The following day, two weeks after leaving the Mediterranean, found Antony, a free man, standing on deck and taking in the view as the liner made its way past Sugarloaf Mountain, which proved to be just one of the improbable peaks dotted in and around the great shimmering blue bay he was entering, with on either shore – but especially concentrated on the western side – a spread of tall white buildings clustered against a background of hillsides dark green with dense vegetation: a sub-tropical New York with an open-armed statue of Christ the Redeemer to welcome travellers rather than Liberty with her torch! The city gradually unfolded and revealed more and more of itself as the ship slowly approached the dock and Antony prepared to disembark with about a third of the passengers who were also leaving the ship here, but who unlike him had had to pay a considerable amount of money to be transported to this breathtaking place.

It was only the beginning of May, the equivalent of November in the northern hemisphere, yet it was nearly seventy degrees, and in front of the skyscrapers he could see people on beaches lined with pleasure craft. What a climate! Truly this was the 'cidade maravilhosa' – the marvellous city. One day, he promised himself with the assurance of a man who had successfully made it to Rio with only a passport and a few pounds in his pocket, he would surely own one of the palatial properties he could now glimpse studding the luxuriantly green slopes overlooking the bay.

As soon as he left the quayside however, his immediate priority was to get somewhere rather more modest to live. He bought himself an English language newspaper from a news stand in the grand palm-lined Avenida Rio Branco and in the small ads found himself a one bedroom apartment in the northern and generally less expensive district of the city. There was also, he discovered in that publication, a considerable demand for English lessons, which seemed promising.

After a few days of sightseeing he gravitated to the liveliest and fastest growing part of the whole of Rio where hotels, luxury apartments, restaurants and places of entertainment were springing up all along the newly fashionable Atlantic beaches of Copacabana and Ipanema. Antony was amazed by the brevity of the swimwear, the amount of young bronzed flesh on display as if it were the most natural thing in the world – which of course it was. All this frank and graceful sexuality was a world away from the awkward embarrassed struggles to change behind a damp towel on a shingly beach that he associated with his annual seaside holidays as a child. (His mother steadfastly refused to remove any item of clothing on the beach, not even her hat, though his poor father, in spite of her contention that he was making a fool of himself, might sometimes go so far as to take of his shoes and socks – though never his coat and tie – roll up his trousers and have a paddle.) It also surprised him that behind Ipanema, as opposed to Bognor, a shanty town of crudely built shacks was clinging precariously to the precipitous hillside less than a mile from all this burgeoning wealth, sophistication and apparently carefree pleasure seeking – a glaring contrast that would be shocking in Europe but which, in the less sedate and possibly less hypocritical New World, seemed to be accepted.

Here, fortified by his experience on the Riviera and having grown a moustache to make himself look older, he hired a tuxedo and spent most of his evenings at the roulette table in an establishment called the Casino de Paris in Copacabana – the gaming, including the calling of numbers was conveniently conducted in French rather than Portuguese. As before he played cautiously betting only on rouge/noir or pair/impair and always stopping to cash in his chips when he was modestly ahead – though his winnings always seemed much larger in cruzeiros! One croupier in particular always seemed to bring him luck. He liked to think of her as his muse, his inspiration, his 'goddess of fortune'; but more than that, though unmistakably Brazilian in appearance and probably several years older, she reminded him forcibly of Rosemary in personality, in her open friendly manner and the deft way she was able to manage all sorts of people. It became his habit, if possible, always to make for her table.

After a week or so she began to recognise him. They got talking at odd moments – when she realised he was British she tried to practise her English conversation on him – and it began to seem to Antony that she was friendlier to him than the other punters. But was he just fooling himself? She was after all such a splendid creature in her shimmering low-cut evening gown, why should she be particularly interested in him? But then she was much more his age than theirs and at times they seemed to be just two young people having a laugh together. One evening when she wasn't there he was quite agitated, but when she winked at him the next day it seemed something of a watershed!

After a month he summoned up the courage to ask if he could perhaps take her out for a meal sometime. He was taken aback by the readiness of her reply. "Not tonight", she whispered, "I'm sorry. Give me a call at the weekend."

"OK but how can I...?

"Faites vos jeux mesdames et messieurs s'il vous plaît. Rien ne va plus... C'est le quarante-cinq rouge, le quarante-cinq rouge qui gagne..."

A quarter of an hour later she slipped into his hand a card on which she had written her name, address and phone number. "Call me first, yes?"

"Thanks, I will."

The following Saturday morning he set out to find where she lived. (The name on the card said Aneta/Annette dos Santos. Perhaps Annette was the name she used at work.) The address led him to a modern apartment block about half a mile from Botafogo Beach, not very far from her work in fact. He stood for a little while on the opposite side of the street wondering what to do. Then a Mercedes drew up and Aneta herself got out. The car drove off. He waved but she didn't notice him so he crossed over to say hello before she disappeared inside.

"It's me, from the casino."

"Yes, I told you to call first!"

"Oh I wasn't coming to see you I just wanted to see where you lived."

"Have been here long?"

"About a quarter of an hour."

Suddenly her mood seemed to change. "That's very sweet, very... very romantic. Well don't just stand there, come on in."

They went up in a lift to Aneta's small apartment on the tenth floor – just a combined kitchen and living room, bedroom and bathroom. It looked out onto other blocks but there was just a distant glimpse of the sea in a narrow gap between the tall buildings if one leant out of a side window.

"You know I don't even know your name."

"Antony."

"Antony, that's a nice name, really English. I'll call you Tony. I'm going to have a shower. Help yourself to a drink. Make yourself comfortable. I won't be long."

He poured himself a generous measure of cachaça and sat back on the sofa. After five minutes Aneta emerged from the shower still drying herself with a small towel which, making no attempt to cover herself up, she then fixed round her hips. Inevitably they became lovers.

Nearly an hour later they were lying in bed together smoking. Aneta was the first to speak. "I noticed you the very first day you came into the casino."

"You didn't show it."

"Ah well you have to be very discreet in my job."

"I can't think why."

"What do you mean?"

"Why you noticed me."

"Because you looked so young."

"I'm twenty, said Antony, slightly increasing his age – he was in fact in his twentieth year.

"You were not like most of the clientele in the casino, the ones I have to entertain sometimes, you know, for the business – so old, so fat, so crude sometimes...

"Do you have to sleep with them?"

"Of course, if that's what they want. They pay well. Some are quite nice, but mostly they treat you like dirt. Have I shocked you?"

"Not really, that's the way the world is I suppose." Then he told her about the money he earned from the contessa for his special services as a steward before she turned on him. "So you see," he concluded, "I can hardly blame you."

"No," she laughed happily, "we're both whores. My boyfriend, he couldn't accept what I do, so we broke up. Brazilian boys, they are very possessive – it's the machismo."

"Machismo?" (Antony was unfamiliar with the term.)

"They have this attitude that they can fuck anyone they like but nobody can lay a finger on their woman. It's all male pride. But you are not like that. I knew you wouldn't be. Are you a student?"

"I was going to university but it didn't work out so I decided to travel the world instead. I want to be a writer."

"A poet?"

"More a novelist."

"You are like me. I trained to be a teacher in a small town in the north, but I couldn't see myself spending all my life in a classroom or just settling down and having kids, so I gave it up and came to Rio. I wanted to get a job in films, the theatre – I wanted to be an actress, a star, fame, bright lights! Does that sound stupid?"

"Not at all, in your shoes I'd have done just the same."

"I should love to travel – New York, Paris, especially Paris... God look at the time! I've got to go to work." She dragged on jeans and a T-shirt and kissed him. "Have you had many girls since you've been in Rio?"

"Just you."

"So English, such a gentleman, my lovely, lovely English boy. Now you must go. Come back tomorrow, not tonight!"

"I may see you tonight though – at the roulette wheel."

"OK, but from now on you must pretend that you don't know me."

A week later he moved in with Aneta and they shared the rent of her apartment, though they never went to or returned from the casino together, and at least three times a week she came back at about three or four in the morning or stayed out all night, only returning in a big shiny car sometime in the morning. Though it was something they never talked about, Antony learnt to live with Aneta's 'entertaining'. She had after all been entirely frank about it and he was now very much more realistic and worldly-wise than he had been when he was with Laura in Crete. In fact, if the truth were told, it gave him a perverse pleasure to think of her abandoning herself totally to other men as she did to him, and made her even more desirable. He even had fantasies of watching her either openly or unobserved, though Aneta made a very clear distinction between her work and private life and it was her rule never to bring anyone home.

They had not been living together more than a month or so when one night Aneta said apropos of nothing: "Did you know the roulette wheels in the casino are fixed?"

"Really?"

"Well not fixed exactly, but there is a button I can press if necessary that vibrates it slightly so that the ball settles in red rather than black, or the other way round of course."

"Why are you telling me this?"

"Because I trust you. I've never told anyone before because I might be putting my life in danger. But I was thinking that if we were careful and as long as nobody suspects I've got any connection with you, we could gradually build up enough money after six months or so for me to leave the casino and go back to England with you."

"But I don't want to go back to England. Besides you wouldn't like it – it's wet and cold and not much fun."

"OK then we'll go to Paris, or the south of France or Italy or the Caribbean – somewhere beautiful and warm. I don't care as long as we're together. And I could wear that bikini you bought me."

"The trouble is I don't think there are many beaches outside Rio where you could wear it without being arrested! You might get away with it in the Caribbean I suppose." Antony was really stirred by this demonstration of her faith in him and their future together but he had something else to propose. Aneta, before we go to Europe there's somewhere else I'd like to see first."

"Where's that?"

"Well ever since I was a kid I've dreamt of being an explorer and discovering a lost city in the Amazon jungle. I don't suppose I'll ever do that, but I would like to go to Manaus and see a little of the rainforest."

"Manaus? OK. I don't mind as long as I'm with you."

So he put Aneta's plan into action, going less frequently to the casino so as not to attract attention. To cover their tracks she allowed him to lose one stake in three or four, and all the time when one of the burly looking supervisors happened to be scrutinising the game. But he never came away with less than the equivalent of about two hundred pounds. Thus by November, the beginning of the summer, they had amassed £15,000. And not a moment too soon, for it had suddenly begun to look as if the management were on to her. Her locker at the casino was broken into and searched and then she was sent for by the manager who questioned her about what he called "excessive losses" at her table. Aneta rather cleverly tried to turn the situation round by tearfully and indignantly protesting her complete innocence but adding that since her integrity was being questioned she had no choice but to resign forthwith! That evening the two of them celebrated their imminent departure for Manaus. But next morning she called Antony to the window.

"Look down there, those three guys; they're bouncers from the club. They're waiting for me. We've got to get away now!"

"But how?"

"There's a back way: down the stairs to the basement and then out through the emergency exit, and over the fence into the land belonging to the block behind which is on a different street..."

They filled two bags and were out of the apartment in less than five minutes. About fifty yards down one of the streets leading to the bay they managed to hail a taxi – or rather Aneta did with Antony lurking in the shadows until it stopped – to take them to the airport.

In those days Manaus, in the heart of the Amazon basin and separated from the more densely inhabited eastern region of the country that ended roughly where the new capital of Brasilia was being built by a thousand miles of savannah, swamp and rainforest, was inaccessible by road or rail. Because Antony wanted to see as much of the Amazon as possible they had decided to fly to Belém on the Atlantic coast and make their way to Manaus by means of a five day journey up river from there by boat. Aneta, who as a modern young Brazilian saw the state of Amazonas and its capital as merely the undeveloped and backward part of her own vast country and not as the ultimate explorer's destination, had not initially been very enthusiastic about the trip but Antony had succeeded in firing her imagination and she was now as excited as he was at the prospect.

Their river journey, however, differed considerably from his expectations. First, nothing had prepared him for the summer tropical climate which even on water was like being in an over-heated greenhouse with the atmosphere so thick and humid as to be almost palpable. Furthermore he had vaguely imagined from the illustrations in his boyhood adventure books that they would be gliding up something like the Thames, only with a wall of im-penetrable jungle on both banks and the constant possibility that some monstrous python-like creature might suddenly rear its head above the tree line and require to be shot before it upset their frail craft and devoured them all. In fact the river was so wide that the rainforest was only visible, mist and low cloud permitting, in the far distance on both sides. The strange cries and chattering noises that reached them over its smooth surface proved for the most part to be nothing more threatening than birds – though they were told that there were alligators and piranhas in the fast flowing waters that surrounded them. The boat too, far from being a frail raft- or canoe-like craft, was much more of a substantial and well equipped river cruiser than he had anticipated.

On the last day they encountered the unique phenomenon known as 'The Meeting of the Waters' where the dark peaty brown Rio Negro having joined the Amazon (at this point rather confusingly called the Solimões) a few miles downstream from Manaus, retains its distinct colour as it flows on side by side with its sister river for around five or six miles, only mixing in occa-sional eddies, before the two ultimately merge.

Manaus too was not what he had expected. He knew that from 1890 to 1920 it had been the Rubber Capital of the World, the Paris of the Jungle, with a splendid opera house and markets copied from Les Halles, only to be subsequently ruined with the development of synthetic rubber and cheaper production in Malaya. Thus he had been imagining something of a ghost town, scarcely inhabited, with dilapidated ruins already reclaimed by the encroaching rainforest. Instead they found a rather charmingly down at heel city of nearly a million people, not the great cultural and commercial metropolis of its glory days certainly – it was many decades since the Teatro Amazonas had staged an opera – but nevertheless a lively place trying to reinvent itself as an industrial and tourist centre.

In order to save as much of their money as possible for France and Italy, they checked into a cheap hotel which had fans but no air conditioning. Antony found it difficult to adjust to the tropical climate but nevertheless enjoyed a two week long journey by riverboat (complete with hammocks, shower, captain, cook and English speaking guide) exploring the Amazon, the Rio Negro and the Anavilhanas Archipelago, which included trekking, camping overnight, bird watching, swimming, alligator hunting and piranha fishing as well as trips by motorized canoe up igarapés (river creeks) and into igapós (flooded forests) and a visit to the native river people to see their way of life. This commercial 'package' trip was to be as close as he would ever get to a real jungle expedition of the sort undertaken, for instance, by Tony Last in one of his favourite novels – *A Handful of Dust*.

He longed to see more of the rainforest and go further up the tributaries of the Amazon but Aneta, essentially a city girl, had had enough. So while they were waiting for the bureaucracy to deliver the passport she had applied for so that she could accompany him to Europe, they spent most of their time on Ponta Negra Beach where she could wear her bikini and, at night, in various louche clubs which pulsated to the beat of a new dance craze called the 'bossa nova' – a quintessentially Brazilian mixture of jazz and samba. This was not really his sort of thing but acquiring such a girlfriend had so completely surpassed his expectations that he was determined to do all he could not to lose her. The whole Christmas and New Year period was one long party and Antony kept as close to Aneta as he could.

Then one evening in January just as they were leaving the

hotel, Aneta was told at the desk that there was a phone call for her. It proved to be from Justina, the girl who had been her neighbour in Rio and a trusted friend – Aneta had sent her a postcard to let her know where she was just in case there was anything she needed to know or any important mail, apart from bills, to be forwarded. Justina was apparently calling because a letter had arrived from England marked 'urgent' and she wanted to know what to do about it. Aneta passed the phone over to Antony who with the faint but distinct hope that it might contain news of his mother's death asked her if she wouldn't mind opening the envelope and reading it to him.

Justina's English was rudimentary but she nevertheless made a valiant effort to pronounce the words, even though she didn't understand most of them. The process took a considerable time, the content however was clear enough:

Dear Antony,

I have been very ill lately and cannot cope on my own. The doctor agrees and has been talking about domestic help and having a nurse come to visit me or even going into a nursing home. But I told him that that was not necessary because I had a son who would come and look after me and I would never, never, consider going into a home. You must come back immediately and do your duty!! I knew this would happen. The way you abandoned me when you did was a disgrace! As soon as you get this, let me know when you are coming back.

Your Mother.

What on earth could have possessed him to send her his address in Rio when to all intents and purposes he had escaped from her. Now her scrawny arm had stretched across the Atlantic to the heart of the Amazon jungle to grasp him by the throat! He explained the situation to Aneta.

"Why can't some other members of your family look after her?"

"There aren't any – just me and her."

"Well you must go I suppose."

She seemed bemused and utterly dejected. Antony grasped her by the shoulders. "Listen, it's not as bad as it seems. She's always imagining she's ill. I'm convinced it's nothing serious. She just needs a bit of reassurance. If I fly to London to see her I can be back within a week and then, as soon as you get your passport, we can go to Paris."

"Do you promise?"

"I swear."

Instead of going to a club they went out for a meal and Antony spent the whole evening trying to reassure her. They parted next morning at the airport with passionate embraces. He flew back to Rio in an ageing VARIG turboprop and then by Air France Caravelle to Paris and on to London by BEA.

As soon as he could, he telephoned the hotel in Manaus to speak to Aneta but was told that she was "unavailable". The next time he rang he was told that she had left the hotel.

"What do you mean 'left', where's she gone to?"

"She checked out, senhor."

"Did she leave a message?"

"No message."

The voice sounded somehow shifty and evasive. He kept ringing the flat in Rio but there was no reply until weeks later a stranger answered who claimed to know nothing of Aneta. He thought of ringing Justina but he did not know her number, and there was no reply to the postcard he sent her. What could have happened? He was tormented by the thought that the thugs from the casino might have caught up with Aneta. The more he thought about it, the more he seemed to recall the odd suspicion that they might have been followed or observed in

Manaus. By leaving her exposed and unprotected had he abandoned her to her fate, giving them a chance strike? The question would always haunt him.

His mother proved, just as he thought, to be not nearly as ill as she had imagined – just having one of her panicky 'turns' – but he never saw his beautiful Brazilian girl again.

II

The fifties turned into the sixties with little discernible change in Antony's circumstances. His twenty-fifth birthday well into the decade when England, to believe the general rumour, was at last shaking off its drab and straight-laced ways (though 'Swinging London' was hardly Rio!), found him still living at home with his mother in what he called a small flat, but was in fact the second floor bedroom he had always occupied.

However much he might try to ignore her and escape from the outward reality of his situation into the inner world of his reading and writing – avoiding as far as possible the humiliation of, as it were, pressing himself up against the bars of his cage – he knew that he was, in the last resort, a prisoner. It made no difference that his mother was now receiving her old age pension and was thus just capable of supporting herself financially, especially if she sold the house and moved to somewhere much smaller; she adamantly refused to move and, in any case, she could not be left.Whatever relative freedom and privacy he enjoyed he had had to fight for every step of the way. (Indeed it was really only to save herself the trouble of getting up to open the front door that she had very grudgingly allowed him to have a latch key when he started work.)

Soon after Rosemary had disappeared from the scene there had been a crucial confrontation with his mother about what she called "disgusting magazines", copies of *Parade*, a comparatively innocent publication by later standards, which she had found at the bottom of his chest of drawers. When he insisted on his absolute privacy in future and demanded that she never enter his room again without his permission and she refused on the grounds that she could go anywhere she liked in her own house, he simply went out, bought a bolt and fixed it to the door. (Though strictly speaking this only secured the door when he was inside, the times when she now felt able to struggle up to the second floor were rare indeed, and the point had been made; so after some resentful mutterings the matter was effectively closed.) For good measure, and in spite of her objections, he subsequently spent several weekends stripping off the old wallpaper and redecorating the room more to his own taste.

A few months later, when his mother criticized the state of the house – she was able to do little more than light dusting while the hoovering, polishing, floor and window cleaning were left to him – Antony retorted that she should get a home help. His mother vehemently objected to paying "some woman to snoop about the house", but in the end after Antony had refused absolutely to do any more cleaning, she tolerated the intrusion on condition that he paid the help's wages out of his earnings.

Then there was a tussle over his father's train set in the attic. When he discovered that she had put it up for sale without consulting him asserting that it was hers to sell and she needed the money, he was clearly so upset that she backed down. Encouraged by this victory he bought himself a portable television for his room – his mother had hitherto always refused to have a TV in the house – took driving lessons and when he passed, acquired himself a little second-hand car. His mother had inevitably proved as negative and discouraging as possible: "You don't want a television set, what do you want to watch all that rubbish for, besides it's bad for your eyes... What do you want a car for, there's nowhere to put it and where would you go anyway?" and so on. In the end however, with very bad grace, she accepted the situation. Whether she was conscious that, considering how much he was giving up for her, it might be dangerous to push him too far or just accepted that ultimately she could hardly stop him spending his own money how he chose, it was impossible for him to be sure.

Nevertheless there were times when he was inescapably confronted with the limits of his condition. Though his mother was generally able to care for herself, walk to the local shops and prepare meals (if he helped her and did the washing up), he had to devote almost the whole morning of his cherished Saturday off, one of the great bonuses of his job in the bookshop, to helping her with the main weekly household shopping which she could not manage by herself and refused to delegate to him. The only advantage of this time consuming chore was that he could ensure that she bought better food, even though her cooking did not improve.

Even after he got his car, which incidentally made the Saturday shopping much easier, spending a night away was not a practical possibility. He tried it twice only to return to find his mother apparently prostrate with nervous anxiety, chest pains and palpitations, so much so that she took to her bed for several days after he returned. As to going abroad during his annual two weeks holiday, to Vienna for instance, even with a neighbour looking in every day to see that she was alright, it was out of the question. In any case his mother would never let a neighbour in the house; this she called "keeping herself to herself". Thus, to change the metaphor of constraint, however long a lead he was allowed, there were times when he encountered its full extent and felt the collar tightening round his throat.

He could never simply abandon her now because he would not entirely give up hope that Rosemary might one day turn to him again – indeed it was one of the few things that kept him going – and thus he could do nothing that might in any way lessen her esteem or affection for him. Her admiration for the way he had accepted responsibility for his mother had inscribed it as a duty in tablets of stone. Nor could he allow himself the luxury of some great showdown with her in which he expressed without reserve and in the greatest detail the full grounds and intensity of his hatred for her. Such things once said could never be unsaid and judging by her physical agitation every time she failed to get her own way, the effect on her would probably be so devastating that he would be reduced to the constant nursing of a bedridden invalid – at the very least he anticipated a major stroke, just to make his life quite impossible! – so he was indeed trapped.

Of course he imagined the showdown scene, refining his attack over the years, nurturing every grievance, polishing and rephrasing every thrust; especially on those occasions when, unable to trust himself after some typically crass or provocative remark of hers caught him on the raw, he rushed out of the house and strode round the neighbourhood muttering furiously. His mother's imagined reaction to this pitiless and well prepared onslaught varied. Sometimes she was stunned, became white and tearful or grovelled for pardon or mercy, which he might or might not refuse; sometimes she sprung into a vicious counter-attack like a cornered wildcat. But her final condition, as he visualized it, was invariably as dire for him as it was for her. With his luck he certainly could not rely on her having the good grace to expire on the spot with a massive heart attack! But these furiously enacted inner melodramas, if allowed to run their course, at least effected some sort of catharsis, giving a certain relief to otherwise intolerably constrained emotions. And one day, he told himself, this episode in his life would be transmuted into great art.

Antony had had no friends at all since he left the Arden Players, merely work colleagues and acquaintances and no social life to speak of. But one spring day about a year ago, one of the other sixth form 'intellectuals' that he had been on speaking terms with at school – his name was Deakin, it had been surnames all the time at school – happened to come into the bookshop to inquire about a textbook. He had done a Geography degree at Cambridge and was now back teaching at his old school. Now that he came to think about it Deakin had always struck him as an unimaginative, unadventurous, nose-to-the-grindstone type, but to return to one's own school as a master to earn one's living joining all the other shabby deadbeats in the common room, struck Antony, who had shaken the very dust of the place from his feet, and saw himself in spite of everything as a cosmopolitan nomad, a citizen of the world, as both sad and incomprehensible. Fortunately Deakin for his part showed no disposition to wonder how one of the leading lights of the Arts sixth at Raynes Park Grammar School came to find himself in the comparatively humble role of shop assistant.

When they had concluded their business, to his considerable surprise he heard Deakin asking: "Do you ever come to any of the Old Boys' dos?"

"No, I don't actually. Not really my sort of thing."

"I thought I hadn't seen you."

"Is Marjoribanks still connected with the Old Boys' Association?"

"Yes, he still produces the play."

"I'd rather not have anything to do with him."

Deakin had some dim memory that Kilroy had been one of Marjoribanks' protégés but being a good chap tactfully tried not to show any reaction. Perhaps he had touched on a delicate area, or perhaps he had simply misremembered.

"Well, you needn't see him if you don't want to. Look, why don't you drop in at the OB's cricket club. You know where it is, off the Purley Road? There are several people from our year in the team. We play at home most Saturdays. I'll send you a fixture list. There are bound to be quite a few chaps there you know and there's a bar in the pavilion if you get bored with the cricket..."

Antony had no intention of taking up Deakin's invitation. He had no particular desire to see his school contemporaries again and he certainly had no wish to be exposed to questioning as to what he had been doing with his life during the past few years, nor had he any great liking for cricket which, based on his school memories, was preferable to football only because for most of the time one was not involved in the game at all. Nevertheless two Saturdays later, as it happened to be a pleasant sunny afternoon and inspired by a mild curiosity as well as the perennial desire to get away from the oppressive atmosphere of the house and his mother, he drove in to the Old Boys' ground just to see what was going on. He fully expected to stay for only a few minutes and drive off again to some beauty spot like Leith Hill without even getting out of the car.

In the event he stayed until about half past nine in the evening. He spoke to at least a dozen Old Boys all of whom seemed to remember and be pleased to see him, including one or two with whom he hardly exchanged more than a few words in his entire school career – and no one asked him any prying questions. He even patronized the rather pitiful little coterie of greying Old Boys and masters (honorary members of the Old Boys' Association) long past their playing days, who nevertheless always turned up to matches because they had nothing better to do and apparently no other interest in life. There was thankfully no sign of Marjoribanks, but given his well advertised contempt for what he called "flannelled fools", Antony felt quite safe from that quarter.

He returned home to find his mother waiting in the hall with the front door open: "What sort of time do you call this? Where on earth have you been? I've had my supper. I couldn't wait any longer..."

"Bonsoir maman!" he replied, not without a certain insouciance. "I've been watching the old school play cricket, don't yer know."

"You've been drinking! I can smell it. Disgusting! Don't think you can start coming back at all hours in that state because I won't stand for it."

"Just a little absinthe, mother dear." (He had in fact in the course of the evening drunk the equivalent of about three pints of beer.)

As he made his way rather heavily up to his room she called after him: "Your supper's ruined and it serves you right!" (The latter phrase constituted one of his mother's favourite expressions. She relished the idea of people getting what they deserved, by which she meant, naturally, something thoroughly unpleasant rather than a reward.)

Her hostility as much as anything else ensured that he became quite a regular visitor to Old Boys' matches, though only in summer and when the weather was suitable. He drew the line at standing on a muddy touchline in the mist and rain and cheering on the football team. He discovered however that there were many worse ways to spend a warm summer afternoon than lazing in a deckchair a few feet from the boundary with half an eye on the cricket and the firm intention of reading the good book he had brought with him, while spending most of the time worlds away dreaming and dozing. The great advantage was that the more he went, the less of a social effort he had to make and before long his presence became totally unremarkable, though not any the less welcome.

III

Antony's current situation – living in one room in a south London suburb and the disappointments, setbacks and humiliations of his life so far, had only served to harden his well-concealed ambition, as well as making it more focused, practical and resourceful, and when it came to planning and launching a bid for supreme power perhaps a bedsit in Raynes Park was a good a place as anywhere else!

As a boy, solitary, friendless, repressed and strictly brought up, despising his parents and his surroundings, overwhelmed with the consciousness of unique gifts and powers of mind that were totally unrecognised and with no outlet for the tremendous dreams that possessed him, he became obsessed by history. It took over from imaginative fiction as the element in which he moved and lived. Here he found his peers and companions, not among mere monarchs and ministers, reformers and revolutionaries but those few whose careers assured him that he was not alone, that men whom he could almost regard as his equals and with whom he could feel a deep affinity, had walked the earth before him – Alexander, Julius Caesar, Augustus, Attila, Genghis Khan, Napoleon, Adolf Hitler, especially Hitler.

The more he got to know about him, the more there had seemed to be an almost uncanny kinship between them – with the sole exception of his strange preoccupation with racial purity which stuck no chord with Antony. Like Hitler he was physically slight (even the curve of his nose resembled that in a drawing of the young Adolf, dreamy, impractical, uninterested in petty detail, essentially an outsider, so unimaginably different from the mediocrities who surrounded him that he felt he belonged to a different species; profoundly musical yet unable to play an instrument (his mother would never have "wasted" money on lessons);

at heart an artist and a bohemian for whom any mundane and conventional course of life would be unthinkable, but also a potential conqueror on a world historical scale, convinced that he could direct vast armies; jerky in his movements and awkward and gauche with others, yet with supreme secret confidence in his destiny and the power of his will to reshape the world according to his dreams – Antony was always looking at himself in the mirror to check on the determination etched on his chin as well as to practise his hypnotic stare – and capable of great rages, hatred and resentment, in Antony's case chiefly directed towards his mother and all the more intense because, for the time being, he had to suppress and stifle them.

It was in the sixth form at grammar school that he first discovered that, like Hitler, he had a gift for public speaking; the instinct for discerning what his audience was feeling even before they knew it themselves and then expressing it for them. Though apparently cool and reserved, in a speech he was able to work himself up to heights of emotion and to elicit it in his hearers. Nothing in his life so far had excited him so much as the moment of connecting with the audience in a school debate and the feeling of having the power to sway and manipulate them, to voice their collective fears and desires.

His failure to get into Oxford where supercilious dons seemed quite unimpressed by his scholarship papers, his rejection by a girl who chose to marry someone else and then invited him to her engagement party, even his humiliation on one of his first visits to a pub – he was provoked and ridiculed by coarse louts who called him a freak and pushed him off his stool and when he unwisely shouted back at them they became so menacing that he was forced to leave hastily, boiling with impotent fury – served only to strengthen yet further the bond he felt with the Führer, given his similar early humiliations in Vienna. If Hitler had been reduced to living in a hostel for the unemployed, he was in a five pound a week bedsit. Even his very name, 'Kilroy', was one that was written derisively on lavatory walls – 'Kilroy was here!' One day he would be there, and everywhere, in earnest; one day the whole world would ring with the sound of his name and nobody would dare to mock it. One day he would be revenged and the world that had ignored and rejected him would acknowledge his power and his genius. An age would be marked with the name of Kilroy!

But Antony was not content to sit in a poky little room and wait for Fate to knock on his door like the first three chords of Beethoven's Fifth. Directly, and through the agency of others, he worked stealthily, unceasingly, remorselessly, single-mindedly, towards his goal. There were several factors in his favour. In the first place he was a natural conspirator, not a team player, but adept at enlisting and exploiting the talents and enthusiasms of his various collaborators without them being aware of what he was really up to. In fact, like Hitler, he countenanced no equals and no confidants; all decisions were his alone. Then again, and also like Hitler, because his personal life was a desert, all his creative and emotional energy was consumed in his quest of power. (Perhaps after all it had been essential for his destiny that he had been rejected in love. The rejection had set him free and caused the iron to enter his soul, but nevertheless, still drove him on to prove to *her* especially, what he was capable of; his parents were by now already dead so he had lost forever his chance of at last impressing them.) Ordinary people, even those few with political or other ambitions who were not content with a quiet life, had some other concerns beside their careers to absorb them – hobbies, leisure, pleasures, girlfriends, wives, families, a domestic life. He had nothing, nothing to dilute or distract his driving burning will. Like Napoleon he could do with only a few hours' sleep and was at his desk far into the night – he was a wolf among sheep!

The time too was ripe for his great enterprise, not perhaps as propitious as the Weimar Republic, but pretty good. The Tories, tainted by scandal, had turned to the preposterously archaic figure of the fourteenth Earl of Home to lead them, and even so had only just lost the 1964 election. The incoming Labour government, with a majority of four, had inherited a large trade deficit and for all its talk of a New Britain 'forged in the white heat of the technological revolution' completely failed to arrest the country's economic decline and chronic underinvestment. A second attempt to join the EEC was rebuffed by President de Gaulle who implied that Britain's economy was now too weak and would be a drag on the other members. This humiliating economic weakness was compounded by a vicious circle of constant strikes, excessive wage rises and mounting inflation – the spectacle of the Prime Minister himself trying to settle industrial disputes 'over beer and sandwiches' at Number Ten, only served to confirm the impression that the unions and the TUC had the whip hand over the government. Attempts at restoring the country's fortunes by indicative economic planning, to nobody's surprise, came to naught. Britain proved not only unable to prevent the white settler government in Rhodesia declaring independence but after much posturing was reduced to negotiating with its rebel colony.

Even with an increased majority after 1966 the decline continued. The pound was devalued but the economy was too inefficient to derive much advantage from having a cheaper currency and Britain had to withdraw from its bases east of Suez largely for financial reasons. The country was drained of confidence, clapped out, bankrupt and in apparently irreversible long-term decline; the froth of 'Swinging London', the 'satire boom' which helped to foster a much less respectful attitude to authority in general and politicians in particular, and the general relaxation in British sexual mores, only serving to add a whiff of Weimar decadence to the period.

This general malaise was epitomized for Antony in the person of Harold Wilson, the quintessential temporizing, 'pragmatic' politician, a consummate manoeuvrer without convictions, concerned only with holding his fractious party together – a party that in this case was constitutionally the creature of the trades unions – and maintaining his base of support. He was thus completely incapable of taking the drastic measures needed to restore the country's fortunes even if he had had the inclination and strength of purpose to do so.

Antony's first substantial move was, after considerable research, to join an amateurish anti-immigration and 'traditional values' group called British Heritage whose principal merit for his purposes was that it was a national organization. He became its secretary, brought his own people onto the committee and revamped and transformed it into the nucleus of his own movement. Then he stood in a by-election in a marginal Labour seat in Essex denouncing the parlous state of the country in a succession of vibrant speeches – in those days candidates still addressed public meetings – and won by a majority of ten thousand. The result attracted national attention which Antony exploited by touring the country where, in a series of theatrically staged gatherings he carried to the nation at large the arguments he had used in the by-election, and was greeted with an enthusiasm normally reserved for pop stars.

Britain was then, much more so than today, a highly centralized country with much less diversity in its media, so that it was easier to dominate the news agenda; thus the almost telepathic way in which he was able to tap into the mood of his audiences who were all too aware of national decline and obviously yearned to believe that Britain could be great again, created a sensation. It was evidently a yearning that was widely shared and when he ended his rallies by quoting, slightly adapted, the lines of Ebenezer Elliott:

When wilt thou save this people?
Oh God of mercy, when?
This people, Lord, this people,
Not thrones and crowns, but men.

the effect was electrifying. Within less than two years, four million people had enrolled in his movement which was renamed the National Regeneration Council – the name was chosen to make clear that it was not just another political party – and the cities of Britain were crammed with his red-shirted followers chanting "NA-RE-CO! NA-RE-CO!"

The political establishment, completely taken by surprise by the national mood revealed in this explosion of support and his extraordinary rise in the polls, were naturally highly alarmed, all the more so as Antony not only mercilessly pilloried the incapacity of the Wilson government but denounced the party system as a whole as merely two cartels of rival vested interests which could never unite the country. He was turning the people against the political class and there did not seem to be much they could do about it except devoutly hope that it was a passing fad, a mushroom growth that would soon collapse. However MPs from both the Labour and Conservative parties, in the first instance with an eye to saving their seats rather than the country, flocked to his banner so that before long he commanded a group of over thirty in Parliament which of course meant that he controlled the balance of power and was able to accentuate the divisions in both the main parties. Though he was courted by both sides and nothing could now be passed without his help, he kept aloof from the mere politicians whom he completely outshone, preferring to keep his powder dry for the general election that could not be long delayed and was so dreaded by what Antony, borrowing de Gaulle's phrase, habitually called "the parties of yesterday".

The genius of his programme was that it appealed across the political spectrum. The right liked the emphasis on law and order and discipline, binding arbitration to end labour disputes, the reintroduction of National Service, a huge increase in defence spending with a wholly national procurement policy, the expansion of the armed forces and the police, making the Commonwealth a reality economically and also militarily by integrating its armed forces under a joint command structure, and the general idea of restoring Britain's self-respect, independence and national greatness. The left liked his anti-American tone, his promise to abolish the House of Lords, disestablish the Church and 'sweep away all antiquated centres of class privilege' including public schools. (He opposed the class system not because he was an egalitarian socialist, but because it was outmoded, inefficient, wasted talent and stirred up resentment – a self-inflicted national wound that urgently needed to be healed.)

He won over the unions with a guarantee of full employment, his plans for a minimum wage and a law to guarantee workers' rights, and both sides of industry by his plans for a massive expansion of the economy with a National Development Bank to finance huge scale public works and incentives for domestic and foreign businesses, though the latter were to be prevented from taking more than a fifty per cent stake in an existing British firm. Most of the newspaper proprietors too, bought into his prospect of a Britain no longer the 'Sick Man of Europe', polarized and divided against itself into 'them' and 'us', left and right, workers and management, but cheerfully marching together in the same direction. Even Lord Mountbatten was rumoured to be a supporter and if true, it probably reflected the enthusiasm of the service chiefs, rather than that of the royal family, for the Kilroy cause.

Once the election campaign got under way his demoralized opponents, divided over what to do with him, found the ground already cut from under their feet. Critics denounced him as a fascist, a dangerous demagogue, a Poujadist, a Peronist, an authoritarian socialist, a corporatist and a puppet of the City of London, without making any impression at all. It was almost impossible to pick holes in his programme. It was coherent and costed and the contradictory charges against him seemed to cancel each other out. In any case the pressure of popular support he was able to generate was overwhelming. He transformed the mood of a country grown used to failure and apparently trapped in a self-fulfilling culture of decline by convincing the voters that there was simply nothing inevitable about it and nothing that he and they were not capable of achieving together. The result was never in doubt. In the event he won four hundred and fifty seats in an unprecedented landslide and the whole of central London and other major cities was given over to wild celebrations. Like Hitler he had acquired power by legal means, only with considerably more élan. He was the youngest Prime Minister since Pitt!

Looking back, given his unrelenting will, unique gifts and, like Hitler, his sleepwalker's ability to turn every difficulty, almost miraculously, to his advantage, his rise seemed inevitable, but was it really so? Of course the world was full of pathetic fantasists impotently dreaming of power, but could there be others who but for ill luck and adverse circumstances might have achieved more or less what he had done. How big a role did chance play in it all? The question was a profound one, a mind numbing and inscrutable problem, which seemed to cast a doubt on everything and especially his conviction of a unique destiny which drove him on. Accordingly he dismissed it.

Though they were in the logic of his programme, Antony had not revealed, except to a chosen few he knew would be supportive, his darker purposes in the course of the campaign – his determination to abolish the monarchy and to counter the influence of the United States whenever and wherever he could. He was more hostile to the United States than the Soviet Union and, contrary to general view, regarded the half-American Churchill as a traitor for, in 1940 spurning an offer of peace from Hitler – who was at least prepared to guarantee the British Empire – and throwing himself on the mercy of Roosevelt and later Stalin who both, for their own reasons, wanted to destroy it! But there were few who understood the full import of the traditional concluding words of the Speech from the Throne at the State Opening of that extraordinary Parliament: "My Lords and Members of the House of Commons, *other measures will be laid before you.*"

Antony immediately began to enact his programme and the effect, both in terms of confidence and first concrete results, was spectacular. But his undeclared intention had of course always been to seize supreme power and establish a new regime and not to be just one more in the long succession of prime ministers of the Crown. What he planned was essentially no different from Louis Napoleon, the Prince President, moving from the Élysée to the Tuileries and proclaiming himself Emperor, or Hitler making himself head of state as well as Chancellor on the death of Hindenburg, except that in his case he would have to remove the royal family. But by the late sixties, with the coronation now a fairly distant memory, the House of Windsor had lost much of its lustre and, especially in the present stirring times of national renewal, had come to seem both irrelevant and part of that old tired Britain that was now being left behind.

Nevertheless Antony knew that he had to act in the honeymoon period while support for him was at its height, and naturally everything would have to be meticulously planned. The Chief of the General Staff and the Commissioner of the Metropolitan Police, both due for retirement in the near future, were replaced by Kilroy loyalists and special cells were formed in the Ministry of Defence and Scotland Yard, drawing on the considerable reserves of support Antony's policies had created at the most senior levels of the police and armed forces, support which he had most assiduously cultivated.

The chosen date was the fourth of February, four months after he became Prime Minister, because on that date the Queen and the Duke would be at sea in the Royal Yacht, the Prince of Wales in Australia, the Queen Mother in France and Princess Margaret in the Caribbean. It was also the day before Antony's birthday so any unusual activity could be disguised under the cover of preparations for that event. Indeed the code name for the coup was Operation Birthday. Secrecy was so absolute that only a handful of his ministers and leaders of NARECO were in the know, even so garbled rumours of what might be planned surfaced here and there in the press. Though it was easy to deny them as complete fantasy, this was alarming even if the leaks did to some extent prepare the ground. At any rate such ominous cracks made it clear that the dyke would not hold for much longer.

On the fateful night Antony made a very public visit to Covent Garden and when he was seen entering his box (not the royal one!) the whole audience rose to applaud him. It was an excellent omen. But a few minutes before the final curtain he slipped away unnoticed, left by a side entrance and was driven with a hand-picked police escort to the Wellington Barracks in Birdcage Walk, the usual base of the unit currently responsible for guard duty at the Palace; that unit had been replaced by a special force and the barracks were now the communications centre for Operation Birthday. Armoured cars were parked all along the road outside and there were police reinforcements in Green Park and St James's Park. Antony spent some time there conferring with senior officers.

At five minutes to eleven, BBC Radio and Television and ITN received what they were told was a special two minute pre-recorded Prime Ministerial broadcast to be put out at eleven o'clock.

The text was as follows: 'My dear friends, I am speaking to you as Prime Minister and President of the National Regeneration Council. This is one of the most historic days in all the long history of our country, for tonight we are setting the seal on the great process of national renewal that began only a few short years ago, by proclaiming ourselves a republic.

'I am sure you will agree that there really can be no place for institutions of hereditary privilege like the monarchy and the House of Lords, which really belong to the Middle Ages and were regarded as outdated even in the seventeenth century, in our new resurgent Britain. We can now endow ourselves, like almost every other country in the world, with a proper modern written constitution which clearly outlines everyone's rights, duties and responsibilities, replacing the piecemeal accretions of centuries which no one really understands. The Americans and the French did it in the eighteenth century; we are doing it today.

'Tomorrow I shall be asking the House of Commons, meeting in special session, to approve these changes and all of you will have the opportunity to vote on them in a referendum before the end of the month, and in due course on the new constitution as well.

'In half an hour's time I shall be appearing on the balcony of Buckingham Palace, which will be reverting to its former name of Buckingham House, and I ask as many of you as possible to assemble in the Mall to celebrate this moment of our national liberation with me and demonstrate to both to our country and to the world how we are achieving it in an entirely peaceful manner without any form of constraint or compulsion.

'God bless our country and God bless you all.'

Antony was not taking much of a gamble in calling for popular support for his coup. Hundreds of thousands of supporters bussed in from all over the country, ostensibly for his birthday celebrations the next day, were already gathering as he spoke, listening to the speech on transistor radios; but their number was soon swelled by ever growing genuinely spontaneous crowds, so that by the time Antony emerged on the floodlit balcony he was greeted by the greatest sea of humanity ever seen in central London, lit by the light of the half a million handheld torches supplied to NARECO supporters. They sang, they shouted, they chanted his name, they waved flags.

Even Antony was surprised by the scale and fervour of the demonstration. When the microphones were switched on (for the first time on that ex-palace balcony designed for a constitutionally mute royal family) he delivered a little speech, in effect proclaiming the republic in similar terms to those of the broadcast. It was greeted with thunderous approbation. His seizure of power had been overwhelmingly ratified. Even his enemies could see that there was no turning back. There would probably be no need for press censorship or internments. His position was unassailable – and all without a single armoured car emerging from the shadows or a single police baton being raised. This was his moment of ultimate triumph.

It soon emerged that reaction from the Commonwealth to the abolition of the monarchy, except in New Zealand, was very largely positive, especially in view of his government's evident determination to make it much more of a coherent group and a force in world affairs. Indeed there was a sense of relief that it was no longer necessary to pretend that somehow that effete and antiquated institution held the whole thing together. The abolition of the monarchy in those Commonwealth countries that still retained the Queen as head of state followed as a matter of course.

So Antony now had supreme power. He could have himself installed as Lord Protector of the Commonwealth – in both senses of the term! – in Westminster Hall at a time of his own choosing. And yet he was minded to walk away from it all. The struggle to win power had been infinitely more enthralling than the holding and exercising of it. He found himself quoting the words of Cromwell, his only true predecessor and the sole figure in English history who really interested him: "No man rises so high as he who knows not whither he is going" and even more appositely: "I can tell you sirs what I would not have; I cannot what I would!" Even as the ruler of a resurgent Britain at the head of a reinforced Commonwealth he was scarcely on the way to becoming a world conqueror. He had been born at the wrong time and in the wrong place! There was now no realistic chance of his being a great war leader – besides did he even want to make Britain a major force in the world again? – the national resurgence he really admired and desired was that of de Gaulle's France. But, in the end, he had an imperial destiny and that he could never abandon... and as a result British history took a different course.

IV

It is true to say that from the day of his coronation as Emperor in Rome, which was followed by coronations on a somewhat smaller scale as King of Hungary in Budapest, King of Bohemia in Prague and King of Poland in Warsaw (the Hungarian one being the most demanding since it involved riding a white horse up an artificial hill wearing Saint Stephen's crown and then brandishing a sword in four directions!) hardly an hour passed when the memory of a certain June night did not occupy his mind. Rosemary remained a constant background to the flux of day to day experience and all his preoccupations great and small. He might be at his coronation banquet in the Quirinal staring at the gilded plate, driving past endless ranks of flashing swords and lowered standards, entering a city en fête or just at the desk of his study in the Hofburg, whose high windows looked out so enticingly over the roofs of the palace to the life of the city of Vienna beyond; but whenever his thoughts wandered and he was no longer concentrating actively on the matter in hand, he found himself asking what she might be doing at that moment, where she was, whether she was happy and if by any chance she might be thinking of him.

He imagined that perhaps, apart from being a dynastic necessity, marrying might help him to forget the past and give more of a centre to his life. The wife they chose for him, or rather that he chose out of a very restricted list, was certainly pretty, delicate, petite and discreetly charming. The wedding itself was a brilliant success and it restored the Emperor to the height of his initial popularity at the Restoration. (Such events are often all that is needed for sovereigns to win their subjects' hearts; for politicians it is not so easy.) The weather was perfect, a public holiday had been decreed throughout the Empire and the crowds packed every vantage point, standing twenty deep at intersections, all along the processional route from the Hofburg to the cathedral and from there to the Schönbrunn where the reception was held, to see the bridal couple pass in an open carriage with a huge cavalry escort. The soaring gothic interior of the Stephansdom was ablaze with candles, filled with the heady scent of banks of lilies and orchids and hung with great loops of white silk and imperial banners. Everyone said that the Emperor looked his best in his Austrian uniform – white and gold jacket decorated with all the orders of which he was sovereign, red trousers and sword – while his bride, the new Empress, so modest and calm, yet obviously radiantly happy beneath her veil crowned with a tiara of flowers and stars, charmed and delighted even the most cynical observers. Anton, who had already been more favourably impressed by her than he had expected, began to fancy himself in love and noted more than once during the celebrations how completely he had forgotten his English rose! The size of the crowds and the overwhelming, indeed somewhat unanticipated enthusiasm, prompted courtiers and ministers afterwards to concede that it would have been better to build temporary stands along the route as for a coronation.

In the long run however marriage only served to increase his longing for Rosemary. In retrospect he could see that the process of disenchantment with his bride had its origins even on their honeymoon in the paradisal setting of the cypresses and marble terraces of the renaissance imperial villa overlooking Lake Garda. It was then that in spite of his good intentions she began to irritate him with her tendency to fuss about trivia, her ceaseless chatter, her tense silvery laugh, her coy smiles, her tendency to wheedle and hint in order to get her own way rather than coming right out and saying directly what she wanted, appearing hurt if he did not immediately comply with her wishes, and lastly with her habit of following him around everywhere even when he had business to attend to. Had he never known Rosemary perhaps it would have been different, but that cheerful, forthright, full-bodied English rose was such a contrast to this slim, simpering and rather flat-chested Portuguese bride! It did not help that she tired easily, was prone to headaches and nervous attacks and turned out to be extremely pious.

Naturally Anton continued to treat his young Empress with every courtesy and to perform his duty as a husband – which was also of course like almost everything else in his life, a public duty – conscientiously. Unfortunately as he rapidly cooled towards her she showed every sign of developing an intense emotional attachment towards him which led Anton to try to keep his distance from her all the more. She took every difference or coolness on his part as a sign of rejection and there were occasionally hysterical scenes when she accused him of not loving her. His answer that they got on as well as most married couples in private life and, he suspected, better than most, perhaps understandably failed to satisfy her. A couple of miscarriages caused further tension in the relationship with the Empress accusing him on one occasion of showing little sympathy for what she was going through and only being concerned that he should produce a son and heir. When at last she had successful pregnancies her narrow pelvis made the births difficult.

Gradually, very gradually, Anton's inability to return her feelings convincingly converted her love into resentment, estrangement and bitterness; though, of course, appearances were preserved. It was a sad business. He would have much preferred it if a civilized friendly relationship could have been established between them but it proved impossible. He did not feel guilty about the way things had worked out considering that as a royal princess of the House of Braganza she should have known what she was letting herself in for. Theirs was a dynastic marriage. If her religious principles forbade her from finding consolation elsewhere that was her problem!

He might have been more sympathetic to her situation if she had not, as he saw it, tried to preserve her predominant influence over their sons as they grew older and even to turn them against him as much as she could; though in fairness it must be said that he had rather left the field to her. By the time his three sons eventually arrived – at eighteen month intervals – he and his wife had separate apartments. He avoided the nurseries as much as possible and seemed only too happy to take advantage of the fact that his daily round of duties, if conscientiously observed, left little time for domesticity.

So it was that as the years passed he thought of Rosemary more not less. From the back of his limousine while smiling and waving graciously he could not help scanning every enthusiastic crowd pressed up against the barriers for a glimpse of her face, and several times a week wondered if he might just possibly have seen her for a second as he sped by. After all her husband, as far as he knew, was a man of means; why shouldn't they be in Vienna, Berlin, Budapest, Prague or any of the other cities he visited regularly in the course of his imperial engagements. Occasionally, in a heart-stopping moment, he thought he had caught a back view of her in the stalls at the opera or in a ballroom, before, that is, she turned round to reveal a stranger's face. So she remained a will-o'-the- wisp. She proved equally elusive at night. In a recurrent dream he and Rosemary lay together naked, cuddling in a massive curtained four-poster bed, the curtains of an open window billowing while a storm outside flashed and thundered. But as he clung ever more tightly to her she had a disquieting way of turning into the slight form of his wife in her long cream nightdress.

As part of the celebrations of his tenth anniversary on the throne his ministers considered it opportune to advise the Emperor to undertake a limited foreign tour for the first time and so, after intense preparation and much diplomatic to-ing and fro-ing, he paid brief state visits to Paris and London. Republican France, to say nothing of monarchists of various stripes, was captivated – even the left wing press wrote of a 'conte de fées'. The imperial couple stayed at the splendidly refurbished Grand Trianon. There was a candlelit banquet in the Galerie des Glaces followed by the most sumptuous operatic entertainment and firework display since the days of Louis XIV. The Emperor even addressed both Chambers meeting together in extraordinary Congress at Versailles, a unique event and an honour never before granted to any visiting Head of State. The Empire was à la mode in Paris; the crown of Charlemagne even became a fashion accessory.

Though the traditional pomp and circumstance of the welcome in London was on an unprecedented scale – the press hailed him as the most important visitor to British shores since Claudius in 43 AD! – it lacked much of the brilliance and breathtaking beauty of his reception in Paris. Nevertheless for Anton personally, rather than for Theodore the Emperor, it was infinitely the more significant stage of the trip, because in London it was virtually certain that even if he did not set eyes on her, she would be looking at him thanks to the blanket media coverage that the visit would receive.

Having been seen off from Orly by the President of the Republic, the Prime Minister and virtually the whole of official France, he landed at Heathrow to a reception by the royal family, the government and the diplomatic corps in a splendid pavilion of red velvet and gold decorated both with imperial eagles and lions and unicorns – shades of the Field of the Cloth of Gold! Two million people filled the Mall when he appeared on the balcony of Buckingham Palace with the Empress and the House of Windsor au grand complet to watch yet more fireworks, this time in Hyde Park, after a state banquet. He addressed both Houses of Parliament in Westminster Hall and visited Winchester to see the Round Table which Henry VIII had had specially painted for the visit of his predecessor Charles V; but all the time during those three days in England his constant thought, however deeply he concealed it, was that somewhere among all the crowds, viewers, listeners or readers witnessing these historic events, must be Rosemary; perhaps at that very moment with him in her mind. It was an uncanny feeling. Though sadly, but to no great surprise, she proved as elusive as ever. Realistically, he told himself, how could it have been otherwise.

He returned to Vienna to paeans of praise for having created new bonds of friendship between the Empire and the major western European powers, laying to rest misgivings, especially in France, about the re-emergence of the Holy Roman Empire which had generally been regarded there as an archaic German dominated structure that had inevitably put an end to all hope for any kind of pan-European economic and political union; but from a personal point of view, determined now once and for all to track Rosemary down, have her put under surveillance, determine the circumstances of her life and discover whether it might be possible, indirectly and with the greatest discretion, for an approach to be made to her.

The Imperial Court in Vienna, a factory and sounding board for rumour and gossip of every sort, was not ideal for such a delicate intelligence operation, but it was in fact many-layered. There were in the first place the hereditary great officers of the Empire who were largely the Electors – heads of princely families and cardinals, then there were the major court dignitaries whose duties were largely public and ceremonial, then the Emperor's personal household – the Master of the Household, secretaries, chamberlains, equerries, aides-de-camp and the other staff and servants that he dealt with on a frequent or even a daily basis. He knew he could depend on the total loyalty of most of his personal household but even here he always followed the rule of the first Grand Chancellor of the Restored Empire, an Italian elder statesman of vast experience and of the chief architects of the Restoration, who had rather taken Anton under his wing early in the reign, and unfortunately resigned two years ago: "Sire, in executing your wishes, only tell each man what he has to know in order to play his part and only when he needs to know it."

In a volume he discovered in a second-hand bookshop – the memoirs of Victor Eisenmenger, physician to Archduke Franz Ferdinand whose assassination precipitated the First World War

– there was a photograph of Schloss Konopischt, a quintessentially central European high whitewashed red-tiled castle with a tower, hidden away in parkland and pine forest in the depths of Bohemia between Budweis and Prague, a place he had often imagined himself to be. It had been the Archduke's favourite retreat from the life of the Court and now it had become Anton's haven too. He went there whenever he could; officially for the hunting, especially in autumn and winter when it was at its most beautiful, above all in the snow. The pretext of hunting meant that he could leave the Empress behind without provoking too much comment. Blazing fires were always maintained there from autumn to spring in case of his arrival.

There he repaired in mid-November after the foreign triumphs which had persuaded his government to plan a similar visit to Madrid and his wife's homeland of Portugal, for what was described as a well-earned rest and to celebrate his thirtieth birthday. But though the party of male friends he had taken with him were happy enough to be shooting game (the Emperor's own lack of interest in the chase was the despair of the Master of the Hunt!) he had come to pursue a different quarry. For here he got his most trusted equerry the Hungarian Colonel Esterházy to brief two special agents in Prague who were immediately despatched to England by private jet; the matter they were told was one of the highest secrecy, too secret even for any regular branch of the imperial security services to be used.

Though they had nothing much more to go on than the report of her marriage in the London Times, a message came back four days later and was delivered to Anton by Esterházy while he was walking in the woods on a frosty morning just as the first flakes of early snow were falling. Steering him discreetly away from the little group that was accompanying him, his trusted friend whispered that she was living near Richmond upon Thames and was under observation. Subsequent reports provided further details but gave him no clear idea of how to proceed, nor was it a matter on which he felt he could ask for advice. He had not even told Esterházy the nature of his interest in this particular English lady, though the Colonel undoubtedly had his suspicions.

V

Then beyond all expectation the problem was resolved in what seemed an almost miraculous way. One evening in the late autumn of 1969 the phone rang on the hall table and he answered it.

"Tony, it's Rosemary, Rosemary Halliwell."

"Rosemary! A voice from the past!"

"Sorry it's been so long. I kept meaning to get in touch, but you know how it is."

"Yes, of course."

"How are you?"

"I'm OK, still working at the bookshop. It suits me I suppose."

"Still looking after mum?"

"Yes, still looking after mum."

"How is she?"

"Oh much the same."

"And the writing?"

"I'm still pegging away. Listen, it's you I want to know about. You sound a bit strange."

"Do I?"

"Everything alright?" (In spite of himself his heart was beginning to pound.)

"Not really. Pretty bloody awful in fact. You were right about your theory of marriage by the way." (With these words Antony's world was transformed, but he tried to not to show it in his voice.)

"What's that?"

"Romantic attraction can blind you to things you only discover later. Listen Tony, I haven't got much time. I'm not at home; I'm in a call box and I'll be cut off in a moment."

"How can I contact you in case...?"

The phone began to bleep and the line went dead.

Real contact at last after all these years, and now he could not get back to her! They had come within an inch of arranging to meet and she had eluded him once again – and after what she had just revealed. How exquisitely, how tormentingly frustrating! Then his mother's querulous voice intruded into his turbulent thoughts.

"Who was that on the phone?"

"No one. Wrong number."

When the first paroxysm of impatient disappointment was over he was able to reflect that even if he could not contact her, in all likelihood she would ring him back when she could. But it was all very well for Rosemary, he thought in calmer mood when he was once more ensconced in his 'flat' at the top of the house, to imply that she had only discovered later what an unpleasant character Guy Halliwell was. She had known from the start and had told Antony so on more than one occasion. How like her to be so objective about the man, to see so clearly and still go ahead and marry him; and then to be so open and honest about her mistake!

He yearned to hear more but a week passed without another call and he was beginning to grow desperate when one lunchtime in a newsagent's at the beginning of his hour off from the bookshop, he heard his name called in a voice that was unforgettably familiar. Hastily replacing the top-shelf magazine he had been furtively browsing, he turned to find Rosemary bouncing up to him with a delighted smile. She was wearing sunglasses in spite of the season and her left wrist was bandaged. Putting down her shopping she gave him the sort of hug that he didn't forget for many a long year.

"This is nice. I thought I might run into you around here somewhere."

"You look great."

"I need to lose weight."

"Not from where I'm standing."

"You were always advising me not to go on a diet I remember."

"Yes and I still would. What's happened to your wrist?"

"Fell off a ladder decorating, would you believe!"

"Have you got time for lunch?"

They had a snack in the café Antony generally used and reminisced over old times with such enthusiasm that he unwittingly overran his lunch break by half an hour. This did not matter as much as it might have done. It so happened that his boss was away and as he was now de facto assistant manager of the shop, he simply had to explain to his part-time colleague that he had had to do something for his mother. He used his mother as an excuse fairly regularly nowadays, mostly to avoid unwelcome invitations. She had her uses after all!

Rosemary did not allude to her current life and what was "pretty bloody awful" about it, though the unmistakable implication on the phone had been that she was referring to her marriage, but Antony did not like to probe. Perhaps she thought she had already said too much and regretted it though she seemed very positive about meeting again soon and not "letting it go another ten years" as she put it. In fact they settled on the following Friday night, the chosen venue being a pub deep in the Surrey countryside and Rosemary explained to him in great detail how to get there, drawing the route on a paper napkin.

When he arrived he found her waiting for him in the saloon bar. The whole business had an air of secret assignation about it which in his inexperience he found quite thrilling. Here he was meeting a woman who had as good as told him that she was unhappy with her husband, and not just any woman – Rosemary! The green shoots of hope were springing up once more out of the scorched earth. He had had a moment of apprehension before he went in that she might have brought her husband with her so when he saw her sitting alone in a corner his delight was obvious. She looked up and smiled at him.

"You looked relieved. Did you think I wouldn't come?"

"No, I was wondering for a moment whether your husband..."

"Oh I see. Don't worry about him. He wouldn't be seen dead in a place like this. (She meant presumably in an unpretentious country pub.) We're quite safe here."

On this occasion she wasn't wearing sunglasses and he noticed some slight bruising round her left eye.

"Where is Guy this evening anyway?"

"I don't know. I never know these days," she sighed.

"You're not happy are you?"

She shook her head. Then suddenly the significance of the bruised eye and bandaged wrist struck him and he said without thinking: "You didn't fall off a ladder decorating, he's hitting you, isn't he?" and in his concern he instinctively moved from his chair to sit on the padded bench beside her. Immediately she flung her arms around him and began to cry; the smartly dressed and apparently sophisticated woman he had found waiting for him dissolved and he found himself comforting someone much more like the girl who had taken him to a coffee bar more than ten years ago, only pitifully frail and vulnerable. But engulfing all his emotions – overwhelming compassion, indignation and tenderness – was the heady sense that this was the moment he had cracked it; that Fortune was finally and against all expectation pouring her treasure into his lap.

In less than a minute, though it seemed much longer to

Antony, she began to recover herself and try to act as if nothing much had happened.

"Sorry about that. Shall we eat? They do quite good hot meals here – my treat."

"That would be great, thanks. How long has this been going on?"

"Oh off and on. It's only occasionally really, but I try to give as good as I get, hit him where hurts, though of course unfortunately he's stronger than me. He broke my arm once."

"But this is appalling! It's grounds for divorce, surely?"

"It doesn't happen very often."

"Once is enough I would've thought. You can't put up with that."

"Very difficult to prove, without witnesses."

"But why?"

"Why does he do it? Well sometimes it's because he thinks I've been too friendly with someone, or because I've been drinking too much, or because I'm too fat, or because I've been criticizing him or putting him down in front of other people – but I'm not prepared to let him bully me into not saying what I think. This last thing was because he accused me of having an affair and I wouldn't answer."

"And were you? (Antony was so shocked by these revelations that he blurted out a question which on reflection he would never have asked.)

"No, as it happens. The thing is if he really thought I was he'd kill me not hit me... You know for a long time I wondered if it might not possibly be my fault; whether there was something wrong with me and that in some way I really deserved it."

"Deserved it!"

"I know it sounds crazy but that's the way he made me feel – most battered wives feel like that apparently. But then quite by chance I came across his first wife, and it had been the same with her!"

"You mean he hit her too?"

"That's why they split up; that and his inability to keep his hands off any attractive young girl who came within reach. She was more his age you see. He told her they were just incompatible, that she didn't understand him – all that crap... (The crisis in her life, the presence of a sympathetic friend from her past, the effect of the meal and the wine plus a couple of gin and tonics all conspired to prompt Rosemary to unburden himself as never before.) You know in a way I feel sorry for him."

"But why?"

"Well I think perhaps he can't help himself. And you know he can sometimes be very good company, very entertaining – never a dull moment when old Guy's around! He can be the life and soul of any party, when he's in the mood that is. I suppose you could call him a Jekyll and Hyde character – typical Gemini. I really think his trouble is that he's a frustrated actor.

"Does he still do any amateur acting?"

"God no. He packed all that in years ago. He only joined the Arden Players to pick up girls; but I think he could've gone on the stage and been a success. He had the talent, but because he's rich he's never had to work at anything. He takes things up and drops them when he gets bored – sports cars, speedboats; now he spends most of his time playing golf. He calls me a lazy cow, says all I ever do is sponge off him and spend his money. I don't want to be dependent on him financially, but he doesn't want me to get a job. It's not his money I want. I'd live in a cave with the right man. I hate my idle life... Tony, I'm nearly thirty. I want a family! I want children!"

"Doesn't he want children?"

"Not interested. He hates kids."

"You'd think he'd want someone to leave his money to."

"Oh it's all tied up in some trust to do with the family firm. You know a few years ago I actually did get pregnant. He wanted me to have an abortion because we'd booked a cruise. I refused and there was a hell of a row."

"Was he violent?"

"Of course. And when I had a miscarriage soon after that he was delighted."

"What about your friends, your social life?"

"He has his cronies and I have my friends. He doesn't like my friends and I have as little to do with his as possible. We hardly do anything together these days, and never just the two of us; yet he always wants to know who I've been seeing. But most of the time I'm alone, rattling around in a great eight bedroom house."

"Have you talked to anyone else about all this?"

"Not really. You don't like admitting to other women that your life is a complete disaster. I've hinted, but they all run their husbands down anyway. Besides all they're really interested in is shopping."

Naturally this reconfirmation after more than ten years of his role as her special confidant at this crucial moment of her life suffused him with intense satisfaction.

"Hmm. If you're afraid of loneliness don't marry – Chekhov."

"I know what he means."

"Do you think he's faithful to you? Do you trust him?"

"Of course I don't trust him; I don't trust myself. But funnily enough, yes, I do think he is..."

In what seemed no time at all it was closing time. As they got ready to leave Antony stretched out his hand across the table and took hers. His whole future and all his hopes now seemed to depend absolutely on the urgent imperative of her getting free of Guy Halliwell and her last answer had rather taken him aback.

"You must leave him you know."

"Oh I'm going to alright, don't you worry – before I get myself killed!" She smiled.

They parted outside the pub and Antony drove home, his heart singing, to find his mother sitting in her straight-backed armchair more than usually grim-faced, waiting up for him long past her almost invariable ten o'clock bedtime and demanding to know what had kept him so long. He spoke airily of catching up with some old friends to which his mother retorted: "Friends! What do you want friends for? If I've learnt one thing in my life it's not to rely on other people. You're getting as soft as your father..."

He did not reply and without apologising retired to his room. It was only when he was lying in bed reviewing the momentous events of the past week culminating in that evening that it occurred to him that he still had no means whatever of contacting Rosemary, and he spent a weekend of restless anxiety till the phone went late on Sunday night.

"Hello, it's me! Sorry I cried all over you on Friday evening. I must have looked dreadful."

Antony laughed happily in the huge relief of their being in contact once again. "No, no, that's what I'm here for".

"You looked so shocked."

"Well I'm not really used to revelations like that; I've led a sheltered life you see!"

"It wasn't the wine. It was your fault for being so nice to me. Anyway it was a lovely evening in spite of me getting all weepy. Nowadays I never see anyone I really like, from the old days."

"We must do it again soon. What about going to the theatre?"

"Tony, I'd love to. I haven't been to the theatre for years. Guy is a complete philistine."

"Really?"

"He practically spits if he hears the word culture."

"Won't your philistine husband mind if I take you out?"

"Oh didn't I say? He's on a golfing holiday – Spain or Florida or somewhere. With any luck he won't be back for a month at least – thank God!"

"That's great news; by the way I went to the Citizens Advice Bureau on Saturday and got a whole lot of information about divorce."

"Thanks, that's sweet of you but I need grounds."

"You've got grounds."

"Yes, but it's not that simple unfortunately."

"Before I forget, can I have your number; otherwise I can't get in touch with you."

"Bit tricky – never know who's going to answer the phone. Just go ahead and get some tickets – anything you like, and I'll ring you in a few days' time – promise. I'd better go now there's someone at the door."

If Antony had ever been inclined to censure Rosemary's motives as opposed to her judgement in marrying the frightful Guy Halliwell, her bitter experience now completely purged and absolved her in his eyes. She had undoubtedly learnt a cruel lesson and his heart went out to her without reserve. And how could anyone who talked of living in a cave with the man she loved possibly be a shallow money grubber!

The next few weeks passed for Antony in a waking dream of happiness. He went to three Saturday matinees with Rosemary followed each time by a meal in an Italian restaurant she knew in Soho. Thus he was able to get home well before his mother's bedtime. Content with the restoration of their old friendship, which was now inevitably richer and more significant than ever, he made no attempt to force the pace of their relationship. But he did use every opportunity to encourage and strengthen her resolve to break with Guy decisively and go for a divorce in the face of what he perceived to be the worrying danger of her backsliding. It was typical of Rosemary – how well he remembered this of old! – that she seemed to draw different perspectives on life from the resources of her complex personality every time one met or spoke to her on the phone;

by turns cheerful, fatalistic, dauntless, detached, decisive, self-questioning, confident, despondent, brisk and business-like, almost frighteningly single minded or apparently paralysed in the face of the range of possibilities she kept raising – and this was never more true than when it came to the prospect of ending her failed marriage. Antony therefore kept repeating mantra-like: "You've got to get out! You simply can't go on as you are. If you want any kind of life for yourself, you've got to get rid of that man!"

Though he was very careful at this stage not to imply that he saw himself sharing her future life, he had convinced himself that after her husband's removal from the scene and with his constant support, this time their friendship would easily and naturally transmute itself into love.

After their second visit to the theatre Antony persuaded Rosemary to come in and see his mother. He opened the front door to find her already waiting. She looked Rosemary up and down suspiciously. Hoping that her married status might make her more acceptable, he introduced her as Mrs Rosemary Halliwell, an old friend that he had met by chance in Wimbledon and who had been kind enough to give him a lift. His mother was frigidly polite.

"Pleased to meet you I'm sure," she said staring at her appraisingly, lips pursed.

"We used to be in the Arden Players together years ago" said Rosemary, doing her best to be friendly.

"I see. You were the one who was always ringing him up I suppose."

"Was I? I can't remember, but when you're that age you do spend most of your life on the phone, don't you?"

His mother, who never received more than one or two phone calls a month, sniffed and continued to stand resolutely in the doorway.

"I won't ask you to come in, Mrs Halliwell, because I expect you'll be wanting to get off home."

"Yes, I think I'd better be going. Very nice to have met you Mrs Kilroy."

She nodded curtly and Antony escorted Rosemary to her car which was parked a little way up the road out of range of his mother's prying eyes.

"I don't think your mother took to me very much."

"Oh don't take any notice of that; she's always on her guard with strangers. It just takes her a bit of time to get to know people, that's all."

Though Rosemary had failed to charm his mother, as he had fondly hoped – he might have known by now that his mother was totally indifferent to charm of any kind – he told himself that he had at least broken the ice, and a few days later he remarked as casually as he could:

"You know mother, Rosemary Halliwell very much enjoyed meeting you."

"Did she indeed," she retorted with another of her classic snorts of disapproval.

"I was thinking I might ask her round for tea on Sunday afternoon." (In the past ten years Antony had invited precisely three male contemporaries from his grammar school Old Boys' Association to tea, so there were precedents for this.) "You will be nice to her, won't you?"

"I'm sure I don't need telling how to behave in my own home. Will her husband be coming too?"

"Eh? Her husband?"

"She is married, isn't she?"

"Er, oh no. He's in America at the moment."

Another snort of disapproval from his mother.

Thus the day after their third theatre and restaurant visit Rosemary arrived at four o'clock. Antony had helped his mother to prepare an elaborate meal with sandwiches, biscuits, a jam sponge, buttered crumpets, potted meat and ham. The occasion however was a fiasco. His mother took little trouble to conceal her hostility and in spite of repeated requests to call her 'Rosemary' insisted, most pointedly, on 'Mrs Halliwell'. Tense silences were punctuated by insistent questioning from Mrs Kilroy as to the whereabouts of her husband, the reason for her being on her own and how she had been occupying herself in his absence. Rosemary, not the sort of person to be easily disconcerted in any company, left almost in tears after half an hour, the large spread that had been prepared left, sadly, almost untouched.

When she had gone Antony rounded on his mother:

"Well I hope you're pleased with yourself."

"I'm sure I don't know what you mean."

"You were very unfriendly."

"What do you mean 'unfriendly'? She's not my friend. I don't know the woman."

"You kept on and on about her husband."

"Well what's so wrong about that? She's a married woman, isn't she?"

"Yes, but she's unhappily married."

"What's that got to do with you?"

"She's an old friend and I've been advising her about getting a divorce."

"Advising her! You've been going out together, haven't you? You lied to me when you said you met by chance. Don't try to deny it! I can see from you face that it's true. Coming between a man and his wife – it's a disgrace! I knew it. Bad blood always comes out! And don't imagine that a woman like that could possibly be interested in someone like you. Old friend indeed! She's just using you, that's all. And you let it happen, more fool you. Coming round here dressed like that, showing herself off...

Well I can tell you one thing, I'm not having her in my house again."

As so often with his mother he had reached a point where words could not possibly heal the situation and he went up to his room in a state of enraged misery. But when they next spoke, at supper, more curious than indignant, he challenged her about her "bad blood" remark. She tried to retract somewhat and went on about only wanting what was best for him, but he insisted.

"I really think I'm old enough to know about the skeleton in the family cupboard. Is the true head of the family by any chance a criminal lunatic walled up at the end of the west wing?"

"There you go again with your nonsense. When will you grow up? If you must know it was your father's older brother. He was a very wicked man and I hope for your sake you never find out any more than that."

On Monday he got a call at the bookshop from Rosemary (she had asked for his work number in case she needed to contact him urgently), asking to meet him after work. They went for a coffee.

During the past three magical weeks (for Antony at least), in spite of Rosemary's troubles, a mood of light-hearted gaiety, almost of festivity, had kept breaking in – looking back they seemed to have spent most of their time together laughing – but now the mood was sombre.

"Guy's coming back at the end of the week. He rang this morning."

"How long for?"

"For Christmas and the New Year, he says, whatever that means."

"But that doesn't change anything."

"No, that doesn't change anything..."

"I must apologise for my mother by the way. We had quite a row about it afterwards. I won't inflict her on you again."

"Look Tony there's something I want to say about that." She reached out and laid her hand on his; "I don't want to come between you and your mother. I won't and I can't. I really admire the way you've devoted yourself to looking after her. You must have the patience of a saint. No other man I know would be so selfless. You're one in a million, you know that; but you can't leave her and that's that."

"But she's only just seventy. She may go on for years!"

"Exactly," she sighed.

There was a lot more Antony could have said at this point but he thought it wiser to hold his peace – something he afterwards bitterly regretted; one of many such regrets of which his life was constituted. So they parted, with Rosemary promising not to weaken in her determination to get rid of Guy and to stay in touch.

But for the next two weeks he heard nothing. Whether this was due to her husband's return or her bruising encounter with his mother he did not know. Then just before Christmas he received a card from her on which was scrawled: 'I'll give you a ring when the coast is clear', inclining him to hope it was the former.

However it was not until one Saturday in early spring, daffodil time, that he heard from her again. He was in the garden which after his father's death had been neglected. Except for the lawn which Antony mowed and some pots on the terrace which his mother tended, nature had been allowed to take its course. Self-seeded trees and shrubs had taken possession of the herbaceous borders that had once been his mild father's quiet joy and consolation, with wild flowers in the long grass.

"Hello, it's me! Sorry I haven't been able to ring before. I just wanted to let you know, I'm getting my divorce."

"But that's wonderful news! How? When?"

"Well I've already got the decree nisi."

"What were the grounds?"

"Adultery. It turned out that he was having affairs all over the place. The wife's always the last to know, don't they say? And he had the nerve to accuse me of everything under the sun. The bastard! He always swore that he was faithful and in spite of all his faults that was the one thing I thought I could be sure of. Why did I believe him with his track record? Why was I such a fool? But he's played right into my hands. I've got a very good solicitor, a woman, and I'm going to take him to the cleaners!"

"But this is all so sudden!"

"Well a friend's been helping..."

"I see."

"Now listen I've got to go. We'll be in touch. Regards to your mum, be good and keep on with the writing."

Though he was delighted to hear from her, her tone and the implication that she was now organizing her life without his help and advice, was gravely troubling and as the weeks became months and he heard nothing further from her he grew more and more convinced that it was his mother's hostility that had in effect driven her away. Then again was the helpful friend that she had referred to, her solicitor, another female friend or, perhaps, a man?

Thus, more acutely than ever, he felt himself trapped, thrashing like a salmon impaled on a hook – the more he wrestled with his situation, the more he was tormented by the cruelty of his predicament. He was like Tantalus or Sisyphus eternally punished by the gods, caught in a perpetual bind from which there was no possible escape. He could not abandon his mother without incurring Rosemary's displeasure, yet staying with her was, it seemed an insurmountable barrier to closer intimacy with Rosemary! And he could not even vent his frustration on his mother without the risk of a disastrous deterioration in her condition which would make his life with her even more onerous.

VI

There was only one way in which he could free himself to take advantage of Rosemary's newly divorced state before it was too late and that was to eliminate his mother in such a way that no blame or suspicion could possibly attach to him. Thus the concept of the 'perfect murder' began to obsess him. At first he questioned whether this course of action could be compatible with his destiny as a great writer. A great writer could be many things: womanizer, adulterer, alcoholic, drug addict, neurotic, melancholy recluse or compulsive party-goer scribbling down poetry in the small hours of the morning after a ball like Byron – but a murderer? However, he argued, 'murderer' as a biographical term implied detection and exposure. But to carry a dark secret successfully to the grave, that indeed might well be characteristic of a supreme artist. Moreover the planning and execution of such a deed, which would demand the utmost ingenuity, was certainly as truly creative as conceiving the plot of a novel, with the added frisson that in this case the slightest mistake or inconsistency would expose him, not just to the odd critical review but to terrible danger! His would be a masterpiece of murder, murder as one of the fine arts indeed – though unfortunately there would be no audience to appreciate and applaud. It was, he told himself, a mere literary conceit – 'murder will out' and so on – and a popular myth fostered by the establishment, that murderers hardly ever got away with it. In any case 'perfect murders' never featured in the crime statistics since by definition they were never recognised as murders in the first place.

What he now began to think of as 'The Deed' would, he reasoned, have to appear plausibly as a tragic accident, preferably in circumstances where the body was never recovered and, if possible, far from the little world where he and his mother were known. It would obviously be preferable if he could exploit and work with the grain of his mother's character. That she was a woman of the narrowest and most rigid perspective on life, inflexible in her habits and mental attitudes, who could moreover be relied on out of contrariness or sheer spite to do the opposite of what he urged, might possibly serve as an advantage.

Everything pointed to taking her on a cruise but persuading her to leave her home let alone visit foreign parts was likely to prove the trickiest part of the whole operation. The attractive Irish nurse who now came to visit her every three weeks agreed that a short and leisurely spring cruise of ten days or so might very well do her good. She added that he deserved a break as much, if not more, than his mother. (The nurse very much shared Rosemary's admiration of him for living with her.)

"The trouble is Mary", he confided, if I suggest it she'll reject the whole thing out of hand; you know what she's like. But if you recommend it and imply that I'm not keen, don't want to spend the money and so on, we may just swing it!"

The strategy worked – if there was one person in the world that she distrusted less than others it was her young nurse. Naturally his mother would have nothing to do with Mediterranean Europe, or Germany because of the War, but clean Nordic Scandinavia just about passed muster. Accordingly she and Mary, Antony keeping well out of it, chose from the vast array of travel brochures which he regularly received and kept stacked in his room, a coastal trip up the Norwegian fjords in a mailboat that doubled as a comfortable cruise liner. As soon as it was booked he sent a postcard to Rosemary's ex-marital address, asking for it to be forwarded if necessary, announcing the plan. Thus he hoped to gain even more credit from her for spending his hard-earned savings on taking his reluctant mother on holiday followed by an outpouring of sympathy for his sad loss which would, as he envisioned it, inevitably bring them together.

Right up until the last minute Antony was worried that his mother would suddenly announce that she was pulling out of what she obviously considered an absurd and outlandish enterprise, and indeed the very idea of his mother being transported to a boat in the North Sea off a foreign shore was almost unimaginable. In the end it was probably the fact that the holiday had already been paid for that induced her in the last resort to go through with it. So they drove to Stansted and flew to Bergen where a well appointed ship was waiting to receive them. His mother naturally regarded the holiday not as a new and possibly enriching experience but as just one more thing to be endured and worse than most for being both dangerous and unnecessary, and she made her feelings abundantly clear at every stage of the journey. Nothing interested her, nothing pleased her and everything she encountered gave her cause for complaint. But Antony, delighted that he had prised her out of her home and thus successfully achieved phase one of the operation, was unmoved. He even amused himself by trying to guess what she might find to complain of next. Inevitably she took strong exception to her cabin on the boat but when Antony offered to swap with her she declared that she liked his even less!

Their route was to take them up the coast north of Norway and beyond the Arctic Circle. They were due to stop at every little harbour beyond Tromsø and Hammerfest all the way to Kirkenes. Unlike his mother who stubbornly refused to leave the boat even in Trondheim, Antony settled down to enjoy what the cruise had to offer. It was not the Nile or the Aegean nor yet the Blue Train (and for once after a few days he found himself agreeing with his mother that the spectacle of deep inlets of green vertically plunging cliffs and pine forests interspersed with indistinguishable little ports of neat well-scrubbed wooden houses began to pall) but he was secretly enjoying the role of both author and protagonist of a 'real life' Agatha Christie or Dorothy L. Sayers murder mystery, one in which the murder and hence the murderer would go forever undetected! As a necessary preliminary he tried to ingratiate himself with as many of his fellow passengers – most of whom to his mother's disgust were Germans or Americans – as possible. As so often when he was abroad he succeeded in making friends with a charming English couple, Richard and Sally Patterson; he a journalist, she a doctor, and their two children – a boy aged ten, a girl aged eight.

At the same time he conceived various scenarios. A possible course would be to blackmail someone completely unconnected with his mother and thus excluded from all suspicion into helping him in some crucial way – a member of the crew caught stealing perhaps or a passenger having an affair – and then to eliminate his unwitting assistant afterwards in case he or she started putting two and two together. But two unexplained cases of 'missing presumed drowned' on one cruise would certainly give rise to suspicion. The use of drugs or poison would only work if her body were never recovered for forensic examination, and how could he possibly ensure that she would collapse where she could be disposed of undetected? Simply tipping her over the side was also an unsatisfactory option. Not only would she certainly make a noise unless chloroformed or knocked unconscious first, but resorting to such a crudely straightforward course offended his aesthetic sense, in that it was entirely lacking in the subtlety and beauty required of a perfect murder, as well as being in practical terms dangerously visible.

Surprising as it might seem, though Antony had been turning over the possibilities in his mind since the cruise idea first occurred to him without coming to any conclusion, he remained serenely confident that an opportunity would present itself. He prepared the ground for his mother's disappearance by confiding in the Pattersons that he was worried that his mother's churlishness and irritability, for which he apologized, coupled with a tendency to perverse and erratic behaviour might be the first signs of Alzheimer's disease. They tried to be reassuring but were evidently inclined to agree. Sally, the doctor, was especially sympathetic.

On the fourth evening his patience was rewarded. His mother, who from the first meal insisted that the food did not agree with her, decided to take a walk around the deck after dinner before going to bed to help her digestion. He offered to accompany her but, though she constantly complained that he was neglecting her for the Pattersons, he was rebuffed, but nevertheless decided to follow at a discreet distance. His new friends were much impressed by such caring behaviour. Antony observed that she paused for a rest at the point where the railings constituted two gates which could be opened outwards to give access to one of the landing gangways, and lent against them for several minutes taking in the view.

The following morning at breakfast he tried to engage her in conversation:

"What are we going to do today, mother?"

"Do? What do you expect me to do? Sit in a deckchair and twiddle my thumbs, I suppose."

"Would you like me to sit with you?"

"What would be the point of that? You go and run after those smarmy people you're so fond of and leave me in peace. I didn't sleep well again last night. How can you be expected to when it's light half the time?"

"That's the tilt of the earth's axis, mother. You can't blame the cruise line for that."

This facetiousness provoked the predictable dismissive sniff.

"You know mother you might enjoy it more if you tried to mix and meet people."

"Enjoy it? I thought I was supposed to be here for the good of my health. Why should I waste my time getting to know people I'm never going to see again?"

"We should be crossing the Arctic Circle this evening." Another dismissive sniff. "By the way, that reminds me, if you go for a walk round the deck after dinner again, I wouldn't lean against the landing gates. It might be dangerous. I happened to observe that you did it last night."

"Nonsense. Don't fuss. They're perfectly safe. If they weren't they'd put up a notice; and I'll thank you not to spy on me in future."

Just as he had hoped Antony's warning ensured that every time she went for her postprandial walk to aid her digestion, which became securely established as part of her daily routine, she deliberately stopped to rest against the gates. He still had the problem of how to exploit this habit, but three days later fate intervened! Early in the morning before breakfast he saw a deckhand painting the portside railings. When he came to the gates he opened them in order to do the job properly, oiled them and left them open to dry cordoning off the immediate area with ropes for safety, as well as leaving wet paint signs along the deck.

After lunch when the paint was dry Antony, making sure he was unobserved, helpfully closed the gates without bolting them (there were four bolts: two securing the gates to the deck and two horizontal ones securing the gates to each other) leaving the rope and the 'wet paint' signs in place. As he had hoped the painter returned in the early evening, removed the rope and the signs in some haste and assuming that another member of the crew must have secured the gates, left them alone. Just before dinner Antony strolled along the deck. The ship was enveloped in a misty drizzle which obscured the coast and there was no one about. He checked the bolts – they were still unsecured. Fate was leading him by the hand!

After the meal he urged his mother, within earshot of the Pattersons, not to go out for her usual walk because of the weather but, fortunately, she insisted. He then offered to go with her but she told him that she was quite capable of going on her own "thank you very much", and donning her coat and the transparent plastic hood that Antony had in vain tried to discourage her from wearing, made her way out announcing that this time, for good measure, she would do two turns of the deck before retiring for the night.

It was only during the second turn that, feeling more tired than usual, she rested by leaning heavily on the point where the two gates met. Before she could do anything to save herself it was already too late. Her falling body was knocked unconscious against the side of the ship and fell into the sea with a discreet plop which on that damp and misty evening passed entirely unnoticed. Antony meanwhile continued in animated conversation with the Pattersons, turning in later than usual – after one o'clock. But before he did so he listened at the door of his mother's cabin. If she was alive and awake he would have expected to hear her moving about, if asleep to hear her snoring, but there was no sound.

At seven thirty next morning the steward who brought round the tea and coffee informed Antony that he could get no reply from his mother's cabin. (She was a habitual early riser and always fully dressed and ready before he entered.) Antony went with the steward while he opened the door. When they saw she was not there Antony, still in dressing gown and pyjamas muttering "she must've wandered off again," went immediately to report her missing and request a search. The search found no Mrs Kilroy but one of the portside gates open.

The conclusion that she had been lost overboard was inescapable and as she was last seen alive at nine thirty the previous evening when she went out on deck and the ship had gone some sixty miles in the night, any chance of a rescue seemed hopeless. Moreover it was pointed out to Antony that the depth of Norwegian coastal waters made even the recovery of the body virtually impossible. Nevertheless the captain called for a coastguard helicopter to do a routine search to see if any traces of her could be found – predictably without success. The 'perfect murder' indeed! But he still had to run the gauntlet of an investigation by the local police commissioner who came aboard at the next port and in true detective story fashion set up a little office and began interrogating the passengers and crew one by one. This proved to be no formality as he was rather a formidable character in a leather jacket with close-cropped blond hair and the traditional steely penetrating gaze who spoke excellent English and clearly regarded Antony with suspicion.

He explained to the commissioner that he lived with his mother because of her delicate health and had taken her on the cruise because he thought it might do her good.

"You were her only close relative?"

"Yes, her only child."

"Looking after her must have been very demanding. Old people can be very difficult can't they? Did you have any help?"

"It's not necessary. She can look after herself. She just needs someone around that's all." (Antony was careful to use the present tense.)

"But didn't you feel trapped?"

"Not at all, I'm happy to do it."

"Is her life insured?"

"No."

"But you are her heir."

"I suppose so, but she hasn't got any money if that's what you're implying."

"I'm not implying anything Mr Kilroy. Can you explain why you waited so long before reporting her disappearance?"

"I didn't wait. I had no idea anything was wrong until the

morning. When I went to bed it was after one. I assumed she was asleep and I didn't want to disturb her. She went for a walk round the deck as she always did... does in the evening after dinner, and I naturally thought she had gone straight to bed as usual afterwards."

"You did not accompany her on her evening walk to ensure that she did not come to any harm?"

"No."

"Why not?"

"She told me not to. She always prefers to go on her own. She doesn't like me fussing over her as she calls it. As a matter of fact I tried to persuade her not to go out at all last night because of the weather but she insisted."

"So where were you when your mother was walking round the deck?"

"I was with an English family all evening – the Pattersons."

"I see. Well, thank you Mr Kilroy, that will be all for now but I may want to speak to you again."

The Pattersons, who were the sort of people whose evidence could scarcely be doubted even by the most suspicious policeman, confirmed Antony's story at all material points; Doctor Sally adding helpfully that Mrs Kilroy seemed to be somewhat irrationally perverse in her behaviour and was very probably in the early stages of Alzheimer's.

A number of passengers mentioned that the portside gates had been left open the previous morning while they were being painted. The painter himself, when identified, was forced to admit in the course of some very tough questioning that, though he found the gates closed when he came to collect the rope and 'wet paint' notices at the end of the day, he might possibly have assumed that the bolts had been secured without checking to see whether in fact they were. The commissioner regarded this as a crucial admission, concluded that the death of the elderly

English lady was obviously an accident and that the sailor was trying to mitigate his own negligence; so it did not surprise him that no other member of the crew would admit to having closed the gates. Accordingly he concluded his enquiry, offered his condolences to Antony and allowed the ship to continue on its way. The gimlet-eyed commissioner had been shrewd and clever, a worthy adversary, but nothing like clever enough and he had comprehensively outfoxed him!

Antony saw no reason not to continue the cruise. The following day the captain conducted a short Lutheran memorial service for his mother and a wreath was cast into the sea. The shipping line, desperately anxious to avoid an action for negligence, offered him an ex gratia payment of £10,000 as well as refunding the cost of the cruise, and the crewman who painted the gates was suspended pending an enquiry by his employers. Antony was only too happy to take the money to the relief and gratitude of the company – the last thing he wanted was for his mother's death to be argued over by lawyers and re-examined publicly in a court case. He even considered requesting that the crewman be treated leniently but reflected that this might not be consistent with the attitude of a grieving son.

Rosemary (he had rung her at the first opportunity with news of the "tragic accident" and now phoned her from every port) was initially all for suing the cruise line, but when he suggested that it might appear money-grubbing and would not bring his mother back, she was impressed by his fine feelings. When the ship returned to Bergen he saw her waiting, as they had planned, in the crowd on the quayside. She caught sight of him and they waved wildly at each other. Then with his heart soaring and muttering the verse that had been obsessing him for a week:

Full fathom five my mother lies;
Those are pearls that were her eyes...

he hurried down the gangway and into her arms, conscious of having triumphantly succeeded in his intention of using real characters in a real situation to create a masterpiece in life rather than art. Now at last his life was beginning!

VII

1970 passed with only a few holiday postcards from Rosemary containing no personal details, and no phone calls. Then at Christmas he received a card from her with a fateful message:

To dear Tony,
Got married in October to Giles – not someone you know.
Sorry I haven't been in touch before; we've just been
round the world!!!
Lots of love to you and your mother, keep up the writing,
Rosemary xxx

Printed on the card were the names 'Giles and Rosemary Whitby-Browne' and their address – a house with a name but no number near Leatherhead.

'Losing' Rosemary again after having been offered an almost miraculous second chance when there was, as he saw it, a much more realistic possibility of them coming together than there had been before, was particularly hard to bear, especially as he was convinced that the loss was due not to any intrinsic deficiency on his part but to a malign external factor beyond his control. The effect was to confirm him ever more strongly in his literary destiny but also, subconsciously, to loosen, now that he had virtually nothing to lose, all the constraints that had hitherto held him in thrall to his mother.

Perhaps obscurely she realised this. Certainly, though her satisfaction was palpable, she received the news of Rosemary's second marriage without any of the contemptuous gloating she might previously have displayed and subsequently was unusually mild, almost conciliatory, as if deliberately trying not to provoke him. In a subtle way the balance of power between them had changed. Antony abandoned even the pretence of caring about her except when other people like the nurse were around, and inevitably his resentment towards her was boiling away dangerously and with unprecedented intensity just below the surface. Only the inertia of custom and routine preserved a fragile status quo, but it would have required only the slightest jolt, a single misplaced word, to provoke an uncontrollable eruption.

The moment came on a cold sunny March day in 1971 – one that reminded him forcibly of the day he received the news of Rosemary's divorce. It was Saturday afternoon and he had just finished the washing up. His mother was standing in front of the French windows of the dark narrow living room with a small green plastic watering can, about to water her potted bay tree on the terrace. Antony announced that he was going to spend the afternoon in the attic with the train set.

"Train set," his mother remarked more in bitter resignation than in anger, "why do you want to waste your time with that? You're becoming just as much of a dreamer as your father, and his life never amounted to anything..."

That was it. He rounded on her shouting with all his strength:

"What do you want me to do? You don't like me going out; you don't like my friends; you make it impossible for me to have a holiday yet you object to me being solitary, to my reading, my writing, my only hobby. How dare you compare me with him! How dare you criticise my life when you've deliberately contrived to deprive me of my freedom with this strange condition that leaves you perfectly well able to look after yourself but means you can't be left for twenty-four hours. Is this the thanks I get for allowing myself to become your slave? Life! You don't know the meaning of the word. And what exactly is this condition anyway? Has it got a name? There's nothing really wrong with you is there? Admit it. Admit it!"

He had now gripped her shoulders and was shaking her so violently that she dropped the watering can. Over ten years of pent up rage and humiliation had finally broken surface and was spurting up with volcanic force into the light of day.

His mother however did not appear to be intimidated by this tirade. Red-faced with anger she reacted stoutly to the general tenor rather than the precise detail of his bitter attack.

"Don't speak to me like that and take your hands off me!"

But there was no stopping Antony now.

"You, you've ruined my life, you selfish, ungrateful, joyless, negative, narrow-minded, friendless, life-hating, venomous, shrivelled old bitch..."

The long rehearsed indictment poured out like lava. He had played out this showdown so often in his mind and lived with it so long that the unique reality of the scene was somewhat blurred. In his imagination somewhere about this point, the merciless torrent of well-honed and thoroughly deserved abuse caused her to wilt and break down in tears begging for forgiveness, and leaving him with the choice of either throwing his arms round her in ecstatic purging mutual reconciliation or pitilessly turning the knife even more in an orgy of revenge, generally the latter. But now his mother conspicuously failed to play her part in this scenario.

More indignant than ever she exclaimed: "You've gone mad! Let me go. I'm going to call the police."

But Antony's rage was not yet spent and her unexpected reaction provoked him to go on to the bitter end, sparing her nothing.

"All my life I've hated you, loathed you, detested you," (his hands were now round her throat and tightening as he started to shake her again) "I hate the very sight of you. If it wasn't for you I might now be a major figure in universal history."

"You are mad..."

At this point the angry red colour drained from her face as she went limp and collapsed striking her head with a dull thud against the wooden frame of the French windows.

Seeing her lying there so still, so motionless, in such an improbably awkward posture, he began to make frantic efforts to revive her. He was dry-eyed but desperate. "Mummy, mummy darling, I didn't mean it, I'm sorry, it's alright, darling mummy, wake up, please wake up, you're going to be alright," he heard himself say as he cradled her in his arms; but all the time in his heart he knew she was dead.

Because he had been in a murderous rage and she had died with his fingers on her throat he naturally assumed that he had killed her. Suddenly all confusion with imagination and fantasy vanished. The dramatic scene of almost Sophoclean intensity which he had just played out was cold implacable truth and he was standing over his mother's corpse.

What could he do? His first impulse was to drag her off and bury her under the crazy paving of the terrace or the bench at the bottom of the garden or to drive out into the country and dispose of her there. But a moment's thought was enough to dismiss such a course. How would he be able to explain her sudden and permanent disappearance to neighbours, tradesmen and above all to Mary, the nurse? 'She's gone to visit a relative and she won't be coming back,' hardly seemed convincing! And if he were to take flight himself that would be tantamount to an admission of murder. No, there was nothing for it but to tell as much of the truth as he could without incriminating himself and to take his chances.

Feeling somewhat calmer now he had made this decision, he dialled 999 and asked for an ambulance: "It's my mother, she's about seventy. She suddenly collapsed... about five minutes ago. I couldn't support her and she fell and hit her head. I've tried to revive her but I'm very much afraid she may be dead... Yes, of course, I'll give you the address..."

He then rang Mary using her home number which was in his mother's address book but there was no reply.

When the ambulance men arrived they had no hesitation in pronouncing her dead and took the body away on a stretcher wrapped up in a blanket; but they were non-committal as to whether hitting her head, and possibly fracturing her skull, might be the cause of death as Antony suggested. They had scarcely gone when a rather grim faced police constable appeared at the door. So soon! Could this be the beginning of a murder investigation which was to lead to a trial and life imprisonment? He assumed the role of a totally innocent bereaved son.

"Officer, I'm afraid this isn't a very convenient time. My mother has just died."

"Yes, sir, I know and I'm sorry to intrude at a time like this, but we had a call from your neighbours at number twenty-seven who say they heard shouting and raised voices coming from here within the last half hour, as if there was some sort of argument going on."

"Argument?" Antony sounded as frankly incredulous as he could. "There was no argument. But I may have been shouting though. I was trying to revive my mother. I was frantic; I didn't know what to do..."

"I see. Perhaps you'd better tell me exactly what happened."

Antony repeated his story but with some extra embellishments. "I knew something was wrong when she dropped the watering can. The French windows were open and she was just going into the garden. I could see she had gone a sort of grey colour. I was only a few feet away and I tried to support her. I was holding her by her shoulders when she just fell like a dead weight knocking her head against the woodwork there. I just couldn't stop her. It was all so sudden – just horrible. I held her in my arms but it was obvious that there was nothing I could do so I dialled 999. I'm afraid I still haven't got over the shock..."

Whether or not the policeman had found Antony's account convincing, his manner softened appreciably and on leaving he came close to apologizing for his visit.

"You do understand sir, we had to follow this up but we frequently get calls from neighbours on occasions like this. They very often get the wrong end of the stick shall we say..."

"Well," Antony added for good measure, "the only time they've spoken to us in the last ten years was to complain about an overhanging branch. My mother couldn't stand them."

Antony thought afterwards that this was a rather incautious remark which did nothing to advance his case, but the policeman went away apparently contented.

Whatever negative consequences his mother's death might still hold for him he still felt inexpressible relief that he was now at least rid forever of the encumbrance that had been blighting and crushing his life. Even though it might be too late for Rosemary, he was at long last the master of his own destiny!

He rang Mary again. This time she answered and he was able to give her the news. "She just collapsed and hit her head. There was nothing I could do, and I've had the police round asking questions."

"You sound surprised."

"Well I am, completely. It was such a shock – so unexpected."

"You mean you didn't know?"

"Know what?"

"Well for the last two years your mother has had a very serious heart condition. That's why I've been visiting her regularly, to keep an eye on her. She was on some drugs but in the long run there was nothing we could do."

"Why wasn't I told?"

"She was most concerned that you shouldn't know how ill she was. She obviously didn't want to worry you; it's very understandable. But I thought you were bound to know anyway so I didn't think I needed to say anything. I'm sorry it's come as such a shock. It was bound to happen sooner or later so you mustn't reproach yourself – congestive heart failure. The surprising thing is that in her condition she lasted as long as she did. I think she must have had a very strong will to live."

There was no reply from Antony.

"Did she have a religious faith?"

"Er, what? No... no, I don't think so."

"I was thinking of the funeral."

"Oh I see. I haven't thought about that yet."

"Well I'll light a candle for her."

"There's going to be a post-mortem of course."

"Of course, but I'm sure there won't be any surprises. I'll try and call in tomorrow evening."

"Mary, you're a dear."

"That's alright. I'm only sorry it had to be so much of a shock for you."

So it seemed he was probably off the hook! But even that now seemed comparatively unimportant. Mary's words had transformed any sense of relief and a new beginning to his life into an emotion of a very different kind; one that could only have been appeased by resuscitating his mother, killing her again and feeding her scrawny carcass to wild dogs. The vicious old bat had been well aware of her fatal heart condition before Rosemary came into his life again. If only they had known how little time she had left. No wonder that she didn't want him to find that his servitude would soon be at an end. She obviously wanted to hang on long enough to deny him his chance of happiness. That was why she seemed so calm and serene after Rosemary's second marriage – she'd got her way! Every word of his attack had been true, truer than he knew. She had indeed quite deliberately ruined his life.

The post-mortem confirmed Mary's diagnosis of the cause of death without any qualification, and striking her head as she fell had apparently nothing to do with it. He could now walk tall, totally exonerated, and despite his now forever unappeasable desire for vengeance on his mother, he was determined to show the world that he had nothing to hide. With Mary's help he spared no effort on the funeral, even advertising the time and place with a notice of her death in the *Daily Telegraph* and the local paper. As a result about twenty people turned up to the nearby parish church and when the well briefed vicar spoke of the exemplary way in which Antony had dedicated himself to looking after his ailing mother, he glared pointedly at the neighbours who had had the temerity to ring the police.

It was not until weeks later that he sent a card to Rosemary telling her of his mother's death though he had nevertheless entertained a fantasy of glimpsing her at the back of the church, a mysterious figure in black at the funeral. Of course she didn't come. In the event the most interesting figure in the congregation was a dapper gent in his late seventies with bushy silver hair and a ruddy drinker's complexion wearing a blazer and a rather bright tie for the occasion, whom he did not recognise as a neighbour or other acquaintance of his mother or himself. Outside the church after the service this unidentified mourner approached and shook his hand.

"Leonard Kilroy; I'm your father's elder brother. You may not have heard of me – the black sheep of the family!"

"As a matter of fact I have, but I wasn't allowed to know anything about you – not even your name!"

"You're busy now. I'll catch up with you later."

Back at the house, where people who had for the most part never set foot while his mother was alive were busily consuming the spread that Mary had prepared, he made straight for his long lost uncle.

"What was it you did that was so terrible?"

"Well the thing is you see, I escaped. Your father didn't, poor chap."

"Sounds very intriguing."

"When we were very young, too young to know what we were doing – still wet behind the ears as you might say – your father and I married sisters. You didn't know that?"

"I had no idea!"

"Well we were very naïve as I said. I wasn't long out of the army – your father wasn't called up because he had a very weak chest – and neither of us knew much about women. Anyway I realised after only a few months that I had made a terrible mistake and I decided that I didn't want to be a shipping clerk either. You haven't got anything stronger than tea by any chance have you, old boy, whisky or anything like that?"

"No whisky I'm afraid but my mother had some brandy kept for medicinal purposes – or I have got some wine upstairs."

"The brandy'll be fine, thank you."

Antony fetched the bottle and a glass. "So what did you do?"

"I left my wife and went on the stage – the variety stage; I became a song and dance man and a comedian – 'Lennie Kilroy'. I've been on the same bill as Dan Leno and Max Miller. My father, your grandfather, was on the stage for a while, I don't suppose they told you that," (Antony shook his head) "but he couldn't make enough of a living at it. He encouraged me though, and he still had some contacts in the business. My wife divorced me and I married a chorus girl. We had forty happy years together. She died two years ago."

"Do you have any children?"

"Two sons, one in Australia and one in Canada. They got away too." He smiled.

"Do you ever see them?"

"Oh yes. As a matter of fact I've just got back from staying with my son and his family in Australia. My son in Canada teaches at McGill University – Astrophysics! Don't know where he gets his brains from, certainly not from me!"

"What about your son in Australia?"

"Oh, he's done lots of things. Now he runs a winery."

Antony excused himself for a few minutes to attend to the other guests and then came back to his uncle.

"Do you think that my father also made a terrible mistake?"

"No offence, but yes."

"I am not offended. I think he did too, but I can't quite see why my mother was so hostile to you."

"Well, not long after I remarried, my ex-wife died. Your mother accused me of killing her, said she had died of shame and grief after I abandoned her for a long-legged harlot – all that sort of thing."

"Yes, I can imagine. But you don't think she did die of a broken heart?"

"No! She didn't go in for that sort of thing. She didn't have an ounce of sentiment in her and she didn't... well, let's just say she should never have married anybody, let alone me. She caught a severe chill and died of pneumonia, as people did in those days. Anyway, I hope you don't mind me gatecrashing your mother's funeral; it's just that I saw the announcement in the paper and well, when you get to my age, you feel like tying up any loose ends in your life if you know what I mean."

"I am delighted you did come. Meeting my long lost wicked uncle has been the highlight of the whole thing; in fact up to now I never really had any family except for my parents. It's very encouraging to find out that the Kilroys are a rather more interesting lot than I imagined."

"You've been looking after your mother for years, I hear. I take my hat off to you. Not many young men in your position would have done that, especially these days."

"Perhaps I should have broken away too... but in your position I would've done exactly what you did." (Antony was determined to make it clear to his 'wicked' uncle that he was made of different stuff to his tame father.)

"Well I suppose you felt you didn't have much choice. Anyway you're free now."

"Yes, I'm free now."

He could quite see now that in view of this family history, his mother would have deplored what she might have regarded as any 'theatrical' tendencies in him, even more than indications that he was taking after her ineffectual husband. But as his uncle had said he was indeed free now to live his life exactly as he wished, to travel and to devote himself without interruption to creating new worlds with his writing, severing forever all ties to an island which had always been alien to him spiritually and imaginatively, and probably making his permanent home in the more congenial lands of Provence or Tuscany.

But his first priority was to dispose of his mother's house with its nosey neighbours and all its dismal memories. That bay tree and those daffodils would, he felt, be marked forever by association with the appalling experience of his mother's death. While clearing the place with a view to putting it on the market he discovered in the furthest recess of the hall cupboard which actually went under the stairs, a region that as a child he had thought of as the lair of some ill-defined monster of ultimate evil and never subsequently investigated, he found an old tin deed box. Dragging it into the light and prizing it open with a screw driver – he had no idea where the key might be and was in no mood for a laborious search – he found that it contained a number of legal documents: the deeds of the house, copies of his father's and his mother's wills, their marriage certificate and his mother's birth certificate as well as three letters tied up like a parcel with faded red ribbon which were at the bottom of the pile.

He studied them with fascination. So remote had his upbringing been from the warmth and openness of normal family life, that until seeing his parents' marriage lines he did not even know that their Christian names were Frederick and Violet. They never used them to each other in his hearing and when speaking to him always referred to 'your mother' or 'your father' – nor until discovering some old sheet music in the piano stool the day before, inscribed 'V. Littlemore' in his mother's handwriting, had he known her maiden name.

He now turned to the little packet of letters addressed to:

Miss Violet Littlemore
2A Stanley Road
Tooting

They were a revelation for they proved to be love letters all written in 1921. The first was dated Monday 16th May:

My Darling Vi,

I hope I didn't surprise or upset you too much with my proposal during our boat trip yesterday. But I didn't want you to be in any doubt about my feelings for you and it seemed the perfect time and place to say what I have had in my heart for a long time. It's always best to speak one's mind; I hope you agree. But darling Vi there is no hurry. Please think about what I said and take all the time in the world before you give me your answer. I just want you to know that I would wait forever for you, but I don't think that would be a good idea because life is short and we could be so happy together.

Your loving cousin,

Will

The second was written on Thursday 30th June:

Dearest Vi,

If it doesn't matter to you that I happen to be three years younger than you are, why should our being cousins make such a difference? I don't like having to disagree with your parents and your sister, but I can think of at least three examples of cousins marrying and royalty do it all the time!!

Please my darling do think about this. My happiness and yours – which is even more important to me – are at stake.

Ever your loving,

Will

The third and final one was dated Wednesday 28th September:

My Dearest Vi,

You said that I shouldn't write to you any more now that you are engaged, but I just wanted to urge you one last time to break it off before it's too late and things have gone too far. You don't have to go through with it. It may mean a lot of embarrassment and a family row, but surely that would be better than spending the rest of your life with a man you don't really love. I used to think how lucky I was to be too young for the War. Now I'm not so sure. I am sorry to have to write to you like this but it's how I feel.

Always yours,

Will

In the envelope with the third letter was a faded brownish snapshot which had obviously once been folded into quarters. It showed a boy of no more than eighteen in flannels, blazer and straw boater with one foot on a bench playing a banjo. His hat was pushed back on his head to reveal a shock of dark hair and he had a cheeky smile. There was a river in the background. On the back of the snap was written: 'W 15/5/21'.

This discovery naturally stirred a whole range of reflections, emotions and questions in him and certainly helped him to understand his mother a little better, though not to forgive her. Being persuaded into giving up her Will for a man she didn't love – presumably his father – must surely have changed her, if not immediately then gradually over the years. Certainly the woman he knew seemed incapable of love and could never have been anyone's 'Darling Vi'. Could she have been aware of this herself? It was difficult to believe that she was the sort of person who was capable of assessing her life with any degree of objectivity and seeing it as a whole, otherwise how could she possibly imagine that her wholly negative, rigid, narrow perspective was in any way normal and anything that deviated from if an aberration. That seemed more of a blind reaction, a mental habit, certainly not something believed as a result of serious thought and reflection. Then again perhaps she had never really cared for Will and had more of her sister's hardness in her than he, as an inexperienced young lad, had recognised. But if so, why did she keep his letters and photograph? Had her natural emotions simply died or were they just deeply suppressed? Now no one would ever know. His dominant reaction however, it must be admitted, was – what material for a novel!

VIII

Although Rosemary did not attend his mother's funeral – he had never really expected her to – its scale and the genuine expression of grief from throughout the Empire that followed her death, had pleased him very much. They had never been particularly close, but she had done her best to support him, especially in those most difficult months when he was first coming to terms with his imperial destiny. Though, in life, she could not be given the title of Dowager Empress or Empress Mother (her husband after all had not been Emperor) Anton insisted, in the face of some reluctance from the Arch-chamberlain's department, that, in death, she should be accorded all the honours of an Empress – lying in state, full cavalry escort at her funeral procession, six weeks of court mourning and so on. He knew she would have wanted it and the arrangements met with universal approbation from the public at large.

PART THREE: ART AND LIFE

I

Antony always experienced a sense of expansive exhilaration whenever he left England, even in imagination, but this time it was different. His mother was dead and all the ties that bound him to England had at last been severed. Now as he leant against the rails of a channel ferry on a sunny breezy June day in 1971 with just a few high clouds scudding across the purest clear blue sky, he was conscious of watching the white cliffs of Dover recede for the last time. The restraints and miseries, the setbacks and disappointments of what his biographers would call one day 'the early years' were definitively over. The time had come to embrace his destiny.

He planned to inaugurate this new life with a journey which would take him far from the superficial getting and spending culture of the West, far from the scientific materialism which reduced everything to meaningless chance, to the remote land of Ladakh in Kashmir, a spiky moonscape of mountain peaks and deep fertile valleys hidden from the rest of the world by the Karakoram and Kailash ranges to the north and east and the Himalayas to the south, variously known as 'Moon Land', 'The Hermit Kingdom', 'Little Tibet' and 'Shangri-La'. There in the heart of Asia along the head waters of the Indus was the meeting point of three great cultures: Hinduism, Buddhism and Islam – and even Christianity, if the Franco-Russian traveller Nicolai Notovitch, who claimed to have found ancient texts in the Hemis Lamasery attesting to the visit of Jesus

Christ to those high valleys after his resurrection, was to be believed!

But Antony was not interested in religions that worshipped some hypothetical being or required the believer to accept some mythical revelation based on traditions or sacred texts that had to be taken on trust, nor in theoretical philosophising that led to endless irresolvable arguments. He was not seeking any specific limited 'truth' at all, but rather something that was almost impossible to put into words – tranquillity, serenity, wisdom, an experience of the infinite, of something that transcended life and death and the limitations of bodily existence, if indeed such things were possible. He was thus attracted to Buddhism, and his choice of destination had nothing to do with any fictitious *Lost Horizon* and dreams of finding some little enclave where ageing was magically held at bay, but was first inspired by a lecture he attended at a Buddhist Society in South London.

Wherever it might lead, such a quest, he felt, was an indispensable prerequisite in the making of a writer of truly Tolstoyan stature and depth such as he aspired to be; and it had to be overland – no hopping about in aeroplanes. First he travelled by rail from Ostend to Munich and the following morning caught the train for the four day journey to Istanbul. Unfortunately gone were the elegant days of the Orient Express with its spies and courtesans; on the second leg of the journey the carriages were filled with Turkish guest workers going home from Germany who held their transistors out of the windows fifty miles from the frontier to catch the first strains of their country's music. There were no wagons-lits and he had to sleep in a cramped stuffy couchette with the other occupants of his compartment.

Antony had planned to stay a week in Istanbul and though he got to rather like the place – the smell of fish being fried on the Golden Horn, the piping hot sweet tea served in little glasses, the minarets on the skyline, the twisting backstreets and wooden houses, the Great Bazaar which reminded him of Oxford Market albeit on a much grander scale – it did not live up to his expectations. No city on earth could have had a more portentous history: Constantine's New Rome, capital of the Byzantine Empire and the Christian East, then capital of the Islamic world, the Sublime Porte of Sultans and Caliphs – heir to Damascus and Baghdad as well as Rome; yet the overwhelming impression was of a sprawling, bustling, half Europeanized and rather scruffy modern Turkish port. Apart from Hagia Sophia and the great mosques that strangely echoed in outward appearance at least what had once been the world's greatest church, with their austerely empty carpeted interiors smelling faintly of socks, the architecture seemed unimpressive; even the Sultan's Topkapı Palace was unexpectedly modest.

On his last full day he took a short cruise on a steamer zigzagging between little harbours on the European and Asian banks of the Bosphorus up as far as the NATO military zone at the mouth of the Black Sea, which it came as something of a shock to realise, was a cold war frontier. It proved to be the most pleasant and relaxing experience of the whole week. Not only did watching the endless procession of tankers making their way up and down those straits give him an appreciation of the of the historic, strategic and commercial importance of Istanbul but as the trip began he glimpsed for the first time, on the European bank, an elegant panorama of buildings including the spectacular Dolmabahçe Palace which did indeed seem worthy of the Sultan's capital. Unfortunately his full appreciation was distracted by a tourist from New Zealand who had no interest in the Ottoman Empire and only wanted to talk about cricket!

Antony travelled by slow train to Ankara then on via Kayseri (once one of the great cities of the Silk Road, that he used as a base for a few days to visit the underground cities of Cappadocia) and Sivas (once part of ancient Armenia) to Erzurum on the spectacular high plateau of eastern Anatolia which, he was amazed to find, had retained the double headed eagle of Byzantium as its symbol. At Erzurum he managed to find a lorry driver – his hitch-hiking days were over – who for a price was prepared to take him on the next stage of his journey on rocky roads all the way through Ağrı, on south of Mount Ararat and over the border to Khvoy in Iran. Here he was able to get another driver – this time with a van – to take him to Tabriz where he caught the train for Teheran.

Teheran, an impressive metropolis of converging motorways and high-rise buildings was, to judge by the number of construction cranes, very evidently in the full spate of the Shah's almost frantic drive to westernize his country in the teeth of opposition from the left as well as the conservative Shi'a clergy, and turn himself into a new Cyrus, Darius or Xerxes with the revenue from oil. In 1971 his regime still seemed virtually all powerful and no one seriously thought that the Peacock Throne might be toppled. Antony spent a few days there taking in the sights – chiefly the Golestan Palace and the main museums, but the city wasn't as interesting as it might have been because most of old Teheran had been or was in the process of being destroyed in the Shah's ruthless modernization.

He went on by train to the city of Mashhad which, he was to discover, was one of the holiest cities in Iran and a major pilgrimage centre, having grown up round the tomb of Imam Reza, the eighth Imam of Shi'ite Islam. It was also the end of the line. From then on he had to rely on a succession of lorry drivers to get him over the border to Herat in Afghanistan, then along the valley of the Hari Rud to Daulat Yar and on to Kabul over terrain that was much higher and more mountainous than he had expected – and cooler too, considering it was the middle of summer.

Afghanistan, a monarchy like Iran (even though Mohammed Zahir Shah had only two years to go before being toppled by his prime minister who set up the first Afghan republic) could hardly have presented a greater contrast to the powerful nation relentlessly modernizing under the leadership of the Shahanshah which he had left behind. This was a poor, rugged, traditional Muslim country of fiercely independent peasant tribesmen. Even the capital was an unlovely place of ramshackle traditional housing and street markets mixed with drab modern blocks and factories which showed more than a little Soviet influence. However he was amused to discover a branch of Marks and Spencer's – those Victorian generals had not campaigned in these parts entirely in vain!

It was not until he visited the National Museum that it was brought home to him what an important crossroads that part of the world had always been. After all the Oxus, now called the Amu Darya, not far to the north, which formed much of the country's northern border was really the frontier between the settled civilizations of the Middle East and the Asian steppe. This was the ancient land of Bactria where Zoroaster was born and chose his first disciples. It was part of the empires of Persia and of Alexander (who having killed the local king, took his daughter Roxanne to be his bride here) and of his Seleucid successors, before becoming a separate Greco-Bactrian kingdom that expanded into the Indus Valley (modern Pakistan), with King Menander (called Milinda in India) actually converting to Buddhism, then the predominant religion of the subcontinent. The Greek kings lasted until the beginning of the first century AD. There were links with China as well as India. Zhang Qian the great explorer visited the kingdom (Daxia to the Chinese) in 126 BC establishing contacts that helped to develop the Silk Road, and centuries later Kabul was briefly the capital of Babur the first Mughal Emperor before he conquered India. This rich and surprising mixture of cultures as well as the country's Islamic heritage was all reflected in the magnificent collections of the museum (later to be so tragically looted and vandalized) ranging from the Bronze Age to modern times. The place was a revelation.

After a few days he obtained transport via Jalalabad through the Khyber Pass to Pakistan – this did not prove difficult because of the constant traffic between northern Afghanistan and the North-West Frontier Province – and once through the Pass he caught the train to Peshawar, another major Silk Road city, whose name means 'city on the frontier' in the Persian language. Now dominated by 'ethnic Afghans', the same Pashtun people as in eastern and southern Afghanistan, it was also once part of ancient Bactria, but Alexander's successor ceded it to Chandragupta Maurya, the founder of the Mauryan Empire and from then on Buddhism became the local religion until the coming of Islam. Under the Kushan King Kanishka, in the first half of the second century AD, it became a great Buddhist centre as evidenced by his construction of the tallest building in the world, a magnificent 394 feet high stupa, to house some of the Buddha's relics. All that now remained was its ruined base just outside the Ganj Gate of the old city which Antony duly inspected. Some at least of the treasures that it once contained were, he learnt, discovered in a chamber under the rubble by a British archaeologist in 1909 and were now on display in Mandalay in Burma where they would presumably be more appreciated.

From Peshawar he went on by train again via Campbellpore (he could hardly believe this name on the station platform!) and the great Victorian railway junction of Rawalpindi to Haripur, from where he was obliged to travel by road to Muzaffarabad, in a narrow strip of Pakistani administered territory in Kashmir. Then he had to cross the so-called 'line of control', the de facto border with the Indian state of Jammu and Kashmir. Such was the current tension between the countries because of Mrs Ghandi's support for East Pakistan's attempt to break away from West Pakistan as independent Bangladesh, that Antony wondered whether he would be allowed to pass – ominously, he appeared to be the only person wanting to cross the line.

In the event, though he was thoroughly searched, his story that he was a Buddhist pilgrim from Britain, supported by several of the books he was carrying with him, appeared to satisfy the Muslim border guards on the one side and the Sikh soldiers on the other. So he was through and able to make his way to Srinagar – a city that with its waterways, lakes and floating gardens is sometimes called the Indian Venice, though its clear air and fresh alpine climate were more suggestive of Geneva to Antony, except that the environing mountains were not the Alps but the great central massif of the world that divides the subcontinent from the rest of Asia.

Here, following the example of the Mughal Emperors, civil servants of the Raj used to come in summer to escape the sultry and unhealthy climate of the plains, but the Maharajah of Kashmir, suspicious of British influence in his territory and not wanting the place to become another Simla, would not allow them to build permanent homes, hence the luxurious and elaborately carved houseboats on Dal Lake which subsequently became one of the great tourist attractions of the city. Antony liked everything about Srinagar: the food, the climate, the relaxed and tolerant multi-cultural atmosphere in which Muslims, Hindus and Sikhs seemed to mix happily and naturally together without difficulty – everything. It was the most beguiling place he had visited in his entire journey so far and he was in no hurry to leave.

He spent two weeks of leisurely sightseeing taking in everything from the Jama Masjid mosque to the Shalimar Gardens.

One place he did not visit however, because it did not particularly interest him, was the Rozabal shrine in the middle of the old town which housed the burial place of Yuz Asaf, believed by the Ahmadi Muslims to be none other than Jesus Christ who had made his way to Kashmir after his crucifixion – an illusion in any case according to the Koran. The shrine was apparently pre-Islamic and so possibly another instance of the legend allegedly preserved in the ancient Buddhist texts in the Hemis monastery.

When at last the time came for him to leave Srinagar for the final stage of his quest he was rested and refreshed. In those days tourists did not visit Ladakh so although it was late August only a few locals availed themselves of the occasional bus service to its principal town of Leh. The distance was just over 270 miles but it was explained to Antony that because of the state of the winding mountain road there was an overnight stop at Kargil which was just about half way. The vehicle itself, which looked like a battered 1930s charabanc with bars on the windows, did not inspire much confidence. But what did that matter, he told himself as he studied his guidebook and prepared, after an early breakfast, to embark on the journey of a lifetime.

The Srinagar–Leh 'highway' followed the historic trade route known as the 'Treaty Road' which, because of the snow, was usually only open to traffic from early June to mid-November. Crossing through the Zoji La Pass (11,500 feet) he passed in a sudden transition from the lushness of Kashmir into the barren contours of a Himalayan landscape – Dras, the first township over the pass had, he read, the reputation of being the second coldest inhabited place in the world in winter. In summer though, the standing crops and clumps of willow gave it a gentler and more hospitable look. After Dras the valley through which they were travelling narrowed to a gorge, occasionally opening up to allow patches of steeply terraced cultivation where a small village population was eking out a precarious existence.

They arrived at Kargil about half an hour after sunset – a small town with a predominantly Shi'a Muslim population which was once a crossroads for travel to Baltistan but now right on the frontier of the Pakistani-controlled Northern Areas of Kashmir – and Antony noted a considerable Indian military presence. The wooden guest house where he spent the night was clean and comfortable and the view from his window in the morning of the sun rising from behind range upon range of vast mountains – truly the Roof of the World – was unforgettable.

When they left Kargil the road plunged down into valleys and over ridges as they crossed the Zanskar Range, then took them over the alluvial plateau of Khurbathang and descended to the area of Pashkyum passing through several roadside villages before reaching Mulbek about 25 miles east of their overnight stop. The first sight that met them in this green and fertile river valley was a gigantic carving of the Buddha Maitreya, 'the One Who is to Come', on a free-standing rock as if to mark the very spot where Islamic and Hindu Kashmir at last gave way to Buddhist Ladakh, and perched on a crag above the village was the first of the many Buddhist monasteries or gompas, of the region. Antony had not expected the land he had been seeking to announce itself in such a dramatic transformation and the lines from T. S. Eliot's *Journey of the Magi*, which he had had to learn by heart many years ago at school, suddenly returned to his mind:

'Then at dawn we came down to a temperate valley,
Wet, below the snow line, smelling of vegetation...
And arrived at evening, not a moment too soon
Finding the place; it was (you may say) satisfactory...'

Leaving the green valley of Mulbek and the Buddha Maitreya, they negotiated two more high passes – Namika La (12,200 feet) and Fotu La (13,432 feet). From Fotu La the road descended in serpentine sweeps and turns past the spectacularly sited monastery of Lamayuru and an amazing wind-eroded landscape of towers and pinnacles that really did look like the surface of the moon, down to the Indus at Khalatse – a descent of almost 4,000 feet in about 20 miles!

From here the road followed the river, passing villages, terraced fields and neat whitewashed houses, roofs piled high with neat stacks of fodder for the coming winter, and a few unfamiliar looking cattle which he thought might be yaks. Here and there he noticed the ruins of an ancient fort or caught a distant glimpse of a gompa on a hill until, at last, on top of a steep slope high above the point where the Zanskar river flowed into the Indus, Leh became visible, spilling out of a side valley that tapered northwards towards eroded peaks, snow-capped even in summer – a huddle of mud brick buildings sprawling from the foot of a ruined Tibetan style palace, flanked on one side by cream coloured desert and on the other by a swathe of lush irrigated farmland. At a distance the seven-storeyed palace, once the seat of the Namgyal rajas of Ladakh, bore a striking resemblance, if on a much smaller scale, to the great Potala of the Dalai Lama which towered over Lhasa – in fact it was said to be the model for it. What a sight to greet him at the end of a journey halfway across the world!

The bus drove up into the town and disgorged its passengers in the late afternoon, and as a rare foreigner Antony received a considerable amount of polite attention. Leh had once been a busy market on the Silk Route with the bazaar receiving more than a dozen pony and camel trains a day – a trade managed mainly by Sunni Muslim merchants rather than Buddhists – but now with the closing of the Tibetan border by the Chinese communist government and the flight of the Dalai Lama (in fact to Dharamsala about 150 miles to the south over the Himalayas in Himachal Pradesh) all that was over and Leh had become a sleepy Himalayan town on the road to nowhere visited only by the occasional intrepid traveller or mountaineer.

Antony's priority was to find somewhere to eat and then a bed for the night. He was not only tired but had been feeling light-headed and dizzy for most of the day, a phenomenon which he attributed not to spiritual excitement but to the altitude, and Leh, he knew, was over 10,000 feet above sea level. It was a only a day or so before he had become acclimatized and was able to explore this magical place where the snow-capped summits of the majestic Stok Kangri Massif, magnified in the crystal clear sunshine, seemed almost close enough to touch.

However he was not there to see the sights, not even the treasures of the Namgyal Tsemo Gompa precariously perched on a peak above the town, or to take in the view however breath-taking; he was after life-changing wisdom. But none of the monasteries in the town seemed at all interested in taking in inquisitive foreigners; either that or he had not managed to make himself understood. But then after a couple of weeks of increasing frustration he fell in with Greg, a young Australian with a closely shaven head who overheard his English voice in the market. Greg, who spoke a little of the local language and apparently knew his way around, had turned to Buddhism to sort out his life after drug addiction, crime and suicide attempts about which he was naturally rather unspecific, and had been working as a sort of lay brother in various monasteries in the old quarter of the town without really finding what he was looking for. He had however heard of a remote gompa about twenty-five miles to the south west of Leh at a place called Sumdahla which had a reputation for giving serious instruction to those who sincerely sought it – even westerners – and even accepted then as novices if they proved suitable. Greg added that he was thinking of trying it out and jumped at Antony's request to accompany him. The Australian had even picked up whispers of an invisible valley somewhere in that region that could only be seen by the eyes of those who achieved enlightenment.

So five days later – it was now the third week in September – armed with a letter of introduction to the abbot, they set off with a driver and a guide in a train of donkeys and camels taking winter supplies to Sumdahla monastery. The journey which followed the narrowest of tracks through hidden passes, over crags and across steep hillsides took the best part of two days. But they were made welcome when they arrived and with very little fuss incorporated into the unvarying routines and way of life of the monks spending many hours each day sitting cross-legged in the prayer hall chanting the mantra 'Om Mani Padme Hum' and sleeping on thin mattresses on the floor.

This, Antony was to learn, was in accord with the Buddhist notion that practice was much more important than theory. But they did however, separately, receive regular instruction – translated by one of the community who spoke English – from a senior monk who acted as a sort of novice master, about the Noble Eightfold Path and the way to Enlightenment. All the Dharma, Antony was told, was based on the Buddha's discovery that suffering was unnecessary. Like a disease, we can discover its cause and when we discover that the cause is dependent on certain conditions, we can explore the possibility of removing those conditions. For this there were many methods but the most powerful of all, for those that had the capacity to understand it – called the Mahayana or Great Vehicle – was based on the practice of compassion.

According to the novice master, within the Mahayana the Buddha had revealed the possibility of benefiting all beings, including oneself, by entering directly into the awakened state of mind, or Buddhahood, without delay. The most powerful and the most accessible way of doing this was to link one's own mind with the mind of the Buddha of Compassion, Chenrezig. By replacing the thought of oneself as oneself with the thought of oneself as Chenrezig, one gradually reduced and eventually removed self-absorption, expanding one's loving kindness and compassion towards oneself and others, enhancing one's intelligence and wisdom.

In most religious traditions, the monk observed, people prayed to external deities in the hope of receiving their blessing. In Buddhism however, the blessing, power and superlative qualities of enlightened beings were not considered as coming from an outside source, but believed to be innate, to be aspects of our own true nature. Chenrezig and his love and compassion were within us. The point of the meditation was to connect with the voice and mind of the Buddha. By posture and gestures one connected with the body, by reciting the words of the liturgy and repeating the mantra, one connected with the voice, and by imagining the visual form of the Buddha one connected with the mind.

Antony asked what was the exact meaning of the four word mantra but was told that it was impossible to translate since there was not a single aspect of the eighty four thousand sections of the Buddha's teaching that was not contained in its six syllables! Through repetition of the mantra of Chenrezig, he was told, one learnt not to cling to the reality of the speech and sound encountered in life, but experience it as essentially empty. Thus the confusion of the speech aspect of our being was transformed into enlightened awareness. That enlightened awareness included whatever one might need to understand in order to save any beings, including ourselves, from suffering. For that reason the entire Dharma, the entire truth about the nature of suffering and the removal of its causes, was said to be contained in those six syllables.

It all seemed rather woolly and vague but after an initial period of adjustment Antony found the monastic life surprisingly agreeable – it was certainly calming, even soporific when the outdoor temperature began to drop and the heat of the basement furnace could be felt through the wooden floor. A blizzard at the beginning of November cut them off from the outside world enveloping them in dazzling white in all directions, broken only by a few faces of vertical rock and a touch of sky above the mountains; but on life within the Sumdahla Gompa, self-sufficient as it was for eight months, the effect was negligible. Nobody even troubled to sweep the snow away from the ancient wooden door.

It was in November also that the abbot himself started to play some part in teaching him and take some interest in his progress. Antony found his teaching in many ways more interesting but also even more enigmatic, more generalized and difficult to grasp than that of the novice master. From time to time he tried to pin him down by respectfully asking a question: was there a difference between Enlightenment and Nirvana? Was it possible to achieve Enlightenment in one lifetime? How did one know if one was making progress towards it? And so on. The drift of the abbot's patient answers was always the same. All this was something to be experienced, not talked about. Enlightenment comes only when you stop seeking it. Suffering is illusory because the world is illusory and the self is illusory. Let go of the self, let go of the world, let go of everything...

Antony could not help wondering what sort of experience there could be without a self to experience it, but he did not ask the abbot this question. Instead he persevered conscientiously, though no epiphany or revelation, not even a sniff of one, was vouchsafed to him. Everybody else, including Greg, seemed to be doing fine. But in spite of all the instruction he had received, he felt an outsider, excluded from some unspoken secret that the others had somehow grasped. Perhaps he was not the only one. Perhaps some of the others were not getting anywhere either; how could one possibly tell? Or was he just an irremediably self-obsessed westerner who couldn't let go, desperately clinging on to an illusory reality?

(The snowbound community of Sumdahla had no idea that from the third to the sixteenth of that December a dramatic – and very real – confrontation was being fought out between India and Pakistan over Bangladeshi independence, with the United States – that under Nixon and Kissinger saw everything in global Cold War terms – illegally arming Pakistan with the tacit support of China, while the Soviet Union as well as France and Britain, supported India. It was a conflict that, before India's rapid and decisive victory, nearly led to a stand-off between the nuclear superpowers. There was even a skirmish in the snowy passes near Kargil which resulted in India taking control of the whole district including frontier posts previously held by Pakistan, but not a word of it reached the chanting monks in that remote inaccessible sanctuary.)

Eventually drinking butter tea and the endless repetition of the mantra 'Om Mani Padme Hum' began to pall, even as a therapeutic routine, and Antony found himself concentrating more and more on the very un-Buddhist activity of writing up and expanding his journal of the trip and recording his day to day thoughts and impressions while waiting for the eventual coming of spring to those high valleys. But he never tired of the beauty of the place – nor did he ever forget it. As he wrote, there was more spiritual exaltation to be found in a few moments gazing at the light changing on the snow and absorbing the silence of the mountains than in all the hours spent in the prayer hall.

By April the snow began to thin and recede, revealing the

rugged contours of a long buried landscape, while expanding patches of vegetation and wild mountain flowers emerged among fields of hitherto unlimited whiteness. In the first week of June a supply train was able to reach the monastery. Antony made his farewells and leaving behind Greg, who looked set to take his vows and become a permanent member of the community, returned with it to Leh, swapping a rather unco-operative camel for a donkey at the overnight stop. It was here that he heard about the war at the end of the previous year and, since his quest was over, decided to make his way back to Europe by the shortest available route – by road to Jammu via Srinagar, then by rail to Delhi and plane to London.

Only a few years later, in 1974, the Indian government opened up the Ladakh district to tourism so that in August and September the streets of Leh are nowadays jammed with climbers, hikers and backpackers doing the 'monastery trail'. Antony was always grateful for the privilege of being one of the last to know the solitude of the 'Hermit Kingdom' before it was irrevocably overrun by the invasion of modernity – truly a Lost World

If Antony did not ultimately discover the 'Meaning of Life', he had learnt that, as in all such quests, it is the experience of the journey itself that can be enriching and life-changing, especially in retrospect, rather than what may or may not be found at its end. And the trip had certainly been fruitful in one crucial respect for he had returned to England (as a very temporary expedient he told himself) from his Himalayan monastery in an intensely creative mood, pregnant with the outline and a considerable amount of the detail of at least two novels. As for ultimate wisdom, it seemed more elusive than ever, though he was convinced that he could have learnt more from one evening in the rooms of his dear late Oxford friend Rollo than in all the months he spent among the snowbound lamas of Shangri-La or more precisely, Sumdahla. If only he had lived! But perhaps the secret of life could only be truly discerned and expressed through art, music and literature – and that would be his mission!

As soon as he was able to acquire a bolthole and an old type-writer, he began to write. With the aid of a pipe which he had last smoked when meditating over essays in his undergraduate days, the words poured out with surprising ease in a fug of Holland House tobacco smoke; and within eighteen months he had completed the two novels and was brooding on a third inspired by his travels. The first, entitled *A Perfect Murder*, was a dark and even philosophical thriller in which the central character for no discernible motive except 'the intellectual challenge and aesthetic delight in any supremely elegant and efficient operation' successfully disposes of his mother on a Mediterranean cruise without her death even arousing suspicion. In the second novel, *A Family Secret*, the death of a mother has the effect of bringing to light a long concealed family secret which radically transforms the lives of her children and grandchildren for good and ill.

II

Having waved farewell to the crowds, the Emperor is now sitting in his gleaming dark purple and gold imperial train, the Kaiserzug, each carriage ensigned with the imperial arms as, at ten o'clock precisely, it glides out of the sumptuously decorated and red-carpeted Westbahnhof in Vienna, past serried ranks of guardsmen presenting arms. Well into the second decade of his reign he is embarking this first of December on the longest of his very rare journeys outside the Empire, one that will go down in history as the 'Winterreise'.

Though he had once flown to Paris, London and Madrid, for reasons of comfort as well as security, he now invariably travels by train. Ever since he was first introduced to his father's train set as a child, and perhaps even before that, he had been fascinated by the notion of long train journeys lasting for days, perhaps weeks – journeys which for all practical purposes never ended with the back-to-reality jolt of arrival at one's destination. There was something so enticing, so comforting about travelling endlessly across the countryside through different cities, regions, countries, even from one end of the world to the other, while all the time remaining secure and cosseted within one's own unchanging domesticated environment. How else could one simultaneously enjoy the pleasures of being both cosily at home and having wheels on the ground in the most far flung and even inhospitable locations? As a boy he spent many happy hours with an atlas imagining and planning such journeys. The imperial train more than fulfilled these childhood fantasies so that even now travelling in it was one of the duties that he most relished.

The train itself was nothing less than a mobile court. There were three central carriages reserved exclusively for the imperial family. One contained a study, a conference room, a sitting and dining room; a second, bathrooms and sleeping accommodation for the Emperor (and the Empress, though she rarely accompanied him) and their personal servants; and a third, half suite, half sleeping car, was for the use of other members of the family or privileged guests – in this case the foreign minister and other members of the government accompanying him. Pullman-style carriages and wagons-lits on either side were occupied by courtiers and staff, kitchens, communications equipment and security personnel.

With surveillance helicopters flying overhead the train gathers pace and speeds on through the Burgenland, over the

Hungarian border via Győr and Komárom on the Danube, and across the Bakony Forest to Budapest. All the stations along the line are decorated and every vantage point is packed with cheering crowds. The train comes to a halt in the Hungarian capital for the Emperor to receive local dignitaries but he does not get off the train, and then on over the frosty landscape of the Great Hungarian Plain and into Romania without stopping at the border.

Here in Transylvania, which formed part of the Hungarian half of the Hapsburg Empire until 1918, the welcoming crowds are, if anything, even larger and more enthusiastic than in Hungary. This is not surprising for the Emperor's mission here is to ratify the accession of Romania to the Restored Holy Roman Empire and personally take possession of his new kingdom and install its first viceroy. The lure of its great and prestigious neighbour has proved too much and the whole country, not just Transylvania, has voted overwhelmingly in a referendum the previous year to join. Snow begins to fall as the Emperor's train makes its way through the mountains to Bucharest for three days of celebrations, but nothing can daunt the mood of popular rejoicing, enhanced by their new sovereign's very creditable attempts to speak Romanian in his address to Parliament. (To tell the truth he found it very much easier than Hungarian; it was, after all, a Latin language.)

The next, and in every way more sensitive stop on this imperial train journey was just across the border in Belgrade, the capital of Serbia. Serbia had for very obvious historical reasons been unhappy with the Restoration of the Empire, particularly as most of the old Yugoslav federation – that strange hybrid created at Versailles, in which it had once held the dominant position – was back under imperial rule. Nor had Serb insecurities been helped by the obvious attraction of its large north-western neighbour towards the Empire, culminating in the current scenes of jubilation in Bucharest. Historically too, the Empire could hardly fail to regard a discontented Serbia as a potential source of instability in the Balkans. But the new political mood created by the Imperial Restoration had profoundly influenced Serbia as well, and no one could doubt that without it the country would scarcely have become a monarchy under its native Karadjordjević dynasty once again.

In the event the two day visit, from the first friendly greeting of the two sovereigns on the platform, exceeded even the most optimistic expectations. In the first place proud little Serbia was delighted to be granted the rare privilege of an imperial stopover with all the international attention and excitement that that involved – it was rather like being awarded the Olympic Games! – particularly when no other countries in the region, Bulgaria or Greece for instance, were so favoured. But the Emperor also played his part – to all appearances modest, always keenly interested, genial, spontaneous but without losing the gravitas appropriate to his great office, he discreetly flattered and charmed his hosts. The effect on the whole country, following every moment of the visit on television, was irresistible. To see their own king playing host to the Emperor and being treated as an equal by him – the double-headed eagles of Serbia and the Empire side by side – was heady stuff! As intended, Serbia, both the political class and the general public, were reassured and apparently entirely reconciled to the expansion of the Empire.

From Belgrade the Emperor's train recrossed Romania bound for Moscow and the main purpose of his trip. En route he stopped for a day in Kiev, once the first capital of Rus but now, since the break-up of the Soviet Union, the seat of a sovereign republic more inclined to look to Vienna than Moscow; then it was north, for the first time through heavy snow, for a meeting with the young Tsar Alexander IV, which as a sign of special respect and with due regard to the historic importance of the occasion – the media inevitably made comparisons with the meeting of his predecessor Alexander I with Napoleon at Tilsit – took place on the station at Kaluga. The Tsar then dined with the Emperor on board the train as it carried them to Moscow together for the formal splendid ceremonial welcome.

It is no exaggeration to say that the successful revival of the Holy Roman Empire, following the collapse of Communism, has changed the climate of world politics giving the greatest possible boost to monarchist and legitimist sentiment everywhere, not least as a way of giving dignity and authority to the state and reaffirming traditional national identity and values in the face of a soulless and corrupting economic free-for-all in which the socially vulnerable, in particular, were left unprotected. In 1918 when the Emperor Charles, having been told 'Herr Hapsburg your taxi is waiting', left the Hofburg for the last time, monarchy seemed an exhausted, decadent and irrelevant institution; now it is the wave of the future. Through all the oscillations of politics the centre of the pendulum's swing is moving rightwards not leftwards, if such terms make sense any more in a highly libertarian world which would have been just as shocking to Louis XIV as to Lenin! So Russia has called back the Romanovs and a Tsar reigns in Moscow and Saint Petersburg, albeit as a constitutional monarch not an autocrat.

Yet never in all its long history has the Great Kremlin Palace seen such lavish festivities as those laid on by Tsar Alexander and his government in honour of their imperial guest. And underneath it all the Emperor's mission is essentially the same as in Serbia: perpetual peace, reassurance and friendship, though this time on a geopolitical scale. For it should not be forgotten that the once Russian Baltic states are now part of the Holy Roman Empire, the independent republics of the Ukraine and White Russia distinctly westward-looking, and with the accession of Romania and with it the mouth of the Danube, the

Empire and Russia have become neighbours across the Black Sea as they were already in the north.

After two days in Moscow, with the Emperor's three carriages incorporated into the Tsar's special train, the two sovereigns set off together on the Trans-Siberian Railway – two imperial eagles flying from the locomotive of the 'Zweikaiserzug', as the media dubbed it – for a five day journey to Khabarovsk, the second city in the Russian Far East, at the confluence of the Amur and Ussuri rivers. The well-heated and luxurious train speeds across vast snowy wastes of forest and steppe to be greeted by large crowds assembled, in spite of the weather, at all the major stations en route: Nizhni Novgorod, Kirov, Perm, Ekaterinberg, Tyumen, Omsk, Novosibirsk, Krasnoyarsk, Taishet, Irkutsk, Ulan-Ude, Chita, Skovorodino and finally Khabarovsk.

Here, less than twenty miles from the Chinese border – in fact on territory that belonged to China before 1858 – the two Emperors leave the train and enter the city for an historic triple summit with the President of China. The meeting is taking place at a propitious time; for China too in spite, or perhaps because, of its frenetic economic growth is feeling the need to stabilize its immense and rapidly transforming society on a base of traditional and indigenous values: in its case Confucianism naturally, and also – such is the climate of the age – with the restoration of imperial rule. Not the Manchu Dynasty, who were never really Chinese, but the Ming who reigned from 1368 to 1644, drove out the Mongols and built the Forbidden City – the last truly legitimate rulers of China. Of course it is not envisaged that the Mandate of Heaven should be exercised other than in a thoroughly democratic context. So here as well there was the same longing that the modern rupture between past and present should be healed and restored, all the nation's history fully validated once again and that the day to day agitations of politics be confined and limited within the enduring framework of hereditary monarchy. And historians will relate that in this process the Summit of Khabarovsk played an indispensable role.

The Emperor returned with the Tsar by train, the latter accompanying him as far as Smolensk, where the 'Zweikaiserzug' was disassembled and the imperial train reassembled, before taking his leave. Then after a brief stopover in White Russia where all the ceremonies took place in a specially erected pavilion on the station at Minsk, the Emperor's train re-entered imperial territory and without stopping at the border made for Warsaw and a triumphal welcome on the afternoon of the twentieth of December, before he returned to Vienna for Christmas the following day.

In retrospect the Winterreise would be seen as inaugurating the most successful period of his reign. A durable entente was established between Russia and the Empire. Spain, the recipient of an earlier imperial visit, though ruled by a Bourbon prince began to show signs of wanting to rejoin the Hapsburg Empire if it could be managed without detriment to the position of the present king and his heir, possibly it was suggested, by a dynastic alliance of some kind sealed by a marriage between the two families; there were, of course, precedents. There was even talk of Serbia and possibly Switzerland affiliating to the Empire in some way, to say nothing of the Empress's native Portugal, which in the aftermath of her marriage and no less than three strictly private visits by the imperial couple and family to her homeland had opted to restore the House of Braganza.

There could be no doubt of the overwhelming, though unquantifiable, effect of the Emperor's personal diplomacy which far transcended whatever concrete results a mere politician, however powerful or skilful in negotiating, might have been able to achieve. It was not the effect of Anton of course, that diffident young man caught up in the great tide of History, but of Theodore, Holy Roman Emperor exercising the unique charism of that great symbolic office. But it was a role that, over the years, he had learnt to play well and confidently, so that by now it had become almost second nature, eclipsing Anton almost completely.

A Hungarian count who served the Emperor Franz Joseph for thirty years wrote: 'I do not, and never shall, feel that I know him. Often when he has been in a good humour... I have thought, 'Now I am going to see the real man', but at that very moment an invisible veil has fallen... insulating him, as it were, from any current of human sympathy. Behind the veil would be, not a man but a monarch, persuaded of his own Divine Right and of his responsibility to none but the Deity. If you want to study the Emperor you must study Austro-Hungarian history for the last 60 years.' Anton did not believe he was answerable to God as Emperor, but he had sacrificed everything to his imperial destiny and vocation, and in other respects they had much in common. But perhaps he had not quite sacrificed everything, for thanks to the good offices of his faithful equerry, contact between himself and Rosemary had been securely and secretly re-established and they were now able to communicate indirectly by letter as often as they wished. And even though she was, by all accounts, happily married, it served to put a certain indefinable spring into the imperial step.

III

The snows of that historic Russian winter melted into spring and found Antony now aged thirty-five walking through the daffodils of the wild part of the gardens of Hampton Court. He was in a cheerful even elevated mood on that beautiful bright Sunday afternoon. The flowers no longer held any sinister association for him. Time had softened and faded the horrific memory of his mother's death aided, however irrational it might seem, by a recurrent dream in which he saw her smiling serenely and at peace as she had never been in life, sometimes in a long dress walking in a garden by a stream and sometimes seated in a kind of throne.

Suddenly he was aware of a woman coming towards him on an intersecting path. Although she was pregnant and pushing a chubby two-year-old girl in a buggy and he had not seen her for years, he recognized her instantly. She was obviously preoccupied. Should he pretend not to have noticed her and turn away? Even then he was aware of making a potentially fateful choice...

"Mrs Whitby-Browne, unless I am very much mistaken!"

"Tony, how lovely!" They embraced. "Thanks for the Christmas cards. Sorry I haven't been in touch more but I've got my hands rather full these days!"

"So I see. Well, you always wanted kids."

"Yes, this is Emily."

Antony bowed and shook her gravely by the hand. "Hello Emily." He then made a funny face which Emily immediately reciprocated. "When's the next one due?"

"June. So you're an author now. I always knew you'd make it. Is it three novels you've published?"

"Only two so far."

"But that's great."

"Oh it's not all it's cracked up to be. Authors are the drudges of the publishing world. The most difficult thing is getting the first one accepted. After that it's relatively plain sailing – they'll take any old rubbish. But you have to go to book signings and literary lunches and stuff. I've even been on television."

"Wow. I had no idea."

"Oh it was only BBC2 – and for a very short time." They laughed. "The trouble is if I get any more successful they might make me go to America and I'm dreading that."

"It all sounds very impressive – to me anyway. I'm afraid I haven't read any of your books though."

"I'll send you copies – signed by the author."

"Thank you. I don't have much time for reading but I'll treasure them... Are you, are you still at the bookshop?"

"Yes, but now I can sell my own books – I think we're blocking up the path. Look, have you and Emily got time for a cup of tea?"

"Why not?"

When they were at last seated in the café with tea and cake, they smiled at each other.

"Are you happy with Giles?"

"Oh he's lovely, he really is. You know he was the only one of Guy's friends that took my side. Of course, Guy accused me of having an affair with him, said he'd seen us talking together..." (Antony did not dare to ask if Guy's suspicions were justified though the words 'I don't trust myself' surfaced in his mind.) "It was thanks to Giles that I was able to get my divorce. He was the one who blew the whistle on Guy. Everyone knew about all his women but no one had the decency to tell me – except Giles. And he fixed me up with a really good solicitor and everything, so I was very grateful to him. I knew I was taking a risk marrying him without your advice," she smiled at Antony again, "but as he was the absolute opposite of Guy in every respect I thought it'd be alright. And it has been. Mind you that's more than I can say for his family – stuffy lot. My mum generally gets on with everybody and even she didn't take to them. And I'm sure they don't really approve of me. I wanted to strip off at the wedding and dance about naked just to shock them..."

"That I should've liked to see. What does Giles do?"

"Oh he works in the City, commodity broker – moves money around. Don't ask me about it. It all sounds very boring. Giles is no intellectual of course. He went to Stowe because he couldn't get into Eton, but he's a really nice straightforward chap. You were always too clever for me." Another smile. There was a somewhat awkward little pause before she went on: "That's enough about me. Let's talk about you. I was sorry to hear about your mum." Antony nodded. "But you're a married man now! How did you and Mary meet?"

"Oh she was my mother's nurse. Mary used to visit her regularly because latterly – for the last two years – she'd developed a serious heart condition that could have proved fatal at any moment."

"Did you know that at the time?"

"Certainly not."

"Why didn't Mary tell you?"

"Mother told her not to, but she naturally assumed I knew anyway so..."

The implication was too obvious and too serious to be made explicit. Rosemary moved swiftly on. "Are you still living where you were?"

"Yes, we're still in the flat in Wimbledon but I hung on to the house. In the end I decided to let it rather than sell. There are three lots of tenants in it – I'm a landlord."

"That was a shrewd move. It must be worth quite a bit more now."

"I wasn't really thinking about that. It was just that when it came down to it I couldn't bear to be parted from my train set and I had nowhere else to put it apart from the attic"

"That's typical of you!"

"Anyway, where's your husband this fine spring evening?"

"Oh he's on his boat in Bosham. Business, he says, rather than pleasure – entertaining clients. I do allow him time off for good behaviour. Where's Mary? Is she working?"

"No, she's gone to church. She's an RC, Irish you know."

"Does that pose any problems?"

"Not really. She can't have children."

"Oh Tony, I am sorry."

"It's sad for her, I think."

"You could adopt."

"Wouldn't be the same. In any case babies and writers don't mix. I think I could just about put up with the noise and disturbance for my own flesh and blood but not for anyone else's."

"You don't really mean that! Emily seems to have taken a shine to you anyway." (Antony and Emily were making funny faces at each other again.)

"Oh, Emily's my friend, that's different."

"I suppose I'd better be getting back. Look, we simply must see more of each other. The first thing is you and Mary must come for a meal – soon."

Antony agreed and they parted; his mood immediately after their chance meeting best summed up in the lines he recalled from *A Shropshire Lad*, which, as with so much of his favourite literature, he had first been introduced to by Mr Marjoribanks:

'I promise nothing: friends will part;
All things may end, for all began;
And truth and singleness of heart
Are mortal even as in man.

But this unlikely love should last
When answered passions thin to air;
Eternal fate so deep has cast
Its sure foundation of despair.'

That seemed to be about it. She was married and starting a family which would keep her absorbed for years to come, and, with no realistic expectation that Rosemary would ever come back into his life, he had married too. The prospect of their eventually getting together now seemed utterly hopeless. And yet (with Rosemary there was always an 'and yet'), she had seemed distinctly defensive about Giles – almost defiantly over-positive – as well as less than unqualified in his praise, to say nothing of her new in-laws! And was gratitude the same as love? The trouble was that, as ever, she was so difficult to read and to pin down. To what extent had she already taken up with Giles when he met her again in the autumn of 1969? Was Giles the reason why Guy had beaten her up even though they weren't then sleeping together, which would have justified her original denial on this point? Or did she only turn to Guy for comfort and advice after Antony's mother appeared an insurmountable obstacle, and was that before or after the divorce? Then again what did she mean by saying that he was "too clever" for her? Would that have ruled him out in any case or was she simply making the best of having had to choose Giles? However the one unambiguous gleam of encouragement, however faint, amid all this confusion and hopelessness was that she had been most insistent on their meeting again.

And meet they did. Rosemary was as good as her word. He and Mary were invited to dinner ten days later at the Whitby-Brownes' rambling mock Tudor house overgrown with wisteria and clematis in the Surrey hills near Leatherhead. It stood in a clearing at the end of a long drive through dense rhododendron bushes as high as trees. On one side French windows opened onto level lawns, while behind the house a wooded slope rose to the horizon.

Unlike Mary, Antony, who habitually frequented much grander places and came bearing, as promised, two signed hardback editions of his novels, was not unduly impressed. They were warmly welcomed and to Mary's relief it became apparent as soon as they were taken into the drawing room – the one with the French windows – that there were to be no other guests.

"What a charming friendly house", pronounced Antony. It's an 'anyone-for-tennis' sort of place isn't it?"

"As a matter of fact", said Giles rather surprised, "there used to be a tennis court out there."

"I rather thought so."

Insofar as he could be, Antony was instantly reassured by Giles whom he read as a good natured, well bred, roly-poly, ex-public school nonentity. In spite of the vast discrepancy in their wealth and respective incomes Antony patronized him from the first and Giles treated him with gratifying deference as a published author and generally 'brainy chap'. Rosemary could see that they had taken a liking to each other and Antony could see that she was mightily relieved.

Antony insisted that they return the hospitality promptly although Mary made it clear that her culinary skills could not possibly compete with the elaborate dinner party fare they had been served chez Rosemary; besides the fact that, as she pointed out more than once, "she has help in the kitchen". They therefore took Giles and Rosemary out to an Italian restaurant in Barnes, an option that, of course, proved much more expensive than entertaining at the flat. The next thing they knew they were invited to spend the weekend down in Sussex in the Whitby-Brownes' charming little Georgian house stuffed with oil paintings and antiques just a stone's throw from Bosham Harbour, where Giles kept his boat

Other invitations followed thick and fast. When it was just the four of them Antony naturally tended to talk to Rosemary while Mary chatted to Giles; but Antony, who always felt that he had the intelligence and wit to hold his own and even impress in any company provided there was no one like Marjoribanks around to upstage him, also felt at ease in the company of Giles's wealthy friends. And even if they did not always understand his jokes he had the feeling that in Giles's social world 'novelist' trumped 'successful corporate lawyer' or 'company director', though he was sometimes pestered with tiresome questions as to 'how you chaps manage to think up your plots' or whether his characters were based on real people and so on. However when they were asked, while visiting Rosemary three days after she had got back from Queen Charlotte's, to be godparents to her new baby Imogen, it came as something of a surprise to everyone except Antony.

"I can't understand it," said Mary as they were leaving and had hardly even got into the car, "there must be dozens of other people they could have chosen."

"Keep your voice down. They might hear us."

"But why us?"

"Well, I think they regard us as their closest friends."

"Do they? Well I must say I've never felt entirely comfortable with them. Don't look so surprised. They're just not my sort of people that's all. I thought you knew that."

"No, not really. I thought we were all getting on so well together."

"Sometimes Antony you have a way of seeing only what you want to see."

"You like Giles don't you?"

"I feel sorry for him. He does his best but Rosemary's always putting him down. Besides," Mary added lowering her voice, "I don't think she likes me very much."

"She does, you know."

"How do you know?"

"She told me."

"If you really want to know, I don't care for their values."

"What do you mean, 'their values'?"

"Well everything's money with them and their friends."

"That's not fair. They hardly talk about money at all."

"They don't need to."

Antony was rather taken aback. "You can't call Rosemary mercenary surely?"

"She likes shopping, I know that. And I can't see for the life of me why they want to have the baby christened. Neither of them seems to have the slightest interest in Christianity."

"It's just something people do. Not everyone is as religiously committed as you."

"Exactly, it's a farce."

"Well I don't think we can possibly back out now."

"No, I suppose not."

When they were in bed that night and the light was out Mary said: "Sorry I blew my top this evening."

"That's OK. They're not that bad you know."

"Yes, well I suppose I just feel they're more your friends than mine."

Though he had no intention of deliberately reversing the process, Antony too was aware that becoming involved again in Rosemary's life had the potential to disturb forever, in a quite unpredictable way, the peaceful even tenor of his life with Mary which had enabled him to get on with his writing, opening the door to forces that might prove dangerously disruptive.

Apart from the christening, to Mary's satisfaction and to some extent Antony's as well, in the weeks following Imogen's birth they saw nothing of Rosemary and Giles. Then at the end of July they had a call from Rosemary apologising for not having been in touch for such a long time. The post-natal period had, she said, been more stressful this time than with Emily, largely because her mother and her mother-in-law, who came from very different backgrounds and both turned up to help, spent most of the time sniping at each other, leaving Ines, the Portuguese au pair, to do the real coping. She added with rather surprising asperity that Giles had proved quite incapable of standing up to his mother. But now, thank God, the coast was clear. However –

and this was the main purpose of the call – as they would not be going down to their house in Sussex at least until the autumn, would Antony like to use it during August as a haven to finish the novel he was working on.

Antony consulted Mary.

"Oh I don't know. The trouble is it's all so one-sided. How are we ever going to be able to repay all this?"

"I'll just give them a signed copy of the new novel."

"No, I'm being serious."

"Well, in fact, I'll be doing them a favour – keeping an eye on the house. You could do some nights at the hospital – get some extra money and come down at weekends. We'd have the whole place to ourselves – no one else about. And I really do need some uninterrupted time to finish. Four weeks would be ideal."

So Mary was won round.

Antony departed the following Sunday – he could now come and go pretty much as he pleased at the bookshop – and Mary was pleased with an arrangement which meant that she had him all to herself at weekends. She would have been somewhat less pleased if she had known how often Rosemary was ringing him up.

The first call came on the Tuesday after he was installed, at lunchtime.

"Hello, it's only me. I thought I'd give you a day or so to settle in. I'm not interrupting am I? How are you getting on?"

"Oh not bad at all, but I love being interrupted."

This was true. He had in fact been typing for three hours and was more than ready to stop.

"I'm just ringing up for a moan really."

"Are Emily and Imogen OK?"

"Emily's missing you, but they're fine. Everything's under control – just about. Thank God for Ines. No, it's Giles."

"Giles? What's he done?"

"Oh just being Giles. I don't want to seem ungrateful or disloyal or anything; he's trying to help but he's always in the way somehow and you have to keep telling him what to do. It's much better when he's not around really."

"Poor old Giles."

"Don't get me wrong. He tries but, well he's hopeless really. With Emily for example, he just throws her about, bellows at her and tries to get her to play cricket with him, and she doesn't really like it. You're so much better with her. You talk to her like, well like a friend."

"That's because she is a friend."

"I know."

"You do give him a rather hard time you know."

"Well he can be very obtuse sometimes and it's irritating. I'm sorry to moan on but I've had him under my feet more than usual recently now he's not sailing."

"Have you ever been sailing with him?"

"Only once, never again. You know he's normally so mild and ineffectual but once 'aboard' as he called it he started shouting orders about jibs and mainsails and making things fast as if I was a sort of cabin boy. It was really quite alarming. I wasn't going to be treated like that just because I didn't know one end of a rope from another. We had quite a row about it as a matter of fact."

"And there was I thinking you two were idyllically happy."

"Come off it!... Oh why am I such a mess?"

"You're not a mess, you're – complicated."

"That's very tactful... No, Giles is OK really. He does his best," she sighed. "Well I suppose I'd better let you get on... Back to the nursery!"

Rosemary "ringing up for a moan" became an almost daily feature of his stay in Sussex as he worked away in a soothing cocoon of gilt-framed oil canvasses and porcelain, deep carpets and softly ticking clocks. It was during those summer weeks that criticising her husband to him became a habit, with Antony inevitably cast in the role of defending 'poor old Giles' – well aware his defence prompted, and even allowed her to become even more outspoken than she might have intended. He was more than willing to lend a sympathetic ear and offer all the support and encouragement the situation permitted, provided that the interruption to his work was kept within bounds, and in particular that her calls did not run on till after six o'clock, which happened once or twice, leaving him having to make some sort of excuse to Mary who always called on the dot of six and had been trying to get through.

Was there a point where Rosemary's criticism of her husband, which Antony was careful never to endorse explicitly, however supportive he might be, actually crossed the line of minimum solidarity between couples which makes a marriage viable, and became a sort of de facto conspiracy between Rosemary and himself against Giles, from which there was no way back? Perhaps it never quite got that far, but Rosemary was so enticingly ambivalent; moreover her mood towards Giles shifted from day to day, sometimes from hour to hour. Was she trying to signal something more to him by talking about her husband in this way or was she just letting off steam to an understanding friend in her typically unguarded and unrestrained fashion? Not for the first time in his life he found himself obsessively weighing and analysing her every word and, as before, reaching no secure conclusion.

By the end of October with the text of the novel duly despatched to the publishers and Imogen having attained the ripe age of five months, meetings with the Whitby-Brownes were re-established at almost their earlier frequency and the question of Christmas reared its head. Rosemary started pressing for him and Mary to come to them, either for Christmas itself at Bosham or the New Year at Leatherhead, or both. Mary however was adamant that they should, as always, go to her family in north London, and Antony felt he had to comply, though the alternative was much more appealing. Nevertheless he was beginning to learn that saying 'no' now and again to Rosemary by no means discouraged her, and over the festive season he received no fewer than three calls telling him how much they were being missed. The New Year was not far advanced before she started talking about summer holidays.

"We've taken a villa at Fiesole just outside Florence from mid-August to mid-September. You will come won't you? The girls would love it and it would make it much more bearable for me..."

Mary was clearly reluctant and there was something of a showdown.

"We just can't accept their hospitality in some luxury villa without paying our share – and we can't afford it. We're just not in their league. Why can't you accept that?"

"I don't suppose it'll be that luxurious – just a glorified farmhouse, I expect. Anyway they're just inviting us as guests. There'll probably be other people coming and going. That's what happens when people have a villa. I shouldn't think we'll be the only ones." (Here Antony was slightly bending the truth, for Rosemary had already assured him that she had made it clear to Giles that as she would have her hands full with Emily and Imogen, his family and friends would not be welcome.)

"If you ask me it's crazy going off to Italy in the summer with two young children."

"Ines will be going too. If truth be told they're probably hoping we'll be helping with the kids as well."

"Hoping you will, you mean. The time and energy you devote to those little girls is unbelievable."

"I thought that's what godfathers were supposed to do. (Rosemary made no reply.) "Well they are very engaging don't you think?"

"I think they get far too much attention. Everything is centred on them, everything they do seems to be filmed and we're invited to watch them eating, even having their baths..."

"I thought you liked them."

"I do. I just think they're in danger of being spoilt rotten, that's all. It wouldn't be my way of bringing up children. And if you like kids so much... you know what I'm going to say, don't you?"

Antony did know what she was going to say and he was only too aware of the justice of her case as well as the thoughtlessness of his own behaviour.

"We will think about adopting, but it's a big decision."

"That's what you always say, but we never do anything about it."

"We'll consider it, I promise."

This was as far as he had ever gone but he felt that in the circumstances he had no choice. In the end with Antony suggesting gently that the villa visit might be considered a quid pro quo for Christmas and conceding that they would "certainly not be staying the whole time", Mary relented.

"You never know," Antony concluded cheerfully, "we might not spend an awful lot of time with them. It's quite a big place, Rosemary said, eight rooms and a pool. We can just use it as a base if we want to, and come and go as we please. We certainly won't be living in each other's pockets..."

In the event they arrived at the villa the best part of a week after their hosts and left only a day or so before them, chiefly because Mary didn't like flying, and when it became apparent that they would not be seeing any of the Whitby-Brownes' wealthy friends she was secretly pleased. Inevitably they did in fact spend an awful lot of time with Rosemary and Giles, though the social pattern varied. For Giles, a self-confessed and happy philistine, the charm of Italy was limited to food, wine and sunshine. Frescoes, tombs, statues and paintings held absolutely no interest for him and he adamantly refused to enter any church or art gallery, even the Duomo or the Uffizi. However he was quite content, while Rosemary and Mary did the cultural round with Antony, to sit in a piazza with a cappuccino or a flask of Chianti. Back at the villa, in spite of Mary's strictures, Antony still devoted a lot of time to the children, especially Imogen who was just beginning to toddle; but when Ines was taking care of them or they were asleep it always seemed to end up again with Rosemary talking more to Antony while Mary was left to cope with Giles. However to Antony's relief the days passed with a remarkable lack of overt tension between them all, though there were occasional snatched conversations in which Rosemary expressed to him her frustration with Giles.

One day they decided to walk down to Florence. Giles in Panama hat, long baggy shorts and sandals was with Mary, a few yards ahead of Rosemary and Antony. Giles's outfit did not flatter him. Florid, tubby and with thinning hair he looked older than his mid-forties and though only eight years younger his wife seemed of a different generation. Suddenly she whispered or rather hissed:

"Why *does* he irritate me so much? He hasn't got a mean bone in his body and he does his level best to be a good husband and father, yet sometimes I can barely bring myself to be civil him."

"I've noticed."

"It makes me feel such a bitch."

"Well, you will marry these people...."

"Oh, shhh!"

"He's not that bad, old Giles, surely?"

"You don't have to live with him."

At this point Giles turned round and waved and the exchange ceased.

The following morning, the first Sunday of the holiday, Giles kindly drove Mary into Florence as she had expressed a wish to go to early Mass in the cathedral, and was going to wait in the piazza until the service was over before driving her back for breakfast. Ines was looking after the children on the sun terrace by the pool. Rosemary and Antony both having had a shower happened to bump into each other in their dressing gowns on the landing between their rooms. Antony was still dripping.

"You're up early," she said.

"Bloody church bells! No point in staying in bed."

"Never mind about that, come and look at the view, it's so beautiful this morning."

She took him by the hand, led him into her bedroom and threw back the shutters. The Whitby-Brownes had naturally chosen the room with the best outlook and the windows opened onto a hillside landscape of cypresses and olive groves – the instantly recognizable background of countless quattrocento paintings – which fell away to a distant but uninterrupted view of Florence spread out around the great terracotta dome in a shimmering haze of heat which signalled another hot late summer day to come. But because there had been a thunderstorm overnight the air was fresh and sweet without the oppressive closeness that had been building over the last few days.

"Yes it is, isn't it? Even better than Wimbledon Hill."

They were standing very close together at the window. Then as he turned round to look at her Rosemary hugged him and they kissed. A minute later they were on the unmade bed making love.

The first words uttered when they eventually finished came from Antony:

"I'm sorry, I'm so sorry."

But Rosemary propping herself up on her elbow looked down at him with a reassuring smile. "Don't be. This was bound to happen sooner or later."

"I can't leave Mary."

"No, of course not. But the most important thing is that it mustn't affect us, our friendship."

"That's exactly what I was hoping you would say."

"Just don't abandon me, that's all. I couldn't live without you..."

At that moment they heard crunching on the gravel of the drive below them announcing the return of Mary and Giles.

"Off you go my love. Remember, from now on we've got to be very, very careful."

"Don't worry, we will be." Pausing in the doorway to look back at her he added, "You know I've always imagined having a secret life."

"Well, now you've got one."

When they returned their respective spouses found them both energetically taking showers and in remarkably good spirits as they prepared themselves for the new day.

From then on Antony devoted much more attention to Mary and Rosemary not only took more notice of Giles but hardly even snapped at him once, and noticeably refrained from putting him down in public as she normally did. All went smoothly until one afternoon two days before Antony and Mary were due to go home. They were all in Santa Maria Novella except for Giles who was outside in a café having a beer; Mary was saying a prayer and Antony and Rosemary were looking at Ghirlandaio's frescoes of the Life of the Virgin. They had latterly developed a technique of exchanging confidences by standing next to each other looking straight ahead so that no one, unless they could hear whispered voices, would imagine they were communicating at all.

"I'm pregnant," said Rosemary, softly but distinctly.

"Congratulations."

"You don't understand. I haven't had sex with Giles since I was pregnant with Imogen. We... we just never started again."

"Are you sure?"

"Of course I'm sure. I've been pregnant twice before."

"And it's not a virgin birth?"

"No!"

"Now would be quite a good time for you and Giles to..."

"Don't worry, I'll take care of that. Anyway, I'm going to have your child. What do you think about that?"

"I think it's marvellous."

Rosemary could not resist touching his arm before she turned to go and even out of the corner of his eye he could see that she was in rather an emotional state.

That evening Rosemary and Giles made a business of retiring early for the night and the following evening, in view of their long train journey the next day, Antony and Mary did so too.

When they were lying side by side in bed Mary said: "You know I sometimes think I can never really reach you, not even when we're making love. It's as if you're not there somehow. It's difficult to explain."

"You married a writer."

"Is that what it is? I thought you were getting bored with me now that we're moving in more exalted circles."

"Never."

"I've not felt it quite so much, just recently perhaps... you know I've enjoyed this holiday more than I thought I would. I think it's been good for us and for Giles and Rosemary too. They seem to be getting on better, have you noticed?"

"Shhh! Listen!"

Antony got up, went to the door and opened it slightly to admit the unmistakeable sounds of strenuous lovemaking reaching its climax in their hosts' bedroom. They both listened with intense interest for a few seconds. "We shouldn't be doing this", chuckled Mary, it's disgusting! Close the door. Why are you looking so delighted?"

"Just happy for them, that's all. Like you said they're definitely getting on better. Romantic Italy working its magic, the voluptuous southern night, studded with stars..."

"Shut up and come to back to bed."

The following morning when they were having an early breakfast before going to the station Rosemary said very deliberately: "I hope we didn't disturb you two last night?"

Giles, who even with Antony's help was struggling with the *Daily Telegraph* easy crossword, had a smug grin on his face.

"Not at all," replied Mary cheerfully. "I hope *we* didn't disturb *you*."

"'Sunshade', seven letters beginning with P is 'parasol'," said Antony.

When they were being seen off at the station Rosemary hugged him so tight that he involuntarily said "careful". In a play, he later reflected, that would have been a moment of revelation to be picked up by a husband or other discerning observer, but in real life on that very noisy and crowded station it passed completely unnoticed. Antony looked out of the window of the departing train and Rosemary watched him till he was out of sight.

They had not been back a week when Rosemary rang up and asked for Mary. From then on she always asked for Mary and only spoke to Antony when she was at work or otherwise unavailable.

"That was Rosemary," said Mary bursting into the spare bedroom that he used as a study in a way that never failed to disconcert him, "she's pregnant again."

"Rosemary? Well that's hardly a surprise," said Antony with the air of one interrupted in the midst of lofty and incommunicable imaginative flights who has difficulty in focusing on some item of trivial domestic gossip.

"No, but it's certainly bad timing. I can't believe it was intended."

"How do you mean?"

"Well, she's really got her hands full now, hasn't she?"

"I expect she was pleased though."

"Oh yes, very. I would have put her on to you but she seemed in rather a hurry. I expect she's got lots of people to ring up!"

Recrossing the Alps back to the distant offshore island of Britain, as he saw it, proved a jolting return to reality in every way for Antony. There was a sudden change of season from balmy late summer to autumn. Wimbledon was a good fifteen degrees cooler than Florence and the dark green trees on the Common were already turning; the first leaves being scattered in the cool drizzly wind. And of course he no longer enjoyed daily access to Rosemary. In fact, by deliberate choice they saw considerably less of each other than before the holiday. Mary, whose jealousy of Rosemary, he sensed had been growing up to the time they went to Italy, to the point where he feared that there might be some embarrassing outburst, had now declined and faded almost to nothing. The pregnancy proved to be difficult and Antony had to follow every twist and turn in the process largely at the end of the phone and often second-hand from Mary from whom he had to conceal his special interest and anxiety.

That autumn also saw the publication of his third novel, *The Valley of the Three Worlds*, in which his young hero, rejecting suburban Britain, embarked on what might loosely be called a quest for the Meaning of Life which took him first, in what turned out to be a prelude, to Crete and the Amazon jungle, and then finally across Asia to Ladakh. It was hailed by lazy-minded reviewers as a modern version of James Hilton's classic, quite inappropriately Antony thought. Though ultimately unsuccessful, his hero's spiritual search culminating in the mysterious remote purity of those high mountain passes where three great religions meet, happened to strike a chord at a time when do-it-yourself so-called New Age spirituality was coming into fashion and also chimed in with the growing popularity of the 'hippy' trail to Nepal, even though that had rather more to do with drugs than mysticism. Antony had simply been using his own experience while trying to make it more interesting by adding fictitious intrigues between monasteries over the possession of a sacred text, against a background of attempted Chinese communist infiltration in league with Pakistan, in an effort to divide and discredit Lama Buddhism and make trouble for India in Kashmir. Quite fortuitously however the wider social context contributed very greatly to the book's success.

With writers a successful first novel can be dismissed as a flash in the pan, everybody after all is supposed to have one novel in them; a second follow-up success and a novelist is regarded as 'promising', the first novel was at least not a fluke. With his third moderately successful novel Antony earned the status of an 'established' author. Moreover while there might be a certain family resemblance between his first two novels, different in many ways though they were, everyone agreed that *The Valley of the Three Worlds* was an interesting departure showing a hitherto unsuspected range and versatility in his work. What he had suggested to Rosemary was quite true: while his first novel had been constantly misread and carelessly dismissed by publishers' readers and agents before it was eventually accepted, once he had two or three books to his name reviewers with equal lack of discernment and discrimination fell over themselves to praise his work. It was ever thus he supposed. The vast majority of people in or out of the book trade had no idea how to tell a good book from a bad one or of the criteria if any on which such a distinction might be based. All they were capable of recognising was success.

Rosemary gave birth to her third child three weeks early, at the beginning of June 1977. There had been talk of a possibility of a breech birth but in the end everything went without a hitch and much more quickly than had been expected. Giles rang with the news but when Antony beat Mary to the phone he sounded even more vague and incoherent than usual.

"... so everything's OK?"

"Sure, everything's fine."

"Giles, you haven't told me whether it's a boy or a girl."

"Oh God no, sorry, of course, it's a boy."

"That's wonderful! She always wanted a boy, didn't she?"

"Well she certainly sounded over the moon. So long as they're both doing well that's the main thing."

"What's he like?"

"Well to tell you the truth," he admitted in his self-effacing way, "I made rather a fool of myself. I passed out during the birth and was given a strong cup of tea and sent home. I haven't actually seen him yet."

This was about ten o'clock in the evening. Next morning Rosemary rang inviting them to come and see the baby. They spent half an hour with her in the hospital and were both invited to hold him. He was very delicate and a little underweight but perfectly healthy.

"Has Giles seen him?" asked Mary.

"Not yet, he's coming in at lunchtime with the girls." She then proceeded to tell the story of his somewhat ignominious collapse in the labour room and removal from the scene. Mary asked if they had decided on names for the baby. Antony suggested Caesar Augustus but was promptly slapped down by the two women.

"I thought Richard," said Rosemary, "after my father, Antony after his – his godfather and of course Giles – Richard Antony Giles. I am assuming you two will be godparents again."

(Rosemary had already cleared these names for a boy with Antony beforehand so they came as no surprise to him.)

"Would that be legal under the circumstances?" asked Antony with a completely straight face.

"What do you mean?" asked Rosemary momentarily alarmed.

"Being godparents twice over of course!"

They all laughed if for rather different reasons, then a nurse came in, Mary said she had to go to work and the two visitors left.

"Don't you think it's strange", observed Mary as they were leaving the building, "that we were asked to see the baby before Giles?"

"Oh I expect he's still recovering from the shock of yesterday – poor old Giles!"

"She was very trusting letting you hold him. I don't think I would have done."

"Well I'm not that keen on babies but he didn't weigh very much so it was quite safe."

"No, but all the same. Do you want me to drop you off?"

"No thanks, I don't want to make you late. I'll get a bus."

Did Mary's rather pointed questions betray the slightest suspicion on her part that there might be some resemblance between himself and the little scrap of humanity that he had just been holding with such intense interest and care? Mary was after all no fool and quite disconcertingly observant. Common sense told him no, absolutely not. Yet the experience of enfolding his own newborn son in his arms and sharing that moment with Rosemary was so palpable and so powerful that it seemed as if it must have been apparent to the whole world, hence his efforts afterwards to be as relaxed and casual as possible. They parted in the car park and Mary drove off. Antony felt a strong desire to go back inside the hospital where the two people he most cared about were in a little room on the second floor, but he suppressed it and walked to the bus stop.

Not the least of the pleasures of being established as a successful novelist was that he felt that at last he was in a position to put Leo Marjoribanks in his place. After each of the first two books Marjoribanks had written him letters which, however they were intended, came over to Antony as condescending. The first one in particular had an 'always knew you had it in you, well done my boy' tone to it and in both congratulations were mixed with some judicious criticism and helpful suggestions; the impression given was very much that of an experienced old hand to a newcomer in the business of authorship. In both letters however he suggested that they meet, and he even invited him to help direct the Old Boys' play. Antony was evasive. On the rare occasions when they both attended the same Old Boys' functions Marjoribanks invariably made a beeline for him; but he was always as cool and unforthcoming as politeness allowed. He had no intention of joining Marjoribanks' admiring circle.

However after the publication of *The Valley of the Three Worlds* he received a more fulsome and unqualified note of congratulations from him (surprisingly, as he didn't think it would have been Marjoribanks' sort of thing at all) and the following June, just before the birth of Richard Antony Giles, a more formal letter on school notepaper asking him to give a talk to the Arts sixth and enquiring on the headmaster's behalf whether he would be prepared to present the prizes on Speech Day. If convenient he would arrange the talk for the same afternoon so that he could then stay on for the prize-giving in the evening. How could he decline this opportunity to take centre stage at his old school graciously offered to him by Leo Marjoribanks? To be standing up in front of the governors and all the staff in full academic dress as the visiting celebrity and distributor of prizes was a fantasy made flesh. In his time one year it had been a bishop, then the mayor, then Lady somebody or other, then a junior Education Minister no less, and now it would be him! Accordingly the day that Rosemary and son went home from hospital he sent off a friendly acceptance. However he more than anyone ought to have known than that fantasy and reality inhabit different worlds.

The great day arrived, Thursday in the last week of the summer term. Antony was greeted effusively at the door of the school by his old English master in a cream coloured lightweight three piece suit and MA gown and taken to meet the new headmaster – a large boned, grizzled looking man of rudimentary social skills who bore a passing physical resemblance to Samuel Beckett – for sherry and pleasantries. Marjoribanks did what he could to keep the conversation going, then after about a quarter of an hour he was taken to meet the intellectual elite of the school – a collection of scruffy adolescents, quaintly and very uncomfortably confined in school uniforms that had not changed for at least fifty years.

He was introduced at some length by Marjoribanks and it was fascinating, if not somehow depressing, to see him successfully deploying, despite a changing world, all his old well tried repertoire to flatter, cajole, intimidate and entertain yet another generation of schoolboys. Marjoribanks referred to him as "a well known writer whom we are honoured to have with us today", and Antony observed that a number of the boys had copies of his novels (which they subsequently asked him to sign). But his host nevertheless contrived to give the impression that as he had taken Antony under his wing from the time that he was in the lower sixth, been his mentor and guide and kept a benevolent eye on his early struggles after he was unable to go to Oxford, it was in no small measure due to him that he had eventually achieved his current stature – one of his many successes over the years!

When he was at last allowed to speak Antony did not try to compete with Marjoribanks in entertaining the boys. He began asking how many of his audience read novels – almost all hands went up; then how many actually wrote poetry or novels – surprisingly about a third of the hands were raised. Finally he asked how many would like to take up writing as a career, either fiction or journalism. At least a dozen indicated that they would.

His talk concentrated in objective terms on the genesis and composition of a novel from first ideas to final draft, and seemed to interest them. But their questions afterwards seemed more designed to impress either him or their contemporaries than to elicit information. Marjoribanks assumed that they were also addressed to him as a fellow writer and authority on all things literary, and so Antony found his answers constantly interrupted, interpreted and amplified. He tried to make light of it but it was very irritating all the same.

"Not a bad bunch, are they?" said Marjoribanks after Antony had signed the last novel and was on his way to tea in the staff common room. "I think I've got at least half a dozen potential Oxbridge entrants there. That's more than I can say for our staff these days. Strictly entre nous they're rather a mediocre lot and with the new head no doubt they'll get worse. And now," he added raising his eyes in mock despair, "we have women. Anyway I don't suppose there'll be anybody you remember."

Antony got the impression that Marjoribanks was enlarging on the shortcomings of his colleagues not so much to apologize for the prospect of poor company as to elicit sympathy for what he had to put up with.

In spite of his contact with the Old Boys' Association he had not set foot on the premises of the school itself since he was unhappily obliged to leave twenty years ago. He dimly remembered the headmaster's panelled art deco study overlooking the drive – the school had been built in the late Twenties – and was familiar with the sixth form study room where he met the boys, but the staff room was now accommodated, with the art room and laboratories, in a new block built in the sixties.

He was introduced to about twenty members of the staff and given a cup of tea and sandwiches from a trolley. They seemed pleasant enough people, mostly younger than he had expected, but understandably preoccupied and harassed. Marjoribanks ensconced himself in what was obviously 'his' chair and proceeded to hold forth to everyone within earshot on the subject of next year's school production which he revealed would be Shakespeare's *Pericles*.

"The boys keep pestering me to take a part myself. Up to now I've always refused but this time, as it will be, believe it or not, my thirtieth school production, God save us, I thought I might take the part of the poet Gower. He acts as a sort of chorus..."

As soon as he could Antony left him to it and talked to the only two members of staff he did recognize. One was the PE master who had given him a hard time in the gym and on the football field. A much stouter and greyer figure now in his tracksuit, he obviously had no recollection of Antony as a schoolboy but was genial and friendly, far removed from the fascist bully of memory.

"I'm not much of a reader myself, "but my wife's bought your latest one; she loves travel books, anything to do with escape, adventure, that sort of thing."

"Did she like it?"

"Not sure it was quite her thing but," he added hastily, "she found it very interesting. Are you writing anything at the moment?"

"It may seem a strange thing to say but I'm not quite sure."

Antony, like most writers, would for choice have happily have chatted about almost anything rather than his work. However he clearly meant well and Antony warmed to him when he said: "To tell you the truth I always feel rather a prat on Speech Day because I'm the only one who hasn't got a gown."

Antony also spoke to the man he remembered as an eager young Latin teacher who had had trouble keeping order, now the rather disillusioned Head of Classics and, Antony was shocked to learn, the only actual teacher of Latin in the school. (In Antony's day Latin was a compulsory subject until the sixth form.) Most boys now apparently did a course called 'Classical Studies' which involved only texts in English translation with a bit of Ancient History and Mythology thrown in!

His carefully prepared speech at the prize-giving contained a few jokes and anecdotes with a little personal reminiscence which all seemed to go down reasonably well with his young audience, but he concluded with a defence of traditional liberal education based on the classics of literature, ancient and modern, which was, he maintained, about cultivating the mind not acquiring skills that might help them get a good job or even contribute to the national economy. He thought afterwards that it might have been wiser to tone down his remarks in the light of what he had heard from the Head of Classics, but he stuck to his script.

When it was all over and he was preparing to go, Marjoribanks said: "Well done, you certainly socked it to them, as they say."

"I don't think it was quite what the headmaster was expecting. He was rather muted afterwards to say the least."

"The head! What does he know? All he cares about are exam results and how long the boys' hair should be. The latest thing is this language laboratory we're threatened with. I told him the boys would wreck it in a week. The man's a complete philistine

– a scientist of course. For example, after our local MP cancelled and I had to find someone at short notice, when I told him about this young friend of mine, quite a well known novelist who happened to be an Old Boy, Antony Kilroy, he said he hadn't even heard of you! I sometimes wonder what I'm doing here when I could have been running the English department at Harrow. Heigh-ho!" Marjoribanks made an eloquent gesture which suggested the wiping of imaginary sweat from a fevered brow. "Now let's shake the dust of this place from our feet and go and have something to eat – on me, of course. There's a rather decent little French place round here that I often use..."

Antony had been trying to contain his irritation with Marjoribanks all afternoon but to be told so carelessly, and with such a complete lack of awareness for his own feelings, that he had been a mere stop-gap, was the last straw. He suddenly realised that to have to spend a whole evening listening to the man would be unendurable.

"Sorry Leo, I'd love to but I promised Mary I would be back as soon as I could."

Marjoribanks was clearly perplexed and disappointed but, Antony felt, not in any way offended since it would have been unimaginable to him that anyone would willingly pass up the chance of spending the evening in his company. So, with a few comments by him about apron strings and married life, they parted with apparent cordiality.

On the way home Antony could not help reflecting on this prolonged exposure to his old English teacher who had seemed more than ever a school institution, although the school itself had changed almost beyond recognition. He might have felt constrained to treat him as a sort of equal who could be regaled with disparaging confidences about the headmaster and the staff, but in all respects he was the same Leo Marjoribanks, still the same upstager, relentlessly focusing every situation, every conversation, onto himself; still acting on the implicit assumption that he was the most interesting person in any company, that he could charm and win over anyone by paying them a modicum of attention and that his vocation was to shed a little light into the lives of the dull and boring people with whom he was surrounded. Any intercourse with Marjoribanks had to be on his own terms. Never once in all the hours they had been together, it occurred to Antony, had he asked him anything about himself or expressed any interest in his life. Was it that Marjoribanks was simply unaware of the impression that he made or did he just not care? Was there, he wondered, any element of self-parody in it all? Did he perhaps ever get bored with the role he played so assiduously or even wish sometimes he was different? Was he like that even when mixing in the more distinguished circles he frequented? Did he patronize *them*? Then there was the perennial question with Marjoribanks as with all malicious gossips that if he was prepared to entertain Antony with scathing comments about friends and colleagues, what might he not be saying about *him* to someone else? After all why should anyone think he alone was in a privileged position as a receiver of confidences?

A few days later Antony received a fulsome letter of thanks from him 'for stepping into the breach so valiantly on Speech Day and for inspiring the Arts sixth'. Marjoribanks then invited him once again to help with the Old Boys' play but this time as co-director and not a mere assistant! Also enclosed was a very brief and formal note of thanks from the headmaster, Mr Ronald Sturgis B.Sc. London. Antony threw them both in the bin and declined Marjoribanks' kind offer.

With Richard being born in June there was no question of a foreign holiday with Rosemary and Giles this year but Florence, the pregnancy and birth had, apart from everything else, proved something of a watershed in his wife's relations with the Whitby-Brownes. To all appearances she and Rosemary had become good friends so that when she rang, Mary automatically assumed it was because she wanted to talk to her. She no longer made any objection to the considerable amount of time they were once again now all spending together and when they were invited to stay for most of August down in Sussex with Rosemary and Giles she was really pleased.

As for Antony and Rosemary, clandestinely sharing and caring for their son together constituted such a deep perpetual and ever-growing bond between them that although they spoke on the phone whenever they could and enjoyed the odd furtive passionate cuddle, in a way nothing more was needed, and they were less overtly friendly than ever. But the situation was inherently unstable. Although Mary now accepted Antony's very evident and continuing closeness to Rosemary's children, it inevitably made his reluctance to adopt all the more difficult for her to understand.

"I just can't see how you can be so fond of other people's kids and not want any of your own."

"Well you can walk away from other people's kids."

"You never willingly walk away from little Richard and the girls."

"That's different, they're friends."

"So you always say... I agree they are very engaging children but..."

"There you are. The trouble with adopting is that you never know what you're getting. They may, I'm not saying they will, but they may turn into little monsters..."

And so it went on.

Then again, although Antony was scrupulous in paying as much attention to Emily and Imogen as to Richard, he obviously had a special bond with him. He called him "my Raggy", from his initials RAG – so did Rosemary when they were talking about him between themselves – but because everybody made such a fuss of that serious brown-eyed little boy who was the latest addition to the family, Antony's particular attachment passed largely unnoticed. The trouble was that the older and larger he grew the more strikingly he resembled his natural father, in Antony and Rosemary's eyes at least, and it was difficult for them to believe that such a resemblance would pass forever unobserved.

In 1978 Mary seemed happy enough to agree to another joint holiday with the Whitby-Brownes, this time in a villa in Provence just outside Avignon. The holiday was a success and if Giles evinced no interest in the Palais des Papes, he certainly developed a taste for the local wine, and came back with several crates of Châteauneuf-du-Pape, not then widely available in England.

The following year when Mary suggested that they went away on their own to Ireland to see some relatives of her mother's, Antony could hardly object; but more concerning to him were certain changes that he was beginning to notice in her. As well as being less cheerful, more withdrawn and occasionally irritable, she was losing a bit of weight and seemed somehow paler and more peaky. There was nothing dramatic about it, but taken all altogether it began to worry him.

Mary was never a very communicative person at the best of times, preferring to keep her own counsel. Did she have some secret trouble, an illness perhaps, or fear of an illness that she wanted to keep from him? Or was it frustration and disappointment with his constant stalling over the adoption question. Was it the change of life? Mary was forty-four after all, a few years older than him. Or had she, the nightmare possibility, become aware of the startling likeness between Rosemary's little Richard and her husband, prompting suspicions that she dare not articulate but which were eating away at her? Occasionally he asked her as gently as he could whether she was alright. The reply was invariably: "Yes of course I'm alright, why shouldn't I be?"

Then again there was intermittent but mounting pressure from Rosemary, who was moreover just crossing the fateful threshold of forty, telling him over the phone that Giles was driving her mad, that she didn't know how much she could stand of him and so on. Nowadays when she quoted his words she mimicked his rather languid plummy voice. (Significantly she evidently never expressed any criticism of Giles when chatting to Mary or even implied that her marriage was in any way under strain.) Antony's constant effort was to try and calm her down and insist on the necessity, for the time being at least, of her staying with Giles and trying to make the best of it.

"...but he's getting so middle-aged – that paunch he's developing, ugh! Sometimes I feel as if I'm going to explode. The trouble is it's almost impossible to rile him, to have a real showdown."

"There must be no explosions and no showdowns."

"I know Tony, I know. But it's all very well for you. It's like having a great big soppy dog all over you, following you about, never giving you any peace. You know, it's awful, the other night I dreamt we were making love and then I woke up to find Giles next to me. I was in a right old state. I couldn't tell him why, of course. He said he thought I'd been having a nightmare – apparently I'd been thrashing about and mumbling in my sleep. Then he tried to comfort me which was really the last thing I wanted. Oh, if only he wasn't so bloody nice!"

"You don't think you said anything intelligible in your sleep, do you?"

"No, I'm sure I didn't. I've got to go now Tony; he's just coming in..."

During 1979 Antony had a growing underlying feeling that something had to give. Given the forces at work the status quo, this half life of deception and concealment could hardly continue indefinitely. And yet the consequences of any kind of revelation of the truth seemed unthinkable and these days he was becoming all too aware that one fateful slip would be enough to bring the whole dangerously precarious structure of his personal life crashing down, a house of cards indeed. However he looked at it he could see no clear or even possible way ahead and the future filled him with such foreboding that he tried to think of it as little as possible.

Looking at Rosemary and Mary chatting together at a party on New Year's Eve Antony had no reason to think that 1980 would be any different to the year before. He had recently been trying to persuade Mary that it would be a good plan for them to buy a little place in Provence now that he was beginning to make enough money from his novels, especially the third one (in those days 'little places in Provence' could still be acquired for a comparatively reasonably sum), but she dug her heels in. Antony had to face the fact that his wife was as averse to living abroad as he was to living in England. So matters stood when only a few weeks into the New Year a violent stroke of fate changed everything.

The crisis came on the sixth of February, a Wednesday; Antony had just got home from the bookshop at a quarter to six. On Wednesdays Mary got off at 2pm, did some shopping and was invariably home long before him, so that he expected the place to be lit up, warm and full of the welcoming smell of cooking. That evening however the flat was dark and empty. As he entered the phone was ringing.

"Mary?"

"It's me, Rosemary. Isn't Mary there?"

"No, not yet."

"Thank goodness. I've been trying to get you at the shop."

"I've only just got in, what's wrong?"

"I'm at the end of my tether, that's all. This time I really am."

(There were days when the contrast between the good-natured, simple-minded and incorrigibly obtuse husband she was stuck with and the sensitive, creative and amusing man whose clandestine love and support she sorely needed was so great as to be almost intolerable, and this was one of those days.) "I tell you, I just don't know how much more of this I can put up with."

"What's to be done?"

"Nothing. That's the point. You know what he's like. I bite his head off then he asks 'what's wrong old girl'." She sighed. "God knows Tony I've been trying to keep this marriage going like you said but sometimes..."

She went on for some time in the same vein and then interrupted herself. "Are you OK? You sound rather preoccupied. Is something bothering you?"

"No, not really. It's just that it's Mary's half day and she still isn't back. Normally she's home long before me."

"Oh, she's probably just stuck in traffic. Look, I'll get off the phone. If she's been delayed for some reason she may be trying to call you."

Antony thought this a sensible suggestion and she rang off. He made himself a cup of tea and went to the casement window in the bedroom, opened it and gazed up the road looking for the first sign of his wife's car. After half an hour in which many cars passed but not Mary's, the phone rang again.

"Mary?"

"No, it's me again. So she's still not back?"

"I just wonder what's happened. It's so unlike her to be late like this."

"You know what I think? She's doing something which she probably told you all about but you didn't take in because your mind was on higher things. You know what you're like."

"Yes, I suppose that must be it. I'll ring round and try and find out if anyone knows where she is, and get back to you."

"OK my love, bye."

So Antony rang Mary's mother, her sister and about half a dozen names that were in the address book as well as the hospital in Croydon where she worked. Nobody had any idea where she was.

He rang Rosemary again.

"She's still not back and I've rung everybody I can think of, but there is an entry on the calendar in the kitchen. I can't quite read it but anyway it's for three o'clock, more than four hours ago..."

At that moment the doorbell rang. Asking her to hold on Antony went to answer it and found a young policeman and a WPC standing in the doorway looking grim-faced and uncomfortable. (Bizarre as it might seem he did not instantly connect their appearance with his wife's absence. His very first reaction was: 'This time I haven't done anything'!)

"Are you Mr Antony Kilroy?"

"That's right."

"I'm afraid we have some very bad news, sir," said the WPC, "may we come in?"

"Yes, of course."

"It's your wife, sir, Mrs Mary Kilroy. She was involved in a car accident this afternoon in Fulham."

"Are you sure? She works in Croydon. She couldn't be going anywhere near Fulham on her way home."

"There's no mistake I'm afraid, sir."

"How is she? Where is she? I must go and see her."

"We're very sorry to have to tell you, sir," said the WPC, "but the accident was a fatal one."

"Fatal? You mean she's dead? You mean my wife is dead?"

"Yes sir."

"Was anybody else involved?"

"Not as far as we know. It seems she lost control of her car for some reason; it mounted the pavement and struck a concrete bollard. She died in the ambulance on her way to hospital – St Mary's Paddington."

"I see."

"When you're ready sir we'll have to ask you formally to identify the body – sometime later this evening if you could. As it was an accidental death there has to be a post-mortem."

"Yes of course."

"You shouldn't really be on your own at a time like this," said the WPC. "Is there anyone, family member, close friend who could...?"

"Yes, that's OK thank you. I've got a friend – she's on the phone at the moment as a matter of fact..."

The police withdrew and Antony picked up the receiver.

"Are you still there? Did you hear any of that?"

"No, what's happened, my love?"

"It was the police. Mary was killed in a car crash this afternoon."

"Right, I'll be with you in under half an hour."

"Listen Rosemary, you don't have to..."

"Not another word. Ines and Giles will have to cope. I'll just throw a few things into a bag."

"You will drive carefully, won't you?"

This terrible event bursting into his life had suddenly made everything seem precarious and, dazed though he was, Antony could not help but be aware that, if anything were to happen to his Rosemary, it would be a disaster of an altogether different order than the death of his wife. Fortunately he had important things to occupy him during what would otherwise have been an intolerably anxious period of waiting for her arrival. First he rang Mary's sister and broke the news to her as gently as he could, asking her to tell her mother. She asked him if he was OK and he replied that he thought he was still in a state of shock, but just about coping. Next he rang the half dozen friends again to let them know what had happened asking them to pass the news on to anyone else whom they thought ought to know. By the time he had completed this rather waring duty it was almost half an hour since Rosemary had said she was coming. Unable to contain himself he ran downstairs and out into the street where a fine sleety rain was now falling to scan the darkness for the first sign of her approach.

Five minutes passed, the longest and most agonizing five minutes of his life, which he spent trying to convince himself that for both Mary and Rosemary to be killed in car crashes within a few hours of each other would be an inconceivably improbable coincidence. At last he saw approaching headlights up the road flashing at him. Rosemary scrunched to a halt and leapt out of the car. She dropped her bag and they flung their arms round each other on the pavement, clinging in a long tight embrace as if reluctant to let each other go. She was wearing a calf-length fur trimmed black coat over an extremely short and unseasonably skimpy dress with bare legs and high heels.

"Do I look like one of the whores on Tooting Bec Common?"

"Yes, but a very nice one. What do you charge?"

"For you, nothing!"

"That's alright then."

"Listen Tony, seriously," she said tapping his chest with the flat of her hand," if you don't want me to barge into your life more than I am already, just say..."

"You know the answer to that, my darling."

"Right, first things first," she said when they eventually disentangled themselves, "I'll get you something to eat. I bet you haven't had anything have you?"

Antony shook his head.

"Well let's get in. It's fucking freezing out here."

They had some sandwiches and then drove to the hospital for

the identification of the body which proved to be even more disturbing than he had anticipated, for though he recognised the cut and bruised face when the sheet was drawn back, nothing could have been more different than the living wife he had said goodbye to less than twelve hours ago. The loyal and loving companion and housekeeper of nearly a decade was simply gone, utterly irretrievable, and replaced by an inert and useless object, no doubt in the first stages of decay – a 'body' which bore no part in life and was fit only to be disposed of as soon as practicable.

Rosemary, he knew, felt the same. No platitudes from her about how peaceful 'she' looked. "That was pretty ghastly", she whispered, as soon as he had done his duty and they were through the swing doors. "Let's get out of this place. You need a drink."

It was some time before the vividness of that macabre scene began to fade in his mind and although he knew that Mary no longer existed and that that was a simple fact that nothing could alleviate or undo, it did seem more than a little incongruous that he and Rosemary should be huddled together in a bright warm convivial pub while his wife's body might even now be being slit open by the pathologist's knife like so much meat.

It felt reassuringly as if she had been reading his mind when she said as he was returning with a second round of drinks: "You've got nothing to feel guilty about you know."

"Yes I know, but it still doesn't make it any easier."

Rosemary held his hand and left him to his thoughts before speaking again. "Tony, this may sound a strange question, but why did you get married?"

"How do you mean?"

"Not just Mary I mean, but anyone. I was so surprised when I heard knowing how important solitude was for you as a writer."

"You think I liked living on my own? Perhaps you're right."

"And why Mary? I wouldn't have thought she was your type."

"Well it was Mary's idea of course, but she was attractive, and I suppose I thought, as I'd lost you, what the hell... and she was very good to me. Yet you know, somehow, part of me at least, always knew that one day we would get together; only I could never quite imagine how."

Rosemary had already rung from the pub to ask how the children were and explain to Ines, and briefly to Giles, that she would be staying at Antony's until further notice. When they returned to the flat it was taken absolutely for granted, without a word being said, that she should unpack and hang her clothes in his room before having a bath.

That night they made love for the first time since Florence and nothing could stop it being a celebration of the fact that they had at long last finally come together and that nothing in the future would ever be allowed to part them. Not that there were any big words or declarations – they simply started living together; and when they eventually stirred the following morning having both overslept, they had breakfast in bed and began to plan their day as if it were the most normal thing in the world.

Antony rang the bookshop to explain why he wouldn't be coming in and Rosemary rang Ines – Giles had already gone to work – to speak to the children. Then Antony spoke to the children which took considerably longer, after which they drove to Stamford Hill to see Mary's sister, who fortunately in the immediate aftermath of yesterday's terrible shock was taking care of her mother.

Although he was careful to introduce Rosemary as 'Mary's best friend' and say all the right things, he was aware that both women were more than a little taken aback by the obvious intimacy and complicity between them, though he did not realise quite how bad an impression they had made. They then went back to see the parish priest at Mary's church and fixed the funeral to allow time for the post-mortem and for the convenience of relations who were coming from Ireland, then on to the undertakers.

The result of the post-mortem proved something of a surprise for, besides the obvious cause of death, cervical cancer in an advanced stage was detected.

"I can't believe it," said Antony. "She was a nurse. How could she not have known? She didn't say anything to you did she?"

"She wouldn't've done that! She was very wary of me really."

"Really?"

"You're not surprised, are you?"

"No, I suppose not."

"Perhaps she did know and was keeping it secret, or suppose she had just found out..."

"Go on."

"Well, you said you didn't know what she was doing in Fulham. Perhaps she was coming back from a hospital appointment when she crashed and she'd just had bad news. You said there was something on the calendar for that afternoon."

"Yes, here it is: Morton, Morden?"

"Why not Marsden, you know, the cancer hospital, that's in Chelsea isn't it? She might well have been coming back via Fulham."

"That would certainly explain a lot of things. I think she must have had worries before but I still don't understand why she didn't tell me."

Twice a day Rosemary rang home and spoke to Ines and the children, and Giles if he was there. Her message was that she was much too busy helping Antony with the funeral arrangements as well as all the other consequences of Mary's sad death – the death certificate, the will, the disposal of her personal effects and so forth – to think of returning before the funeral. But in truth such matters occupied very little of their time or attention which, as Antony had also taken a week off from the shop, was overwhelmingly given over simply to enjoying being a real couple, living together and sharing everything.

Although he had told Rosemary that he did not feel guilty – indeed he was in principle opposed to what he considered such an essentially futile and self-destructive emotion – the very way in which they had become a couple so easily, so naturally, so totally, with Mary not to mention Giles, simply dropping out of the picture, did make him when he thought about it, somewhat uncomfortable. The core of it was that Mary's death had been so convenient that it was important that he convinced himself that he had never wanted or hoped for it, even unconsciously. There was no doubt of course that she couldn't have come back into his life now, there was just no place for her, but that didn't mean, so he tried to tell himself, that he was pleased she was dead.

The funeral mass at the Sacred Heart Church, Edge Hill was followed by the burial in Wimbledon Cemetery, after which Rosemary had organized an elaborate finger buffet back at Antony's flat. In the church it was notable that, as at a wedding, Mary's family, friends and work colleagues sat on one side of the aisle with Antony in the front row next to Rosemary on the other side. The rest of their bench was occupied by the children, with Ines and Giles at the far end. This was the first time he had seen his wife for a week, but so absorbed was she in whispering to Antony that he barely succeeded in attracting her attention, though Antony as usual kept making faces at the children. Behind them were a few members of the Old Boys' Association of Antony's school, the manager of the bookshop and a contingent of Rosemary's girlfriends, none of whom seemed surprised at the obvious intimacy between her and Antony; indeed there were some encouraging looks when either of them looked round. The service itself by Antony's special request was in Latin, which he thought might add a certain extra dignity to the proceedings, an arrangement resented by Mary's family as high-handed chiefly because he had omitted to consult them.

At the buffet afterwards, if Antony was the host, Rosemary was very much and in every way the hostess, plying people with food and drink and trying to get them to mix as at a party. She was unsuccessful in this with Mary's family who, though consuming more than their share, looked extremely uncomfortable and kept entirely to themselves. Apart from the Latin business, the way in which Rosemary and Antony were apparently flaunting their relationship 'with Mary hardly cold in her grave' was more than they could endure. Even seen in the best light, they felt it was tasteless and offensive. No wonder then that Antony never heard from any of them again, not even so much as a Christmas card.

During the proceedings Giles made several hesitant attempts to ascertain from Rosemary exactly when she was coming home, but was rebuffed.

"Not now Giles," she snapped, "I told you we'll talk about it later."

"But I just thought, now it's over... The kids are missing you."

"Giles, this simply isn't the time."

It was the middle of the afternoon; Antony and Rosemary saw off 'their' guests, those who were speaking to them that is, including Giles, Ines and the children. Alone at last they cleared up and then – went to the pictures.

That night in bed Rosemary said to Antony: "You know I've got to go back sooner or later. We must keep a stable environment for the children. Don't you agree? After all Emily is only seven, Imogen five and Raggy's three. We can't expose them to all the upheaval of a divorce can we? Besides you need a haven for your writing." (Now it was Rosemary's turn to defend her domestic status quo, yet it must be admitted that an unruly little devil suggested to him that what she was really attached to, was her more than comfortable lifestyle and her two attractive and valuable homes all financed by her husband. But he dismissed this malign voice. What she said made perfect sense. How could he possibly disagree? And he did need a haven for his writing. She was quite right about that.)

"Yes, of course, but you'll have to keep it going with Giles. Can you manage to do that?"

"Easily, because now I've got you, haven't I?"

The next day Antony went back to work and Rosemary went back to Giles and the children, though significantly she left behind some of her clothes, two pairs of shoes and a pair of slippers, a toothbrush and a dressing gown! Giles, who was only too delighted to have her back, did not go in for any complaints or recriminations. He had told himself that there could be nothing untoward in his wife's prolonged absence. Rosemary, he recognised, felt protective towards Antony in his sudden bereavement and she also happened to admire him and find him amusing. They were friends, good mates; the very idea of anything else was out of the question, ridiculous. And how could they possibly have embarked on an affair immediately after Mary's death? Anyway all three of them were friends. Rosemary's return in any case was sufficient in itself to banish all such concerns for the time being.

Giles's joy and relief were however soon mitigated by the realisation that Rosemary was determined to go on 'looking after' Antony now that he was a widower and apparently incapable of taking care of himself. Thus Antony almost invariably came to lunch on Saturday and Sunday – the length of his visit depending on how the writing was going but the kids always wanted him to stay as long as possible – and to supper on

Wednesday. If the Whitby-Brownes went to Sussex at the weekend Antony always went with them. Mondays and Fridays Rosemary reserved for her friends, an arrangement which could always be changed if necessary, but on Tuesdays and Thursdays she drove to the flat to see if Antony was coping alright and to cook him something, or so she explained it to Giles – in fact for rather hurried sex followed by a bath and a meal in what became their favourite trattoria in the High Street.

In spite of all this Giles was firmly convinced that there was 'nothing going on' chiefly because, as he reasoned, if there were Rosemary would scarcely be so blatantly obvious about it. He knew she was cleverer than him but that beggared belief, and even though Antony had practically become one of the family, he seemed much more interested in the children. When he spoke to Rosemary it was generally to tease or make fun of her, though surprisingly she did not appear to resent this. In fact he was continually surprised by what Antony got away with. He knew all too well that he would have got his head bitten off for much less. Be that as it might, the one thing they didn't seem to be, as far as Giles was concerned, was romantically attached.

Ines however was not so easily fooled. She had had her suspicions since Florence and partly because she had something of a crush on Giles whom she considered a perfect English gentleman and partly because of religious scruples, she was not happy. Events since Mary's funeral seemed amply to have confirmed her suspicions and she had recently said to Rosemary that she was 'not very pleased with the way things were at the moment'. Rosemary pretended not to understand what she was talking about, though she knew all too well. This presented her with a ticklish problem. Ines was very good at her job and very helpful and reliable; she also got on well with the children.

She discussed the situation with Antony whose advice was clear: "She'll make more trouble if you sack her and in any case you've got no reason that you can give for doing so. Much better keep her on side."

Accordingly she raised the matter with Giles: "Darling I've been thinking, perhaps we ought to pay Ines a bit more – she's a treasure and we don't want to lose her do we?"

"Why, is she unhappy?"

"No, of course not. But I'm sure she would appreciate it and she has more to do these days. Besides a lot of nannies round her get more."

"Whatever you think, my love."

When Rosemary gave her the good news that she was raising her wages by fifty per cent she was careful to add: "Everything really is alright you know, Ines."

Whether she was convinced or not was another matter but there were no more mutterings. It was however tacitly accepted among Rosemary's circle of friends that she, Antony and Giles constituted something of a ménage à trois which in those more tolerant days seemed unobjectionable, interesting rather than in any way scandalous, particularly as Antony was a writer.

One spring evening down at Bosham after the weekend guests had left, and Antony was reducing Emily and Imogen to hysterical laughter upstairs with a bedtime comic song, Rosemary announced: "Tony's going to move back to his mother's old house in Merton." (She didn't say Raynes Park!) "He's getting rid of the last of the tenants at the end of the month; do you think that's a good idea?"

"Oh very," said Giles, with some interest and enthusiasm lowering his Sunday paper, "he did well to hang onto that place with property prices the way they're going." (Giles of course was well aware that Merton was hardly a mile or more from Antony's flat in Wimbledon and even a little nearer to Leatherhead; but a move from the flat where he had lived with Mary back to his old family home suggested that he was now ready to begin a new life and would be less of a permanent guest.) "How soon do you think he'll put his flat on the market?"

"Not straight away. He's got to do up the house first. He's going to knock through and make some of the rooms bigger, redecorate from top to bottom, put in a new kitchen, and build a conservatory across the back. There's a lot of work to do. He's already applied for planning permission."

"Good for him. I suppose he can afford it now with all the money he's raking in from his books."

Rosemary did not add that these plans were largely hers but Giles soon discovered that the redecoration of the Wimbledon flat prior to putting it on the market, and then the total refurbishment and re-equipping of Antony's family home in Raynes Park with new windows, doors, carpets and furniture, so that virtually nothing remained to recall the miserable environment of his childhood and the years with his mother – except of course the train set in the attic – was to engross his wife's attention fairly completely through that spring and summer until early October (builders being what they were) when Antony was finally able to move in. Indeed such was the extent of her involvement that for the first time Giles took his summer holidays separately from the family, sailing with some friends to Ireland and back.

Times were changing. Rising property values and increasing affluence were having their effect on the post-war dinginess of Fullwell Avenue though none of the neighbouring properties was as expensively and tastefully improved as number twenty-five. If for the sake of proximity to Rosemary and the children he was obliged for the time being to live in the London suburbs, Antony reasoned that he might as well make himself as comfortable as possible. But there was more to it than that. Returning to his family home now that he was successful and in control of his destiny had the effect of exorcising, of healing his past of all its bitterness and frustration and making his life seem whole and coherent at last. He was thankful now that he had preserved the link with 25 Fullwell Avenue, and not only for financial reasons. The house offered him the best of both worlds – a base in which he could live and work alone, together with the possibility of seeing Rosemary and the children more or less whenever he wanted.

During the period of the upheaval he felt he had not been able to get down to prolonged serious work but what time he had was employed in preparing some children's stories for publication. As they were based on tales he had made up to entertain Rosemary's three, they practically wrote themselves. The first dedicated to Emily and called *The Magic House,* was about an apparently normal house in a normal street that could change its shape and move through time and space; the second, for Imogen, *The S.S. Bountiful*, concerned a group of children who slowly piece by piece build an ocean liner out of discarded household goods and sail off round the world; and the last, for Richard Antony Giles, *The Underground Empire*, was the tale of a little boy who tries to dig down from a flower bed in his garden to Australia but finds a whole subterranean civilization instead.

Though with every month Raggy seemed to be growing more and more obviously like him in appearance, Antony did not find him as easy to get close to as his half-sisters. The little boy was precociously intelligent with a keen sense of the ridiculous and it was easy to make him laugh but, although it was natural to him to charm and entertain, he was more introverted than the girls and apparently wanted admiration and applause rather than affection from his 'godfather' and the world at large. Had he been like that, Antony wondered, when he was Raggy's age? Perhaps they were too alike. Nevertheless he seemed quite prepared to be cuddled by his mother and sisters. Thus while

Antony was delighted that his son was enjoying the female affection he had been so deprived of as a child, he could not help but feel on occasion a mild pang of envy and exclusion.

When Richard Antony Giles joined his sisters in full-time schooling at the age of five, Rosemary's visits to Antony could take place during the day rather than in the evening – he was working on a long novel now and only part-time at the bookshop – and though he almost always spent weekends and holidays with Rosemary and Giles en famille, he was less of a presence with them during the week, something that Giles could only welcome, albeit silently. In spite of these easier circumstances there were times when Rosemary, in bed with Antony, suddenly became aware that she was late for the school run and would have to dash off without even taking the time to dress, clad only in an all-covering raincoat, to collect her unsuspecting children from school. Happy days!

IV

That October day when Antony at last reclaimed his family seat had a significance which for him far transcended his own brief existence. After inspecting the interior of the house he made his way to the secluded stone seat surrounded by trees touched by the first tints of autumn – his favourite place on the whole estate – and took in the scene in the mellow afternoon sunlight. The lands, the homes, the history – what a romance it was, what a story, what twists and turns of fortune, what vicissitudes, not least in the twentieth century when the last of that heritage was almost lost for good. His grandfather, who had failed to return to his wife after the Great War, settled in France and spent most of his time on the Riviera. Having already disposed of all the outlying farms, in 1923 he finally sold the Hall, which had stood on land held by the family since soon after the Conquest, to pay his gambling debts and died eighteen months later.

His father had left England to farm in Africa in the Thirties but Antony had only dim and incoherent memories of him and his world having returned to London with his mother as soon as the Second World War was over, aged only six. His parents subsequently divorced and his mother remarried. He never saw his father again; he died in Kenya in 1956. Antony was sent to boarding schools from the age of eight, but the one sustaining passion of his lonely childhood and adolescence was the House of Beauregard and his inheritance. It was a passion all the more intense in that no one around him seemed at all interested. It had all the allure of the most extravagant fantasy and yet it was true. No wonder that his school books were doodled over with coronets.

Brede Hall had meanwhile become a convent for French nuns, then when they moved to smaller premises in Bexhill, an agricultural college (as well as serving as a military headquarters during the Second World War). The college had moved to more modern buildings in the early seventies leaving the old Hall with no buyer in sight. The local authority purchased the estate intending to demolish the house and 'develop' the site, but they were frustrated by the fact that the place, ramshackle though it might be, was a Grade I listed building containing as it did traces at least of the architecture of every period from early Plantagenet to late Victorian; the ensemble could not be said to be beautiful but, lying in a hidden fold of the Cotswolds, it did have a unique charm and a sense of rightness reflecting centuries of extension, restoration, refurbishment and adaptation by owners who never had quite enough money in hand to knock the house down and rebuild it from scratch according to their conception of the latest style.

But having withstood siege and fire as well as the less than successful improvisations of its proprietors down the ages it was now, in the later twentieth century, faced with the prospect of slow dereliction. Nor was there any question of Antony, then a freelance journalist with only a modest private income, being able to buy it back on behalf of the family. All he could manage was discreetly to acquire one of the lodges, which were not down for demolition, as a sort of vantage point from which to keep an eye on the place. Then Antony met up with a very bright young History don whom he had known as an undergraduate and invited him to stay during a vacation to put some sort of order into the family papers which were still in his possession.

One never to be forgotten spring morning he burst into Antony's study in a state of some excitement: "Did you know that there was an entail on the property when your grandfather sold it – an entail created by his father and lasting for five generations. Look!"

"What does that mean exactly?"

"It means quite simply that it wasn't his to sell."

"But how did he get away with it?"

"Well he appears to have used a firm of English lawyers in Paris, not the family solicitors. Perhaps they didn't know about the entail, perhaps he didn't. Anyway he was desperate for money wasn't he? But that's irrelevant. Don't you see what this means? If the entail still holds, the estate is yours!

Antony was determined not to become too euphoric too quickly. In any case aristocrats didn't go in for euphoria. "But perhaps he broke the entail or cancelled it or revoked it or whatever you call it."

"That would be an immensely complicated business and there's absolutely nothing about it in the papers. They're all here and they record an entirely straightforward sale. It's early days of course, but I'd say that your right to the property is unassailable."

So it was, after legal proceedings that had taken less than six months (it seemed that the council had rather lost interest in the site and they put up a half-hearted case for ownership) that he, Antony James Arthur Kilroy de Verrayne Beauregard, ninth Duke of Castlemayne, Marquess of Everland, Earl of Longstaffe and Baron Brede and Beauregard, came to be savouring the repossession, against all the odds, of all that remained of his family's ancient patrimony. What if all he had of the old furnishings, apart from a handful of rather battered family portraits which used to hang in the long gallery, was a Victorian roll-top desk, a dinner service marked with family arms, a small collection of silver, two carpets, a cupboard full of photograph albums, a trunk full of documents and two suits of armour – all of which were in store when his father died – he was determined to do whatever it might to hang onto the house, to restore it and to ensure, insofar as he could, that henceforth Brede Hall would remain in his family's hands forever. 'Forever' of course was a relative term. How many of his ancestors had promised, even sworn, to secure the lands of the House of Beauregard with varying degrees of success. Nevertheless in all of that noble line there could scarcely ever have been a greater and more significant day than this!

Though not by any means the grandest, Brede Hall, the last remaining of the family seats, was also the first. Geoffroi de Beauregard, a Norman knight who did not literally come over with the Conqueror but five years later, was granted the manor in 1071 and then proceeded to marry the lady who would have been the Saxon heiress of the property, an arrangement that occurred more often than is generally supposed. Why it happened in this case was not clear, but the marriage had the effect of ensuring a continuity of ownership stretching back generations, and possibly even centuries, into Anglo-Saxon England – a rare distinction indeed.

Geoffroi was described in some of the earliest records as 'cueilleur du roy' variously translated as the king's gatherer, arrester or picker – no one seemed to know exactly which. But whether his services were agricultural, military or legal they were evidently rewarded. It also seemed that in the course of time the hereditary office of 'cueilleur du roy' attached to the family, had generated the name 'Kilroy' – it was not for nothing that Antony had devoted so much of his life to family research. And if for all their quarterings and titles the Beauregards had not always been wise or lucky, showing an unfortunate and recurrent tendency to pick the losing side, they had so far enjoyed down the centuries one almost unparalleled piece of good fortune, that of always producing a male heir – son, grandson, nephew or cousin – to carry on the line; hence one explanation of the family motto: 'jamais défaillant'!

The Beauregards supported Matilda rather than Stephen in the anarchic period when they were fighting for the crown, but managed to hang onto their lands and prospered when her son, the Count of Anjou, came to the throne as Henry II, acquiring a barony. However Baron Beauregard, by joining his fortunes to Richard the Lionheart and going off on the crusade with him, antagonised Prince John and, when he became King, the Beauregard lands were confiscated and he was forced to go into exile in France. The family fortunes were more than restored under Henry III however, together with a second barony bearing the title of their original manor of Brede and they naturally never wavered in their support for the King against Simon de Montfort.

The sixth Baron Beauregard distinguished himself in the first phase of the Hundred Years' War and was rewarded by an earldom by Edward III. But the family stayed loyal to Richard II to the very end and were consequently out of favour with Henry IV. Though the third Earl of Longstaffe fought valiantly in the

Agincourt campaign, true to form, the Beauregards somehow contrived to be almost always on the wrong side in the Wars of the Roses ending up as very late converts to the cause of the House of York. No less than three members of the family were with Richard III at Bosworth when he went down in defeat to Henry Tudor.

The Tudor age was generally a lean time for the family. First because they despised this parvenu and scarcely royal dynasty and the new men who served it – after all had they not been proud tenants of mighty Beauregard Castle on the Marches when the Tudors were petty Welsh squires! – and second because of a partiality for the Old Faith, albeit based more on a firm attachment to venerable tradition as well as a detestation of the Protestant mentality which encouraged every Tom, Dick and Harry to read the Bible in English and voice his opinion on religion, rather than any special loyalty to the Apostolic See on theological grounds. This partiality never went quite so far as open opposition and rebellion – the eighth Earl had, after all, accepted from the King at the Dissolution, Everland Abbey in Gloucestershire with its orchards, farmland and rolling pastures stretching almost to the Severn. Nevertheless the Beauregards, unlike the Howards, wisely kept their heads down in these dangerous times and attended court as little as possible. Under Elizabeth, the tenth Earl – having in any case little desire to rub shoulders with the new nobility of Cecils, Thynnes, Cavendishes, Russells and the like – spent most of his time building the magnificent Longstaffe Hall in Wiltshire, outdoing even Hardwick in its profusion of glazed widows and chimney pots. The money came largely from his fortunate marriage to the heiress of the ancient de Verrayne family but needless to say the Great Queen never included it in any of her progresses.

With the Stuarts, it was different. While the de Verrayne Beauregards were disappointed in James I, the twelfth Earl made Charles I's quarrel with what he regarded as the rabble of Puritan lawyers that made up the so-called House of Commons very much his own and was vocal in denouncing their impertinent demands and remonstrances. His strong support for the Personal Rule was rewarded by his being created first Marquess of Everland by a grateful sovereign. A splendid masque was held at Longstaffe Hall in July 1637 to celebrate his elevation, but unfortunately the banks of candles illuminating the ingeniously elaborate theatrical spectacle started a fire which took hold so rapidly and so fiercely that it could not be extinguished until it had reduced the whole house to a shell with nothing remaining but the walls. Thus the de Verrayne inheritance and much more besides went up in flames. At the time with the way the country was going, the disastrous fire that summer on what was supposed to be an evening of celebration seemed peculiarly ominous. The great house was never to rise again, for before the Marquess could even contemplate the huge expense of rebuilding, the King had raised his standard at Nottingham and the Civil War began.

Being such a prominent champion of the royalist cause brought the Beauregard family close to ruin. Beauregard Castle, whose towers had dominated the Welsh borderland for more than four centuries, was slighted by the New Model Army and reduced to rubble, and although Amelia, the first Marchioness, valiantly and successfully defended Brede Hall against a Parliamentary siege, the property became derelict during the seven years when the Beauregard family went into exile in France and subsequently Holland with the future Charles II after his defeat at Worcester in 1653.

The Restoration, if only briefly, raised the family to a position of prestige and influence at court and in the counsels of the realm, that their predecessors had not enjoyed since the Middle Ages. The Merry Monarch was a frequent visitor to Everland

Abbey, and to Brede Hall, when it had been brought to life again and a new wing added, and the beleaguered James II created the second Marquess, Duke of Castlemayne. But in spite of this signal honour the new Duke did not follow the King into exile in 1688 as his father had done over thirty years before.

The Beauregards, though never active Jacobites, despised the House of Hanover even more than they had the Tudors, and deterred by the long and, as it seemed at the time, permanent ascendancy of the Whigs in national politics, took little further part in the public life of the country. In fact they came to the capital so seldom that the fourth Duke, who divided his time between the family estates and a palazzo in Tuscany, sold Castlemayne House, the family's London residence in the Strand, in 1786. The only speech he ever made in the House of Lords was against the 1832 Reform Bill, and its passage so vexed him that he took to his bed and died a few months later – or so it was said, but he was in fact eighty-one years old!

The fifth Duke, who succeeded his grandfather in 1832, was to become the very model of an earnest Victorian, a complete contrast to that old roué notorious for his extravagance and mistresses. He even restored the chapel at Brede Hall and gave it over to Catholic worship for the first time since a brief period in the reign of James II, and later financed the construction of several churches in the new Gothic revival style. But his first endeavour had been to pay the debts that he inherited from the profligacy of his grandfather, who in pursuit of a life of pure self-indulgence had not scrupled to sell off family treasures including four van Dycks from the dining room at Brede and, most notoriously, in order to finance the purchase of a thoroughbred which in the event just failed to win the Derby, the so-called Beauregard Chalice. Believed by some to be the Holy Grail itself, it was in fact Byzantine in origin and probably brought to the West after the sack of Constantinople in the

Fourth Crusade. The family received it from Edward II after the suppression of the Templars, as a special mark of favour from a monarch who needed all the friends he could get, sometime in the second decade of the fourteenth century. It was now in the British Museum.

The fifth Duke found himself obliged to sell not only his grandfather's palatial Italian villa but Everland Abbey as well, disposing of it to cousins of his mother, so that although it remained in the family it passed out of the hands of the male line and was to all intents and purposes lost to the de Verrayne Beauregards. Thus by the accession of Queen Victoria, the Dukes of Castlemayne were left, after centuries of expansion and contraction, with nothing but their original estate of Brede, for all its charm hardly a ducal seat, which had started life as a mere fortified manor house.

The fifth Duke's life was visited by tragedy. His beautiful, much painted but flighty Duchess, whom he adored – the Lady Alice Trefoil, or 'Alice the Bolter' as she became known, evidently tiring of her worthy husband's attentions, ran off with her riding instructor abandoning their young son and daughter. He also was eventually succeeded by his grandson (his son, Lord Everland, a leading campaigner for sanitary improvements for the poorer classes, having died in the great cholera outbreak of 1854 when his son, the future Duke was only four years old).

The sixth Duke, Antony's great-grandfather, had little interest in religion or social reform (on his accession he promptly turned the chapel into a billiard room). Lacking the steady influence of his father and spoilt by his doting mother, he seemed in character more of a throwback to the fourth Duke and to his notorious grandmother, Lady Alice. He succeeded to the title in 1875, but not before he had brought yet more grief to the old Duke's declining years by running off to Buenos Aires with a Spanish dancer who had been the toast of Second Empire Paris before the fall of Napoleon III. He only returned to England when he received news of his grandfather's death, and subsequently married a famous society beauty several years older than himself. They started a large family beginning with Antony's grandfather Henry, who was born in 1879.

All seemed to be going well until, in 1885, a certain Señora Miranda Ramirez de Verrayne Beauregard arrived in London with a handsome fair-haired boy of ten, whom she claimed was the heir to the dukedom. There was no doubt that he bore an unmistakable resemblance to the Duke and that his mother was indeed the Spanish dancer with whom he had once eloped. She was also to produce evidence that they had married in Buenos Aires so that it seemed as if the English Duchess was not really his wife and all her children illegitimate.

To say that these claims caused a sensation in London society, and indeed in the whole country, would be an understatement. The resulting law suit, heard in the Court of Common Pleas, proved even more than dramatic than the Titchbourne case. Prior to the action the majority opinion was that she had justice on her side and would win. Even the Prince of Wales, who had no time for the Beauregard family in any case, let it be known that he was inclined to believe the alluring Señora's claim. But while she seemed to be captivating all hearts, including those of the all-male jury, with her dignified bearing and mature beauty during the first week of the trial, the Beauregards were not to be so easily thwarted. Documentary evidence was produced that her marriage to the future Duke had only lasted two years and that he had subsequently divorced her for desertion in, of all places, Colorado; a fact of which Señora Ramirez claimed to be unaware. But the coup de théâtre that finally destroyed her case, brilliantly orchestrated by Sir Rufus Cleverly-Pritchett, the most celebrated advocate of the time, occurred of the morning of the ninth day:

"I put it to you, Señora Ramirez," Sir Rufus began, "that by the time your son was born, you were living under the protection, shall we say, of a Canadian businessman in Montreal."

"That is a lie!"

"Very well, Señora, I will call a witness to refresh your memory. Call Charles Scott McKenzie..."

When the witness entered the box a gasp went round the crowded court, for everyone could see that he was the father of the boy who sat in the front row of the gallery. The unfortunate Señora Ramirez, who had not imagined that the long arm of the Duke was capable of stretching as far as Canada and suborning her former lover, fainted. That very afternoon after hearing McKenzie's evidence the judge instructed the jury to find against her claim. Señora Ramirez returned to Paris still protesting that her son had been cheated of his rights, dying there in obscurity ten years later.

Victory in this case however did not solve all the sixth Duke's problems. Once again the debts piled up; all but two of his children were girls and the youngest, Lucius, seemed to be interested in nothing but dressing up in female clothing and performing in amateur theatricals. The junior branches of the family were all childless apart from a smattering of daughters, so all hopes for the solvency and indeed the very survival of the family rested on the elder son, Henry. This sensitive, reserved and serious-minded boy, much closer to his mother than his father who did not understand him, was at her insistence tutored at home rather than being sent to Eton and Oxford. It was arranged that as soon as possible after he came of age, he should be married to the Honourable Pamela Frances Harding, heiress of one of the local county families and a healthy horsey girl considerably more robust in every way than her intended husband.

A great ball was organized at Brede to mark his twenty-first birthday at which the engagement was to be announced, the most splendid occasion the old place had seen for a generation. The Hall blazed with lights and the terrace with torches; a vast marquee half covered the south lawn and the unaccustomed sounds of revelry reverberated far into the close August night, even to Beacon Hill, the highest point in the Home Park, where following the centuries old tradition a bonfire blazed and an ox was being roasted for the tenantry. (Bonfires had always been lit for the accession of a new Duke, the coming of age of his heir and on occasions of national rejoicing from the defeat of the Armada to the relief of Mafeking.) The evening was to culminate in an elaborate firework display organized by a London firm.

Unfortunately this particular son and heir happened to have reached a crisis in his young life. Over the past two years he had grown close to the daughter of his tutor, a Miss Virginia Cutler, a very independent young woman of about his own age who was a chemistry student at London University. To someone of Henry's background, aristocratic and unusually sheltered, she was a revelation. In the vacation when she came to visit her father they went off on bicycling trips together and discussed socialism, women's rights and the works of new writers like Bernard Shaw and H. G. Wells. Inevitably he fell in love.

Henry was fully sensible of all the hopes and responsibilities incumbent upon him as the future seventh Duke and head of the House of Beauregard, but when it came to it he found that he simply could not give up Virginia and declare his love for the Honourable Pamela Frances in spite of what he knew would be his mother's anguish and his father's uncomprehending and intransigent rage. So with deep misgivings on both sides the couple hatched a plan by correspondence. On the night of the ball under cover of the festivities Henry was to leave the house and make his way through the woods to the edge of the estate, where there was a halt on the Great Western Railway that ran from London to Birkenhead. Here, where the trains invariably slowed right down to walking pace even when they did not actually stop to set down passengers for the Hall, at approximately 9.38pm, he would climb aboard the 7.30pm from Paddington on which Virginia would be waiting for him in a second class compartment (it was against her principles to go first class) with a flask of coffee and sandwiches and the couple would thenceforth never again be parted. They intended to get off at Chester and after several changes of train, arrive at Gretna Green, where in the time-honoured fashion they would be married and face the consequences of what they had done, together.

Henry had underestimated his father who had recently thought the boy's behaviour odd, not to say suspicious, and was having him watched and his letters intercepted with the help of the compliant postmistress in the village of Brede, most of whose family had worked at the Hall or on the estate for generations. Thus, when on that fateful night Henry was in sight of the train and could actually see Virginia at a lighted window of her carriage (though she could not see him thirty yards away in the darkness), he found his way barred by the head keeper and his two well built young assistants who, with due deference and the minimum of force, led him back to the ball as the train inexorably gathered pace and bore Virginia away from him forever.

In the end it was with a strange relief that Henry accepted his destiny. Virginia too, in spite of her modern ideas, had been increasingly daunted, as the decisive moment approached, by the enormous responsibility of luring a young man she loved and respected away from his parents, his family, his world and all he had been brought up to be and do. The matter was irrevocably sealed by Henry's father having a severe stroke a few hours later from which he never really recovered. Naturally Henry blamed himself for this and he knew that his mother did too. The old

Duke died sixth months after the Queen and it was thus Henry as seventh Duke of Castlemayne who paid homage to the new King Edward VII at his coronation in August 1902. He then duly married the Honourable Pamela Frances who after several false starts and one miscarriage occasioned by falling off her horse while hunting, at last produced a son in 1909, to much local rejoicing. The Duchess was well liked and the Duke practical, energetic and open to new ideas, but with a sound head for financial management. In spite of the demagogic antics of Mr David Lloyd George, who seemed determined to pick a quarrel with the peerage for his own political aggrandizement, everything, at Brede at least, seemed to point to the onset of the most stable and prosperous period in the whole history of the Beauregard family.

Then came the Great War. As Colonel of the local regiment, the Duke of Castlemayne's Light Infantry, Henry saw it as his duty to serve with 'his' men on the Western Front. His brother Lucius, who had a staff job and spent the War in various picturesque chateaux well to the rear of the action, was killed in a German air raid in 1917. But though Henry survived the War physically unscathed, the terrible slaughter on the Somme, the years of trench warfare, the futile sacrifice of millions of young lives in pursuit of military stalemate, depressed him profoundly and, as with so many others, undermined his faith in the old certainties and values he had been brought up to maintain. Perhaps Virginia had been right after all, though after those four years he could find no more faith in her Brave New World than in the Old Order that the War seemed to have destroyed. In any case there was no question for Henry of returning to Brede Hall and resuming a life which would have seemed a pretence and a charade, however difficult it might be to explain the decision to his family. Without making any great melodramatic show of it he lost all heart and moral compass and began drinking heavily.

So, although in contrast to so many landed families, the male line of the de Verrayne Beauregards did not actually perish in the Great War, it came to much the same thing. Their household gods were scattered, and Brede was abandoned. The eighth Duke, Miles, lived most of his life in the scandal-ridden, pleasure-seeking society of wealthy and upper crust expatriates in the White Highlands of Kenya, not even returning to England for the War, or the Coronations of 1937 and 1953, and when Antony became the ninth Duke of Castlemayne at the age of seventeen, very few people seemed to care.

When Antony was eventually able to move into his ancestral home he found that only about a quarter of it was habitable; but he had spent a lifetime planning what he would do if, by some extraordinary chance, this moment ever came. Besides the progressive restoration of the house to its earlier glory with the aid of old photos and plans, he intended to revive the walled garden, currently part car park, part junk yard, giving it back to fruit and vegetable cultivation, and to restock the park with deer. But his most cherished project was to rebuild, and make into three storey accommodation, the ruined tower – all that remained of the early Norman manor which stood twenty yards from the house as it was now constituted – joining it to the to the rest of the property by a discreet and tasteful modern gallery of glass and stone. This would be his contribution to the changes that successive owners had made down the centuries and he saw it, in a sense which he found very satisfying, as restoring the integrity of the house, for however much its fabric and appearance might have been altered with time there was a continuity which made it the same place, not unlike that of a living body which persists even though its constituent cells are constantly being renewed.

Even if it meant having to share his home with builders for a generation and resorting to every kind of expedient to raise the cash, he had achieved the essential. He was there, he was staying, he had reunited his august title with his ancient home, the past with the present and the future, healing and restoring the destiny of his family and ensuring that the last sixty years of exile and desolation were not the end of the story but just one more comparatively brief episode in the ever continuing history of the Beauregards, lords of the manor of Brede, 'cueilleurs du roy' and lineal descendants of the Saxon thanes who held those lands before them. And now at last he was able to try at least to assume a role that he had aspired to all his life, that of grandly phlegmatic and imperturbable aristocrat secure in his estates. It was a pity that he didn't have the limitless funds to go with it. Perhaps he should marry an heiress...

V

The five years after the move back into his family home were to prove in some ways, even though he was hardly aware of it at the time, the happiest and certainly the busiest and most productive of his life. Though he and Rosemary were constrained to keep their relationship an unacknowledgable secret, he was able to combine creative solitude, which she was happy for him to enjoy, with a ready-made family waiting to receive him whenever he needed to relax. His children's books were, rather to his surprise, a huge success. Not only did they sell better than his adult novels, but stories for that age group with their larger print and copious illustrations – he was fortunate that his agent found him a very sympathetic illustrator who added a new dimension to the text – were only about a tenth of the length of a book for grown-ups. It was money for old rope! *The Magic House* was turned into a cartoon, something for which his artist deserved much of the credit, and there was even talk of making Richard Antony Giles's tale *The Underground Empire* into a big budget feature film with American backing. But Antony was dubious about it. He made various conditions and was quite relieved when the plans fell through.

His major work during these years was a sequence of novels – more pretentious reviewers used the term 'roman-fleuve' – of almost unprecedented scope, chronicling the story of a noble family from the Norman Conquest right up to the twentieth century: 'a never quite broken thread, running all the way through the rich brocade of English history' as he liked to put it. When he really got into his stride he was producing a three hundred page volume every six months or so. The whole thing was so vivid in his mind and it poured out of him at such a rate that the main problem was getting it down quickly enough. First to appear was *A Saxon Marriage*, then *The Beauregard Chalice*, followed by *Lords of the Marches* and *A Castle in France*. Afterwards there came *The Upstart Welshman* (about the Wars of the Roses and Henry VII), *Dangerous Times* (about the Reformation years and their sequel), *The King's Companion* (about the Civil War period), *The First Duke, The Brink of Ruin, The Spanish Claimant, Brede Hall Deserted,* and finally *Homecoming*.

The Beauregard Chronicles as the sequence was called were almost embarrassingly well received. The twelve volumes of that constantly unfolding story, appearing at regular intervals and awaited with ever-growing eagerness, became something of a publishing sensation and established Antony as a major and unique figure in contemporary English writing. Those who made slighting comparisons with the historical romances of Georgette Heyer and Anya Seton, or tried to dismiss them as a dated throwback to works like Hugh Walpole's *Herries Chronicles* were not heeded. There was some muttering about the 'facility' of the writing, prompted chiefly by the speed with which the volumes were produced and the dramatic immediacy of the narrative, but nobody was really able to suggest how, in their own terms, they could be significantly improved.

In fact the Chronicles acquired something of a cult status and in those pre-email and internet days he was constantly getting fifteen page letters from students at obscure American campuses, asking him unanswerable questions about minor characters and details of locations, revealing a minute knowledge of English history, to say nothing of his own story in all its ramifications, that far exceeded his own! He found it very strange that he had been able to create a vast domain, now quite independent of himself, in which everyone was free to wander and able to find things that he, the author, never knew were there. But as far as his own literary career was concerned this sequence of novels, impressive though it had obviously been, was only the trial run for another great multi-volume epic that he had been planning and preparing for all his life: the story of the centuries long rise, fall and restoration of a family compared to which the de Verrayne Beauregards were nobodies, the greatest of all noble landowners – the Hapsburgs.

For good or ill however Antony was now a literary celebrity. There were of course irksome duties involved – promotional tours, publisher's receptions, interviews with obtuse journalists – but one event he did enjoy, because it really did represent the 'return in triumph' to his old school that he had been variously imagining ever since he left in such unhappy circumstances all those years ago, was the dinner given in his honour in the spring of 1985. There had only been one such occasion before in the school's history and that had been for an old boy who had won a gold medal in the Olympics for clay pigeon shooting.

Although the event was organized by Marjoribanks, who made a long, witty and well received introductory speech to which

Antony had to reply, and who clearly saw the whole thing as part of the celebrations marking his retirement that July, there could be no mistaking the fact that Antony was the guest of honour. The dinner even made the front page of the local press.

Having stayed on well past the usual retirement age just to teach the upper sixth, Marjoribanks had finally decided that it was time to leave the classroom, to the intense, if unexpressed, relief of the head and some of the younger members of the staff who regarded him as a slightly absurd anachronism, even if they would not have dared to say so openly because he was still, to all appearances, hugely popular and one never knew who was a fan and who wasn't. Although he had been fêted in the spring, Antony refused, as it were, to return the compliment and attend either Marjoribanks' final school production in June – *The Tempest*, in which inevitably he played the part of Prospero – or his leaving party in July, a decision which he afterwards rather regretted.

Though in his own estimation Antony's achievement had so far been modest, after the Chronicles he was more convinced than ever that writing a novel – creating a human world that was permanent, intelligible, significant and available to anyone who chose to read the book, out of the meaningless flux of so-called real life where the present was continually being burnt away into the past – was the one supremely worthwhile and self-justifying activity. And he never felt so much himself as when sitting at his desk he faced the prospect of an uninterrupted day's work. Through his work his imagination at least would survive him and live in other minds, as it evidently did now, as long as the text itself survived and anyone wished to read it.

Of course, according to the philosophy of his marvellous Oxford friend, nothing was lost and the passage of time was itself an illusion, a misunderstanding, and who was he to say that Rollo could have been mistaken; certainly no one who had heard him could fail to have been convinced inasmuch as they could follow the profundity of his thought. But in any case, Antony recalled, Rollo had specifically cited works of art as examples of timelessness. In his literary success he often thought of that luminously charismatic boy who died so young. What would Rollo have thought of his novels so far? The world might applaud, but would they have had any merit in his eyes? Would Antony be in any way ashamed for him to read them? At any rate Rollo functioned as a sort of artistic conscience, preventing him from going for the easy compromise and the short cut, always urging him to the limits of his powers. He meant to dedicate his future magnum opus on the Hapsburgs to him.

But Antony's solitude was not completely engrossed by writing. One of the great benefits of moving back to his family home was regaining access to his father's train set which had remained locked in the attic out of the reach of the tenants. As soon as he reacquired it he cleaned and restored the whole thing and spent the succeeding years buying new rolling stock, almost doubling the size of the track and changing the landscape setting from English domestic to a more Central European scene with mountains and a great river with bridges to represent the Danube. Here with his staff he could spend hours planning the details of his journeys all over the Empire in the Kaiserzug.

He never forgot the delight in the five-year-old Raggy's eyes when he took him up and showed him the train layout for the first time. The girls had been impressed but showed nothing of their brother's intensity of emotion. Like father, like son! Emily and Imogen on the other hand were more interested in his writing and always clamouring to know when he was going to put them into a book.

Although he was only around at weekends and holidays, as far as the girls were concerned, 'Nony' as Antony was called from Emily's first unsuccessful attempts to pronounce his name, was as much a part of the family as mummy or daddy, a virtual parent – all the more so as he was by far the most entertaining and least critical of the three. He might defer to their mother when they asked if they could do something but then so did their father. It was a situation that, when they were young, taking their cue from their mother, they accepted as quite normal because it was what they had been brought up with. Antony was the main adult male figure in their lives. He was the one who made things happen. He fired their imaginations, invented games and projects for them, told them stories and composed songs and poems for them. Even Rosemary was a little jealous of his relationship with the girls.

Giles did his best during the week in Antony's absence but was often tired after a demanding day's breadwinning in the City and the children found him kindly but dull. Rosemary too tended to be restless and irritable when it was just Giles and the kids. At weekends and holidays by contrast, the mood with Nony was relaxed, high-spirited and often hilarious. It was a world of private jokes, illusions and role play which increasingly Giles felt had nothing to do with him. Somehow they all seemed to be talking a different language, Rosemary included, and he had no idea what they were laughing about. It was not that there was any deliberate attempt to exclude him but that, sensing that it was not really his thing, no one took the trouble to incorporate him, so he that grew more and more awkward, peripheral and out of touch with the life of the family.

Richard, who disliked being called Raggy by his mother and Antony, was something of an exception to this tendency. Though he joined in the fun, ironically, his first loyalty remained steadfastly with the man he had been brought up to call his father, but even he did not show it very obviously. However Antony was all too well aware that he had still not really succeeded in winning him over.

Quietly despairing Giles asked himself how he could possibly compete with the glamorous figure of Antony who could even take the children to the launches of the books he had written them. He still clung to the conviction that there was nothing 'going on' between Antony and his wife; not merely because no one would dream of carrying on a secret affair so blatantly, but also because if something were going to happen it would have already happened a long time ago, and it clearly hadn't. He did however think that, deliberately or not, Antony was alienating his children's affection and there seemed nothing he could do to stop it. If he so much as hinted at the idea to Rosemary, taking Antony's side as she always did, she would retort that it was the most ridiculous thing she had ever heard and he would end up in the doghouse.

So Giles tended to become rather withdrawn with the kids and, since he didn't appear to be wanted at home, tended to spend more and more of his free time with clients, or just sailing. Moreover when he was at home he tended to drink rather too much which only lowered the girls' opinion of him and provoked scathing criticism from Rosemary. And though he sometimes took Richard out in his boat when he was old enough, his relationship with the children inevitably deteriorated further.

As they entered their teenage years Emily and Imogen began to feel that the situation they had grown up with and simply accepted as children, that of having in effect two fathers, with the adopted one so to speak eclipsing the real one, and which their mother apparently continued to regard as entirely normal, was in fact highly anomalous – though in a very intriguing way.

One Sunday morning early in 1987 when Emily was fourteen and Imogen twelve, Antony came upon them sitting on the stairs having evidently been in deep discussion.

"Secrets?" asked Antony sitting on the step below them.

"Sort of," said Emily. "You ask him."

"No, you," said Imogen.

"OK then, we were just saying that we wished you were our dad, our real dad."

"What's brought this on?"

"We were just thinking, that's all."

"You've got a real dad. You don't want anything to happen to him, do you?"

"No, nothing terrible. But he could just sail off in his boat somewhere," this was Imogen's contribution, "and you could marry mummy. She wouldn't mind. I'm the only girl in my class whose parents haven't split up," she added encouragingly.

"Richard wouldn't like it."

"Oh he's too young to have an opinion."

"Why do you want a new real dad anyway?"

"Well mummy's always in a good mood when you're around. You can tease her and laugh her out of it when she's over the top. She always does what you say, with Daddy there's just a row."

"You say things to her that no one else would dare to and she doesn't mind. It's so much more fun."

"I get it. You want me just to keep your mother in order."

"No, no," they chorused. "We want you anyway. But it would be nicer if you were our real dad too. It would sort of make it official."

They could tell that he wasn't angry as Imogen thought he might be.

"You won't tell anyone that we've had this conversation, will you?"

"Mum's the word."

"Especially not mummy!"

That conversation was never forgotten, for two and a half years later in September 1989 a strange and tragic circumstance seemed to give a prophetic resonance to Imogen's words. Giles had decided to sail from Sussex over to Waterford in the south of Ireland. (For the past few years he had stopped taking holidays with the family altogether. They didn't like sailing – even Richard now seemed bored with it – and Giles evinced little enthusiasm for going on what he called "one of Antony's cultural tours".) So Rosemary and the children went with Nony to the south of France and Giles went sailing when the school holidays were over. Such was the state their relationship had now reached, that Rosemary did not expect to hear from her husband till he returned in ten days or a fortnight and, to tell the truth, she thought so little about him during his absence that she failed to register the news of a storm in the Irish Sea, and it was only when she heard three days later from the yacht club in Bosham that his boat was out of radio contact and had not arrived in Waterford, that she began to be at all concerned.

The yacht club tried to be reassuring – the boat was eminently seaworthy and well equipped, Giles was a good skipper and the crew very experienced, it was possible that he had been blown off course and would make contact in due course from some other Irish port further along the coast, in any case sooner or later he was bound to be spotted, and so forth. Then as days passed with no news and an air-sea rescue search brought no result, Rosemary and her family began to come to terms with the worst. There was no sudden shock, no moment of grief, just a gradual dying away of hope, tempered, it must be admitted, by the fact that he had already become something of a marginal figure in their lives.

The names of the five crew members who had been presumably lost with him, including a young woman of twenty-eight, were all totally unknown to Rosemary, which made him seem even more distant to her. Though she told her inquisitive daughters that the mystery girl was the girlfriend of one of the crew, she couldn't help wondering whether her husband had been living a double life these last few years as well.

Thus, although it was a very disturbing time for them all – twelve-year-old Richard was the most deeply affected and Rosemary and Antony, who was now around all the time, did their best to console him – when, after six weeks wreckage from Giles's yacht, which happened to be called the Rosemary, was washed up near Cork, it felt like the closure rather than the beginning of a period of mourning. Even though no bodies had been found, his death could now be taken as virtually certain, and an inquest held. Only Richard remained silent and alienated in a way which worried his mother. "I'm sure he blames me," she kept saying to Antony.

The well attended memorial service in Leatherhead parish church was packed with Giles's friends and colleagues from the City and the sailing world whom Rosemary knew only slightly or not at all. Here again the lack of a coffin to bring his death into focus and the remote and unknown location of his disappearance, contributed to the impression that he had somehow simply drifted off into the sunset.

Rosemary had declared well in advance that she was not going to hold a reception back at the house for upwards of two hundred people; after all as she said, it wasn't really a funeral. Nor did she think it necessary to entertain Giles's 'stuffy' family whom she felt had never really approved of her. So afterwards, it was only she, Antony and the children who adjourned en famille to their favourite country pub where they had booked a table for lunch.

The mood was one of palpable relief that it was all over. Antony sat at the head of the table with the girls on one side and Rosemary and Richard on the other. She kept her arm round her son until a waitress appeared with menus. "Isn't this nice, just us!"

"Well I don't know about anyone else", declared Emily, "but I'm starving."

"I thought you were on a strict diet," said her mother.

"Oh that was only because of Will really. He was always on about how he wanted me to be slim – like he was trying to control me or something. We had a row about it. I've dumped him."

"Good for you," said Antony, winking at her.

"I didn't know anything about this. That's why he wasn't at the service I suppose."

"She only told him last night, mummy," said Imogen.

"Well I can't say I'm not pleased, darling. He was too old for you. Besides you've got a lovely figure – there's absolutely no need for you to lose weight."

"Mummy," said Imogen, "who was that lady who read the lesson on hope?"

"That was daddy's secretary, Sally Ryder, nice woman."

"She seemed very upset. Do you think they were having an affair?"

"Imogen! What on earth gave you that idea?"

"I thought perhaps that was why we didn't see much of him recently."

"No I don't think so at all. She's married; she introduced me to her husband. You can put that idea right out of your mind. Now, before we start I'm going to change." (Rosemary was the only one in funereal black). "Order for me", she whispered to Antony, and made for the loo. When she returned as the starters were being served her daughters were aghast.

"Was that what was in the carrier bag?" said Emily.

"Nony bought it for me."

"You shouldn't encourage her Nony, you really shouldn't!"

"What's wrong?" asked Rosemary.

"Mummy it's so embarrassing", said Imogen, "and those heels!"

"When I wanted to go out in something like that," said Emily, "you made me change, remember."

"That's because you're only sixteen and I'm – in my forties.

(Even before she had finished the sentence Rosemary was aware that she was on somewhat shaky ground.)

"Exactly!"

"Don't go mad mummy, but I think what Imogen means", put in Emily helpfully, "is that it makes you look like an old slapper."

"Less of the old, I'll have you know that I'm in my prime..."

"Talk about mutton dressed up as lamb", muttered Imogen.

"What's that? Listen young lady, if I want to go around stark naked..."

"Ladies, ladies, please. As I feel I'm partly responsible for this – these questions of taste and fashion are always very ticklish – I propose we settle the matter by democratic family vote, and abide by the result. Agreed?"

"Agreed!" (Rosemary calculated that with Tony and Richard on her side she could outvote the girls.)

"Right, who thinks mummy looks like a slapper?" (He was careful not to say 'old'). "Hands up!"

Emily and Imogen shot up their hands. Richard, who was mortified by his mother's outfit too but trying not to show it, took no part in the voting. The argument, which everyone else seemed to be revelling in, made him very uncomfortable and he just wanted the whole thing to be over as soon as possible. All eyes now turned to Antony who slowly and deliberately raised his arm. The girls cheered and Rosemary turned on him in mock fury, raining down blows on his chest; "traitor, traitor, you set me up. I'll never forgive you for this..." until Antony restrained her by holding her so tightly that she couldn't move.

"You're in public now, people are looking. Behave!"

Rosemary relented with bad grace. "OK. You can pass me that

bottle. If my family thinks I look like a slapper I'll behave like a slapper. You're driving by the way."

"Oh mummy, you're not going to get pissed are you?"

"Don't talk to me like that Emily, I'm your mother."

"Now come on", said Antony giving her a conciliatory squeeze, "you know we all love you really. I was just thinking when we came in how your children derive all their best qualities from you."

"Really?" said Rosemary, already slightly mollified.

"Yes, really. Look, here's Richard: mimic, performer, actor, thinker, touched by genius. We don't know what sort of genius yet, but it's there."

"He certainly doesn't get that from me."

"Oh yes. Then there's Imogen: outspoken, warm-hearted, impulsive, mercurial..."

"What's mercurial?"

"It means moody," said her sister crushingly.

"No, no," said Antony, "many-sided, complex. You never quite know what she's going to do."

"And finally, Emily – the passionate romantic. Always looking for something, or more likely someone, wonderful; wishing on a star, chasing a dream..."

Emily and Imogen tried to assume the appropriate pose and expression for each attribute, to general laughter.

"And I'd also like to say, seriously, we've all been through a very difficult time lately, especially mummy, so I'd like to propose a toast – to us all, especially mummy!"

"To us all, especially mummy!"

At this point Rosemary became a little tearful but from then on the meal proceeded in an almost festive atmosphere. Everyone was on good form, even Richard to whom Rosemary continued to pay close attention, though the girls winced occasionally at their mother's ringing laughter. Nony's egging her on to be outrageous, and sometimes she didn't need much encouragement, could cause some embarrassing episodes for her teenage daughters, but on the whole, as they well appreciated, his influence gave them a much freer, happier and more easy-going home environment, to say nothing of a more exciting and entertaining one, than they would otherwise have had, and their friends, they knew, envied them.

Their late father had not only been something of an outsider to the life of the family, but also, quite unfairly, found himself cast in the role of naysayer. Rosemary also laid down the law, often most emphatically, but generally relented and was always open to persuasion, while Antony was gloriously permissive and subversive. He sometimes scored minor rows between her and the girls like a tennis umpire – by the time he got as far as 'advantage' in the first game both parties generally dissolved in laughter – but his preferred method of undermining Rosemary in more substantial disputes was to ask if she had ever got up to whatever it was that she was currently taking issue with them about, when she was their age. As the girls were in some ways very like her, especially in being rather advanced for their years, the comparison was often too close for comfort. In fact she was, as ever, contradictory – always encouraging them in their relationships with boys and then fretting and worrying about them getting too deeply involved too soon. Poor old Giles by contrast, had come over as harassed, worried, negative and boring when, in fact, he only had his children's interests at heart.

After the sweet, Emily and Imogen disappeared conspiratorially returning about ten minutes later with the air of having reached a decision.

"Mummy and Nony, we got something to say," said Emily. "Promise you won't be angry."

"Of course we won't be angry," said Antony.

"It depends what it is," said Rosemary.

"You say," said Imogen.

"No you," said Emily.

"OK. Well, you two are obviously an item," began Imogen tentatively, looking at her mother.

"An item?"

"You're together, you're a couple. It's alright we don't mind."

"How do you know?"

"Mummy! We're not children anymore" said Emily. "Look, you're obviously in love with him." (Rosemary made absolutely no attempt to deny this.) "All we're saying is that's it's OK with us if you two decide to get married."

"Yes why don't you?" pleaded Imogen.

Rosemary and Antony looked at each other with a resigned smile and held hands in a gesture of mutual support. "It doesn't look as if we've got much choice does it?" said Antony. "Right, family vote again. Who thinks your mother and I should get married?"

Four hands shot up instantly, then Richard's as he accepted the inevitable, making it unanimous.

"Carried nem. con.," said Antony.

Rosemary for once said nothing but glowed with satisfaction. Had she been a cat she would have been purring her head off. The girls whooped with delight and hugged each other. Such a quick and conclusive decision had totally exceeded their expectations.

"Why are you so excited?" asked Antony.

"Because it's what we always wanted," said Emily.

"And now you really are our dad", said Imogen.

"I'll be as much of a dad as I can possibly be, but I can never replace your father."

"No, no, of course. I didn't mean that."

With that they both hugged and kissed him.

"What about you, Rags?" asked Antony. "Are you OK with this?"

Even if he didn't share their enthusiasm, Richard had clearly foreseen this turn of events when his sisters were only dreaming about it, and was therefore prepared.

"I suppose so, as long as you never call me Rags or Raggy again."

"It's a deal."

He and Richard solemnly shook hands. Then after some whispering Emily and Imogen stood up.

"Are you two off to the loo again?"

"No, we're going to leave you two lovebirds together and wait in the car. Come on Richard!"

Left alone Rosemary and Antony gazed at each other, just savouring the moment and trying to take it all in. It was Rosemary who broke their silence. "Are we doing the right thing? Not too soon is it?"

"It had to happen. Sooner or later it absolutely had to happen. The great thing is that it's not too late."

"I know, I know. But you don't think it'll spoil everything do you?"

"How could it?"

"Well, me invading your space."

Antony shook his head. "Of course you'll be marrying a friend. You once said that friendship and marriage didn't mix."

"I don't think I said anything about marriage. Anyway we're not just friends are we?"

"I think we've earned it, if anybody has."

"So do I."

They clinked their glasses and drank to each other from the last drop of their wine. In all the myriad versions of this scene he had imagined over the years it invariably ended with his telling her at this point that the other men in her life, unlike him, never really knew her, or found her interesting or funny – they might have fancied her, but they never understood her or even tried to, and Guy Halliwell didn't even like her! – and that that was the ultimate justification for their partnership. Quite simply they belonged together. But before he could do so a young man from another table, recognising him from the photo on the back of the book, approached and asked him to autograph his copy of *The Beauregard Chalice* and the much rehearsed words remained forever unuttered. Perhaps, he reflected afterwards, it was just as well – after all, they went without saying. Instead he asked if she had been aware that Richard didn't like being called Raggy.

"No I had no idea."

"Nor had I. We must remember in future. I thought he took it quite well; but you know how important it is for me that we get on."

"And for me, but he's going to need careful handling... By the way I really love this outfit; bugger what the girls say about mutton dressed up as lamb!"

"Amen to that. I haven't seen anything so sexy in years. If you want to know it's the real reason why I agreed to marry you. No chance of a quickie round the back I suppose."

"On yer bike! Now come on or they'll be wondering what's keeping us."

Antony drove Rosemary and family home and for the first time shared her bedroom at Crossways, the house in Leatherhead.

Just a few weeks later, on Saturday 11th November 1989, a party was held there to celebrate their quiet register office wedding earlier in the day, and also, belatedly, Rosemary's fiftieth birthday. Most of the sixty or so guests were Rosemary's friends for whom the occasion was simply the public acknowledgement of a union they had accepted for years. There was nevertheless with all the congratulations a palpably liberating sense of the air being cleared.

In an impromptu speech, in which he tried not to sound too

triumphant, Antony remarked that anyone who so much as hinted at the phrase 'third time lucky' would be shown the door. This briefly alarmed Rosemary who had not told her children about her first marriage. In the event, as soon as they learnt that they had no half-brothers and sisters, they were barely interested and even Richard took the news in his stride. The happy couple then spent a brief honeymoon in Paris.

This was the climax of what proved to be something of an annus mirabilis for Antony, for not only had he and Rosemary at the beginning of their fifth decade finally, publicly and irrevocably come together, but in those last weeks of 1989 when, following Poland and Hungary, the communist regimes of Eastern Europe collapsed one after another, it seemed that public events were beginning to conform to the world of his imagination, that the outer and inner realms of his universe were, in some almost miraculous way, converging and merging! But though the momentum of this glorious convergence was maintained with the reunification of Germany and the shattering of the Soviet Union, it was no more than a few months before the first signs of discord appeared in his marriage.

The first specific clash occurred early in the New Year. The issue was Rosemary's assumption that now they were married, Antony would sell his family home and move lock stock and barrel to Crossways where she contended there was plenty of room for him to write in complete privacy; he could have a study, an office, a library, anything he wanted. Antony was evasive, but it eventually became clear that her husband had no intention of abandoning his bolthole and putting it on the market in the spring as she had anticipated. She was disappointed and more than that had the feeling, justified or not, that it signalled that Antony was not totally committed to married life, that he was withholding something from her.

A second and more serious clash arose over whether and when Richard should be told that Antony was his father. Here it was Antony who felt that he was in some sense being rejected, for Rosemary, to his surprise, was adamant that for the time being nothing should be said, insisting that it would be far too upsetting for him when he was just coming to terms with his father's death and her remarriage. This could of course be argued, but to Antony it seemed strange, to put it no higher, that she should be so attached to preserving the fiction of her late husband's paternity when there was no longer any compelling reason for secrecy, in effect denying that they had ever created a child together.

These overt disagreements were however symptomatic, to Antony at least, of a more general and disconcerting change. He had implicitly assumed that their marriage would simply be a public ratification forever of the status quo ante, a happy ending, a homecoming with Ulysses, all wanderings over, finally claiming his Penelope. It was soon borne in upon him however that Rosemary saw their marriage rather as a new beginning than a culmination and that for her a husband was by no means the same thing as a confidant/best friend/lover. For example it was made clear that she expected him to pull his weight domestically and support her against the kids when required; sitting around making drole comments and playing the subversive funny uncle was no longer good enough.

Moreover she was no longer so biddable, no longer easily teased and laughed out of things, but rather seemed almost to look for clashes and positively to demand rows which Antony refused to rise to, thus provoking her even more. At one time or another she accused him of leaving everything to her, burying his head in the sand, living in his own dream world and irresponsibly undermining her authority with the girls. But on occasions when he did try to put his oar in and be assertive in family matters she tended to resent it, making no bones about overruling him if she didn't agree. It appeared that he couldn't win and when, after six months, he remarked only half-jokingly that he could quite see why her first two marriages hadn't worked, it did not go down at all well.

For years he had watched Giles taking the flack while he had been her constant ally. Now, in a reversal which until recently he would have considered inconceivable, he was finding himself in the firing line. For years he had been, or so it had seemed, her rock, her support, her counsellor, the one who cheered her, who listened to her secrets, her problems, her moans, the one constant and point of reference in her life. Now he felt he was being cast as her adversary and the obviously private phone calls he kept coming in on suggested that she was turning elsewhere for the confidential advice which she no longer sought from him, presumably because he himself had now become, in her eyes, a problem. When sometime in June he finally asked who the recipient of one of these endless calls might be, she rounded on him:

"You've never really liked my friends have you? Never really tried to get to know them, always kept them at arm's length like you do everyone – just because they're not intellectuals who like spending their time in art galleries and museums or going to the opera or some incomprehensible play! Well let me tell you, they think you're peculiar. All those ironic comments and subtle allusions you come out with – they don't know what you're talking about. It might have been funny or original years ago but now it's just bizarre."

"It's nothing to do with whether I like your friends or not, or whether they happen to find me entertaining; I was merely wondering what you can possibly have to say to them that you so obviously can't say to me. Besides I thought you liked going to the theatre and opera."

"Did you? Well it just shows how little you know about me. You always thought you could educate me, improve me, didn't you? Well if you must know I find your attitude smug and patronizing. I'm happy with the way I am and I don't want you to change me," she paused to pour herself a generous measure of wine from the bottle next to the phone, "and before you start on about it again, I shall continue to drink as much as I like without your permission."

"I only suggested that if you're serious about losing weight you might think about cutting down on the alcohol. I thought you agreed."

Antony was clearly getting nowhere by sounding like a pompous prig, so not wishing to inflame their disagreement further, and seeing that she was impatient to resume the phone conversation he had interrupted, he walked away. As he did so he heard her voice saying: "Sorry about that... no nothing... oh, only Antony."

Rosemary subsequently apologised for her attack and said she didn't mean it; but though it was true that she had a habit of flaring up and seemed to take rows in her stride, for Antony the words remained said. How could he believe they had hadn't reflected her attitude to him, at least partially; more than that, they clearly sprung from a long held grievance and seemed to undermine basic assumptions about their past relationship. And the question of who her new confidential friend or friends might be, and what exactly she was discussing with them, remained unanswered.

One underlying source of the tension between them, it must be admitted, concerned sex. For years they had had to be content with brief, intense sessions of love making, and Antony, for his part had found these clandestine, occasional encounters exciting. But now that they habitually slept together and could make love whenever they wanted, the business lost something of its savour for him, whereas Rosemary, now that all restrictions were removed, clearly wanted and expected more sex than before. He therefore began to make excuses, she to feel rejected and resentful, to say nothing of frustrated – an old, old story! But now Antony was beginning to suffer from the gnawing suspicion that it was this that his wife might be discussing so earnestly over the phone, and he found the very possibility of it particularly galling. Even worse, could the new confidant with whom she was on such intimate terms, or one of them, be a man?

There were naturally some lighter moments between them, some echoes of the old days but these only served to highlight the overall pattern which was one of gradual but inexorable estrangement from the one person that Antony had always thought of as his soulmate. But even out of this deep bitterness and disappointment he found a new work sprouting and shaping itself in his imagination, transmuting his pain into the objectivity of a work of art.

The new novel, *The Man Who Liked to Break Things*, was partly a detailed and utterly candid account of the whole of his relationship with Rosemary and her family with only minimal changes of name and place, and the analyses of character, including that of the narrator and eponymous hero, for whom he inevitably drew on certain aspects of himself, were much more forensic than anything he had attempted before. The difference was that when the narrator finally achieves his goal of marrying the Rosemary character – called Melissa in the novel – he gratuitously, and from a pure love of destruction, breaks up their marriage at the very height of their happiness. When the distraught Melissa asks him finally why he hates her, he replies that, in spite of all her shortcomings and weaknesses which he details at some length, he does in fact not hate her at all, but that he has always liked to break things – the more perfect, the more beautiful, the more delicate, fragile and tender, the greater his pleasure in smashing them. So his destruction of their marriage was in a sense a compliment to her.

Though the brutality of the dénouement was intended to shock the reader as much as Melissa, Antony was careful to include enough clues to indicate that consciously or unconsciously his hero was all along bent on the brutal action he eventually took and also how such a predilection for 'breaking things' might have had its origins in his childhood.

Was the new novel in any sense a form of literary revenge on Rosemary, his way of restoring his dignity in the face of his rejection, of getting his own back, to put it crudely? Antony would have denied it vehemently, preferring to see the work as an unprecedentedly honest study of a type of character that had never been explored in fiction before. Of course he had exploited his intimacy with Rosemary and her children. This caused him some misgivings and he knew he would have a certain amount of explaining to do when the time came; but in the last resort he was a writer, and using his life as raw material for his art had to take precedence over all other considerations.

The role of pitiless destroyer was one that in 'real life' Antony had aspired to play as far back as he could remember. When under his parents' roof, he had often imagined causing all manner of havoc: setting fire to the house, wrecking the train set, dashing all the crockery to the floor during a meal or even committing murder, though not – unlike his hero – out of pure motiveless malignity or sheer love of destruction for its own sake, but in an attempt to provoke some kind of emotional reaction from his mother even at great cost to himself.

Work on the novel progressed well, continuing into the summer months and keeping Antony and Rosemary apart for long periods which incidentally had the effect of lessening the tensions between them, but the matter of summer holidays was beginning to surface. This year the children, including Richard, were making arrangements to go away with friends and it was a sign of how far things had moved that there was a question as to whether Rosemary and Antony would be holidaying together or separately, something that would have been unthinkable in the years before their marriage.

With this issue in mind Rosemary drove over to Antony's on the afternoon of the second Saturday in July – these days he spent most of the weekend at his old home writing – in conciliatory mood. She was going to propose that they went back to Florence for two or three weeks in September: a sort of compensation for the briefness of their Paris honeymoon which had scarcely been more than a weekend, and a chance, as she saw it, to 'begin again'.

It was a beautiful day and finding the French windows open she preferred to go up and surprise him in his study rather than interrupt him by ringing the bell. (Antony had never got round to giving her a key to the house.) She made her way up the stairs to his study on the first floor but found it empty. Antony in fact had been sitting and writing on the stone seat at the bottom of the garden out of sight of the house, but hearing Rosemary's car he had come indoors. Not finding her downstairs he too had made his way up to the study and found her sitting at his desk which was covered with notebooks and typed manuscript, reading.

"What are you doing in here?"

"I came to see you, the French windows were open." She answered him in a small distant sounding voice without looking up from the page she was studying. "Is this really how you see me?"

"Er, it's just some notes – for a character in the novel I'm writing," Antony began, but he knew that it was already too late either to divert or to convince her.

Ignoring this feeble disclaimer she sat quite still, her face tense and pale as she examined the contents of one notebook after another.

"Is that what you've been doing all these years, spying on us all? You bastard!"

"It's just the way writers work," Antony remarked hopelessly. "It's nothing personal."

"Nothing personal! Nothing personal! You wormed your way into our family, tried to turn my children against their father, tried to turn me against him. He was a good man and a good father. If he sometimes didn't get on with the girls it was all because of your influence. You drove him away. If it weren't for you he'd probably be still with us!"

Unwilling to listen to any more Antony went down to the kitchen and with trembling hands made himself a cup of tea. His life had suddenly become a waking nightmare that he found it impossible to come to terms with. But at the moment his overriding emotion was one of searing resentment and indignation. He returned to find Rosemary, who had so recently metamorphosed into a wholly alien and hostile figure that he did not know and perhaps had never known, skimming with rapt attention through the typed pages.

"Is this your novel?"

"It's a long short story really, more a novella."

Rosemary ignored the literary distinction. "This man who likes to break things, who spends years planning and scheming to marry someone and when at last he gets what he wants, wrecks the whole thing just for the fun of it – it's you, isn't it?"

Antony could have defended himself by saying, with a pardonable economy of the truth, that however closely the actual characters were drawn from life – and he had incidentally been more unsparing with himself than anybody else – his hero's nihilistic attitude had no more to do with his creator than Iago had to do with Shakespeare or the Satan of *Paradise Lost* had to do with Milton, and that she was quite misreading the novel. But why should he have to? Reeling under what he saw as a completely unjust attack from Rosemary, based on an utter travesty of all their life together, he was stung into playing the merciless destroyer for real.

"Yes," he said, "it's me!" (This was the ultimate act of vengeance. There could be no going back now. He was over the cliff.)

"Well, I always thought you were cold-blooded, but this, this is unbelievable!... And all that so-called advice you kept giving me, now I know what was behind it all. You deliberately set out to undermine my marriage, you planned it from the start – that was all part of this breaking things business! It's all so obvious now! You're sick, you know that, psychopathic! You need psychiatric help. You're much worse than Guy Halliwell. He was a complete and utter shit but he was fun and he used to bring me flowers. In all the time you've known me you've never once brought me flowers; you even criticised Guy for it if I remember. That should have been a warning! Well, at least he had warm blood in his veins. He wasn't a cold, smug, self-absorbed, ineffectual, scheming little monster like you. However did I let myself be taken in by you? I don't ever want to see you again!"

With that she rose quietly and left the room. They were never together again except for a few brief moments when he was clearing his things out of the Leatherhead house. The situation as it stood being totally irretrievable and with neither side showing the least inclination towards a rapprochement, divorce soon followed. A lifelong friendship – Rosemary had once told him that he was the only man she had ever met that didn't bore the pants off her – had ended in a disastrous marriage lasting less than a year!

His very first impression of her, uncontaminated as it were by physical attraction and their growing friendship, that she wasn't his type, had been vindicated. But Antony's efforts to fortify and console himself by interpreting Rosemary's character in the most negative possible way, representing her as coarse, philistine, money-grubbing, a mass of contradictions for which other people were made to suffer, and assuring himself how much better off he was without her – even entertaining the dreadful thought that his mother might have been right about her all along – were not in the end very successful.

He had hoped that in spite of his break-up with Rosemary, he would be able to stay close to Emily, Imogen and of course Richard. The girls were very different to their mother, he told himself. Though lively and uninhibited, they had a grace and refinement that she lacked and he had, after all, always been their intimate friend and ally against her. Moreover they had seemed sympathetic and encouraging while the marriage was deteriorating, even though they had no idea how bad things were and were naturally much more interested in their own lives. He was to discover however that when the crunch came, blood was thicker than water and they unhesitatingly sided with their mother.

When he attempted to maintain contact with them after the divorce they even turned on him in a way that he could never afterwards recall without tears coming to his eyes, saying how much they had resented his interference in their lives, how he had exploited them, filled their heads with a lot of nonsense and tried to make them fit his mould – "instead of being ourselves we felt we had to play up to you all the time" – and much more in the same vein. A lot of this, he afterwards considered, must have reflected Rosemary's influence and, though they didn't mention it specifically, she had must have told them how he had used them as characters in his novel. They even echoed Rosemary's accusations about his having driven their father away – Imogen perhaps now feeling guilty for having expressing the hope on the stairs a few years before that he would just sail off on his boat and leave them all.

Henceforth Antony was to be totally excluded from their lives and from Richard's, his claim to be the boy's father now acknowledged by no one except himself. And how could he ever prove it? From time to time he thought about writing to Rosemary to try to put her right about the novel – he did not care to be thought of as a monster – but then what would be the point? In any case she would probably not believe him. In due course *The Man Who Liked to Break Things* proved a brilliant critical success but he feared its publication had burned his bridges with Rosemary and her family forever.

VI

By 1990 with the children almost grown up it seemed appropriate that the Emperor and Empress should officially separate and the pretence that their marriage was still a reality in private as in public, no longer be maintained. And not before time for, in spite of the couple's appearances together whenever protocol required, for years there had been persistent rumours of estrangement which had found their way into the foreign press. It was a great relief that it could now be acknowledged openly before the whole world. Accordingly the Empress, who kept all her titles, dignities and household and continued to fly the imperial doubled-headed eagle as her standard differenced with her personal arms as before, ceased to reside at any of the imperial palaces; it being considered unseemly that they should continue to share the same roof however large. She was however given, for her own exclusive use, the renaissance palazzo overlooking Lake Garda where she had spent her honeymoon, a

Palladian villa in the Veneto, castles in Bavaria and Hungary, as well, of course as enjoying the royal estates in her native Portugal. She also continued to perform public duties on her own and, when it was deemed appropriate, with her children. The separation nevertheless cast a certain shadow over the mature years of the reign.

PART FOUR: ANOTHER DAY

I

Having lain awake most of the night he finally lost consciousness as dawn was beginning to filter through the shutters of the high palace windows and was eventually stirred from a light doze by a nurse who leant over him, hers the only distinguishable features out of that great indistinct sea of faces that filled the imperial bedchamber and surrounded the bed.

"Majesty, majesty, a friend, an old friend would like to speak to you".

"Man or woman?"

"A man, majesty, an old school friend."

"I don't want to see him. I'm waiting for a lady, I told you – it's very important. There's no time to lose."

"Yes, majesty, we're doing everything we can to find her."

"When you do she must be brought here as soon as possible."

"Yes, majesty."

"What time is it?"

"It's half past nine in the morning, majesty. Will you have something to drink?"

"I don't want anything to drink; I just want you to find the lady."

II

Now that he was launched into his fifties Antony found that most of his contemporaries either openly or by implication envied him his apparently trouble-free and solitary bachelor life, and all he heard from them tended to confirm that he had chosen the better course. By dint of regular attendance at Old Boys' cricket matches – for years now he had been umpiring the games of the 'Seniors' XI' – and his increasing involvement in other OB activities (he even played an active role in the successful campaign to prevent the school going comprehensive), he was elected to the Association Committee, eventually becoming, inevitably it seemed, Hon. Sec. in the September after Marjoribanks finally retired. Thus Antony, who at school was known as Kilroy A. (only Marjoribanks had called him by his Christian name), a marginal and virtually friendless figure as far as the other boys in his year were concerned, an outsider, a member of no gang or clique or set, now found himself, if only by sheer benign perseverance, at the centre of the web – an indispensable point of contact for all those of his generation who wished to remain in touch with their old school friends – learning incidentally that he was not the only one in the community of Old Boys, parents and friends of the school to be less than totally impressed by the great Leo Marjoribanks.

At fifty-one he was now at last the manager of the book shop. He had put on weight, he was comfortable, respected, sought after, smoked a pipe, drank convivially but not to excess, drove an old Jaguar and on suitable occasions wore the OBA tie – in short the quintessential 'Old Boy', that he had once, on his first visit to the Saturday cricket game, so much despised. Had he been told then, in all the ardour of his youthful ambition, that this was how he would end up, he would have been appalled. But these days the role suited him pretty well. He had nothing in common with most of the other Old Boys intellectually but within limits he enjoyed the camaraderie.

Those who thirty-five years ago were the leading lights of the school, the lads, the sportsmen who would have scarcely given him the time of day had they passed him in the corridor, now as defeated middle-aged men, not only accepted him as an authority on the LBW law, but confided in him as a trusted friend who had somehow managed to remain above the battle, about their failing marriages and divorces, furtive affairs, alcoholism, impotency worries, mothers-in-law, inconsiderate and unreasonable partners, insufferable teenagers, and all the anxiety, pressure and stress that nowadays seemed inseparable from family life. No wonder he looked so young they thought, his face so smooth and unlined, "the lucky bugger's got nothing to worry him". And when he saw the treachery with which men and women treated each other, how 'wedded bliss' degenerated into bitter squabbles about weekend access to children, Antony could only congratulate himself on not having been caught in that particular trap. But he listened sympathetically and gave judicious advice.

Nor did it now seem to him that there was anything particularly meritorious in being successful with women seeing the smarmy, shallow types they generally seemed to fall for; people whom, sexual attraction apart, they did not even like and inevitably ended up bored and frustrated with. No doubt men made more or less the same mistakes about women but by and large they seemed to expect less from marriage and were consequently more prepared to put up with what they were stuck with, having the odd affair on the side if they were lucky. But it was a sorry business. Marjoribanks had at least been right about trying to dissuade him from becoming ensnared in domestic life all those years ago – or so he told himself.

In the autumn of that year, instead of an outside speaker it was decided that Antony himself as Hon. Sec. should address the annual Old Boys' dinner. Though much of it was over the heads of the company his was generally agreed to have been the most entertaining speech in living memory; even Marjoribanks appeared to concur, making it clear when he detached himself from his circle of admirers and sought out Antony for a private chat, that he had registered and appreciated all the historical and literary allusions. He then tried to persuade him to take over the Old Boys' play, to inherit his mantle as he put it. But Antony, averse to inheriting any mantle from him, demurred.

Marjoribanks, though still resplendent in the blue velvet frogged smoking jacket he always wore on black tie occasions, seemed to Antony that evening, in a way that he had not noticed before, a somewhat diminished figure, his impregnable confidence muted. He had not seen him to speak to for eighteen months and the change was unmistakable. Was he worried about his health? He wasn't smoking his usual cigar and spent some time giving an account of the various fugitive symptoms that had prompted him to have a complete health check. It had proved satisfactory so far though there were still a few results to come. How typical of the man, thought Antony, as he made the required sympathetic noises, to be so obsessed with the minutiae of his own health.

In any case retirement didn't seem to be agreeing with him and this was a real surprise to Antony. Because he had always taken it as given that for Marjoribanks trying to broaden the cultural horizons of the brighter and more responsive boys in a south London grammar school had only been a very peripheral part of a crowded life spent largely among the rich, well born, famous and talented, Antony assumed that he would have flourished once he had finally shed the constraints of sixth form teaching and became totally absorbed into his true milieu. But whatever else he might be up to, Marjoribanks had remained just as much involved with the Old Boys' Association as before, and when Antony enquired whether he intended to profit by his retirement by taking a luxury cruise around the world, or some other glamorous holiday, he had brushed the suggestion aside with a throw away remark about 'abroad' being overrated. Leo Marjoribanks, for all his flamboyant manners remained, it appeared, a very private as well as enigmatic person, or at least one who kept the different compartments of his life firmly separated.

For the first time in years Antony spent Christmas alone instead of being obliged to join in someone else's family jollity and found it a refreshing, even liberating, change. Then on the afternoon of the twenty-ninth of December, in the middle of that dead time between Christmas and New Year, he received a call from a lady with a West Indian accent asking if he was Mr Antony Kilroy, a friend of Mr Leo Marjoribanks.

"Yes, I know him."

"Well, the gentleman died this morning you see, and I wonder if you would be willing to come over and sort out his things..."

It would have been difficult for Antony to say what he felt on first hearing this totally unexpected news. Irritating or not, a constant presence in his life, as well as a potential audience for any success he might achieve, had been suddenly removed. It was, more than anything, disorientating. However the invitation to delve, for whatever reason, into the Marjoribanks enigma was irresistible, all the more so as he, along with all the rest of the world, was just then at a seasonal low ebb.

Laura, the West Indian lady whom Antony assumed must be Marjoribanks' housekeeper, gave him the address – a number and a street in SW12 – and he set off straightaway imagining his destination as a large elegantly furnished Victorian house near Clapham Common. Like most people he took it for granted that

Marjoribanks was, or rather had been, a man of substantial private means. If he chose to spend the working day schoolmastering it was to amuse himself and shed a little cultural light in the process but certainly not because he needed the money! Astonishment was therefore too weak a word to describe Antony's reaction when he found himself in a back street in Balham, ringing the bell on one of the doors in a dingy porch between two shop fronts. It was already dark when he got there and everything was closed up, but there was no mistaking what sort of place he had come to.

For a moment he thought he must be mistaken, then he told himself that this must be where he was to meet Laura who would then escort him to Marjoribanks' residence. But no, Laura opened the door, welcomed him warmly and led him up a narrow staircase to a bed-sitting room, on the first floor – Mr Marjoribanks' room. Laura explained that she was his landlady (not his housekeeper!) and that she owned the two floors over the cycle shop.

The astonished Antony entered gingerly, half expecting to see Marjoribanks laid out on the bed, and was relieved to find himself in quite a large empty large room with two sash windows overlooking the street. It was clean and tidy and filled with cheap furniture. There was a wardrobe with a battered suitcase on top, a radio by the bed, a desk, a sofa, a bookcase stuffed with books, a portable television on the table he obviously used for eating, a washbasin and threadbare carpet. The impression it made was drab and impersonal. At first glance there appeared to be no photographs, souvenirs or mementoes of any kind.

Prompted perhaps by Antony's obvious surprise at this austere lodging Laura said: "He used to say he liked to travel light."

"Has he lived here long?"

"About twenty years. He told me he that if he could afford it he would like to have lived at the Ritz, but apart from that, one room was very much like another." She smiled. "He called it his pied-à-terre."

"That sounds like him. Was he very sociable?

"Not so as you'd notice."

"Really? I must say I find that a bit surprising."

"Well hardly anyone ever came to see him here. He spent most of his time in his room reading and watching the TV – when he stopped going to work that is."

"I see... Er, can you tell me how he died?"

"Well now, I found him this morning when I brought him a cup of tea because I hadn't heard him moving about and I was a bit concerned – and there he was. It was such a shock. Big heart attack the doctor said, but there will have to be an inquest. He hadn't been well for months really. I think he must have known it was serious because he said to me that you were a lifelong friend and that if anything happened to him I was to get in touch with you. I want him to have my things, he said. Anything he doesn't want he can get rid of; that's what he said – in fact he said it several times so it must have been on his mind. I shall miss him, you know. He was a real gentleman, one of the old school, always so smartly dressed and everything – and so amusing."

"Yes I know."

"You're quite a bit younger than him."

"He was my old English teacher years ago."

"Oh I see. Well he certainly thought a lot about you, that's for sure. He told me that if he was cast away on a desert island you were the one person he'd want as a companion... I'll let you get on then and I'll bring you some tea in a little while. You just take as much time as you want."

How petty, how mean-spirited, his treatment of Leo Marjoribanks had been, thought Antony as soon as he was left alone.

Just because he had resented being undeservedly outshone by someone he regarded as essentially unserious who just happened to be more quick-witted and infinitely more socially self-assured and who, he felt, had patronized him and failed sufficiently to acknowledge his talent (with Marjoribanks he had never quite grown out of being the promising schoolboy eager for his admiration and encouragement), he had continually rejected a fellow human being, a fascinating, cultured, intelligent and evidently lonely man who had in fact admired him, regarded him as a friend and over the years made persistent efforts to get close to him.

Latterly he had even less of an excuse for his rejection in that, more mature and self-confident, he was no longer so intimidated by Marjoribanks or bothered about trying to compete with him. So what if Antony was irritated by the way that Marjoribanks only had to go through the same old performance to have most people eating out of his hand. Any form of social interaction was after all a performance. Perhaps one was too apt to assume that those who did it badly were more 'sincere' than those who did it well: 'person', 'personality', the very words derived from 'persona' – an actor's mask. It was futile to try and unmask people, to speculate that Marjoribanks might have had a shy, diffident soft centre. People were what they were. He was at any rate – or rather he had been – an interesting man to whom Antony had owed a great deal and now through his own pettiness he had irretrievably lost the proffered opportunity of what might have been a very rewarding friendship. All he could do was to try to discover any clues which might help him to understand a little better, posthumously, the Marjoribanks he had so culpably failed to get to know in life and who was now turning out to be an even more surprising and enigmatic figure than Antony could possibly have imagined.

The first thing he noticed was that the cabinet above the

washbasin was filled with dozens of boxes and bottles of pills, drugs and assorted medicines as well as several bottles of hair dye. The wardrobe contained his frogged velvet dinner jacket and dress trousers and five other suits together with waistcoats, shirts and a line of well-polished shoes – all in immaculate condition. The books were the usual collection of plays, novels, poetry and criticism from Chaucer to T. S. Eliot that one might expect any long serving English master to possess. The only items of special interest were a shelf of what looked like prompt copies of every play he had ever produced and an unmarked 1970 edition of Burke's Peerage. There were no copies of his own books.

Antony then turned to the desk as his last hope of finding something a little more revealing. In the deep drawers at the bottom he found a roll of thirty years' worth of school photographs – eleven in all, together with dozens of individual class photos and play programmes. Most of the other drawers contained, of all things, his old mark books! (Antony now remembered that even his critics among the Old Boys always conceded that he remembered the details of everyone he ever taught.) It really was beginning to seem that his schoolmastering, instead of being merely a peripheral day job, had been central to his life and that instead of the glamorous weekends and holidays that everybody had imagined, he had in fact been spending most of his leisure time in this sad little Balham bedsit. Marjoribanks as a down at heel Mr Chips! How bizarre it seemed to visualize him here; how difficult to adjust to. And could he have really have been so isolated that Antony, who had always kept his distance from him, counted as a close friend? Perhaps Marjoribanks' highly polished social persona repelled intimacy generally, even as it impressed and attracted an admiring audience. Perhaps it was intended to. Perhaps after all it really was designed to hide something: if not a soft centre then some sort of secret life. Or perhaps he had come to find the role of social entertainer, which he was invariably expected to play, irksome, and preferred to be at home with a good book.

Then he made a discovery – an old photo album so large that it was jamming the one drawer he had not yet investigated. He eventually succeeded in extracting it by removing the drawer above to find the record of Marjoribanks' life that he had been searching for – albeit a tantalizingly fragmentary record – for there appeared to be many pages from which the pictures had been removed.

The first entry was a grainy photo cut from an old newspaper. The quality was poor but it was quite possible to make out a beautiful bride leaving a church on the arm of her husband, who looked like a Guards officer, about to pass through an arch of drawn swords. The caption read: 'The marriage of Captain the Honourable Lawrence Foljambe Marjoribanks and Miss Henrietta Marchant-Fellowes'. Underneath Marjoribanks had written in his bold cursive hand: 'Mummy's Wedding Saturday 5th June 1909'. So he *was* out of the top drawer! That much was real, genuine and incontrovertible. And if his father was an Honourable that made him a younger son of a peer.

On the next few pages there were pictures of a plump little Leo with his mother – on her lap, on a velvet stool and under a cedar tree in a sailor suit on the lawn of what looked like a charming small eighteenth century house. There were pictures of him on a pony and sitting with an older couple, as well as his mother, in a rather grander setting – on a terrace with a stone balustrade at the top of a flight of steps flanked by two enormous urns with high windows behind. Could this couple be his grandparents – Earl and Countess or Marquess and Marchioness, and the setting, their ancestral seat? Leo was obviously an adored child and probably an only one as there was no sign of any brothers and sisters, nor for that matter, after the initial wedding picture, any sign of his father. Could he have been one of the hundreds of thousands of young officers who had perished on the Western Front? If Marjoribanks was seventy when he finally retired in 1985, he must have been born in 1915. Perhaps he never knew his father.

There were a number of holiday snaps taken both in the country and by the seaside, sometimes with his mother and sometimes with a lady that Antony imagined to be a nanny, and a little collection of school photographs – one of him standing, again with his mother, in front of what was obviously his prep school, and one of the top class. Prep school (presumably boarding) was followed by Harrow, and there were various blurred snaps of Leo and unidentified friends disporting themselves in boaters, short jackets and Eton collars. The school section ended with several pages devoted to the 1933 school production in which Leo played Lady Macbeth. He had also stuck in the programme a review cut out of the *Harrow Record* with certain laudatory references to himself underlined in red.

Then followed about a dozen pages relating to his years at Gonville and Caius College, Cambridge – a mild surprise for Antony who always thought he went to Oxford. But that was not the only surprise. The pictures consisted of young men at parties dressed up as women – there was one of Leo in blazer and flannels playing a tennis racquet like a banjo, but this was an exception – and of photos of various Footlights productions, complete with programmes, showing that he was a leading light of the company. Here again dressing up in drag seemed to be the order of the day! Unlike the party photos which were largely captioned with nicknames or first names, the cast lists enabled Antony to identify at least half a dozen individuals who had subsequently became well known in the wider world.

What had really attracted his attention however was the heading at the beginning of the Cambridge years – 'Gonville and

Caius October 1934 to March 1937'. March 1937! Did this meant that Leo Marjoribanks had not stayed up for the third term of his last year, that he had not sat his finals, and not, in fact, graduated? Did this explain why he could only teach at a suburban grammar school that might then have been sufficiently impressed to accept him at face value without asking questions, whereas a major public school would have delved into his qualifications more thoroughly?

It also raised the question as to whether he had been sent down and why? Had he been involved in some scandal? Was it some sort of sexual offence? Had he been caught in bed with a young lady or, more likely, with one of the androgynous young men who featured in the photographs? Or, was it political? After all here he was, an undergraduate at Cambridge in the mid-Thirties at exactly the same time as Guy Burgess, Donald Maclean and Kim Philby, when Anthony Blunt was a young don recruiting likely lads to be Marxist 'moles' in the British establishment? Although Leo had not been at Trinity or Kings and seemed to have moved more in theatrical than political circles, it was an intriguing possibility, and hadn't there always been rumours among the boys at school that 'Marchers' was, or had been, a spy and even that he groomed or vetted the occasional protégé for the security services? Gonville and Caius was right next to Trinity too, and there was one snap of him in a sleeveless sweater that could have been mistaken for the young Guy Burgess at his most cherubic. But on second thoughts it seemed unlikely that a Cambridge college in the Thirties would have sent an undergraduate down merely for being a communist or fellow traveller. If that were so half the university would have been asked to leave!

Could it have been Leo's being sent down from Cambridge under a cloud – particularly if it were a sexual scandal – which initially brought about his estrangement from his aristocratic family, or did he deliberately break with them? Tucked away among the Cambridge pictures was a photo labelled 'Mummy's second marriage', taken during his first summer term at the university. It showed her, a still attractive middle-aged woman, with the elderly, distinguished looking, but distinctly old school Lieutenant Colonel Forbes-Greville. Perhaps he didn't get on with his stepfather. Possibly he disapproved of young Leo's antics and turned his mother against him. At any rate the photo had obviously once been folded in half separating the two figures before being mounted in the album.

Of course, he might just be letting his novelist's imagination run away with him. The anomaly of the date might simply mean there were no photos from his final term. But then again it would have been strange for him not to have included some pictures of his final summer Footlights Revue, which would have been the climax of his theatrical career at Cambridge, nor had any photos been extracted thereabouts. But after all perhaps he just wasn't in it.

The following few pages, from about October 1937 till the start of the War, complete with a set of theatre programmes, indicated a career as a juvenile lead in provincial rep in casts that again included a handful of names that were later to become stars of stage and screen. Though his undergraduate years in the Footlights had obviously given him the entrée to this career, he imagined it was scarcely one which, in those days, his mother and especially his stepfather would have approved of. Could it have been this that caused the breach with his family?

On the evidence of the photos, the War severed his contact with the theatre but was it, Antony wondered, an episode in that period of his life which had given rise to the persistent school legend of a liaison with a famous actress (though probably not famous at the time) resulting in a child – and perhaps a brief unsuccessful marriage? Any such goings on would undoubtedly have caused an estrangement from his family and he could well imagine the Lieutenant-Colonel insisting that the boy never darken their door again. Perhaps a "pram in the hall" had blighted Marjoribanks life, hence his warnings against being ensnared by domesticity. But here of course he was piling speculation upon rumour.

At any rate whatever differences he might have had with his family did not prevent him getting a commission and having what appeared to be an interesting war. The couple of pages of wartime snaps showed a dashing young officer with a mane of thick black waved hair and the rather excessively good looks of a matinee idol, his cap at a jaunty angle, and somewhat incongruously clad in battledress. Generally he was on his own but he also appeared with his arm round a young Flight Lieutenant, with other officers looking at a map which was spread out on the table in front of them, sitting at a desk and walking down a street in London. There were also several pictures of him in 'civvies' – a light-coloured suit and a bow tie. Interestingly these had somewhat exotic captions: Cairo, Algiers, Lisbon, and in the first one there was a plane in the background. The rest had no captions at all except for the staff conference (or whatever it was) which was labelled 'GHQ/ops 40'.

Unexpectedly the first picture after the war, which filled most of a page following half a dozen from which all the photos had been removed, showed Marjoribanks still in uniform and was dated June 1951. It looked like an official group photograph with Marjoribanks, two other officers, one Navy, one Air Force and half a dozen mature looking civilians surrounded by about sixty young men in their early twenties. But what sort of group? Then by a stroke of good fortune he found, when he prised the photo free from the patches of glue which held it, an inscription on the back: 'Joint Services Russian Course, Bodmin, Cornwall'.

The rest of the book was taken up with school, Old Boys' and Arden Players' productions (including the *Twelfth Night* he had been in with Rosemary) and those of a few other theatre groups he had evidently been associated with. There were also some pictures of other school occasions – Old Boys' dinners, Speech Days and so on – but nothing more that could be called personal, though a large number of gaps in that part of the album might possibly have recorded moments from his private life or lives.

Antony's thoughts returned inevitably to the earlier pages – the Cambridge years, the wartime army career with the maps, the exotic locations and civilian clothes and his presence, indeed prominence, at a Joint Services Russian Course. Taken altogether did not this give credence to that other Marjoribanks legend linking him with espionage? Perhaps his otherwise puzzling decision to give up a service career in the early Fifties and become an obscure grammar school master was a matter of assuming 'cover', and the obscurer the better – hence Raynes Park rather than Harrow – while all the time he continued to do whatever it was that spies did. But if so who had he been spying for, his own country or perhaps Russia like some of his Cambridge contemporaries? Estrangement from his class might well have been the cause or the result of a conversion to Marxism, as it had been for so many others of his generation in the political climate of the Thirties, and what better disguise for a communist mole than that of a flamboyant and distinctly elitist schoolmaster in a suburban county grammar school.

There was no end to the speculation because there was now no way that he could see of conclusively proving anything. There was though, at the very least, a strong possibility that he had had something to do with spying and he was certainly an aristocrat. Antony, who had always aspired to noble birth, which he felt was his by right, as well as longing to live the purposeful double life of a spy – how well he understood those who despised their own country and were secretly dedicated to another allegiance – felt that even in death Marjoribanks had outshone him. Certainly Marjoribanks had made no attempt to recruit him!

Another undoubted fact emerged from the album; the year Antony entered the grammar school Marjoribanks was still in the army and, although when he at first encountered him as an English master in the sixth form he had the impression – such was his air and reputation – that he must be a very well established member of the staff, if not coeval with the school itself, so that it was difficult to imagine the place without him – in reality Antony must have been there before him. According to this record his first school production was in 1953 – a sort of patriotic fantasia celebrating the coronation, which he wrote himself.

Antony was later to learn that the Joint Services School for Linguistics was the place where bright National Servicemen were sent to learn Russian in the Cold War Fifties so that they could work as translators, interpreters, and intelligence and signals officers, and that alumni included Alan Bennett, Dennis Potter, Michael Frayn, Peter Hall et al. Here too, it seemed, Marjoribanks would have made contact with names he was later able to drop so nonchalantly.

So engrossed had Antony become in Marjoribanks' story that he was not even aware that Laura had brought him in a cup of tea. He only discovered it later when he finally closed the book and prepared to go. She was waiting for him in the door of the kitchen when he emerged onto the landing.

"Sorry I've been so long."

"Oh that's quite alright. Would you like something to eat?"

"That's very kind of you but no thanks, I must be off now. There's only one thing of his I want to keep really and it's this photo album. You could just get rid of the rest. I don't think his suits would fit me anyway. He didn't have much stuff, did he?"

"No, like he said, he believed in travelling light."

"Do you think I should do anything about the funeral or find out if he left a will? He must have had some money somewhere..."

"Oh no, don't worry, Neil's organizing all that."

"Neil?"

"His godson."

"Oh I see. Well, you will let me know about the funeral, won't you? I'd like to go. Thanks for the tea by the way; I'm afraid I forgot to drink it."

"That's alright. I'll give you a ring."

Antony drove home with the album on the front seat beside him unable to stop musing on the total change that death makes to our appreciation of anyone known to us. Whereas one was naturally aware of a living person in his or her current age and circumstances, once a life was over all its stages were equally 'real', equally part of the whole completed picture, with the same claim to our attention – Marjoribanks in his sailor suit, at Harrow, at Cambridge, the juvenile lead in rep, the young officer, the retired schoolmaster. The dead were neither young nor old; their whole lives were spread out in a sort of eternal present. That of course did not mean that the picture itself was always clear, especially in the case of a life as ambiguous as Marjoribanks'. But what fertile material for a novel! It was already taking shape in his imagination, a sort of *À la recherche d'une vie perdue*, a gradual teasing out of the true story of a Leo Marjoribanks figure; if indeed there could ever be a true story about anyone's life. It would be an exercise in trying to recover the irrecoverable.

The funeral was in the twelve o'clock slot at Mortlake Crematorium on the third of January. Antony gave Laura a lift and they sat together near the back of the chapel. A well dressed and socially polished middle-aged man had a general air of being in charge.

"That's Neil," whispered Laura, "Mr Marjoribanks' godson that I told you about."

He smiled vaguely at Antony as if unsure whether or not he ought to recognize him. Could godson Neil, who might be said to bear a very striking resemblance to Marjoribanks in face and to some extent in manner, be in fact his son, the product of his youthful fling, or was this merely Antony's wishful imagination at work?

In less than five minutes the congregation had assembled and the clergyman on duty began to read the completely anonymous routine service witnessed by a total of seven people excluding Neil, Laura and himself. There was a group of three wealthy looking women, probably a mother with two daughters in their forties: Marjoribanks' ex-wife and family perhaps, or his own relatives – a sister and nieces? (The 'ex-wife' wore dark glasses so that it was difficult to tell whether she was a well known actress or not!) At any rate Neil seemed to know them though he sat at some distance apart. There were two casually dressed and distinguished looking grey-haired men, widely separated and obviously not together, one of whom was wearing a long knitted scarf. They had an actorish appearance but gave the impression of having somehow just wandered in. They could even have been waiting for the next slot or have come to the wrong place altogether. Laura, at any rate, had never seen either of them before. She did however identify a couple of furtive and disreputable looking youths in tracksuits and trainers who mooched in at the last minute and, evidently feeling out of place, hunched down at the end of a bench as far as possible from everybody else.

"Those two," she said, "were always coming round. I think

they were sponging on him for money. He felt sorry for them I suppose."

The boys were a surprise. Of course if Marjoribanks had been an active homosexual in his youth it would have explained the breach with his family – if indeed there had been a complete breach. But in spite of his obviously camp 'theatrical' manner, which seemed if anything to become more obvious as the years wore on, and Rosemary's confident assertion all those years ago that he was obviously gay – though in those far off days the word she used was 'queer' – Antony continued to have doubts. For one thing, as far as he was aware, there had never been any sign of a partner and certainly never any suggestion of anything 'inappropriate' in his relationships with the many boys he had taken under his wing down the years. For another, Marjoribanks had always seemed too narcissistic, and also somehow too fastidious, for the give and take of any kind of loving relationship, straight or gay – indeed the very word 'relationship' would have provoked some caustic comment from him. Not only was he flagrantly cynical about all the couples of his acquaintance however apparently happy, confessing that he simply could not understand how two people could endure being constantly in each other's company for a week let alone a lifetime, he once let slip the remark apropos of some avant-garde play containing a simulated sex scene, that coitus was the most unaesthetic as well as the most ridiculous of all human activities. So in spite of the mooching boys and the youthful transvestitism, Antony remained unconvinced. But perhaps he was being naïve.

Marjoribanks at any rate had retained his mystery. Had he lived a life like Proust's Swann moving in several, or even many, completely different worlds, each one unknown to the others, some remnants of which were finally assembled in this sparse congregation? Or had his life outside school been empty, uneventful and largely solitary, at least in recent years? Had he deliberately tried to keep a certain distance from people, if so why? Was it simply his character to resist intimacy and never give too much of himself away or was he for some reason or other living a lie, harbouring secrets he could never reveal? Had he perhaps regarded Antony as one of the very few people among all his associates and protégés for whom he felt some kind of affinity and genuinely wished to know better? If Antony had reciprocated, how close would he have got to him? A sadly futile question, as at that very moment Marjoribanks' coffin was receding from view for the last time, making an almost comic exit bumping along rollers and through the little curtains that suddenly parted and closed again as in a toy theatre. Emerging into the anteroom already filled with a considerably larger crowd waiting for the twelve fifteen slot, he still expected to hear Marjoribanks' high commanding but subtly modulated voice making some scathingly flippant comment about crematorium funeral arrangements.

When the school reassembled a few days later, Antony as Hon. Sec. of the Old Boys rang the headmaster about Mr Marjoribanks' death learning to his surprise, as Antony had already notified the OB Association Committee, that it was the first he had heard of it. The head was persuaded of the need of some kind of memorial service on condition that the Old Boys took charge of the arrangements and it was held two weeks later in the neo-Gothic parish church round the corner from the school. The school was an ordinary county grammar with no special religious affiliation, but this was where the annual carol service took place.

The pews in all three aisles were full as well as all the portable chairs and there were even people standing at the back – the vicar, whose usual Sunday congregation was about twenty, had never seen the church so full. Apart from the staff and the current sixth form, everybody in the congregation – Old Boys, parents, ex-parents, old staff and friends of the school – were there on a weekday afternoon because they wanted to be. Antony, who had largely organized the proceedings – for him it was a way of making some sort of amends – was amazed at the turn out, but not nearly as much as the headmaster. There followed a carefully chosen series of apposite literary readings and music from the school orchestra, which Antony hoped Marjoribanks would have approved of, interspersed with some lively recollections of him by former pupils.

The headmaster spoke last and it must be recorded that his contribution was, to say the least, not commensurate with the occasion. He regarded himself as an educationalist not a teacher (and certainly not a schoolmaster) – he never actually taught any kids – and saw his role as the essentially managerial one of raising standards and 'delivering' results which would equip his charges for the modern competitive labour market. He had no time for any sentimental attachment to the school or its past (in fact he would much rather be running a brand new comprehensive), nor for that matter for antiquated elitist notions like culture and the liberal arts; consequently he was all at sea amid this overwhelming demonstration of regard for someone who, in his mind, epitomized these things along with all the amateurish inefficiency that went with them. He saw Marjoribanks as a relic of an age when Raynes Park Grammar was, absurdly, still pretending to be a minor public school. (In this he was largely mistaken as Marjoribanks had stood out quite as much among his shabby time serving colleagues in the Fifties as he did against the sharper, more professional and career-minded young staff of the current school.)

But now Mr Sturgis felt he had no choice but to make the best of it and so he delivered an address in which he actually referred to Leo Marjoribanks as representing "all that is best in the spirit and traditions of this school which he served with such loyalty and devotion for so many years". His address was only saved from sounding totally hypocritical by its inept and clichéd flatness and the singular lack of conviction with which it was delivered. As the service wound up with a blessing – the vicar had insisted on that minimum of religious content – Antony was left imagining Marjoribanks' derisive reaction to such a tribute. As for 'loyalty' and 'devotion', however important schoolmastering and producing plays might have been to him, his attitude to the school itself as an institution – 'this place' as he called it – had never, in Antony's experience, been anything but subversive and contemptuous.

III

So Marjoribanks, the enigmatic figure that none of the hundreds he had impressed and entertained down the years really knew, had departed leaving all the questions and ambiguities surrounding him forever unresolved. But Antony's intense and eternally frustrated curiosity was compounded by the sense of having failed his old mentor, a failure that could now never be remedied. Even though he was eventually to get a much admired novel out of it, the whole episode, following as it had hard on the heels of his break-up with Rosemary, seemed overwhelmingly sad and dispiriting. What after all, had Marjoribanks' life amounted to? What did any life amount to? Antony, at fifty-one, was a well established and successful novelist but far from the supreme artist he aspired to be; his work was far more impressive to others than to himself, knowing as he did all too well from the inside, as it were, the processes by which it was all, not faked perhaps, but confected. He began to take stock, to feel his age and to be oppressed by searching questions.

After the book inspired by the Marjoribanks enigma, which was well received even though against his agent's advice he stuck to the French title he had initially thought of, he published a novel that he had been working on intermittently for many years and consequently took little time to complete – the story of a social misfit who succeeds in overturning the British political system and acquiring supreme power. Though received with interest, because it was set in the Wilson years, this piece of alternative history seemed to have less relevance to a more prosperous and confident post-Thatcherite Britain. Needless to say the rather lukewarm reception of his latest novel did not improve his mood.

IV

His life jogged on relentlessly according to its habitual rhythms and routines until in no time at all he was nearing sixty – strangely though his days often dragged, the years passed faster and faster. His fellow Old Boys might continue to regard his life as enviable, but was it? On those long summer Saturdays when he umpired their cricket matches and the last pint after the game was sunk – nowadays they always adjourned to Antony's local afterwards – the others at least had someone to go home to, however unsatisfactory their domestic life might be. He went back to an empty house. He had no one with whom he could share his impressions, his thoughts, his experiences, to give them a kind of objective reality, no one with whom he could share a secret, no one he could even argue with.

Setting out on life he had taken it as a given – and Marjoribanks' advice had merely confirmed it – that if he were to fulfil the greatness he felt within him and fulfil his own manifest destiny, manifest to him at least, he would have to travel alone.

This was not simply for practical reasons. Great men were in his estimation essentially solitary. They breathed the clear air of the summits far above the common run of human kind; there was something almost ludicrous in the conjugation of greatness and genius with cosy domesticity. Could one imagine Hamlet settling down comfortably with Ophelia or Nietzsche happily married to Lou Salomé! Kierkegaard would not have been Kierkegaard if he had not sacrificed his fiancée Regine and with her his chance of ordinary human happiness. But apart from all other considerations travelling alone through the world had a certain irresistible glamour about it and the possibilities of such a life had seemed limitless.

He had devoted his whole life, apart from the unavoidable business of earning his living, to becoming a great writer – in fact he had never seriously considered doing anything else – and in practice this had meant that, instead of exotic holidays, going out and meeting people or just enjoying carefree days wherever the fancy took him, he had spent his free time hunched up over pads of paper and sheaves of notes. Life for him was something to be observed, recorded, analysed, rearranged, made use of, not lived. His experiences and emotions could never really be enjoyed for their own sake because in the last analysis they were only the raw material for his work – even his friendship with Rosemary and her family, the exploitation of which for literary purposes had cost him the trust and friendship of the only people he had ever loved.

This sacrifice of his whole life to his literary ambition might have been worthwhile – though the older he got the more he doubted it – if he had produced some enduring masterpiece; but what had he achieved so far through a lifetime of trying to recreate life at second hand? Nothing! Worse than that, a creative genius might be well advised to eschew domesticity but this did not exclude mistresses, passionate episodes, even Babylonian orgies; they might indeed enrich his art. Picasso after all reinvented himself each time he found a new girl and Balzac might have worn a cowl to show his monk-like dedication to his work but he had lovers too; to be famous and to be loved, that was his aim! Here too Antony, in spite of having the signal advantage of living in an increasingly sexually permissive culture and being entirely unencumbered with Kierkegaard's moral and spiritual baggage, had lost out all along the line. Though he told himself that rather like Philip Larkin he had been born just a few years too early to belong to a generation that took sexual freedom for granted, he knew in his heart that it was a lame excuse.

If he were honest, and these days he found that honesty was being more and more forced on him, his conspicuous failure to achieve the glittering success that Marjoribanks had, seriously or not, once predicted for him when he was a schoolboy, had contributed to the tension in their relationship – from Antony's point of view at least. The consciousness that he had failed to live up to Marjoribanks' expectations had made him especially sensitive to any hint of patronage or condescension on his old English master's part.

How could he, of all people, have missed so many opportunities at crucial points of his life? Perhaps it was true after all that character was destiny. It was a proposition that he had argued passionately against in the sixth form debating society in the days when he was convinced that he could achieve anything he chose if only he willed it with sufficient intensity; but now, looking back, it seemed as if he had been dealt a bad hand, with Nature, or rather his genetic code, endowing him with just the wrong concoction of mutually antagonistic qualities. He was highly intelligent, vastly imaginative, remarkably emancipated in his world view from the limitations of his particular culture and period, had a highly original, though very subtle, sense of humour, and a certain discreet charm, as well as a great capacity for happiness. He was industrious, nimble-witted, capable of speaking coherently and persuasively to large crowds and of entertaining an audience with or without a script. He had all the potential to make his name as a journalist, travel writer, best-selling author, actor or politician; but not only did he have far too high a sense of his own self-worth to settle for such modest and inevitably compromised success, he was averse to that thick-skinned and single-minded pushiness involved in selling oneself and breaking into a highly competitive world. Or, as he told himself, he was not prepared to demean himself by slugging it out in the dirt for any such comparatively paltry reward.

For there had been nothing modest about Antony's ambition, however reticent he might have been about it. Lord Rosebery set out to become a millionaire, prime minister and owner of a Derby winner, expiring at the last to the strains of the Eton Boating Song – and had done so – but this would not have been anything like good enough for Antony. As we have seen, his ambition was almost metaphysical. In his secret imaginings his only true peers, apart from world conquerors, were the very greatest writers: Aeschylus, Euripides, Vergil, Dante, Goethe, Tolstoy, Proust, and it was their ranks that he aspired to join. Striving to do so, insofar as he could, had seemed the only worthwhile objective given that he had only one life to lead.

Unfortunately, though he knew exactly what Alexander felt when he crossed into Asia or Napoleon when he entered Moscow, could, he was convinced, have prosecuted the Second World War more ruthlessly and more effectively than Hitler or, for that matter, have committed the perfect murder or been a criminal mastermind, Antony would have been too embarrassed to challenge a barman who had blatantly short-changed him in a pub, and though he had never had any inhibitions about acting on stage, he still found parties and all informal social gatherings something of an ordeal. He was uneasy with strangers, had no natural bonhomie, no easy spontaneity and even in late middle age continued to be acutely self-aware and sensitive to the reactions of others, even bores and people he despised. Truth to tell, in spite of rather half-hearted efforts to be sociable, he had always really preferred his own company, though whether this lack of sociability was due to his own peculiar upbringing or because he was he was more like his parents than he would have cared to admit, he could not possibly say.

Finally, although he had become, in his own imagination at least, a most consummate voluptuary, he had never been able to take the initiative in asking a woman out or making any kind of sexual advance, even when, as sometimes happened, he was fairly sure she was attracted to him, as he was quite unable to cope with the indignity and mortification of a possible rebuff; nor could he ever summon up the nerve to approach a prostitute. Although as he matured into middle age, he was able to establish more confident and friendly relations with women, the older he got, the more anomalous his position became and, in his eyes at least, the more impossible to resolve. It can thus be imagined, in spite of his ardent desire for the most grandiose possible self-fulfilment, with what reluctance and trepidation he had submitted each completed novel to the judgement of publishers and agents.

So here he was in his late fifties, asking himself how it had all gone wrong. In the past he had been able to overcome the disappointments and failures of his life so far by anticipating the love and glory that, he was able to convince himself, must be awaiting somewhere down the road which stretched out almost limitlessly before him; but now his days were beginning to run out, his energy was diminishing, that 'anything can happen' feeling, which had supported him and borne him along, confident in his own genius, his luck, his destiny, in spite of everything, was fading. There now seemed every likelihood that the future would be worse than the past and there was no refuge or immunity in reading, in the bygone splendours of History or in all the resources of his imaginative life from this relentless process. There was no life in books and museums as such. What vitality they had depended on the experiences of real people. That was where he had made his great mistake. And even if his lifetime of waiting were, by some incalculable stroke of fortune, to be ultimately rewarded and recognised, how could that recognition compensate for all the empty years? Would it not now be too late for him to enjoy?

He had always dreamt of attaining a serene stage in his life when he could withdraw from the bustle of the world to a secluded country estate – either deep in the English countryside or within sight of the Mediterranean – where he could enjoy the fruits of his success, entertain, read, reflect and watch the seasons pass unchanging year after year more or less indefinitely. But his future now was all too short for the mellow enjoyment of such open-ended expanses of time whatever his circumstances might be.

If only he could be granted another go at life knowing what he knew now, how differently he would live! Life did not stretch out almost indefinitely, barring some terrible accident, as he had assumed in his youth – on the contrary it was terrifyingly short. Given a second chance, there would be no dreamy procrastination, no fastidious standing back from everyone and everything that did not exactly suit some lofty preconception of his own, no excuses for standoffishness: he would make an effort to mix and get to know as many people as possible – there was no virtue in being supercilious and solitary as he once so mistakenly affected to believe. He would face up to every challenge and take advantage of what every precious day had to offer. But above all he would seek normal happiness. Though how possible that would be, given that to be himself he would still have to be saddled with the same genes, the same parents and the same upbringing, was something else altogether. Was it ever possible to escape from or transcend oneself?

As it was, he found himself nowadays staring with yearning envy at young couples and pregnant mums and even walking the suburban streets at night looking in at families grouped round the television or up at bedroom curtains where the shadows suggested a wife might be undressing for her husband. Thus he was reduced almost to being a stalker, a voyeur of other people's happiness – that whole feathery, frilly, silky feminine world of nighties, pink bows, babies and nurseries, now seemed a paradise from which he was forever excluded. Those things which he had once despised, that he thought he had no need of, were now eating his heart out.

In addition to all this he was haunted more and more by the fear that his dark secret might erupt at any moment. Every phone call, every knock on the door, even every quickening of footsteps behind him in the street, now held the possibility, however remote, that stony-faced police officers might intervene in his life with new and unanswerable 'evidence' concerning his mother's death, so that by a hideous irony his remaining years would be wasted in the living hell of prison for a crime of which he was perhaps morally guilty but legally innocent! Sometimes in his dreams he had already been arrested and more than once Antony had woken sweating after shouting desperately at his interrogators in the dark dungeon where he was being held: "but I've seen her since and she's happy now!" There was another irony of course. That fierce little tragedy had, in fact, been quite unnecessary. His mother would have died soon anyway and, in any case, her death had not really liberated him since in the event it made comparatively little difference to his way of life.

V

Thus from being one of the most remarkable and promise-filled people ever born, however unapparent it might have been to others, capable in favourable circumstances – or so he was convinced – of encompassing, ruling and creating whole worlds, he was now faced, against all expectations, with final disappointment, failure and perpetual obscurity, without even having been able to find those ordinary commonplace comforts and consolations that were open to almost everybody. He had nothing realistically left to look forward to but the gradual waste and decline of his physical and mental powers as the sands of his life ran out grain by grain leaving nothing to mark his presence in the world at all, not even children perpetuating his genes and bearing his name. Looking back, with what horrifying speed it had slipped through his fingers, that precious gift of life and youth and all his unprecedented and superabundant talent! 'Gaudeamus igitur juvenes dum sumus' – it was a bad joke! Yet even apparently happy, successful, fulfilled people declined into humiliating infirmity which seemed to cancel out everything that had gone before, reaching a state in which extinction seemed a 'merciful release'.

He had thought of old age as a sort of rare disease that afflicted a few unfortunates on the fringe of life who constituted almost a different species, from which the vigorous, the attractive, the daring, the brilliantly gifted, and a fortiori himself, must be immune, but not anymore. He had now lived long enough to see glamorous figures that he took for granted as securely enthroned in a sort of eternal middle age suddenly appear shockingly charmless and decrepit, and even young stars lose their looks. He had also become aware of the dreadful cocksure annihilating ignorance of the generations advancing behind him. He now heard supposedly educated adults talk of the Sixties and Seventies – for him more or less the contemporary world – as if they were practically the beginning of recorded history. But in due course everything would be forgotten, everything would decay, crumble, vanish: whole civilizations, human life, the planet, the universe itself – at some measurable distance in the future – with nothing left to say that sentient life had ever existed: cold infinite silence, forever.

It was a time of complete despair for Antony – what possible justification could there be even for the efforts he made to preserve his existence? Then one day after a terrible night when it seemed that he had reached the end of his tether, he saw with blinding certainty, as if by inspiration, that the only way to break the grip of this all-enveloping fatalism was simply not to accept it: to be the creator and shaper of his own life, an actor, a free agent, and not the passive victim of mere external physical laws – a subject and not an object; to change his whole way of life and mentality, utterly, radically, totally.

It was as if, trapped deep in an underground cave, unable to see so much as his hand in front of his face and with the knowledge that the air was inexorably running out, he had suddenly, miraculously, been confronted with a narrow ring of light and that on inspection it proved that the light outlined a boulder which, when rolled away revealed that he was not hundreds of feet below ground but on a hillside surveying a vivid summer landscape, warm and welcoming, with birds singing, bees buzzing in heavy-scented flowers and wooded hills in the distance.

And he simply walked out on that bright midsummer morning like Bunyan's hero in *Pilgrim's Progress* leaving behind his house, his possessions, his work, all the baggage of nearly sixty years, into a new world that it seemed he was seeing for the first time – a new world and a new life beyond hope and despair, one of total self-abandonment and acceptance in which he wanted nothing and needed nothing, and therefore failure, disappointment and even death didn't matter, and everything was beautiful. By recreating himself out of the ashes of his past he felt he was experiencing the reality that Rollo's philosophy had tried to put into words, as well as achieving the 'letting go' that his Buddhist teachers had counselled in the snowbound monastery in the Himalayas. That was all there was to it – all the religion and spirituality down the ages was essentially nothing more than this!

On his way he stopped at the estate agents to dispose of his house. When told by the girl he dealt with that she and her partner were having trouble as first time buyers finding a place they could afford, he simply gave it to her, leaving the keys on her desk and left. He then took trains until he found a congenial spot and then set off walking round the country, trusting that he would find a bed for the night, possibly in return for some casual work, in a pub, farm or hotel. Failing that he would be quite happy to sleep under the stars.

On the first evening, in the Yorkshire Dales, descending a gentle slope with the sun behind him throwing a long shadow, he came upon the garden of a little pub and was invited to sit down at a table by two kindly disposed gents of about his age kitted out for a walking holiday. With the new benevolence towards others that flowed from his conversion to total selflessness, Antony insisted on buying a round of drinks with the last money he had in his pocket and engaged them in conversation. It transpired that they were both widowers, one a retired headmaster and the other a former accountant. Both too had been diagnosed with cancer and in spite of conventional treatment their prognoses were not encouraging. As a result they had turned to an alternative therapy centre in north London and had joined its associated support group which was where they met.

They were impressed by Antony's account of how he had achieved a new life beyond hope and despair and he made the suggestion that instead of roaming the Yorkshire Dales with no particular object, the three of them should set themselves the challenge of walking the six hundred and thirty miles of the South West Coast Path from Minehead in Somerset all the way round to Poole in Dorset. At first they thought he was joking but he convinced them by implying that they had nothing to lose and could always drop out if they didn't feel up to it. Swept along by the force of his positive energy, they eventually agreed and, in the event, instead of regretting what they had rashly taken on, they found to their surprise that they felt themselves growing in strength and physical well-being as the six week walk progressed.

When it was over they went back to their respective consultants for check-ups to learn that amazingly, as far as could be ascertained, neither of them had the slightest trace of cancer and were remarkably fit for men of their age. On the strength of this, Antony was invited by Pete Nielson, the retired teacher, to address their support group. He had no desire to put himself forward but felt he could hardly refuse to share with others the possibility of transforming their lives.

His talk was extremely well received and he was asked to give more, many of his hearers reporting not only a psychological boost from adopting his radically new perspective on life, but also an alleviation of physical symptoms. Very soon Pete Nielson was receiving requests for Antony to address other support groups and, as word spread, his meetings were swelled by all kinds of people who felt there was something lacking in their lives or who were troubled for any reason.

At first nothing was planned since the demand for Antony's message could not possibly have been foreseen, but very soon, as his popularity continued to grow, it became apparent that some sort of organization was required if only for answering phones, planning and advertising meetings, booking halls, providing transport and collecting and investing the donations which began to flow in. There was no shortage of enthusiastic volunteers but Pete Nielson, now fired up with an evangelical zeal and energy that taxed his younger helpers, acted as a sort of coordinating secretary and spokesman and Andrew Stillman, the ex-accountant and Antony's other companion on the coastal walk became the treasurer of what, largely because a name of some kind was inevitable, became known as the New Life Movement. A derelict farmhouse and some outbuildings were acquired in Cornwall which willing hands rapidly converted into the Movement's permanent base and headquarters.

Antony, who would never in his wildest fantasies have imagined getting caught up in such an extraordinary phenomenon, had nothing whatever to do with the organizational side of things. All he did was try to communicate his message to whoever was prepared to listen and do what he could to offer comfort and advice to the innumerable people who came to see him. That message was always the same: we live lives driven by desires that can never in the nature of things be satisfied – for success, recognition, approval, fame, love, security, wealth, power and even for happiness, but at the same time, as if every step was on the thinnest ice or on the crust of a smouldering volcano, in constant fear of the sudden and uncontrollable eruption of the disaster – accident, misfortune, disease, and ultimately, death – that will take everything from us. Therefore abandon all wanting, hoping, planning, possessing and controlling, for those who have nothing to lose have nothing to fear. No need for mysticism, prayer or meditation, just do it and rejoice in every moment of existence – 'gaudeamus igitur juvenes dum sumus', but not only while we are young – now!

His luminous sincerity, compelling oratory and dramatically simple message had an extraordinary effect on his hearers and undoubtedly changed many lives. His fame spread through the then developing internet and crowds wishing to hear him began far to exceed the capacity of suitable indoor venues in the West Country, so he began addressing large outdoor gatherings in such places as Avebury, Glastonbury, Cerne Abbas, Maiden Castle, Cadbury Castle, Athelney and on the Wiltshire Downs. Because Antony's 'change life' teaching was essentially simple it attracted a large number of different groups who saw in it a reflection and affirmation of their own beliefs – or at least found it compatible with them, so the Movement became a home for Buddhists, evangelical Christians, pacifists, environmentalists, utopian socialists, hippies and pagans among many others.

Thus, though Antony was solely concerned with transforming individual lives and never mentioned God or current affairs, there was growing pressure to politicize and theologize the Movement that supported him. Factions, tendencies and personal rivalries began to develop and, as far as he was concerned, the whole thing seemed to be getting out of hand. What he was doing had nothing to do with politics, religion or morality in the conventional sense – his message was that people could transform their own lives without the aid of some outside power and when he was alone he felt no need to pray, though he did try a few times without any success. Moreover he was finding that giving himself completely to all those who came to him seeking help and advice was severely taxing even his capacity for self-transcendence and he was minded to walk away from the New Life Movement altogether. Though his two principal lieutenants Pete Nielson and Andrew Stillman managed to argue him out of it by telling him how desperately he was needed, it was really the support of the crowds he addressed that kept him going and revived his flagging faith that it was all worthwhile.

Then one day about six o'clock on a warm September Saturday evening as he was being greeted on his arrival by a crowd of at least ten thousand people at the earthwork of Old Sarum (courtesy of English Heritage) – Antony habitually spoke from a simple platform using the lie of the land to make himself visible – something very remarkable happened. A mother pushed a little girl in a wheelchair right in front of him and they were both looking at him imploringly. Without thinking he laid his hands on them and said: "You can change your life." To the amazement of the by-standers, including Antony, the little girl got out of the chair and embraced him. He moved swiftly on but word of the 'cure' spread so that as he was leaving at the end of the meeting, stewards brought to him an elderly lady painfully bent and crippled with arthritis and a youngish man with such poor eyesight that he carried a white cane. He laid hands on both of them as before and once again the old lady straightened up and seemed ten years younger while the partially blind man began to weep saying that he could see clearly and distinctly for the first time since his childhood. The crowd became so enthusiastic at this point that it was only with difficulty that his minders managed to get him to his car and drive him away, totally exhausted.

Although innumerable people, starting of course with Pete Nielsen and Andrew Stillman had reported being transformed mentally as well as physically as a result of Antony's 'new life' teaching, sudden and dramatic 'cures' like these apparently accomplished just by the laying on of hands were something completely new. From now on at every meeting he was asked to touch sick people and the cures continued.

In fact not everyone he touched was cured, but only the spectacularly successful instances –the instant recovery of a man with advanced Parkinson's disease for example – were noted and remembered, so that the belief grew that he had only to lay hands on somebody for them to recover. Understandably this phenomenon dramatically changed Antony's mission. The pressure to turn him into a quasi-religious figure became overwhelming and the custom developed of calling him the Master – that was after all how the crowds now acclaimed him. A Council of Elders, including Nielsen and Stillman, was established to insulate him from the rest of the Movement and access to his person was severely restricted. This was necessary in any case because requests to see him from those seeking guidance had become overwhelming.

For the ever growing multitudes that followed him and now sought to touch him as he passed, faith in his message had become faith in him as well, and how could Antony fail to be warmed by their faith, to embrace it and grow more and more to believe it himself? Surely all those people could not be deceived in him. After all he had transformed his own life and the lives of so many others and he was working miracles all without recourse to prayer or any exterior higher power. Surely therefore he must be a source, perhaps the source, of transcendent power himself – a Messiah, a World Redeemer, an Avatar, a Buddha? (Perhaps the last was the closest analogy, since his teaching had had nothing to do with any supernatural god.) It would certainly explain his inability to pray. But these were thoughts that he could reveal to no one and increasingly he kept apart from others, even his closest collaborators.

Not long after the healings began a visitor arrived at the Movement's HQ in Cornwall who was most insistent on being admitted to see him. She would not have succeeded had not Antony himself, hearing a familiar voice, looked out from the stone tower that formed his private quarters, seen her at the gate and sent word that she be allowed to pass. The visitor was

Rosemary. As soon as she entered his room he opened his arms to her and she flung herself at him. Overcome by the intense emotion of that moment she broke down and like the penitent Magdalen admitted that her whole life had been a mess; Antony had been right all along, she should have listened to him and not married either of her husbands, he was the only man who had ever really meant anything to her, she had been attending his meetings and was trying to follow his teaching and change her life completely but finding it difficult...

The scene would once have been the fulfilment of the dream of a lifetime but now he had to explain to her gently what in her heart she already knew, that as Master of the Movement he was wholly devoted to others and could not possibly allow himself to be involved in a private relationship. Rosemary, who now wanted nothing more than to remain close to him, offered her services full-time to the cause and became an invaluable personal assistant to Andrew Stillman. Before long, with Antony's encouragement and blessing, a more than professional relationship developed between her and his trusted lieutenant.

As Antony grew naturally into the role of miracle-working Master, the more closely his every utterance was scrutinized, interpreted and analysed both by his own followers and by outside observers. Although he taught no doctrine and had no programme, his message was in itself essentially subversive since if taken seriously it would undermine the whole culture of getting and spending, individualism and the pursuit of happiness on which contemporary society and the economic system were based. Now that his ever growing Movement was numbered in hundreds of thousands – perhaps even more than a million (it was difficult to say as there was no formal membership) – and could no longer be ignored or dismissed as some sort of alternative hippy cult, serious concern began to be expressed by politicians and the media. Though some saw merit in what were taken to be the 'green' elements in the Master's teaching, the consensus was that there was something distinctly un-British about the emotional fervour that surrounded him, and that the prospect of the country being overrun by what one journalist described as 'an irrationalist sect combining the worst features of CND, Christian Science and Falun Gong', was nothing short of alarming. At any rate it gave the scaremongering industry something new to work on. Religious authorities, conscious of being upstaged, were also concerned. The Muslim Council of Britain branded the Movement as 'un-Islamic' and the Catholic bishops of England and Wales declared that no Catholic should join, though Buddhists and Hindus were less hostile and some in the Church of England even went so far as to welcome it as evidence of a deep spiritual hunger that still persisted even in modern secular society.

The problem for opponents and critics however was that the healing miracles showed no sign of stopping, the New Life Movement continued to grow and worse, Antony seemed to keep 'upping the ante'. His style of preaching and his references to himself became constantly more exalted and grandiose. He began to talk of changing the life of the world in addition to changing individual lives since, as he declared, one could not be accomplished without the other. But it was when he announced to some five hundred thousand people at Glastonbury that in a few weeks' time, at Easter, less than three years after his now legendary Coastal Path Walk, he was going to 'take over' London and posters started appearing on billboards all over the capital reading: 'The Master is Coming To Set You Free!', that the political authorities decided that he had to be stopped. In this they found a timely ally in the Cardinal Archbishop of Westminster who preached a sermon denouncing the so-called 'March on London' which was widely praised even in papers not unusually sympathetic to the Church. His text, from Matthew 24, practically chose itself: 'Then if any man shall say to you, Lo, here is Christ, or there; do not believe it. For there shall arise false Christs and false prophets, who will show great signs and wonders; so as to deceive, if possible, even the elect. Behold, I have told you before. Therefore if they shall say to you, Behold, he is in the desert, go not forth; behold, he is in the secret chambers; do not believe it. For as the lightning comes out of the east, and shines even to the west, so shall the Son of man be.'

Of course there were quite a number, especially of those who had been associated with him in the early days who were disillusioned by Antony's failure to do anything to stem what they saw as a creeping tendency to divinize the leader of a Movement that they saw as essentially about helping people to transform their lives. Some observed that he was beginning to behave as if he believed the most extravagant claims made about him. But not only were these defectors jumping off the band wagon vastly outnumbered by those jumping on, they had no scandals to reveal, nor had any of the moles planted in the Movement by the security services. Repeated meetings in the Home Office and Downing Street had difficulty in finding any grounds on which to proceed against it given that there was no obvious evidence of conspiracy, corruption or the infringement of any other law. Moreover there was an awareness that any heavy-handed action against a hitherto peaceful sect could lead to potentially uncontrollable protests. But in the end it was decided, with some trepidation, to ban any more mass meetings by the Movement for a period of three months on the grounds of public order.

Antony's 'advance' on London had been marked by a rally of seven hundred and fifty thousand on the Hog's Back near Farnham. Two days later and just after the ban came into effect he decided to go ahead with another already planned mass meeting at Polhill on the North Downs near Sevenoaks in Kent, not far from the M25. What power on earth could prevent him?

It was arranged that he would stand on top of the disused Polhill quarry and address the crowd gathered far below. (Hidden in the woods behind it was the secret weapons research establishment of Fort Halstead and it was the fear that some of the groups attached to the Movement might use the meeting as cover to take some sort of action against it, that had induced the government to move quickly to introduce the ban before the Polhill rally.)

The police tactics of blocking off all roads leading to the site had partially succeeded in reducing the numbers but nevertheless there were at least a hundred thousand people to give him a frenzied welcome when he appeared on the edge of the vertical chalk cliffs that beautiful April afternoon. Truly nothing could stop him now! He had microphones to speak into even though the giant screens that had been used at his recent meetings had been intercepted by the police. He began as was now the well established custom by laying hands on the sick and at his touch a completely paralysed man, his greatest ever challenge, rose from his stretcher and embraced him. This most spectacular of all his healings conducted in full view of the whole assembly produced an extraordinary reaction. Then almost immediately five uniformed constables pushed their way through the stewards and Elders standing around him and attempted to arrest him under the Public Order Act. Their words echoed round the quarry on the public address system and a great rhythmic chant of protest rose from the crowd, who, however, could do nothing to intervene.

Antony called for calm. This was his moment of destiny. He could make a paralysed man rise from his stretcher. He was master of the laws of nature. How could he allow himself to be tamely led away by policemen? He would display his power yet more wonderfully and hover in the air above them all. This would be the ultimate miracle. After this no one would be able to oppose or even doubt him. This would be his apotheosis. He would be revealed as the Lord of the Universe.

"Have no fear", he announced. "I will rise above you all and descend amongst you. Stand back and bear witness!"

Everyone fell silent. There was scarcely a soul who did not expect that as he walked off the cliff he would he would be somehow borne aloft. The alternative was simply inconceivable. He felt the faith of a hundred thousand, amplifying, if that were possible his own utter confidence in his power as he prepared to soar upwards as one mightier than an archangel.

He gave a little leap then the silence was transformed into a terrible groan. Fortunately no one ever saw the look of amazement on his face followed by terror when he realised that he was subject to the law of gravity, but they all heard his despairing cry before he was dashed against the face of the chalk as he plummeted the hundred feet or so to the unyielding ground below.

The spell was broken. The bewildered, despairing and disillusioned gathering melted away with surprising speed as if ashamed of the belief that had united them only moments ago, and then, from the almost deserted quarry floor rose the inconsolable wail of a grieving woman as Rosemary cradled in her arms the broken body of the only man she had ever loved.

The Movement broke up in mutual recrimination and confusion – a case of striking the shepherd and the sheep being scattered. Some maintained he had not really died, that it was all a conspiracy and that it was a stand-in, a lookalike, who had been killed. A few others predicted his eventual Glorious Return to Earth. He was even said to have appeared to various people. But all this was confined to an insignificant fringe. The establishment breathed a brief sigh of relief, the world moved on and one of the most remarkable episodes in recent British social history was over.

PART FIVE: REUNION, RETURN TO VIENNA, LAST THINGS

I

Rosemary and Anton had continued to correspond almost weekly down the years. The need for absolute discretion was just as necessary after his formal separation from the Empress as before because Rosemary had never told her husband or family anything about the illustrious connection. How could she? There are some secrets that override even the ties of marriage. But for all its undisclosable secrecy this correspondence could hardly be described as love letters. It began as a simple catching-up with the news about each other's lives since they had parted but gradually, as complete confidence was restored between them, their letters became a much more intimate and personal form of communication in which nothing was held back, especially by Rosemary, except any direct reference to their own relationship – though she no longer called him Tony, as she had done when they were students.

Thus Anton felt he knew everything about her daily life and was able to follow all the excitements and anxieties of every stage of her children's growing up. At appropriate moments he sent discreet gifts, as when in 1966 her elder daughter, Emily, interrupted a promising career in publishing to produce Rosemary's first grandchild. Writing, they both felt, enabled them to express things that it would have been difficult, if not impossible, to say directly. They did in fact speak occasionally to each other by mobile phone from 1990 onwards (calls by landline were too insecure and difficult to arrange) but such exchanges were necessarily brief and largely confined to an exchange of greetings on special occasions – Christmas, their birthdays and so forth – though she did ring once after seeing a television report of a failed attempt on his life in Vilnius. In general, however, all the personal and gossipy stuff was kept for the letters.

When her children were at last off her hands – her son Richard finally left home in 1998 – a plan was mooted and gradually hatched between them that they should somehow arrange a reunion. Rosemary was somewhat less enthusiastic than Anton, but concealed her misgivings and went along with the idea without demur. It transpired that her husband was to attend an international business fair in Vienna in the spring of 2002, one of the innumerable events organized as part of the year of celebrations to mark the Emperor's forty years on the throne – his *first* forty years as it was loyally expressed – planned to culminate on the anniversary of that September morning when he had been elected and proclaimed King of the Romans to huge rejoicing in Frankfurt and in all the capitals of those countries which had completed the ratification of the constitution of the Restored Empire.

These fortieth anniversary celebrations, which, unlike those that Musil's anti-hero Ulrich spent his time organizing for the seventieth anniversary of Emperor Franz Joseph, actually took place, were intended to far outdo those for his Silver Jubilee, when he had his Empress and young family at his side, or even those for his wedding. They were also intended to focus especially on Vienna, which, though it was the 'de facto' capital of the Empire, with Rome the 'de jure' capital, had the feeling that it had been somewhat deprived of imperial favour in recent years.

That is not to say that the Emperor did not continue to

observe the demands of the court calendar most punctiliously – attending balls, gala performances at the opera and the annual Corpus Christi procession, holding investitures and garden parties, hosting state visits, presiding as Sovereign over chapters of the Order of the Golden Fleece and the Teutonic Knights, taking the salute at the military ceremonies to mark his birthday, receiving the Imperial Chancellor and other ministers and transacting high state business in the Aulic Council, the Reichshofrat. (In the Restored Empire the Aulic Council no longer functioned as a court or a council of war but as the supreme organ of the executive in which the Emperor formally assented to acts of the Imperial Council of Ministers – rather like the Privy Council in Britain – while the Reichskammergericht functioned as the ultimate court of the Empire in all criminal and civil, as well as constitutional, cases.) But although the good burghers and loyal subjects of Vienna could see the Emperor's standard with its black double-headed eagle on yellow ground and characteristic triangulated border floating at regular intervals high over the Hofburg or the Schönbrunn, it was remarked that he preferred more and more these days to take refuge in the country, especially at Konopischt, unquestionably his favourite residence. And when he wasn't at Konopischt he seemed to be forever travelling from one palace to another round the Empire by train. Moreover, though he never failed to open the Imperial Diet at Regensburg with due pomp every five years, and had done the same at one time or another for almost all the other landtags, assemblies and other legislatures of his vast Empire, he had never, as it happened, opened the Austrian parliament, a task which he always left to his Viceroy, who in the case of Austria was by tradition always an Archduke of the imperial family.

There was another, darker, reason for making so much of the fortieth anniversary of the Emperor's election instead of waiting, as might have been more usual, for his golden jubilee in ten years' time, or even the anniversary of his coronation which was just over a year away. It was a reason that was undisclosed, indeed never explicitly acknowledged – the Emperor's health was beginning to give rise to serious concern. The concern had been communicated by the Emperor's doctors to a few chosen and totally trustworthy courtiers and thence to the Imperial Chancellery which fortunately or otherwise was immediately adjacent to the imperial apartments in the Hofburg.

The Emperor himself, though naturally aware of certain disquieting symptoms, did not appear to realise how serious their possible implications might be. And who was going to tell him? At any rate for the moment he refused all tests that might clarify the matter, suggesting that his doctors were, as usual, making a fuss about nothing. All the doctors could do was wait. So concern persisted and intensified, a dark secret that could not be indefinitely contained, like a fire deep in the hold of a mighty liner whose passengers are blithely unaware, as she steams on apparently serene and invulnerable, of desperate and growing danger in the very heart of the ship. But the formidable communications resources of the imperial household were mobilised to stress that nothing could be more natural than to celebrate the Emperor's fortieth anniversary in an exceptional way. After all had not exactly the same thing been done for Franz Joseph in 1888, the occasion for which Johann Strauss had composed The Emperor Waltz and Wilhelm Gause painted his famous picture of the 'Court Ball at the Hofburg'?

The long dreamt-of meeting – the reunion between Anton and Rosemary – did indeed come to pass on a beautiful but chilly April day in 2002. With her husband occupied all day at the business fair Rosemary, like any tourist, took a taxi to the Augustinerstrasse and entered the Church of the Augustinians, which, though accessible from the street is an integral part of the Hofburg. As arranged at twelve o'clock precisely an equerry, who would have shown the same exquisite courtesy to anyone from Pope to bag lady, graciously introduced himself and, after remarking that the chapel in which she was presently standing contained fifty-four silver urns that preserved the hearts of many generations of the House of Hapsburg – 'a custom now discontinued' – offered to escort her to what, with most delicate discretion, he called 'her appointment'.

Unlocking a side door he led her out of the church, along a corridor which turned into a narrow stone tunnel and up a wrought-iron spiral staircase which, he explained, took them up to a maintenance passage through the high-pitched roof space. Thus, as he informed her, they were able to pass over the halls housing the great collections of the Imperial Library (the National Library of Austria in the days of the Republic) and then over the Secular and Sacred Treasuries until they reached a shallow flight of marble stairs which they descended to a corridor of brilliantly polished parquet along which ran a strip of red carpet. They stopped at the third set of double doors on their right where a liveried footman was waiting. He opened them and then another pair of doors and suddenly Rosemary and Anton were face to face. The equerry meanwhile, having accomplished his mission, vanished like a ghost.

As soon as the door closed behind them they embraced then held each other at arm's length. It was not that their present appearance was unfamiliar – after all everyone knew what the Emperor looked like and he had seen recent photographs of her – that caused them to gaze so intently at each other, but rather that the simple fact of their being together after forty years was so difficult to absorb.

"I can't believe this is happening," said Anton.

"But it is," said Rosemary.

They were in a little sun filled rococo sitting room lit by a single high window on the third floor of the imperial apartments looking out onto the 'in der Burg' courtyard and the skyline of Vienna beyond. Anton pointed out the intricate patterning of the glazed tiles on the high roof of the Stephansdom, less than half a mile away and the double-headed eagle at the top of its slender spire, adding with a faint smile: "My predecessors' entrails are buried in the crypt under the high altar."

"Don't. I have already heard about those hearts in that other church."

"You don't know Vienna, do you? There are so many beautiful things to see: churches, art collections... I can choose someone really good to show you round. Christmas is really the best time to be here – Christmas in Vienna, April in Paris, that's what they say isn't it? But the spring is..."

"I am afraid I'm not very good with churches and museums, unless you could show me round. You always made things interesting I seem to remember."

"How I wish I could." He sighed and then said with a renewed effort at liveliness: "Anyway you chose a lovely day. Shall we sit down? We can talk while we eat."

Beside the window was a round dining table covered down to the floor with a white starched linen cloth laid for a meal with crystal glasses and silver cutlery, a Chinese 'famille rose' vase of spring flowers at its centre, and two gilded white and red velvet chairs. As soon as they had taken their places and shaken out their napkins, as if by magic, white-gloved figures appeared from a side door with champagne, an ice bucket and oysters, and as rapidly disappeared. When they were alone again there was a short period of silence then they both began speaking at the same time, and laughed.

The oysters were followed by poached salmon and a salad served with a dry Riesling, then fruit and a rich layered cake called a Dobos Torte, accompanied by a bottle of Château d'Yquem. The serving and clearing away was performed with wonderful dexterity and despatch so that they were left as far as possible undisturbed throughout the meal and they talked incessantly as if anxious to avoid any more silences or pauses for reflection, but giving nevertheless a fair impression of cheerful happiness. However the conversation generally led, contrary to all protocol, by Rosemary, in which they spoke about everything they could think of, but chiefly her children and grandchildren, seemed more designed to fend off intimacy than to promote it. Anton, who did not mention his health anxieties, did his best to entertain and amuse her, making an effort that was never required with courtiers, even if it sometimes proved necessary with politicians.

At about three thirty Rosemary looked at her watch. "Goodness how quickly the time's gone. Anton it has been lovely but I ought to be thinking about getting back. I've arranged to meet my husband about five..."

For a moment he was bemused. It was the first time for forty years that anyone had indicated to him that they wished to leave his presence; but then for the last few extraordinary hours he had no longer been the Emperor, just Anton. It ought really to have been a liberating feeling

"Yes of course. I hope you didn't find the lunch too heavy. I chose it myself."

"It was lovely. Sorry I didn't try the torte – it would have been a disaster for my waistline. Now don't try to say anything complimentary. I know I'm overweight." She stood up as did Anton. "You know I think I've had a little too much to drink!"

"At least let me send you back in a car."

"Alright, thank you, provided I can tell the chauffeur where to stop. I don't want to draw attention to myself."

Anton pressed a button and prepared to escort her from the room.

"Before you go, I have got something for you – a little present." He produced a red leather jeweller's box embossed with the imperial arms. She opened it to find a gold and ruby necklace. "I had it made specially. It's an ancient Egyptian design. I thought it might suit you."

"Oh Anton, it's beautiful, but I can't possibly accept it. You must see that."

"Have you ever thought that if things had turned out differently we would be coming up for our ruby wedding now?" (For the first time he had broken the implicit mutual taboo on talking directly about their past.)

"Anton, I don't regret not becoming an Empress – it would never have worked – and besides how could I wish away my family, but I want you to know... I want you to know that I have never loved anyone as I loved you."

She laid her hand briefly on his arm and turned away, her eyes full of tears. "I knew this was a bad idea," she muttered and abruptly left the room, the two sets of double doors opening unbidden in front of her. Out in the corridor she found Colonel Ferenc, the Hungarian equerry, waiting for her. He clicked his heels, kissed her hand and seeing her distress gently guided her on her way. Soon they were in what appeared to be a service lift and then passing through a side door into a courtyard where a Mercedes with one-way glass in the windows was parked. Ferenc took his leave, the chauffeur ushered her into the car and in no time they were speeding over cobbles, through gateways where guardsmen saluted and out of the palace by the splendid Michaelertor entrance to rejoin the Viennese traffic.

'It was a mistake', she kept thinking as she was being smoothly conveyed back to her hotel, 'I wish I'd never gone. Pickled hearts,' she heard herself saying, 'all those pickled hearts in silver urns,' and shuddered.

Anton meanwhile stayed in the rococo sitting room – once used by one of Maria Theresa's daughters – gazing out of the window. He had been completely bowled over by her unforgettable parting words which, it seemed to him, had been wrung from her as in a last agony – 'I never loved anyone as I loved you'. The words were terrible. He knew now for certain, inescapably, what he had missed; what he had given up for History, for other people's dreams. But it was worse than that. Their meeting had seemed to him completely unreal. It had felt like a scene played out between two people at which he was a spectator, rather than a real encounter. They had kept telling each other how enjoyable it was and how neither of them had changed, but in reality everything had changed for he had realised that afternoon when they met face to face, that his desire for her had faded. It was no more than a memory and could not be revived. The agonising thing was that she was still remarkably attractive – the deficiency was entirely his! Their love for each other had been unfulfilled, but now even that love itself, which had in a way secretly sustained him all these years, had silently, and without him ever being aware of it, died. Life and love were wasting assets. There was no stasis, no plateau, no way in which they could be securely preserved and hoarded to be perpetually enjoyed at one's leisure like miser's gold, or the regalia in the Schatzkammer. Everyone knew that in theory but now he knew it in his heart, in his very soul.

Emperors however, perhaps fortunately, do not enjoy the privilege of being able to remain alone with their thoughts for very long. A few minutes later his Principal Privy Chamberlain, whose duty it was to know at all times exactly where his Emperor was, interrupted him with a respectful reminder that at four thirty he was granting an audience to the Minister for the Navy together with the entire Naval High Command and the Admirals in charge of the imperial fleets to discuss the great Naval Review, in the Adriatic off Trieste, planned to celebrate his forty years on the throne.

That night, by some meteorological freak, the most violent storm for years broke over Vienna and Anton found himself in the Wienerwald – the Vienna Woods – but a Wienerwald that had taken on the aspect of some far more sinister and more ancient forest, for all the trees seemed to be dead and gnarled and twisted into monstrous shapes. It was a landscape under a curse. He was an old man with a straggling white beard, his hands thin and wrinkled, his limbs aching, stranded far from home in torrential rain, a wasted Merlin-like figure approaching his dotage, burdened with long and bitter memories of ancient convulsions, terrible upheavals and 'old unhappy far off things and battles long ago'. His cloak was so sodden and heavy that he could scarcely drag himself along, so he paused to rest against a hollow oak and take advantage of what meagre shelter it afforded.

At that very moment a thunderbolt sundered the tree behind him with a hard-edged ear-splitting explosion, but it was accompanied by a flickering radiance in which he saw a huddled figure beside him throw off its tattered cloak to reveal a young woman of dazzling, irresistible beauty – his Morgan le Fay, his Nimue, his Rosemary transfigured! Suddenly the forest around him was green again and flooded with sunlight. He was young again too; youthful blood was coursing through his veins. They looked at each other in an eternal moment of love and, overwhelmed with a passionate mutual yearning to unite, a feeling more intense than anything he had felt before, they embraced, never to be parted again. There was another clap of thunder, the sky darkened, the rain returned and he immediately recoiled in horror as he found that instead of his beautiful mistress, he was clutching a toothless and shrivelled old crone in a nest of rags, and he was a cold, tired, bereft, hopeless old man once more. His groan of anguish for youth, beauty and passion glimpsed once and lost forever reverberated around the forest.

It alarmed his valet who slept in a room next to the imperial bedchamber and the guards and security men within earshot. As he came to his senses Anton found himself gazing up at half a dozen anxious faces and collecting himself with some difficulty realised, with his forty years' experience as Emperor, that it was his first duty in all circumstances to reassure those about him and put them at their ease. He acknowledged their presence with a smile.

"Is your Imperial Majesty quite well?"

"Quite well, Joseph. You can all go back to bed. It was the storm. My sleep was disturbed."

II

In the summer of 2002 at the age of sixty-three Antony was still working at the bookshop but facing the prospect of retirement in two years' time. To himself as well as to others he claimed to be looking forward to it as an opportunity to be at long last the master of his own time and to be able to think, write, read and travel without any constraints, if indeed, as he joked with his cronies in the old boys, he actually made it to sixty-five! Nevertheless he did have misgivings amounting at times to panic, which he refused to acknowledge, about the loss of any publicly recognised role and function to give a structure to his day and indeed to his life; in other words having no compelling reason to get out of bed in the morning, however bitterly on any given morning he might have resented having to do so over the years.

As for his literary career, he was now counting on success and recognition after his death – after all had not Nietzsche said that some men were born posthumously. That was about all, realistically, that he had left to hope for, but though this was a bleak enough consolation it seemed like quite a good bet. Many of the greatest painters and composers had only been truly appreciated after their deaths – sometimes long after, and in any case it took at least two generations for a literary reputation to be securely established. Only the winnowing effect of time could separate enduring merit from the transient popularity of the best seller.

He was now determined on one thing however; he was not going to wait for his retirement to start travelling. That summer he was going to spend some of his savings on what he called a 'now or never' two week holiday in Vienna – the city he had longed to visit all his life – from the twenty-fifth of August to the seventh of September. (Conveniently enough he had just finished and sent off to the publishers the novel on which he had currently been working. Ironically entitled *Gaudeamus Igitur* it was the strange and tragic tale of a man of mature years who almost unwittingly becomes the leader of a quasi-religious movement and is finally destroyed by coming to believe in the messianic powers that his followers attribute to him. When he came back from Vienna he was resolved finally to get to grips with the masterpiece that would constitute his enduring legacy and claim to greatness.)

Incredible as it might seem for such a knowledgeable world traveller who so despised his own island, this was to be his first trip abroad in the physical sense and he planned it meticulously, making a comprehensive list of everything he wanted to see on each day so as not to waste a single hour. Averse to flying he arranged to go by Eurostar to Brussels then take the Thalys high-speed train to Cologne, before going on the following day via Frankfurt and Nuremburg to Vienna. (Coming back he intended to take a day trip from Brussels to pay his respects at the tomb of Charlemagne in its Romanesque sanctuary in the cathedral of Aachen.) One of his guide books mentioned tick-borne encephalitis, which could possibly cause brain damage or even death, as a very rare danger in deciduous woodland areas, so, as he wanted to visit Grinzing and the Vienna Woods, he decided to take out the most expensive form of health insurance which provided for his being taken home by air ambulance in an emergency.

On all the previous occasions that he had planned a foreign holiday something had cropped up, generally a bout of flu or a stomach upset – the sort of thing that he always seemed to succumb to whenever the pressures of his job, such as they were, relaxed and he had a long anticipated week or two off. Then with regret, but always with a certain unacknowledged relief, he had cancelled his trip, or rather postponed it to the indefinite future. On this occasion too he was feeling unwell, but he had been feeling unwell off and on for months, and now he was absolutely determined that nothing should stand in his way – it really was, as he told himself, now or never.

As soon as he emerged from the Westbahnhof after his long and tiring rail journey and was bowling along in a taxi on a blazing hot Viennese late summer afternoon to his hotel, he knew he had done the right thing to come. All symptoms of illness had lifted and he was in exultant spirits. He had the overwhelming feeling of having returned at last after sixty years of exile in a remote and alien land. Vienna was everything he hoped and expected it to be – the epitome of the great European metropolis, the worthy capital both of culture and imperial and royal majesty. His hotel, a charming old world establishment was ideally situated right in the heart of the city just off the Kärntnerstrasse, one of the main shopping thoroughfares, very near the Stephansdom, handy for the U-Bahn and surrounded by cafés and restaurants.

Antony spent the first few days in a delighted daze. He took a coach trip into the surrounding countryside, he strolled in the Prater, he wandered into churches, museums, palaces and theatres. He watched the world go by as he drank his coffee and ate his torten. But though in a lifetime's loving study of the city he had imbibed and lived with every detail of the architecture of old Vienna and its monuments – the red marble tomb of Frederick II in the Stephansdom, the copies of Trajan's Column on either side of the Karlskirche, the staircase of the Opera, the four commanders at the feet of the statue of Maria Theresa holding the Pragmatic Sanction, the statue of Athene in front of the Parliament building – nothing had prepared him for how conveniently close and interrelated were all the gardens, squares and grand buildings round the Ringstrasse in their rich variety of architectural styles, even the Schwarzenberg Palace and the Lower and Upper Belvedere. Only the Schönbrunn was beyond walking distance. The sole discordant note was the coach loads of American and Japanese tourists that infested these cherished places of his dreams but were really only interested in the Spanish Riding School and the graves of the famous composers!

III

Catching a widespread mood the media spoke, with pardonable exaggeration, of the Emperor's 'long awaited homecoming to his own city' or, more fancifully, of 'the renewal of the marriage between Vienna and the imperial crown' and even of his 'return from exile', which, it was universally hoped, would be permanent. On Friday the thirty-first of August Anton arrived late in the evening at the Schönbrunn from Konopischt, where he had spent most of the summer, for what the almost frantically excited popular press were calling 'Ruby Jubilee Week'.

The following morning he drove under a cloudless sky the Stephansdom for a Te Deum celebrated by the Cardinal Archbishop of Vienna, who had been named Papal Legate to the celebrations, through a city en fête as perhaps it had never been before in all its rich and momentous history. From the cathedral he was to drive round the Ringstrasse to the Rathaus to dine with the mayor, the city fathers, the imperial government and representatives of all the nations of the Empire – a signal honour for the city which in turn was to present him with a silver model of the Rathaus studded, appropriately, with rubies to commemorate the occasion. After this he would proceed to the Hofburg to host a reception for all the foreign royalty, heads of state and government and other official delegations attending the festivities.

It was estimated that the population of Vienna had doubled for the occasion and all along the imperial route the special stands that had been erected were crammed with people. Elsewhere crowds stood thirty deep; every window, every balcony was filled, every vantage point occupied. The whole way was decorated officially and unofficially with floral arches, garlands, flags and tapestries, and everywhere floated banners bearing the full or greater imperial arms – the crowned and nimbused double-headed eagle bearing on its breast the arms of the House of Hapsburg-Lorraine and on its wings shields representing the traditional titles of the Emperor and the constituent states of the Empire. (Though naturally no one mentioned it the crowds far exceeded even those of the fourteenth of March 1938 that had welcomed Hitler's entry into Vienna.)

He was preceded by marching contingents representing every part of the Empire and by members of his family in open carriages. Then came the procession proper: an entire regiment of the Imperial and Royal Horse and Foot Guards escorting the Emperor in his gilded coronation coach drawn by four pairs of greys, their plumes like the coats of the coachmen, postillions and footmen in the imperial livery colours of black and gold.

Beside and immediately behind the coach where Anton sat alone wearing the full dress uniform of Supreme Commander of the Armies rode the Elector of Saxony, Grand Marshal of the Empire, the Master of the Horse, the Imperial Standard Bearer and the aides-de-camp of his military household.

The Viennese had never before seen his coronation coach on their streets – he had been crowned in Rome, and in Budapest, Prague and Warsaw as King of Hungary, Bohemia and Poland respectively, but never in Vienna for Austria was officially only an Archduchy, not a kingdom – and as the cavalcade advanced at walking pace he was greeted on all sides by an unbroken sea of delighted faces and one continuous roar which drowned out the constant pealing of bells and the strains of the Kaiserlied (Hayden's tune now firmly established once again as the imperial anthem) taken up by band after band along the route as he passed by. It was an overpowering, heart-warming and humbling outpouring of gratitude to a man who symbolized the august political order, both ancient and at the same time new, that had given them forty years of peace, prosperity and prestige and, at least as far as the Viennese were concerned, raised their capital permanently to a status that it had always deserved but never really enjoyed before, not even during the Congress era, that of undisputed metropolis of the heartland of Europe, with Paris and London very much in its shadow and relegated to the outer fringe by comparison.

This display of fervour – there was no other word for it – which he was quite unprepared for, made him feel that it might all have been worthwhile – all the sacrifices he had made, all the limitations he had accepted, all the burdens he had borne in the great and glorious role which had been assigned to him – even giving up Rosemary, everything. And though not naturally demonstrative or given to bold gestures, he did his best to return it.

That evening after dark when the imperial cavalcade returned to the Schönbrunn his carriage was escorted with torches and this time every face in the immense crowd seemed to be illuminated with a flickering candle – another unforgettable experience of communion with his people, and today for the first time he felt they really were *his* people. That night there was a ball at the Schönbrunn. All traffic was banned from the centre of the city and streets, squares, parks and gardens, all specially decorated with lights were thronged with celebrating and dancing revellers. The night ended with a breathtakingly magnificent firework display from two to three in the morning from the hill of the Gloriette for the benefit not only of the Emperor's eight thousand guests but of the city and the worldwide television audience. Hardly anyone in Vienna slept that night; fortunately the following day was a Sunday.

Anton felt so exhausted the following morning that he deputed his eldest son to officiate at a ceremony in the Burgkapelle of the Hofburg at which he was to have bestowed the Order of the Golden Fleece on twelve visiting sovereigns. However he could hardly miss the march and fly-past in the afternoon and the gala performance of *Don Giovanni* at the Opera in the evening – both very public occasions where his absence would cause concern. For the march-past he took his place in the central bay of the Neue Burg with his sons, all the imperial Field Marshals and the Chiefs of Staff, while for over two hours an apparently interminable column of regiments of cavalry, infantry and military bands passed by. The crowds loved it, every nation and region cheering on their favourites. The parade got off to a lively start with the running Italian Bersaglieri in their feathered hats and ended with a fly-past in which an elite squadron etched trails of black and gold smoke in the sky over Vienna. Fortunately for Anton he was only required to stand and salute as each new standard passed by and for the rest of the time he could sit in comfort as he was also later able to do at the opera.

The following day, Monday, his only unavoidable duty was a state banquet at the Hofburg for which the finest historic table decorations from the Silberkammer were used, including the hundred foot long gilded bronze centrepiece with its accompanying candelabra dating from about 1800 and the Sèvres dinner service which had been the gift of Louis XV to Maria Theresa. But Anton had little appetite and only picked at the ten courses set before him, though he did his best to play the host and his short speech was well received.

It was on the Tuesday the fourth of September while he was in the Schatzkammer of the Hofburg looking at a special exhibition of the ruby-encrusted gifts he had received from all over the world to celebrate the fortieth year of his reign that he began to feel distinctly ill. The feeling was accompanied by an implacable pain deep down below the pit of his stomach. He had experienced this particular symptom regularly over recent months, though not as intensely – the first time, as it happened, was during the Review of the Fleet in the Adriatic not long after his reunion lunch with Rosemary.

That was a glorious occasion very different from the coronation Review of the Flee almost forty years before. Then the Imperial Navy had been an amalgam of a number of quite modest sized national fleets which he steamed past in a destroyer that for the first time in his life made him feel seasick. Now the Imperial Navy strung out in line astern and dressed overall off the Dalmatian coast was the largest in the world in surface ships consisting of six grand fleets with headquarters at Gdynia, Kiel, Wilhelmshaven, Genoa, Naples and Trieste respectively – the flagship of each fleet being an aircraft carrier named after an Emperor: the Charlemagne, the Otto the Great, the Charles IV, the Maximilian, the Charles V and the Franz

Joseph – and he had conducted the Review from the bridge of his own imperial yacht, the Maria Theresa, which was the size of a small liner, while the massed ranks of the sailors lining the decks on each vessel greeted him with three hearty cheers as he passed. He did not really care for life aboard the yacht and rarely used it, but at least with its specially designed stabilizers it never made him feel ill. (There had been some talk that he might get rid of it following the example of the Queen of England but he had firmly rebuffed the suggestion. Whatever the distaff side of the House of Hanover, merely the family of his Arch-treasurer, might choose to do could be of no concern to the Emperor!)

The world had in all probability never seen such a display of maritime power and all with entirely peaceful intent. As he had striven as Emperor to assure his neighbours, the Hapsburg Empire had now, as always, only one objective – to exist in glory at the heart of the world. But the Review had been ruined for him by that sudden intimation of infirmity which, however, he had done his very best to conceal from all those admirals and naval officers.

IV

He left the Treasury, made for the toilets and finding to his acute distress that he could not urinate, collapsed on the floor. When he came to he was lying in an ambulance desperately trying to explain his condition in English over the noise of the siren to two paramedics as they sped rocking and swerving through the traffic to Vienna General Hospital. The next thing he knew he was in a ward with tubes sticking into him. When an Austrian doctor who spoke excellent American-accented English told him he was very seriously ill, he insisted on using his health insurance cover to be flown back to Britain and the doctor, having warned him of the risks involved, reluctantly agreed in principle. The formalities and arrangements took forty-eight hours to complete before he was returned, heavily sedated, to Heathrow and taken to the West Middlesex Hospital.

Two days later an overworked registrar did not mince his words:

"Mr Kilroy I am sorry to have to tell you that you're suffering from an advanced stage of prostate cancer."

"What can you do about it?"

"Very little, I'm afraid. If we had caught it earlier it might have been different but now it looks as if it's spread. You must have had it for a year at least. Why did you ignore your condition for so long?"

"I don't know. The symptoms kept changing. I told myself they were unrelated, different things – and they came and went. When I was passing blood I thought it might be cystitis."

"Cystitis!"

"So what you're saying is that there's no hope?"

The registrar said nothing but gently nodded his head. "We'll do all we can to make you as comfortable as possible", he added as a passing shot, and moved on down the ward.

So it had come to this. He was going to die. After so many months of increasingly unequal struggle to convince himself that nothing serious could be happening and trying to account for and explain away each new set of symptoms – their very variety, he tried to assure himself, indicated that they could not all be related! – it was almost a relief to know the truth at last. Then it occurred to him that though he was separated by a whole universe of thought and experience from his poor wretched father he was dying at exactly the same time in his life and for exactly the same reasons as he had done. Perhaps they had more in common than he had ever liked to think. And he was dying leaving his greatest literary work, to which he had subordinated and sacrificed his whole life, unwritten and in a state in which it could not possibly be completed.

V

The sudden illness of the Emperor in the middle of his happily triumphant fortieth anniversary celebrations in Vienna, followed, unbelievably, by the news that his condition was so serious as to leave little ground for hope, caused consternation throughout the Empire. For decades, through all the churn of crises, scandals, sensations, conflicts and changes of fashion, the rise and fall of governments and the waxing and waning of reputations, he had remained the one fixed point in an unceasingly turning, changing and sometimes chaotic world. Only those well into middle age had any real memory of life in pre-imperial times or the Interregnum, as the period between the abdication of the Emperor Karl in 1918 and the election of Theodore as Holy Roman Emperor, was officially known. Until a few short days ago it had naturally been assumed that he would go on to celebrate his golden, and in due course his diamond jubilee and eventually, God willing, to equal, if not exceed, Franz Joseph's sixty-eight years on the throne. The prospect of life without him was almost unimaginable; hence the tense and grief-stricken vigil throughout the Empire and beyond, but especially among the Viennese who felt they had got 'their' Emperor back at last only to have him snatched away from them again forever by a cruel fate. Even his estranged Empress had now joined the children at the Emperor's bedside, a development which was taken as revealing the desperate gravity of the situation.

About ten o'clock in the evening, on the day following the Empress's arrival, a private jet of the Imperial Flight landed at

Vienna Airport bringing a very special person from London. She was driven immediately with a police escort to the Hofburg and taken to the Emperor's bedroom from which the Empress and her children had just been discreetly escorted away for the night (chamberlains are very practised at arrangements of this sort); so it was that when Anton opened his eyes he saw Rosemary.

"Am I dreaming?"

"No, my darling, I'm really here," she said, squeezing his hand.

"Forgive me for what I said to you when we had our little quarrel. You know I didn't mean it."

"And you forgive me for the terrible things I said to you. I didn't mean them either. I've always loved you."

"So have I. We never really mean what we say, do we? It's all a comedy... that doesn't mean it's always funny..."

Anton kept trying to talk and Rosemary, with a kind and loving smile, kept saying: "I know, I know," and holding his hand until he fell asleep.

The next morning the Cardinal Archbishop of Vienna insisted on anointing him and celebrating a Mass in his room. Though he remained personally untouched by orthodox religion, these events prompted him to try to concentrate his mind on his approaching death, for sooner or later he was going to die; that was what the doctor had told him.

Although he had spent so much of his life alone, writing and living the life of the imagination, he was all too well aware, for all his wide reading, of having merely glossed over the surface of things, with the vague idea that there would be time enough to go into all the really deep stuff later on. But now, if ever, was the time to think seriously and strenuously and penetratingly, and he couldn't! He just couldn't, however hard he tried. He wasn't even sure whether he was conscious or not.

Could it really possible that he had some sort of immaterial ghostly inner core that would survive death? What could that core possibly be or do? How could he be himself without his body? Surely all such speculation was just the mind crying out against annihilation. His near death experience, he seemed to remember, had proved a delusion. What if death resolved nothing? What if it were just a meaningless interruption, fixed forever? If only his dear friend Rollo were here. He had been so convincing, so compelling, about the unreality of time and death. If only he could remember what... but now he seemed even to be losing touch with thought itself...

Around him in the ward he heard snatches of conversation, phrases where words were separating from their meanings – "sorry to cause the poor girl's health... their three colour is afternoon... ranger deep and coffee wanting" – and things were separating from their names, substance from accidents – so things really did have essences. He knew the words or rather the words were there – words, things, happenings, without a subject, without anyone or anything they were happening too. Now he was completely bodiless, personless, infinitely small, not there at all, in fact not anywhere, in a limitless void, then falling towards a huge and terrible face, the face of his mother, not smiling and at peace as he had seen her in his dreams, but a hideous avenging gorgon, a fury. And this was real, more real than anything he had ever experienced before, indeed a new kind of reality. She was all that existed, she filled the whole universe. He was powerless to stop what was happening. He had no power to do anything at all, a dead leaf in a hurricane. He was nothing... nothing. Then, with a start he woke up. "Thank God I'm alive" he said to the nurse, "I was having a really horrific dream...!"

VI

"This one's dead," said the ward sister, drawing the curtains around the bed. "Tell the doctor."

"Mr Chatterbox?"

"Why do you call him that?"

"Because he was always talking away to himself as if there was a crowd of people around the bed. Funny the way the drugs take some people."

"Any next of kin, do you know?"

"I think so, some woman. She's supposed to be coming to see him today. Can't remember the name – sounded Italian."

"Right, well let's get on with it."

An hour or so later a plump well preserved middle-aged woman in a T-shirt and orange-coloured suit with a luxuriant crown of rather improbably curly reddish auburn hair breezed into the sunny ward carrying a huge bouquet of lilies and a basket of fruit. Though in her very early sixties, at a glance she could have passed for ten, or on a good day, fifteen years younger. And if anyone had been bold enough to remark on the lowness of her top, the shortness of her skirt or the height of her heels, she would have replied that this was the way her husband liked her to dress – it gave him a buzz to have a wife who could still turn the occasional head. But of course nobody ever did. The fact was that with her confident, direct and cheerful manner, she invariably carried it off and she had the advantage of the bloom that robust health, money and leisure, to say nothing of HRT, inevitably give.

"I've come to see Antony Kilroy," she announced to the young nurse who had just finished clearing his bed. "I was told he was in this ward."

"Oh yes, Mrs Ricardo, I've just been trying to contact you. I'm very sorry to have to tell you that he's just died."

"Has he? Oh dear. I knew he hadn't been very well recently but I didn't expect that. Well, you'd better give these to someone else."

"Are you the next of kin?" asked the nurse rather stiffly.

"Lord no. He was just an acquaintance."

"Well, I'm very sorry we've troubled you, Mrs Ricardo."

"Please call me Rosemary," she said, touching her arm with a warm smile. "And what's your name, dear?"

"Meadows, Janice Meadows", she said, finding it impossible not to smile back. "Well Rosemary, we rang because he kept asking for you. We found your number in his wallet and a photo, so naturally we thought..."

"A photo of me? In his wallet?" Janice nodded. "Well now. You did exactly the right thing, darling; it was you who rang up, wasn't it?" Janice nodded again. "I thought so. Thank you, that was very thoughtful. I'm only sorry I was so difficult to get hold of. We're in the process of moving to Spain at the moment and we've only just got back. Poor old Tony. Come to think of it, I was probably the only friend he had apart from his old school chums. He lived with his mum for years. She was a bit of a trial but he was very good to her. I thought he might branch out a bit when she died, but he carried on living in the same house – he lived there all his life, and he had the same job, working in a bookshop. Sad isn't it really? But I think he was quite happy, in his own way."

"We thought you might be his ex."

This struck Rosemary as very funny and she and Janice broke into laughter. Though Janice had initially been inclined to resent this brash intruder, the irrepressible Rosemary, as was her wont, had by now completely won her over.

"What an idea! No, Tony was you might call a confirmed bachelor, very set in his ways."

"You mean he was gay?"

"Heavens no. I just can't imagine him having a girlfriend that's all – a bit of a loner really, I suppose. But he was a very nice man, very well read, very fond of his mum. It was after she died that I tried to take him under my wing a bit, asked him round for Sunday lunch, that sort of thing, you know how you do. And he was very good with our kids. But when my second husband was drowned in a sailing accident he got rather too involved – always hanging about, couldn't get rid of him – so I had to draw the line a bit, if you know what I mean. After that I only saw him occasionally, when we bumped into each other. But we kept in touch. He could be quite amusing sometimes. Come to think of it he might have been gay I suppose. I never thought of that before... You said it was prostate cancer?"

"Yes, but he neglected it and by the time we got him in here it was far too late. He collapsed somewhere abroad on holiday and he had to be flown back home."

"Abroad? Tony? That must have been a first. First foreign holiday of his life and wham! Poor chap..."

After another ten minutes in which Janice started telling her all about her policeman partner and their wedding plans, Rosemary suddenly looked at her watch.

"I must go, love. My husband's waiting for me downstairs. And I told him I was visiting an old boyfriend!" Thus with a cheery wave she breezed out.

The following day Rosemary received a postcard from Vienna:

'Having a wonderful time. This city is a revelation. I feel as if I have been here all my life. I should have started travelling sooner. It certainly agrees with me. I've never felt better.

With very best wishes, Tony.'

A much greater surprise awaited her a week or so later when she learnt from a solicitor that she was Antony Kilroy's sole heir – she got his house and contents, his savings, everything!

Within hours she was round with her husband to size up her inheritance. Rocky Ricardo was a multi-millionaire cockney property developer and medallion man given to chunky male jewellery, a good five years younger than herself. Rosemary was well aware that her children, especially Richard, didn't care for her "toy boy" as she called him; but as she had given up the best years of her life for them, and her daughters now had children of their own, she reckoned she was entitled to a little happiness. And the truth was she had never been happier. Nor had she had to join a dramatic society to meet him. Their paths had crossed when his company – or rather one of his companies – was extending her house in Leatherhead. He was no culture vulture certainly, but so far he had done his very best to please her – though what poor old Tony would have made of Rocky she dreaded to think! However one thing he did know about was doing up houses.

"Get rid of the eighties kitchen," he was saying, "clear out all the junk, put in a couple of en-suites, lick of paint, ten thousand tops, and we could be looking at four fifty for this place."

"There's a model train set in the attic," said Rosemary.

Looking round the study she found on the shelves the completed manuscripts – all typewritten without a computer – of at least twenty-five novels in box files, another file filled with thirty-five years' worth of rejection letters from publishers and agents and another whole shelf of card indexes and notes for a multi-volume novel set against the background of the fortunes of the House of Hapsburg, past, present and future on which he appeared to have been working for most of his life. She browsed through some of the novel typescripts but they seemed wordy, over descriptive and full of literary and historical allusions, and did not engage her interest.

So this explained what he meant in his will by appointing her as his 'literary executor', charging her to do everything she could 'to ensure that all such works as I leave behind on my death may achieve publication' – he had even set aside a large portion of his life savings, a sum of £10,000, for that purpose. But realistically what could she do?

Opening the central drawer of his desk she came upon a hand written volume of sonnets dedicated to a certain 'R'; an introduction declaring that they celebrated a 'higher love' which, because it remained unconsummated, like Petrarch's for Laura or Dante's for Beatrice, could symbolize man's transcendental longings. In another drawer she found, carefully preserved, what looked like every note and postcard she had ever sent him together with about twenty different photos of her and her children all annotated and dated on the back. Others were filled with assorted diaries for every year of his life back to 1948, and the bottom one on the right, she was quite shaken to discover, was stuffed with top-shelf soft porn magazines. How extraordinary, how very incongruous and unlike any picture she had of him. On reflection she would somehow have been less surprised to find paedophile material. What a terrible thought! To her intense relief there didn't seem to be any.

With an acute sense that she was prying into secrets that were no business of hers, she slammed the last drawer shut just as her husband was coming into the room, and picked up a packet of pills that she happened to notice on the desk.

"Look at these; I never knew he suffered from gout."

"I thought you said he was one of your old boyfriends."

"And you believed me?"

"He left you everything didn't he?"

"Well he was never my boyfriend in any sense, just someone I've known for a long time that's all. I felt sorry for him more than anything, but if you must know, though it sounds awful to say it, I never really liked him that much. He was a bit creepy and a bit too much of a cold fish for me. But you can never really know people, can you?" (This observation failed to interest Rocky.) "Anyway these are all the writings that he wanted me to try and get published. I knew he wrote in his spare time but I'd no idea he'd done so much! It's amazing."

"Well we can chuck it all away with the rest of the junk, though that train set ought to be worth something."

"It seems such a terrible shame – after all it was his life's work."

"Would you want to read it?" (Although her taste only ran to Maeve Binchy and Jilly Cooper, Rocky regarded his wife as a reader and an authority on literature.)

"No, I suppose not."

"Then nor will anyone else."

VII

The last stage of the imperial funeral rites are being played out in the Capuchin Church of the Hofburg in the heart of Vienna. Among the very select congregation consisting of Maximilian, King of the Romans and Emperor-Elect, the Empress Dowager and the rest of the family, Cardinals, the highest court and government officials, foreign royalty, heads of state and government, and sitting right in the front row on the opposite side to the Hapsburgs, is a woman of uncertain age heavily veiled in black yet still attractive who was widely rumoured in the foreign media (so naturally everybody knew) to be the late Emperor's lifelong English companion and mistress; the woman he really loved.

Daringly the television camera lingered on Rosemary's veiled face for most of the time that the Arch-chamberlain was proclaiming the departed Emperor's titles of which she understood not a word: "... His Imperial, Apostolic and Royal Majesty, Theodore the First, by the grace of God, Holy Roman Emperor and King of Italy; Apostolic King of Hungary, King of Bohemia, Poland, Romania, Lombardy-Venetia, Dalmatia, Croatia, Slavonia, Lodomeria and Illyria; King of Jerusalem, Sovereign Prince of Lithuania, Latvia and Estonia; Archduke of Austria; Grand Duke of Tuscany and Kraków, Duke of Lorraine, of Salzburg, Styria, Carinthia, Carniola and of the Bokovina; Grand Prince of Transylvania; Margrave of Moravia; Duke of Upper and Lower Silesia, of Modena, Parma, Piacenza and Guastalla, of Auschwitz and Zator, of Teschen, Friuli, Ragusa and Zara; Princely Count of Hapsburg and Tyrol, of Kyburg, Gorizia and Gradisca; Prince of Trent and Brixen; Margrave of Upper and Lower Lusatia and in Istria; Count of Hohenems, Feldkirch, Bregenz and Sonnenberg; Lord of Trieste, of Kotor and in the Wendish Mark; Grand Voivode of the Voivodship of Serbia...."

Finally, after the Emperor's mortal remains were at last interred with those of his great predecessors, the rite closed, as he had specifically requested, with the singing of a traditional German student song. Rosemary who could not join in was lost in her own thoughts. So it was really true after all. She had loved an Emperor and an Emperor had loved her. And nothing at all could *ever* alter or undo that!

Gaudeamus igitur,
Juvenes dum sumus;
Post jucundam juventutem,
Post molestam senectutem
Nos habebit humus!

Bodmin, Cornwall 2007